Mission of Love . . .

"You go into that mission talking about everybody being equal, and believing it, and you've got trouble coming, lady. You won't last a month there. Hell, you won't last a week!"

"Yes, I will," Beth said. "This time I'm not going to—I mean, there's work that needs to be done here, and I'm going to do it."

Jerry was still shaking his head. "We'll see. The school's just over that rise." He pointed to the sandy hill before them. "Road goes down into a canyon—you can't see it from here."

"Then why did you stop?" Beth asked.

He moved imperceptibly closer, and she knew the answer before his hands closed over her shoulders. "Some things you can't do in the mission," he murmured.

SUNSET AND DAWN

KATE ASHTON

PINNACLE BOOKS NEW YORK

SUNSET AND DAWN

Copyright © 1985 by Margaret Ball

An original Pinnacle Books edition, published for the first time
anywhere.

First printing/March 1985

ISBN: 0-523-42350-0
Can. ISBN: 0-523-43353-0

Printed in the United States of America

PINNACLE BOOKS, INC.
1430 Broadway
New York, New York 10018

9 8 7 6 5 4 3 2 1

Chapter One

$\mathscr{A}$s the train passed over the last miles of parched New Mexico landscape before pulling into the Gallup station, Beth Johanssen felt a mounting excitement that could hardly be explained by the vista of cactus, sagebrush, and red cliffs rising in the distance to the north. She was on her way to a new home, a new life. She fought down the quiver of apprehension in her midriff, the little voice that whispered she'd been foolish to come this far alone. Perhaps she should have stayed in Iowa until she knew that the job near Gallup was hers. But it was done now, and in a few minutes she'd know her fate.

She stood, rocking slightly against the motion of the train, and pushed down the dusty window to get a clearer view of the desert landscape.

"Here, miss. Let me get that for you." The only other occupant of the compartment, a well-dressed man who had boarded the train at Albuquerque, jumped up and offered his help as she wrestled the stubborn window down a few inches. His hands closed over the frame and pushed it down as he smiled at her. Beth smiled back, impressed with the ef-

I

fortless display of strength even though she felt irritated that he so obviously expected it of her.

"Allow me to introduce myself. Lawrence Hudson, banker, rancher, and—" He broke off and grinned. "Well, I guess I have a hand in most everything that goes on around Gallup!"

The boyish grin gave an edge of youth and spontaneity to Lawrence Hudson's smooth face. Beth found herself prepared to like Mr. Hudson. She hoped the other residents of Gallup were as friendly.

"You must be a busy man, then," she said meaninglessly. For all she knew, Gallup was a whistle-stop, one-horse town like Albuquerque. But one had to say something. She extended her hand. "I'm Beth Johanssen. Perhaps you can tell me something about Gallup. I'm going to be staying there for a while." She hoped that was true.

Hudson's large hand enfolded hers while his delighted smile redoubled in intensity. "You don't say! It's not often we have a lovely young lady honor our town with a visit. I thought you must be going on to California. You have family in Gallup? I don't recall any Johanssens."

His open inquisitiveness was too innocent to be resented, too blunt to be turned aside. Beth had heard westerners were less formal. "I'm planning to teach at the mission school on the Indian reservation," she said reluctantly. She was a little shy about discussing her plans in case they didn't work out.

Hudson laughed. "Not for long you aren't."

Beth felt as though she'd stepped down onto a stair that wasn't there.

"I mean," Hudson hastened to add, seeing her stricken face, "ladies are scarce in the West. I predict you'll be married and retired from teaching in six months. Why, as soon as they hear you're in town, every single man for fifty miles around will be standing in line to court you."

He was still holding her hand. The gentle pressure increased slightly. "I count myself fortunate, Miss Johanssen, to be first in line."

Beth withdrew her hand, laughing. She'd been nervous about the wild ways and rough manners of the West, but nobody had warned her that her first problem would be hordes of lovesick men at her door. "Is this a proposal in form, Mr. Hudson, or are you just leading me on?"

That set him back for a moment, as she'd meant it to. Beth knew her own weakness; she was lonely after the long trip and just a little bit nervous, and Lawrence Hudson was a handsome man with an air of determined charm. She didn't want to get into Gallup already involved in a heavy flirtation with somebody who might be difficult to handle.

Leaning against the open window, pretending to look out, she appraised him out of the corner of her eye. He dressed like any conservative banker, in a gray silk suit, with the gleam of a gold watch fob and the flash of a diamond in his ring to show that there was money in his background. But under the formal suit was a strong, confident man. Regular, slightly tanned features; smooth hair that gleamed like melted butter; and a devastating, confident smile. Beth guessed that Lawrence Hudson had not suffered any setbacks that his money and charm couldn't cure. Yes, he could be difficult to handle—and rewarding.

Pretending still to be engrossed in the desert landscape, Beth hund on to the edge of the open window, automatically balancing her body against the jerky rhythm of the train. During the long journey from Iowa it had become second nature to brace herself against the train's swaying motion. She wondered if she would stagger when she got off onto the station platform at Gallup, as ocean travelers were said to do after a long voyage.

"I've never seen the sea," she said over her shoulder to

Lawrence Hudson. "But I think it must be something like this."

Hudson laughed at her comment and hooked his thumbs into the armholes of his gray silk vest. His butter-colored hair, combed back smooth and thick from his forehead, gleamed as he shook his head. "Not much, Miss Johanssen. It's wet!"

Beth flushed, bit her lip, and turned back to the window. Tit for tat; she'd been asking for it. No doubt he thought her a silly, naive little girl, venturing so far from home to teach for low pay on an Indian reservation. Well, perhaps she was. But she still thought that the wide plain with its speckles of greenish-gray vegetation must be something like the limitless expanse of the sea.

"Nervous?" Hudson said unexpectedly. "Don't be, Miss Johanssen. I venture to predict that Gallup will welcome you with open arms."

Beth turned from the window and gave him a slightly shaky smile. It was kind of him to try to allay her nervousness. Of course it would be all right once she got there. "It's only that everything is so new and strange," she excused herself. "I've never been out west before."

"Very few young ladies have." Hudson gave her a patronizing smile, and Beth fought down a growing sense of irritation.

"What is Gallup like?" she asked. Not that she'd be seeing very much of the town—she assumed the mission school lay somewhere outside of town—but it would be a starting point.

"A growing metropolis, one of the bright cities of the future." Hudson leaned against the window to balance himself and went into a speech so smooth he must have practiced it before many civic groups and newspaper editors.

"We are blessed not only with fertile and easily worked soil, but also with mineral wealth as yet hardly tapped. Prospectors have reported rich deposits of copper, silver, and even gold—untapped veins lying just below the surface." He licked his lips and stared past her with a strange light in his blue eyes. "Gold! Incalculable wealth for the right man." He gripped her arm as if to force her to share his compelling vision.

"Yes, that's very interesting," Beth said. It made her nervous, the way Hudson's bright blue eyes seemed to be looking right through—or past—her. And her arm hurt. She gently disengaged herself.

"But I was wondering more about what the town is like. To live in," she added, hoping to forestall another disquisition on the economics of the territory of New Mexico. Lawrence Hudson was a disturbingly handsome man, but she was beginning to think he looked better with his mouth shut.

"The town? Now? Well . . . it has a great future," Hudson said lamely.

Beth would have rather heard that it had a library.

"In a few years," he went on, seeing her disappointed expression, "it should be a metropolis to rival Albuquerque or even Santa Fe."

Albuquerque! Beth's mind flashed back to the huddle of shabby, false-fronted buildings where the train had stopped and Lawrence Hudson had boarded. If Albuquerque was a metropolis, what was Gallup? And what *had* she gotten herself into? Somewhat uneasily, she wondered if she would be stepping off the train straight into an empty desert.

Lawrence Hudson began lifting his calfskin suitcases down from the overhead rack as the train slowed for the Gallup stop. Beth leaned out of the window, feeling both eager and apprehensive as the first buildings of Gallup came into view. To calm herself, she took in deep breaths of the hot, dry, exhilarating desert air.

Her tight-fitting blue cloth basque strained at the seams, and the breeze whipped wisps of black hair out of her high-piled pompadour. In her head she could hear her school superintendent back in Iowa, scolding that a schoolteacher should present a picture of decorum at all times. Sticking one's head out of a railway train window had never been mentioned in their frequent talks, but she could imagine what he would have said about such behavior.

Beth grinned at the red rock cliffs, still visible behind the ugly town buildings, and raised one hand in mocking salute. Thinking about those little talks on propriety and decorum made it easier to believe that she'd come out west to find freedom and adventure.

And so she had, really. There was no need to tell the people at the mission school that she'd been fired from her last position for gross impropriety of conduct, leaving her with no references and a choice between going back home in defeat or taking up this work at the mission. Why burden them with irrelevant details? She was here, and she was the qualified and competent teacher they were said to need. Naturally they'd be delighted to see her.

Beth's face burned as she remembered that last scorching interview with the school board in Iowa.

"All children deserve a chance at education," she'd protested in defense of her actions.

"Not children like *that*," the head of the board had replied self-righteously.

Beth had lost; she supposed that was predictable. The good people of the town had felt no responsibility toward a prostitute's ragged child. In fact, they had been downright outraged when Beth had impulsively bought Whiskey Kate's Johnny a new pair of pants and invited him to join the primary class. And now Beth could see that it might have been wiser to go slower, talk a few members of the school board into sympathy with her side, rather than presenting them with a *fait accompli.*

What you need, she told herself sternly, is to stop and think before you act. From now on, no more impulsive actions. No more jumping in before you understand the situation thoroughly.

Of course, spending nearly the last of her savings on the train fare from Iowa to New Mexico might be construed as impulsive. Beth recognized that now. She recognized it more and more as the gritty reality of this isolated mining town intruded on the desert vistas outside the train window. But at the time it had seemed like a heaven-sent answer to her problems.

There she was, jobless, disgraced, about to creep back to her family and humbly admit they'd been right when they'd said she was too hotheaded to succeed as a teacher. And there was that pale, interesting young missionary, giving such a moving speech about the poor Indian children with no teachers at the mission school. His health forced him to return east, he had said, and now all he could do was speak at church gatherings like this one, where he solicited their contributions for the mission.

Beth had been about to empty her purse into the hat they passed around when it dawned on her that she could make a much more practical contribution than her scanty savings. Why not go out and teach at the mission herself? They needed people; she needed a job. It was a perfect match.

Or so it had seemed at the time. Now Beth felt a quiver of doubt in her midriff as the train screeched to a halt before the Gallup station. Perhaps it would have been wiser to make sure that the Griscoms were expecting her at the mission school, instead of just sending that telegram and impulsively taking the first train out of Vinton. Why, she didn't even know how much it would cost to get from here to the school!

Lawrence Hudson was already halfway down the aisle. She should have asked him about hiring a carriage. He might even have offered to transport her to the school himself.

As she drew her skirt up to keep the hem free of the dust and ashes that littered the carriage floor, Beth hesitated for a moment. "Mr. Hudson," she began as she made her way to the door, "do you happen to know how I can hire—"

A wild burst of shouting and gunfire interrupted her half-formed question. Beth paused with one foot on the folding steps at the end of the carriage, her hand frozen to the iron handrail, as a laughing crowd of dirty, unshaven cowboys burst onto the platform and came crowding up to the train.

"Need help, lady?" one of them asked. Without waiting for an answer, he reached up, took her by the waist, and neatly swung her to the platform. The instant her heels touched the planks he let her go, to the accompaniment of derisive moans from the rest of the crowd.

"What's the matter, Jerry," one of them shouted, "don't you know how to hold a girl?"

"Well," Beth said faintly, too astounded to be afraid. She turned and looked for Lawrence Hudson and found to her astonishment that he had already stormed over to the side of the station to wave his fist at some man in a buggy over there. "Well, he did say I'd be greeted with open arms, didn't he?"

Chapter Two

The crowd at the station seemed to have other things on their minds besides welcoming the new lady schoolteacher to Gallup. While Beth stood uncertainly on the platform, the lean, redheaded roughneck who had unceremoniously lifted her down from the train dove back into the crowd and extracted a weedy man in a rumpled gray suit.

"On the train, Carruthers," the redhead ordered, "and don't let me see your face this side of Santa Fe again!"

Beth gasped and stepped back as he shoved the other man toward the train—toward her. Her left heel came down on emptiness. She rocked backward and felt the sickening certainty that she was about to go over the edge of the platform. Hard fingers caught her wrist and jerked her back to safety with a yank that left her breathless.

"Sorry about that, ma'am." The redhead touched two fingers to his hat. His other hand still encircled her wrist. "Didn't mean to scare a lady."

"You didn't scare me!" Beth retorted. She yanked her arm free of his grasp. Somewhat to her surprise, she found it was true. She was too astounded to be afraid. She couldn't believe these greasy bullies were any real threat to anybody. But they were repulsive. She couldn't remember having been so casually handled in her life. "I was just startled by your western hospitality."

The redhead's deep laugh amazed her. She looked up at the six feet of bone and sinew, tanned flesh and corded muscle that stood before her, coiled and dangerous. She was disgusted by the slovenliness of the man, with the prickling of red stubble on his cheeks, with his dust-caked pants that released a cloud of reddish dust every time he hitched them up on his lean hips.

"Don't you have anything better to do with your time than to get drunk and bully an innocent stranger?" she demanded. "Let me pass."

The redhead stepped back a pace. "Anybody stopping you?" he inquired with a sweeping gesture.

Beth eyed the motley crew that crowded close behind him. For all Lawrence Hudson's words about how women were cherished in the West, she didn't relish pushing her way through that crowd. But as she looked them over, the men dropped their heads and shuffled their feet uneasily.

"Didn't mean no offense to a lady, miss," offered an anonymous voice from the back of the crowd.

Beth nodded and bent to pick up her case. The redhead forestalled her with one swift motion; their fingers met on the handle.

"You see, ma'am," the deep voice said, "you're making a mistake. Several mistakes." He held her case and enumerated them. "I'm not drunk, and I'm not bullying an innocent stranger." He made no move to let go of her case, and her fingers tingled where they met his on the handle. She was damned if she was going to give in first.

A disturbance to one side saved her. The redhead let go of the handle and the weight of the case jerked her arm downward. "Back here, you!" He wheeled, reached one long arm to fasten on the man called Carruthers, and hurled him toward the train. Carruthers tripped and fell.

Several of his followers yipped approval and shot their guns into the air. One aimed at the station platform where Carruthers was struggling to his feet. Beth closed her eyes, sure that her last moment had come.

"Let's see him dance first!" Bullets thudded into the platform; Carruthers whimpered and Beth opened her eyes again. No one seemed to be hurt. But one man was waving his revolver around far closer than she liked.

The redhead knocked the gun up so that the next shot went harmlessly into the air. "Cut that out," he ordered, one fist clenched as if he were prepared to enforce the order on the spot. "We don't need any shooting to get rid of this city feller. Ain't that so, Mr. Carruthers?"

He grasped the weedy man's collar and held him upright, almost choking him in the process. Beth felt a blazing rage crackle through her, obliterating caution. What a disgusting scene to have walked in on, all these great big men bullying one little fellow who was obviously scared to death of them! Her fingers itched to slap this redheaded outlaw into next Sunday.

Calm down, she told herself. It's not your fight. Remember about turning over a new leaf? No more impulsive actions. Remember?

"It's all . . . right," Carruthers gasped as the redhead shook him by the collar. "I'll go peaceably, Jerry."

"Mr. Dixon to you." The man called Jerry dropped him and Carruthers sagged with relief. "All right. On the train!"

"I thought you didn't bully innocent strangers," Beth heard herself saying. Calm down, she told the quailing spirit inside her. They won't hurt a woman . . . will they?

"This man ain't a stranger, and he ain't innocent," Jerry Dixon contradicted her.

Beth moved so that she stood directly in front of the door to the carriage. Her better self seemed to have fainted dead away; at any rate, it had stopped nattering on about look before you leap and other time-worn principles.

"If you'd just kindly step aside, ma'am?" He waited, unsmiling, for her to obey.

Beth glanced around the station platform. Two porters were unloading luggage from the train, and the station master was sitting at his desk behind a partition at the end of the platform. A pair of unshaven men, their faces streaked with coal dust, were standing in the street with their elbows resting on the high platform, watching with undisguised interest. Across the street to her left, a woman in a red silk dress twirled her sunshade and watched from the steps of a clapboard building.

The number of people reassured her. She couldn't believe that these men would dare shoot anyone in front of so many witnesses. They were just trying to intimidate this Carruthers man.

"N-no," she said. "No!" Good, that was firmer. "Why should I help you?"

"Actually, ma'am," Jerry Dixon said pleasantly, "I don't need your help." His voice hardened. "I don't need your interference, either."

"You can't put this man on the train if he doesn't want to go!" Her large dark eyes flashed with determination and she nodded emphatically at her opponent even while she wondered, with a chill of fear, what she would do if he reached for his gun.

"Oh, yes, I can," Jerry said in the same pleasant voice. "But I don't need to. He's going peaceably. Ain't you, Carruthers?"

He didn't turn his head to glance at Carruthers as he tossed the question out. All his attention was focused on Beth, and she felt as if a powerful spotlight had been pointed directly at her. The force of his will, blazing from hard steel-gray eyes, made her feel as if she were melting inside. He put up one hand toward her shoulder, as if to move her away. Beth shook her head, and shook it again as he moved closer, glaring at her.

Now she was standing so close to him that the starched ruffles on the front of her basque brushed his chest when she breathed. He was tall enough to look down on her, an unusual experience for her. For the first time she looked him full in the face. His narrowed gray eyes met hers and she felt a shock of something like recognition. The young, lean, tanned face with its firm chin and unsmiling mouth seemed to have come from out of her dreams, the embodiment of something she'd longed for and never found.

"It's all right, miss," Mr. Carruthers said in a weak voice. "I want to go back. Honest I do."

They both ignored him.

"Who . . . are you?" Beth murmured. For some reason she was having trouble breathing.

Jerry stared back at her, his mouth set as though he'd just received a mortal wound and had yet to feel the shock of it. The air between them quivered with the heat rising from the baked desert ground, and all she could see was the firm line of his lips, set against some deep internal pain—or was it pleasure?

"Just a wrangler with a job to do, ma'am," he answered at last. "Now if you'll kindly get out of my way, I'll see that it's completed."

"You can't do this!" Beth cried. She looked around at the people on the station platform. The men who'd accompanied Jerry had backed off, as if acknowledging that the battle was between the two of them. She raised her voice, hoping to attract the attention of the station master, still busily scratching away with his pen behind the partition.

"You can't just come in here and push innocent people around and force them to do anything you want."

Jerry's eyes twinkled as though he found her more amusing than anything else. "Just applying a little gentle persuasion, ma'am. I'd surely hate to push a lady around, but I've asked you twice now to step aside."

As he moved toward her, Beth put up one gloved hand to keep him away. He captured the hand she raised and folded strong brown fingers around it. His touch seemed to burn right through the thin material into her skin. She would have stepped aside now without fighting. Her knees felt weak and there was a buzzing in her ears.

"Now let me give you a word of advice." His fingers caressed the blue-veined skin under her wrist and sent shuddering thrills all along her arm. "It doesn't do to be interfering in matters you don't understand, ma'am. Señor Galvan and I found this man surveying a section of the Galvan ranch.

"We don't take kindly, in these parts, to strangers coming on our land without asking permission. Especially strangers hired by some smooth-talking land shark who's been trying to get his hands on the Galvan land grant for three years. Most men in these parts would have shot him first and asked questions afterward. We just escorted him to the train. And now, if you've no further objection, I'll see that he gets on it."

He released her hand and it fell limply to her side. Beth's wrist felt cold where his fingers had burned into her skin. But the strange intoxication was gone. "No," she said flatly. "How do I know you're telling the truth?"

"You don't," Jerry allowed. His eyes were as cold and

gray as the winter sky at home, incongruous in this land of hot red dust. "Some way, you're just going to have to make up your mind who to trust."

He waited, his own hands at his sides, as if to say he wouldn't force her. Beth bit her lip and wanted to look away, but his cool eyes held hers. She felt helpless, mesmerized by his straight unsmiling stare. He was, she realized, as certain he was right as she was. But he didn't flash his eyes or shout at people or threaten them. He just waited. And she couldn't bear another moment of the waiting, and she couldn't move aside and allow him to run this stranger out of town, and she could hardly breathe in the stillness between them.

Then he broke the tension with a laugh. "Reckon the man you're defending has settled matters for himself, ma'am." He pointed at the train. Beth whirled and saw Carruthers peeping from a window. As she watched, the departure bell clanged again and the train slowly pulled out of the station.

The man who'd followed Jerry onto the platform slowly moved away, talking in low voices. As they left, Beth saw Lawrence Hudson standing at the end of the platform, talking to a short, dark-haired man whose dark coat glittered with silver buttons.

"You won't get away with this again, Galvan," Hudson snapped. "Bringing in hired guns to run my men off! The courts will have something to say about this!"

The tubby, dark little man bowed slightly. "The courts have already decided the matter, Señor Hudson. My claim to Galvan North has been confirmed."

"Spanish land grants!" Hudson sneered.

"Upheld in an American court." Galvan spoke with softly menacing emphasis. "This land has been in my family for a long time, Señor Hudson. I do not intend to sell it." He paused. "I do not intend to lose it."

Hudson stared at Galvan for a moment, scowling and clenching and unclenching his fists. Then he gave a sharp laugh and turned away. "We'll see about that!" He jumped from the platform into the padded leather seat of a light-weight buggy with gleaming black woodwork and drove away without looking back.

Beth looked up at Jerry Dixon. "I don't understand."

He shook his head, unsmiling. "No. You wouldn't."

"But why—"

Ignoring her, Jerry strode across the platform and nodded to the tubby little man who stood staring after Hudson's wagon. "Señor Galvan."

"Jerry." The man nodded. "Rather an impetuous action. Mr. Hudson has just been complaining to me of your high-handed ways."

"Notice he didn't have much to say to me about it," Jerry said with a slight smile.

Beth trailed after Jerry. Everybody else around the station seemed to have vanished, including the porters who'd unloaded her heavy brass-bound trunk while she was arguing with Jerry. "Excuse me," she said loudly to get their attention. "Would either of you gentlemen know where I can catch the stagecoach to the reservation?"

Jerry turned, his red brows shooting up into his forehead. "Stagecoach? Reservation? Ma'am, the stage company don't run lines into the Indian reservation."

"Oh!" Beth looked back at the uncompromising bulk of her trunk, far too heavy for her to lift herself. "Then . . . perhaps," she decided aloud, "I had better stay at a hotel until I find some way to get to the school. Would one of you gentlemen be so kind as to call the station porter? I need help with my luggage."

"Porter." Jerry Dixon was grinning broadly as he fanned himself with his hat. "What then, ma'am? Do you reckon to take a *hackney cab* to the *station hotel*? This here is Gallup, ma'am. A mining town, whistle-stop station, fifty miles from nowhere in the middle of the desert. Not Chicago. We don't have all the amenities you might be accustomed to.''

"Oh!" Beth looked in dismay at her heavy brass-bound trunk. "I never thought—that is, I didn't—"

Señor Galvan rescued her from her confusion.

"All right, Jerry," he reproved his companion, "stop teasing *la señorita*. Miss, there is a hotel in Gallup, but I don't think it is a good place for a nice young lady like you to stay."

With an expressive glance he gestured toward the clapboard building across the street from the train station. The woman in the red silk dress grinned and waved back with a shrill laugh. She leaned forward to display a generous expanse of bosom under the low-cut, clinging bodice.

Beth followed the wave of his hand, took it all in, and gulped audibly.

"Are you sure," Galvan asked gently, "that this is where you meant to come?"

It was a good question. Even if one ignored the gaudy woman in front of the hotel, the town itself was depressing beyond words: one street of shabby square buildings, half of them saloons with swinging doors.

But for backdrop, there were the magnificent red cliffs rising to the north. And it wouldn't be quite like this at the school. They might have planted trees. She would start a garden; the children would enjoy helping her, and it would be a good way to teach them English. One could improve any situation.

"Quite sure," she said faintly. She reached into her reticule and drew out the paper handed out at the missionary meeting. "I've come to teach at the missionary school on the reservation. The gentleman who addressed our church said this was the nearest train station to the school.''

"The mission school.'' Jerry Dixon's face hardened and he turned away from her. Beth felt suddenly and inexplicably chilled. "If she's part of that outfit,'' he addressed Señor Galvan, "seems funny the Griscoms wouldn't have sent the wagon for her.''

Señor Galvan shrugged and spread out his hands. "Maybe it is late. Someone will be here for her soon, I trust.''

Assailed by a sudden fear that the two men might simply walk off and leave her standing on the platform beside her baggage, Beth plucked up her courage to address them as they stood looking down the street away from her.

"Señor Galvan? The Griscoms weren't exactly expecting me. You see . . . well, actually,'' she admitted, blushing, "they don't know I'm coming.''

It was Jerry who whirled back to her, his dark face alight with inner amusement. "You come all the way out here and they don't even know it? Say, what is this, some kind of a joke? Ma'am, nobody comes out to Navaho country if they don't have to! Even old Griscom—''

"That is enough, Jerry,'' Señor Galvan interrupted him. He bowed to Beth. "Señorita, I think you did not perfectly understand the difficulties of travel in this part of the country. It will take half a day for someone to take a message to the school, and another day for Mr. Griscom to come with the school wagon. In the meantime, there is no place in Gallup suitable for an unattended young lady to stay.''

Beth gulped again as the full difficulty of her predicament struck home. Oh, why hadn't she written to the Griscoms and applied for the teaching position in the regular way? What on earth was she going to do now? Wait for the next train back?

No. How cowardly that would be, to admit defeat before

she'd even set foot on this challenging desert land with its dry, spicy wind off the mesas. And how they would laugh at her back in Iowa! Beth raised her chin a fraction of an inch. She would just have to find some way of getting to the school.

Señor Galvan was watching her face as if he knew exactly what thoughts were passing through her mind. Jerry Dixon retreated a few paces and lounged against a post, staring into the distance and occasionally giving her a sidelong glance.

When Beth lifted her chin, took a deep breath, and picked up her straw case again, Señor Galvan stepped forward and took it from her hand. "Allow me to introduce myself," he said with a slight bow. "I am Eleuterio Galvan, proprietor of the Galvan Ranch, and this gentleman is Jerry Dixon, one of my wranglers. We will be happy to drive you to the mission school."

Jerry Dixon started upright at this statement and opened and closed his mouth several times as though he meant to say something but then thought better of it. Galvan's head turned and he gave Jerry an emphatic nod. Turning back to Beth, he extended his hand.

"May I say, Miss . . . ?"

"Johanssen," Beth said reluctantly. "Beth Johanssen."

Señor Galvan nodded. "Miss Johanssen, I should be honored if you will permit me to do you this small service of furnishing transportation to the school."

"You're very kind," Beth said, "but I don't think . . ."

Desperately she glanced at the impassive figure of Jerry Dixon. His long form was slouched against the post again; his arms were folded and he was surveying her between slitted lids with eyes that held a glint of amusement. From the toes of his scuffed boots to the silver-mounted pistol dangling from his gunbelt, he was the very picture of an outlaw in a dime novel. How could she go riding off into the

desert with a man like that? She swallowed, her mouth suddenly dry, and tried to find a polite way of refusing Señor
Galvan's offer.

"I really couldn't accept such a favor from a stranger."

Señor Galvan smiled. "You mean that no gently bred
young lady from the East would consider riding off alone
with a strange man. I assure you, Miss Johanssen, Eleuterio
Galvan is a name honored and respected in this part of the
country. No harm will come to you while you are under my
protection."

He took in her doubtful glance and smiled slightly. "Mr.
Dixon is not always so dirty; he has just returned from riding
the boundaries of Galvan North. You may have noticed that
he encountered something there that called for immediate
action."

Beth smiled at this description of the scene at the station.

"The station master will vouch for my character," he
added, gesturing toward the clapboard shed at one end of the
platform, where a blue-uniformed man sat quietly making
entries into his ledgers. At a gesture from Señor Galvan, he
rose and came forward to join them.

A slightly built man with white hair long enough to brush
the collar of his blue uniform, he walked with a slight hitch
in his stride. "Jim Maxwell, at your service, ma'am," he
said in a deep voice, extending his hand.

"Beth Johanssen," Beth replied automatically.

"Miss Johanssen requires transportation to the mission
school," Señor Galvan told the station master. "I have offered her a ride with Jerry, who is freighting supplies up to
Galvan North, but she is dubious about traveling with two
such desperate characters."

Jim Maxwell nodded. "Mission school? Fine group of
dedicated people, Miss Johanssen. Done good work with
civilizing the Indians. I'm sure they're looking forward to

your joining them. Surprised to find you helping out, though, Eleuterio. Thought you didn't approve of educating the red devils.''

"It's Miss Johanssen I am concerned with helping," Galvan said. "She can't wait in the hotel until they send transport out from the school."

"No." Maxwell turned toward Beth. "Miss Johanssen, I can assure you that it's quite all right to ride out to the school with Señor Galvan. He is one of our best-known citizens and I would trust him with anything—except my vote."

Eleuterio Galvan smiled. "Mr. Maxwell and I differ on some political questions. But let's not get involved with those matters now. I am sure Miss Johanssen is tired of standing on this dusty platform, and it will be a long ride out to the school."

Jim Maxwell nodded and stuck out his hand again. "Pleasure to meet you, ma'am. I hope to see you again. Please convey my best wishes to those fine, dedicated workers at the mission school."

While Beth was saying good-bye to the station master, Jerry Dixon and Eleuterio Galvan heaved her trunk into the back of a wagon already loaded high with supplies. The wagon was hitched at the far end of the platform, some distance from the steps. Jerry Dixon vaulted lightly down to the ground with one hand on the platform, then turned and held out his hands to Beth.

"You don't want to walk all the way around the station, do you, ma'am?"

His teeth flashed white in his tanned and dusty face, and before she remembered her dignity, Beth pulled off her gloves, bent to take his outstretched hands and jumped from the edge of the platform. She landed in a drift of sand that spurted up around her shoes and left eddies of white dust in the air.

Jerry's hands were firm and warm and dry against her palms. For a moment she stood with her hands on his, finding it oddly difficult to catch her balance—or her breath—in the cloud of dust that swirled around them.

Then the dust settled onto the hem of her dark blue traveling costume. Jerry laughed. "That's a territory baptism! They say you have to get an acre of New Mexico on you before you're a citizen."

"Then you must have earned enough citizenship to vote three times over," Beth retorted before she could stop herself, looking at Jerry's dusty pants.

He didn't seem offended. Still laughing, he placed his hands around her waist and swung her up into the wagon without waiting for permission. He jumped up beside her and took the reins from Eleuterio Galvan.

"So long, Eleuterio. See you next Saturday." Clucking to the horses, he turned them and the wagon rolled forward on the slowly rising, dusty road that led to the red cliffs of the north.

Chapter Three

"Wait a minute!" Beth turned in her seat and Eleuterio Galvan gave her a cheery wave. The hard edges of the plank bit into her leg as she twisted around to call to him. "Señor Galvan! I thought you were coming, too!" Already they were several yards away from the station.

Señor Galvan cupped one hand to his ear and raised his brows with an inquiring look. Beth leaned perilously far over the edge of the wagon and took a deep breath to shout again.

She felt a hand slip into the minute gap between the waistband of her blue skirt and the small of her back. She was yanked back down to the wagon seat with a painful thump.

"Sit down!" Jerry ordered her. "You're scaring the horses."

Beth looked back as Señor Galvan crossed the street, bowed to the woman in the red silk dress, offered her his arm, and pushed open the hotel door. Her mouth fell open as she realized the meaning of his actions.

"I thought Mr. Maxwell said your employer was a man of good character!"

"He is," Jerry said. "He's also a widower. Wife's been dead fifteen years. Don't come to town but once a month. Lorena's good to him, and he's good to her." He glanced at her, and his lips twitched with involuntary amusement at her straight-backed indignation.

When she'd defied him at the train station he'd felt some spark in him leap to answer the fire in this girl. But now, indulging in her righteous disapproval of poor old Eleuterio, she'd lost that inner fire that attracted him. Perhaps he should tell her she wasn't half as pretty when she was being righteous—that might soften her virtuous disapproval some. Then again, maybe not. There was never any reasoning with these mission people. Too bad she'd turned out to be hitched up with that crowd. "You want to jump out and walk back to town?"

"I'm not accustomed to associating with people like that," Beth said stiffly.

"Well, ma'am," Jerry drawled, "you jump off this wagon, you're going to associate with a powerful lot of them right soon. That's the Gallup Hotel and the only place in town to stay." He chuckled. "Mebbe Lorena'd let you share her room." He regretted the crack as soon as he'd made it. Being a girl alone, and a missionary to boot, she was probably scared enough already at the prospect of driving out to the mission with a sinner like him. No need to make it worse for her.

Beth stared straight ahead at the dusty road before them. The horizon seemed to shimmer, as if it were under water. But close by there was only the heat and dust and the scrubby gray-green plants that gradually succeeded the irregular line of houses. He wondered what she was making of it all. Must look pretty grim to a girl from back east, where things were green—she wouldn't see the beauty in it that he did.

She was still sitting poker-backed! He couldn't resist the urge to tease some kind of reaction out of her. Missionary or not, she was a pretty girl, and warm-blooded under that stiff blue costume. He wasn't accustomed to being so thoroughly ignored by the few girls he saw out here.

"Matter of fact," he said, picking up on his previous comment as they passed the last buildings and headed out into the desert, "you stay around here, won't find much else to associate with, and that's a fact." She might as well understand what she was getting into. " 'Ceptin' those good folks at the mission school, of course. You must be right eager to get out there and be with your own sort."

"I am," Beth said stiffly. She glanced at Jerry out of the corner of her eyes. He was slouched on the rough plank seat, seemingly absorbed in guiding the horses. It did seem excessive to jump out of the wagon and walk back to town. Besides, how would she get her luggage back? Something told her this strange, quiet man would not be agreeable to the suggestion that he should turn back to deposit her and her trunk at the hotel.

Actually, she thought, if you cleaned him up a little, he wouldn't be so bad-looking. His long, lantern-jawed face, if not precisely handsome, suggested the inner strength she found more attractive in a man than conventional good looks. The bright flash of his red hair made a striking contrast with his dark-tanned skin. And the eyes . . .

Beth caught her breath as he turned his head and she caught the full force of those cool gray eyes. A man shouldn't look like that, she thought over the hammering of her heart. It wasn't fair!

"What's the matter?" Jerry asked. "I got something on my face?"

Beth blushed. She realized that she had been staring at him for quite a long time while she mulled over what to do.

"Or are you afraid of me?" he asked.

"Certainly not!" Beth sat very straight on the plank and tried to ignore the mocking smile on his face.

It was not quite a lie. She was not afraid of him—only intensely aware of his presence beside her. As they left the shabby town, the desert stretched before them, a rolling expanse of sand and twisted bushes climbing slowly to the red and ochre cliffs ahead. Beth felt both exhilarated and overpowered by the grandeur of the vista. And the man beside her affected her in the same way. Slouched on the wagon seat, guiding the horses, eyes narrowed to scan the horizon, he seemed to blend into the landscape. She couldn't imagine ever belonging to it the way he did. And she could not forget how alone they were under the dazzlingly blue sky.

She tried to convince herself that this was no different from being alone in a railroad car with Lawrence Hudson. But her body told a different story. The palms of her hands still tingled from Jerry Dixon's casual touch, and it seemed to her that she could feel the imprint of his hands about her waist where he had lifted her into the wagon.

Beth glanced down at her wrist and was surprised to find that there was no dark ring of bruises encircling it. Perhaps her reaction to his touch had been nothing more than surprise that anyone would dare to handle her so. She was a tall girl, and people told her she had a commanding presence— whatever that meant. She knew that her striking coloring, her thick black hair and eyes so dark blue that they seemed black in most lights, impressed men. Plenty of them had told her so.

This redheaded roughneck who now slouched on the wagon bench beside her, driving his team into the desert, did not look as if he had been struck by her beauty. He treated her with casual disrespect; she remembered the moment of shock when he'd swung her down from the platform with that easy, wiry strength and they'd stood face to face, laughing, in the miniature dust storm that swirled around them. When he'd reached for her waist to lift her up into the wagon, she had actually thought for a moment that he was going to kiss her.

Now, remembering that moment of shock, she felt something strangely like regret. She peeped at Jerry, sitting impassively behind the horses with his eyes narrowed to stare at the horizon, and wondered what it would be like to be held and kissed by this man who took what he wanted with such casual ease.

But I don't even like him! she reminded herself, startled. Look at the way he'd bullied that poor man at the railroad station.

She frowned, remembering the scraps of conversation she'd overheard. She couldn't quite understand what had been going on. It sounded as though Señor Galvan had been accusing Lawrence Hudson of trying to steal his land. But Mr. Hudson was a respectable man, a banker. He wouldn't need to swindle some poor Mexican out of his land. Besides, who'd want this land! Beth glanced around at the barren vista of broken cliffs and jagged hills sprinkled with cactus and sage.

"Mr. Dixon?" she asked. "Would you mind telling me what all that was about—back at the station?"

"Yup," Jerry said.

They rode on in silence.

"Well?" Beth asked after a few minutes.

"Yes, I'd mind telling you," he translated with a touch of impatience. "Nothing to do with you."

Beth could feel the ends of her hair crackling with irritation. Well, maybe it was just the dry air. Still, she hated his superior, don't-worry attitude. "It's everybody's business when innocent citizens are being pushed around and bullied!'' she exclaimed.

Jerry sighed. ''Ever think of waiting a while—maybe ten minutes or so—before you leap to your conclusions? Maybe the innocent citizens in this case aren't who you think they are. Hudson's been after that land a long time, and I bet he's behind the latest—''

He stopped and clamped his mouth shut as though afraid of saying more.

''Latest what?'' Beth asked.

Jerry shook his head. ''What I tell you, you tell the Griscoms out at the mission, and they tell Hudson.''

''You told me back at the station,'' Beth argued, ''that I'd just have to make up my own mind whom to trust. How about giving me some evidence on which to base the decision?''

''How about you tend to your business,'' Jerry replied, ''and I'll tend to mine?''

Beth bit her lip and stared out at the desert landscape. They were laboring up the steep road to the top of the mesa now, and she had to hold on to the plank with both hands to keep her seat as the wagon lurched and heaved over the boulder-strewn track. It was probably a good thing that her hands were busy. Otherwise she would have been sorely tempted to hit this taciturn, annoying man. For heaven's sake, what would it cost him to explain his side of the story to her? She'd been prepared to believe there were good reasons for his behavior at the station—well, prepared to listen, anyway. But naturally, a woman's opinion wasn't important enough for him to take the trouble of telling his story.

''Typical!'' Beth fumed through clenched teeth. She resolved not to speak to Jerry again until they arrived at the mission. Then she would thank him, politely and very coldly, for his services. She would make certain he had no doubt where he stood in her eyes—somewhere lower than a dung beetle.

When they reached the top of the mesa, though, she was unable to restrain a cry of delight. An entire new world was spread out before her, a world shimmering with blue-and-lilac shadows across rolling green and red-and-purple hills. Far in the distance a wall of mountains rose up to form a sharp, serrated line against the sky. "Oh, how beautiful!" Beth exclaimed. She leaned forward to see more. In the sharp, clear air of this high altitude, every detail seemed crisp and precise as if etched in glass.

"Beautiful?" Jerry sounded amused. "You don't sound much like a missionary. Griscom calls it barren and desolate." He twitched at the reins to guide the horses around a huge boulder that blocked the road. "See how much you like it after a week at the school, missionary lady. No shops, no neighbors to visit. No amusements but doing good to the Indians—the ones that can't get away, that is."

"You hate the mission, don't you?" Beth asked slowly. At first she'd thought his hostility was only directed at her. But the sarcastic tone of his voice when he spoke of the mission reminded her of his reaction when she'd said she was going out there. That puzzled her. "Why? What harm does it do you if we help the Indians?"

"There's help," Jerry said darkly, "and then there's help."

"What exactly does the mission do that you find so terrible?"

Jerry glanced at her, and she was momentarily chilled by the cold look in his eyes. "Same as most missions, I guess. They save souls. Isn't that what you come out here to do? Do good to the poor naked Indian savage, and all that?" The mockery in his tone cut her like a fine wire slicing through her dreams.

"I take it you're one of the people Mr. Farragut warned us about," she said, remembering the missionary talk that had inspired her to come out here. Savages indeed! Without thinking about her manners, she let loose at him in a blaze of indignation.

"You don't think the Indians are good enough to be educated—you don't care if they stay ignorant and on the reservation all their lives! Well, I don't make those distinctions, Mr. Dixon! I don't care if my pupils are red or white or—or green! These children deserve the same chance as any other American citizen, and neither you nor anybody else is going to stop me from giving them that chance!"

Her eyes flashed and she brought her hand down on the plank between them with a resounding thump at the end of the statement. Jerry's eyebrows shot up until they disappeared under the crisply curling red hair that fell over his forehead. "All right, don't get so het up about it," he muttered. "Just believe in letting people live their own lives, that's all."

Beth gave an unladylike snort of disgust and settled down on the hard plank again, arms folded. For the next few miles indignation kept her back straight as she kept mentally adding statements to her impromptu speech.

"You'll see what I mean when you get there," Jerry muttered as they reached the valley floor.

"Just don't believe in going out of your way to get involved," he added after they'd driven in silence for a while longer.

Beth sniffed and feigned absorbed interest in the circles of a great black bird in the sky. With her arms folded and her face lifted to the sky, she was taken by surprise and almost fell off the wagon bench when Jerry directed his team across the sandy valley at right angles to the road.

"What are you *doing*?" she panted, grasping the plank with both hands as they bounced among sand and sagebrush.

Jerry's chin jerked toward the base of a red mesa. "Saw Pahie over there. Looks like she's in trouble."

Beth strained her eyes but saw nothing, and Jerry urged the team forward until all his attention was needed to keep control of their bumpy ride.

In a few minutes they were at the foot of the mesa. Jerry pulled the horses up just short of a deep gully that ran between this and the next mesa, a jagged red scar in the earth. A little girl wrapped in yards of faded calico, her black hair twisted into an untidy knot on the back of her head, was kneeling at the edge of the gully, reaching down to something just beyond her reach. Her pony browsed placidly on a prickly mouthful of gray-green brush.

"*Ahalani*, Pahie," Jerry greeted the girl. She scrambled to her feet and began explaining something to him in a strange, guttural language augmented with many gestures. With a thrill of excitement Beth realized that this was the first Indian she had ever seen. She leaned out of the wagon and stared shamelessly. Was this what her pupils would look like? Ragged, dark-skinned, speaking with their hands?

Jerry broke off the conversation and came back toward the wagon. "One of her sheep strayed and fell down the arroyo," he said. "Landed on a ledge about halfway down. I think I can get it out, but I'll need the bench plank for a lever."

Beth took the offered hand and scrambled out, ruefully noting that she was adding a layer of red dust to the white sand that already ornamented her traveling costume. Perhaps she shouldn't have been quite so critical of Jerry's dusty appearance. She was beginning to realize how difficult it was to stay clean.

"Were you talking Indian?" she asked.

"Navaho," Jerry corrected her. "There's a good many Indian tribes in these parts—Zuni, Tewa, Apache—or didn't your missionary fellow get into that much detail?"

Beth shook her head, her heart sinking at the thought of having to learn so many different languages just to communicate with her pupils.

"Figures. All Indians look alike to a missionary."

"All *people* are alike to a missionary," Beth countered, following Jerry as he carried the heavy plank to the edge of the arroyo. "We are all children of one God—whites, Navahos, Zanys, or . . . whatever." She couldn't remember the other names he'd mentioned.

"Zunis," Jerry said. "Never mind. It'll be mostly Navahos at your school. But you sure are going to raise some hackles around there, Miss Johanssen, if you go around talking like that!"

Beth glowered at his back as he knelt where Pahie pointed and leaned down into the arroyo. It was just too bad if she annoyed this Jerry Dixon by caring about what happened to the Indians!

He strained farther and farther down, reaching and tugging at something. An indignant bleat drifted up from the depths of the arroyo and Jerry gave a pull that inched his body even farther across the lip of the gully. Beth put the back of one hand to her mouth to restrain a cry of fear as she saw how far down he strained. When he came up, red-faced and with a smear of red dust ornamenting his shirt, she felt quite limp with relief.

"I can get a hold of its tail," he said, slapping his hands together to clean them, "but the damn fool beast—'scuse me, missionary lady—the intractable quadruped don't seem inclined to walk up the side of the arroyo backwards while I hold its tail. Can't say as I blame it." He grinned through the dust, and Beth thought how hard it was to keep disliking this man.

"If you're going to do that again," she said, "at least let me hold your feet."

Jerry's eyebrows danced up and down. "Why, Miss Johanssen, ma'am! I didn't know you cared! You think we been acquainted long enough for such goings-on?"

Then again, Beth thought, sometimes he made it easy to dislike him. "Nothing of the sort," she said. "I just don't want to be stranded in this barren, desolate place without a guide."

"Oh, Pahie'd guide you out all right," Jerry said. "But I don't aim to break my neck over a sheep. We'll have to get the board under it and lever it out. Might take some time." He eyed her doubtfully. "I'd ask you to help me, but I'd hate to muss up that nice dress. Maybe Pahie can take the other end."

Beth didn't have to glance at the slight frame of the little girl to make up her mind. "Nonsense," she said, picking up one end of the plank. "A little exercise is just what I need to unkink my muscles after that long train ride. Now, what did you want me to do?"

Jerry looked her up and down with a long, slow, lazy grin. "Ma'am, you better learn not to ask that question of a lonesome wrangler. What I might want you to do is something we better not go into."

Beth bit her lip and turned away. "What I need you to do," Jerry went on, "is to balance the weight of this plank while I climb down to the ledge where the sheep is."

By the time Beth had helped Jerry to maneuver the plank down into the arroyo and partially under the sheep, she was covered with red dust from head to toe and her black hair was falling out of the pompadour in loose, damp strands that clung to her face. But she felt an incredible sense of accomplishment when Jerry, standing precariously balanced on a ledge a few feet under the one where the sheep lay, called up, "Got it! You can put your weight on it now!"

Beth leaned on the end of the plank that projected over the lip of the arroyo while Jerry, the muscles in his arms and shoulders standing out like taut cords under the strain, pushed his end of the plank up and kept the frightened sheep from sliding off. The sharp edge of the eroded gully began crumbling under the pressure of the plank.

Her arms aching with the effort of holding the plank steady, Beth watched helplessly as clods of red earth tumbled down the sides of the arroyo. The plank gave a sickening lurch as the edge gave way. It swung sideways and Beth felt her arms being pulled after it. But it was almost level now. She pushed down with all her strength and felt no response. "Help me, Pahie!" she panted.

The little girl added her efforts to Beth's, but the plank still did not move. In desperation, she threw herself bodily over the end of the plank. The sharp corners of the wood bruised her ribs and the force of landing knocked the breath out of her. But she was lying facedown on safe ground, the plank securely held under her body, while Jerry shoved the bawling sheep to safety.

Once the sheep was on solid ground, Jerry helped Beth pull the plank back from the edge of the gully. "We did it!" Beth wiped the back of one hand across her face and tasted grit. It didn't matter. She hadn't felt so good about anything since she'd received her teaching certificate.

"We sure did. Pretty good work, partner." Jerry grinned at her and Beth felt an unfamiliar warmth rising from her midriff. "Guess I owe you an apology, missionary lady. I couldn't have got that sheep up without your help." He offered her a dusty hand and they shook hands solemnly.

"Apology accepted—partner," she said. But she couldn't resist one last needle. "You should have expected a missionary lady to be good at saving lost sheep."

Jerry's clothes were streaked with the red dust of the arroyo, and the sweat trickled through the grime on his face. "Do I look anywhere near as filthy as you do?" Beth asked.

Jerry's grin broadened as he surveyed her disheveled appearance. "Worse, missionary lady. Worse."

"Oh, dear." Beth glanced around the barren plain. "Is there any place where I can wash?"

"At the mission," Jerry said.

Beth shook her head, ruefully looking down at the wreckage of her neat traveling costume. What a way to arrive at her new job—a job she didn't even have yet! "Oh, well," she said with more optimism than she felt, "I'm sure the Griscoms will understand when we tell them how it happened."

Jerry blinked. "You think they'll approve? You got something to learn about mission folks, ma'am." He shook his head as they climbed back into the wagon.

"So do you," Beth said. She held on to the side of the wagon as they careened over a boulder-strewn dip. She was beginning to think she might have misjudged Jerry. He might even have had some good reason for the actions at the train station.

"Why don't you tell me some more about your philosophy of life? Don't I recall something about not going out of your way to interfere?" she teased lightly.

"Ain't interfering to help somebody when they need it," Jerry mumbled in some embarrassment, pulling his hat down over his eyes and slouching down over the reins.

"Exactly!" Beth said in triumph. "And that's what I'm going to do at the school."

Jerry shook his head again. "It won't work out that way."

"Look," Beth said in exasperation, "exactly why do you hate the mission so much? And don't give me these generalities about saving souls. I don't believe you care what church people go to. And neither do I. I'm going out there to help the children learn reading and figuring so they can have a better life. What's so terrible about that?"

Jerry shrugged. "Nothing . . . as long as you don't mess up the rest of their lives while you're doing it."

Beth stared in blank incomprehension as the wagon moved slowly through a plain littered with scrubby cedar and sage, yellow rocks, and red mounds. "How on earth can reading and writing hurt anybody?"

Jerry slapped the palm of his open hand with the end of the reins. "Don't you know *anything* about how the boarding schools operate?"

"How can I?" Beth snapped back. "I just got off the train, remember? What am I supposed to do, absorb local knowledge through the pores of my skin?"

"Well . . ." Jerry stared out across the mesa, visibly collecting his thoughts. "They take the kids away from home. Ten, maybe twelve years. Make 'em speak English. They forget how to live like Indians. Then they turn 'em loose when they graduate, tell 'em to get jobs and live like white men. Only they mostly can't get jobs, 'cause you missionaries haven't done much about educating the whites, and not many men in Gallup want to hire the red savages. And it's worse for the girls. Only one kind of work for a girl in Gallup—besides teaching school, that is!" He brought the reins down against his hand with another slap and the horses twitched nervously at the sound.

"What's so bad about learning English?" Beth cried. She hadn't really understood the rest of his speech, hadn't really heard it. "Do you want them to be prisoners of their own language forever, on the reservation, quaint and primitive and unthreatening?" She remembered something else. "Mr. Farragut explained about having the children board at school. They mostly come from too far away to go home every night. And they're allowed to go home in the summer. He said so!"

Jerry shook his head. "Bet he also said they weren't encouraged to go home, because they revert to heathenish ways."

Beth sat back. There had been something like that—but why was Jerry making such a big deal over it?

"Thought so," he said with satisfaction when she didn't answer. "I heard that speech, too. More times than I care to count. And you know what it adds up to? Griscom hates the Indians. He wants to paint them white and dress them in suits and make them pretend to be white men, but he doesn't really believe they can ever be anything but savages. The kids at the school spend more time working in the laundry and the garden than they do having lessons. After they've done their ten years of free labor, they're turned out to be hired hands or maids—if anybody'll have them."

Every line of his body was taut with anger, and his eyes were cold and burning at the same time. Beth shrank from the fury she had unleashed.

"It . . . it doesn't have to be like that," she said.

"Maybe not." Jerry relaxed slightly. "I'm telling you what it is like."

He turned his head and stared at her as if he were trying to read her thoughts. Why had she thought his eyes were cold? They burned her; she could feel the heat wherever he glanced.

"I'm here to teach," she said lamely at last. "I want to add to what the children have—not take anything away."

"See how it works out," Jerry suggested. She wished he would stop looking at her like that. "I got to admit you were some help with the sheep. Could be . . ." His voice trailed off and the horses, sensing his inattention, slowed to a walk. Beth felt as though those piercing eyes were looking right through her now, discarding all the frivolities of black curls and large dark eyes and tailored traveling costume to find out who she really was. Not the schoolteacher. Not even the pretty girl. Just herself.

Somehow that was worse than being physically stripped. Beth felt as though he could see right through to all the doubts and fears and inadequacies that plagued her whenever she thought about doing something instead of jumping right in and doing it. She dropped her eyes, but that didn't help. There was nowhere she could hide.

"I thought," he said slowly at last, "I thought you were another la-de-da missionary lady from the East, come out to show us ignorant yokels where we went wrong. Maybe you're not. Old Griscom talks a good fight about loving your neighbor, but I never seen him get dirty to help his neighbor get a sheep out of trouble.

"I wasn't going to say anything. Didn't want to make you any madder than you already were." He shook his head and reined in the team till they came to a slow, ambling halt just before another hill.

"But you go into that mission talking about everybody being equal, and believing it, and you've got trouble coming, lady. You won't last a month there. Hell, you won't last a week!"

"Yes, I will," Beth said. "This time I'm not going to—I mean, there's work that needs to be done here, and I'm going to do it." She wasn't going to jump in without thinking and get in trouble the way she had in Iowa. Jerry's criticisms of the mission might be justified; she'd see after she'd been there a while. She couldn't believe it was as bad as he said.

Jerry was still shaking his head. "We'll see. The school's just over that rise." He pointed to the sandy hill before them. "Road goes down into a canyon—you can't see it from here."

"Then why did you stop?" Beth asked.

He moved imperceptibly closer, and she knew the answer before his hands closed over her shoulders. "Some things you can't do in the mission," he murmured.

He held her firmly and competently, not hurting her but giving her no choice. As his face came close to hers, Beth stared into his eyes and felt as if she could lose herself forever in that gray sea. She closed her own eyes, but that wasn't enough to block out the sensation of his lips coming down on hers with a demanding pressure that scorched and dizzied her. She was floating, falling, and only the whipcord strength of Jerry's arms about her held her safe. Her lips parted under that insistent pressure; she was sinking into the gray sea now, drowning, totally encompassed by it.

When he released her, her mouth burned from his possessive kiss. Breathless, feeling her heart hammer in her chest, she sat facing him with parted lips from which no words came.

Jerry shook his head, smiling. "Okay, that settles it. You'll never make it at the mission. They've got no place for normal warm-blooded people there."

He flipped the reins over the horses' backs and they started laboring up the slow rise of the last hill. Beth clutched the edge of the plank she sat on, somehow reassured by the gritty reality of the sand in her hair and the sharp edges of the board cutting into her palms. She was still in the real world. It hadn't changed into something else in that one magic, intoxicating, frightening moment.

"A week should be long enough for you to figure out that you don't belong here. I'll pick you up on Saturday and take you over to Galvan's ranch. You can stay there while you're figuring out what to do."

Beth sat open-mouthed in amazement. The nerve of the man! Did he think he could plan her life, herd her around like a cow? She bit down hard on several scathing retorts. It was high time to stop talking—and acting—without thinking.

"Thank you very much," she said at last, "that won't be necessary. I don't run away from a job that quickly."

"A week," Jerry repeated. "And that's about three days too long, but I want to give you time to be good and sure."

Beth shook her head. Jerry grinned but offered no more words to change her mind. Unspeaking, they started down the long tilt of the road into the canyon where the mission was.

❧ Chapter Four

_J_ erry's estimate that Beth would be ready to leave in four days was not quite correct. She actually made it through four and a half days before her first major clash with the Griscoms.

Her first sight of the school had been rather disappointing. In contrast to the rolling vistas they had traveled across, here the wagon track dipped sharply into a red-walled canyon with a flat sandy bottom. The mission buildings were set squarely in the middle of this sandy area, surrounded by a three-strand barbed-wire fence that gave the school the look of a military encampment or a prison. Worst of all was the discovery that the high canyon walls cut off the spectacular view Beth had been delighting in on the journey into the reservation.

Mr. and Mrs. Griscom had been somewhat surprised to have a new teacher drop in out of thin air, and they had clearly been suspicious of anyone who traveled with Jerry Dixon, even though Jerry tactfully departed as soon as he had introduced Beth and unloaded her trunk from the wagon. Beth was surprised to find that she felt just a little bit lonelier after the annoying redhead had driven away. She stood by her trunk, looking uncertainly at the man and woman who had started this mission school and who had the power to keep her or reject her.

They were not an attractive couple. Mr. Griscom was tall and thin, with a red-wattled neck like a turkey gobbler's; his wife was a massive woman with arms as thick as Beth's waist, her stout body encased in a stiff column of black bombazine that crackled when she moved. Beth reminded herself that good works and a good heart didn't necessarily show on one's face. But did they have to frown so much?

After Mr. Griscom had lectured her for a while on the dangers of choosing improper traveling companions, and had read over her teaching certificates several times, he grudgingly allowed that they could use another teacher right now. Of the two men and two women who had accompanied them when they took over the mission school, only one remained. The others had gone back east, finding the work too hard and the life too lonely.

"I won't complain of the isolation," Beth promised. Fewer people around meant fewer people to annoy. She didn't want this teaching job to be marred by the kind of dissension that she'd inadvertently caused in Iowa.

"Very well." Mr. Griscom raised his balding head and looked at her over the silver-rimmed spectacles that perpetually slipped off his nose. "You will take over the mixed primary class and the girls' senior class. You may sleep in the attic bedroom with Miss Clare."

He jerked his head at a slender young woman who came running out of one of the long school buildings, almost tripping over her skirts and her words as she apologized for not being there to greet Beth.

"But how could you?" Beth said, amused. "Nobody knew I was coming!"

Mr. Griscom ruthlessly interrupted Miss Clare's breathless, endless apologies. "Addie will show you your room.
Classes begin at six sharp." A nod of his head dismissed
them both.

Addie Clare led Beth up the narrow stairs to the attic bedroom. "What a blessing you are!" she exclaimed as soon as
they were out of earshot of the Griscoms. "I've been driven
to distraction trying to handle the classes, and dear Reverend
Griscom does so need my help with his correspondence!
Now I will be free to take some of the burden of the mission
work off his shoulders."

Addie was tall and thin, with a long neck and a long thin
nose, red from constant sniffling, as she was allergic to the
dust and pollen that filled the desert air. She wore her mousy
brown hair at the back of her neck in a depressed-looking
bun, where it bounced in time to her emphatic nods as she
chattered to Beth about the school routine.

Beth was surprised to learn that there were only twenty
pupils at the school—mostly Navahos, with a few Hopi and
Tewa children from farther away. They slept on the upper
floors of the two long adobe buildings that Addie pointed
out from the window of the attic bedroom; boys in one
building, girls in another. The lower floor of one building
was used for classes; the other one was devoted to a dining
hall and what the Griscoms called "industrial arts," which
translated into cooking, laundry, and carpentry work for the
school.

Beth was somewhat surprised at first to learn how little of
the school routine was devoted to what she considered
teaching. At half-past five every morning Mrs. Griscom
rang the bell, which was the signal to wash and dress, and at
six the children marched into the dining room to the accompaniment of Addie's energetic poundings on the old piano.
They were required to keep absolute silence during meals.

As soon as breakfast was over, the older boys went to work in the vegetable garden or in the carpentry shop, while the girls did the school laundry and prepared the meals for the rest of the day. Beth was supposed to teach the younger children during this time, but the morning's instruction was continually broken up by Mrs. Griscom's classroom visits and little homilies on civilized behavior.

In the afternoon the older children had two hours of lessons, the boys with Mr. Griscom and the girls with Beth. She found that they were often too tired and sleepy from their morning's work to pay attention, so after a few days she began to search for ways to make the lessons more entertaining and less demanding than the traditional school curriculum.

Both classes were frustrating at first. The older children sat dumb and morose on their benches, some unashamedly napping, none volunteering a word in class unless she virtually dragged it out of them. And the little ones! There were times, that first week, when Beth seriously wondered if the task was entirely hopeless. More than half of them seemed to understand no English at all, and even those who'd been at the school for a year or two spoke only in monosyllables. It was like trying to communicate with a classroom full of Pahies—without Jerry's help.

Her first breakthrough came on the Friday morning after her arrival. She'd been called out of the classroom to discuss the linen stores with Mrs. Griscom, and when she came back she was astonished to hear her mute, sullen children babbling happily among themselves. She stood outside the door for a moment, listening to the voices of at least half a dozen of the thirteen children in the classroom and wondering at the strange liquid flow of unfamiliar syllables. How bright and happy they sounded! And yet, when she tried to teach them the first lesson in the reader, they sat like so many little lumps of dough.

She wished that she could understand what they were saying. Why not? she thought suddenly. On that thought, she threw open the classroom door and marched in.

Immediately the children fell silent, looking up at her with big, scared eyes as though they expected to be punished. Beth clapped her hands for silence, quite unnecessarily, but it was the way she had always begun in her Iowa classroom, and the familiar gesture helped her to get started.

"Children. I need your help." She spoke slowly and clearly, knowing that at least some of them could understand her, even if all the faces looked uniformly blank. "Some of you speak a little of my language, but I don't know any of your languages. I would like to learn the tongue of the People. Will you help me?"

A dazed silence greeted her. Beth looked from one shuttered face to the next, her brief excitement ebbing as she looked without success for some light of understanding. She beckoned to George, a boy of ten who would be going to Mr. Griscom's section next year and whom she had heard speaking some English with Addie Clare.

"George. Do you know what this is?" She pointed to the book she had been trying to use as a reader before Mrs. Griscom had called her away.

"Book," George said after some moments of thought.

"And what is it in your language?"

George screwed up his face in agonized contortions. "Book?"

"No," Beth said patiently, "what do you call it when you are at home?"

George shook his head. "Don' call it nothing. Don' see it."

Of course, Beth thought, and nearly laughed aloud at her

own foolishness. Books must be very foreign objects to a
Navaho hogan. What could she use, then? She looked
around the classroom. Desks, pointers, slates, chalk—
wasn't there anything here the children could remember seeing in a Navaho hogan?

For the first time Beth began to appreciate what a very
foreign world the school was to them. Well, that shouldn't
stop her. Picking up a piece of chalk, she sketched the outline of a sheep on the blackboard. "What's this?" she ap-
pealed to the class in general.

"Uh . . . cloud?" suggested one of the girls on the back
row.

Beth hurriedly added four legs and a tail. "Sheep. What
do you call a sheep?"

There was another silence. Then the tiniest girl in the
class, Mary Neez, started vibrating up and down on her
bench with excitement.

"Dibe!" she cried out. *"Dibe!"*

It was the first word she had spoken since Beth had taken
over the class.

"Dibeh?" Beth imitated the word after her. Her halting
mimicking raised gales of laughter from the class, and two
little boys vied with each other to correct her.

Now that the ice was broken, Beth found it easy to get the
children to continue this fascinating new game. Before long
the blackboard was covered with sketches. She had learned
that a knife was *beesh,* a coat was *eetsoh,* and a coyote was
something that sounded to her like *mayee.* If her pupils had
learned the reverse, she'd be happy with the day's work.

Tomorrow, she thought as they rocked with laughter over
her attempt to pronounce the word for coyote, tomorrow she
would have to test them on the English. But only if they
were allowed to test her on the Navaho! And she had a feel-

ing this was one time when the teacher wouldn't show up
any better than the students.

"Mahnee?" she tried again. Mary Neez jumped up and
down and launched a long, complicated critique of which
Beth understood less than one word in ten. Once again she
was humbled, thinking what impossible feats of learning
and comprehension she and her fellow teachers expected of
the children pitchforked into this strange world.

Mary Neez was still involved in her speech when the
classroom door flew open and banged against the wall. Mrs.
Griscom marched in, arms folded. Her stiff black bombazine dress seemed to be spitting sparks and her snowy-white
pompadour quivered with indignation.

"Miss Johanssen! What do you think you are doing?"

The animated children seemed to fold in on themselves.
A hush fell over the classroom and with despair Beth saw the
children turning back into the "little lumps of dough" she
had imagined them as earlier.

Mrs. Griscom beckoned imperiously. "Come outside. I
wish to speak to you."

Feeling like a naughty child herself, Beth followed Mrs.
Griscom out into the dusty yard that surrounded the school
building. The heat and glare of the noonday sun was blind-
ing after the shady classroom. Blinking against the assault of
light, she put up one hand to shade her face.

"Don't you understand," Mrs. Griscom demanded,
"that the children are never, *never* to be allowed to speak
their heathen language in our school? They come here to be
taught civilized ways, Miss Johanssen—not to drag us down
to their level! I was very pained to hear you imitating their
speech and inviting them to laugh at you."

Beth couldn't help laughing. "Oh, come now, Mrs. Griscom. Surely my first task is to teach them enough English so
that they may learn their lessons? Does it matter if they have

some fun while they're doing it? I certainly don't mind if
they make fun of my accent . . . and did you hear Mary
Neez?'' Surely even Mrs. Griscom would appreciate that
small victory. ''Today was the first time she's talked since I
took the class.''

''Talking Navaho,'' Mrs. Griscom said with a sniff.
''That is *not* the purpose of this school, Miss Johanssen! I
have made it a very strict rule that from the day a child ar-
rives here, he is not to use his native language on pain of
punishment. It is the only way to wean them from their savage life. In one hour you may very well have done incalculable harm.''

Her spectacles flashed in the sun as she glared at Beth.
Groping for words with which to defend herself, Beth was
relieved to hear the ringing of the dinner bell break off their
discussion. The children came marching out of the classroom in their well-disciplined lines and she had to lead them
to the dining hall.

Over dinner she had time to calm herself. Mr. and Mrs.
Griscom would not have established the rule against speaking Navaho without good reason. They had been working
here for years; they must know better than she. Besides,
hadn't she resolved that this time she would curb her unruly
tongue and get along with her superiors? There must be no
more scenes like the one in Iowa.

Beth suppressed a small sigh. She had imagined the West
as a place of wide-open skies and free people—a place
where her impulsive nature wouldn't lead her into so much
trouble. But the mission school, with its rules and regimen-
tation, was a more confining environment than her home or
the school in Vinton.

That afternoon, while Beth heard half a dozen senior girls
give their stumbling renditions of a poem by Shelley, the
back of her mind was busy trying to reconcile the new inter-

est shown by the children with Mrs. Griscom's absolute ban on using Navaho in the classroom. Surely there must be some way to help the children link their life in the hogan with the classroom, even if they had to do everything in English.

It was a shy comment from the oldest girl in the senior class, Lucy Tso, that opened the way for her.

"What do you think Shelley meant by 'Like a poet hidden in the light of thought,' Lucy?" Beth asked without much hope of an enlightening answer. She would settle for knowing that Lucy had understood the words.

"I tink . . . he mean by writing poem . . . he make light." Lucy tugged on one shiny black braid, her face screwed up with the effort of concentration. "Like—like Changing Woman sing to make light come to world."

Beth sat up a little straighter on her hard-backed chair. Not only had Lucy understood the poem, she was relating it to something in her own culture. "Who is Changing Woman?" she inquired.

"White Shell Woman," whispered a girl at the back of the room.

"Born to Water's mother!" another volunteered.

"Lucy?" Beth looked at her and the other girls fell silent. As Lucy began, in halting English, to explain the age-old story, they nodded in silent approbation.

Beth, too, sat silently, gripped by the unfolding beauty of the story as she glimpsed it through Lucy's stumbling translation. Changing Woman, mother of the twin heros, mother of the People, had made light come to the world when the People came up to the earth level and found only darkness. White she spread for dawn light, blue for morning, yellow for sunset, and black for night; Turquoise and White Shell, the twins, made a magic circle, and over this circle Changing Woman held a crystal that blazed into light.

"Lucy, that's wonderful," Beth said when the girl had finished. She turned to the other girls in the class. "Do you know more stories like that? Perhaps we could turn this into a class project for the month. Each of you will write down one story of your people, in English. I'll help you with the words," she promised as faces fell. "And then we can copy the stories, very neatly, and get the boys in the industrial arts class to bind them into books that the younger children can use for readers."

Her imagination caught fire with the beauty of the idea. The senior girls would learn English through working on the translation, the children would have readers that meant something to them, and she herself would learn something of the life of these people who inhabited the red-rock desert. She spent the rest of the class time discussing plans for the projected book with the girls. Perhaps they could illustrate the readers with watercolor paintings. How many stories could the girls think of?

Lucy Tso, the last to leave when the bell rang for dinner, stopped by Beth's desk. "Teacher . . . good idea," she said. "But don' tell Griscom, okay? He won't let us do it."

Beth smiled. "I'm sure he will. The Griscoms want you to learn better English, Lucy, so you can get a job outside when you graduate. They'll be very proud of this project."

At dinner, Mr. Griscom disabused her of this notion in no uncertain terms.

"These heathenish legends, Miss Johanssen, are among the greatest evils that lie in the way of their becoming civilized. They are infected with the poison of dark superstitions and profane ceremonies of a system as gross as that of darkest Africa. I am deeply shocked that you would even think of allowing the children to discuss such matters. If you had seen the unbridled evil of the orgiastic sings where they celebrate their pagan ceremonies, you would understand why I utterly forbid this translation project.''

Beth clenched her hands under the table, reminding herself of her vow to keep quiet and stay out of trouble this time. It was no good. She couldn't do it.

"Have you," she inquired in a voice of syrupy sweetness, "witnessed these 'orgiastic ceremonies' yourself?''

Mr. Griscom blinked, astonished, and his glasses slid to the end of his nose. "Of course not!''

"Then how do you know they are so evil?'' Beth followed up her advantage while he was still too startled to speak. "Mr. Griscom, I made notes of the story Lucy Tso told me today. If you would just read it, you'd see what I mean. There is nothing evil there—it is a beautiful, poetic, moving account of their creation myth, as meaningful to them as Genesis is to us.''

"Miss Johanssen!'' Mr. Griscom's glasses fell entirely off and hung suspended around his neck on a thin silver chain. The purplish-red folds of skin that hung down from his neck quivered as he tried to control his anger, making him look, Beth thought, exactly like an enraged turkey gobbler. "How can you make such a comparison? The Book of Genesis is part of the sacred truth which we are bringing to these people!''

"Maybe you are bringing them sacred truth,'' Beth snapped before she could stop herself, "but I'll settle for teaching them to read and write.''

"So that they can read the glories of Holy Writ.''

"So that they can read whatever they choose!'' Beth pushed back her chair and stood up in one furious movement. "Please excuse me, Mr. Griscom. I don't think there is any point in continuing this conversation.'' She marched out of the dining hall, leaving the uneaten stew congealing on her tin plate while twenty pairs of black Indian eyes followed her departure with interest and regret.

Too agitated to go to her stifling little room under the eaves of the Griscoms' house, Beth paced back and forth along the barbed-wire fence that marked the boundary of the mission for a while, staring at the red canyon walls that rose high overhead.

The walls of the canyon seemed to her to symbolize the irony of her trip out west. Seeking freedom and wide skies, where had she landed herself? Trapped at the bottom of a canyon, that's where! Well, she wouldn't stay! If that Jerry Dixon came tomorrow, she'd go with him as he'd suggested. . . . No, she wouldn't. That was running away. Besides, she wouldn't take Jerry Dixon's orders. She would, she would—

Beth marched up and down along the line of barbed wire, wearing out her furious energy in the soft sand. Before long her sense of proportion returned and she regretted her hasty words to Mr. Griscom. Of course, as a man of God, he would be dedicated to spreading the Word. In the morning, when they had both had time to cool down, she would go to him and explain that she had not meant to jeer at his faith. She was a churchgoer herself; it was just that her mission in life was teaching, not converting. But after all, they both had the same aim—to help the Indians. Surely they could find some way to work together.

Beth lifted her eyes to the canyon rim again. Now, instead of a prison barrier, it seemed like a challenge to her. She need not spend all her days at the bottom of the canyon. Tomorrow, on her half day, she would climb the steep wagon trail to the top of the mesa. Finding a way to work at this school was just another challenge, another hill that she had to climb. Eventually she'd reach the top!

By the time night fell over the canyon, with soft velvety

skies and stars that seemed low enough to reach out and touch, Beth had walked herself back into good humor. She was relieved to find that Addie Clare was already asleep when she returned to her room. She had no desire to discuss the quarrel with Mr. Griscom until she had settled matters with him.

Beth woke the next morning with a sense of bubbling anticipation. What was so wonderful about today? Then she remembered. It was Saturday, and Jerry Dixon was coming back! She smiled as she dressed, thinking of his confident prediction that she'd be ready to leave the mission after a week of teaching! "Nothing of the sort," she said decisively, sliding one foot into her high-buttoned boot and yanking the button hook through with quick, deft gestures.

"What sort?" mumbled Addie Clare from her bed.

"Oh . . . . I'm not going to quit this job," Beth said, starting the long task of hooking up the buttons on her other boot.

Addie sat up in bed and bumped her head against the low roof. "Ow! I certainly hope not," she said with feeling. "If you did, I'd have to go back to taking the primary class—little devils. They made my life miserable. Of course, they're really very sweet children when you get to know them," she added hastily, remembering that she was supposed to be persuading Beth to stay. She blew her nose with a doleful honk and began unplaiting the neat brown braids in which she tied her hair each night.

"Oh, they're not so bad," said Beth absently. Forgetting the task of putting up her own hair, she knelt with her arms on the windowsill and gazed out at the panorama of dawn in the canyon.

The view from her window was always breathtaking. The rest of the room . . . well, the thin roof let all the summer heat through to make it unbearably hot during the day, and

the slanting ceiling made it impossible to stand upright anywhere but in the exact center of the room between the two
beds; but Beth loved looking out the window over the flat
bed of the canyon to the red-and-yellow rim with its tracing
of scrubby junipers. She lingered morning and evening to
watch the shifting play of light and shadow across the canyon wall, marveling in the way the colors changed through a
whole spectrum from blue and violet to gold and red. The
sight reaffirmed her joy to be in this strange, harsh land with
its heart-stopping beauty. It was almost enough to give her
the patience she needed to get through the long, frustrating
days.

At the moment, the flat sandy plain and the school buildings were still shrouded in blue-and-violet shadows, but the
sun coming over the canyon rim touched the rocks with
gold, making the rough wagon trail that snaked over the
edge of the canyon into an enchanted path. ''I wonder when
he'll get here. . . .'' Beth murmured.

''Jerry Dixon?'' Addie gave a sharp sniff and pinned her
lank brown hair into a knot on the top of her head. ''I
thought you weren't going to leave.''

''I'm not,'' Beth said, ''but I'd like to talk to him.
There's a lot I don't understand.'' She tugged thoughtfully
at one of the long coils of black hair that fell down her back
and covered her white blouse in a shining blue-black cape.

Last week Jerry hadn't trusted her enough to explain the
quarrel between his employer and Lawrence Hudson. And
the Griscoms, when she'd asked them, had told her that
Lawrence Hudson was a good man and Eleuterio Galvan a
godless sinner, which didn't quite clarify matters. Maybe
today Jerry would tell her what he was so worried about.
Somehow, Beth realized with shock, in the course of this
frustrating week, she had begun feeling as if Jerry's worries
were also hers.

Addie sniffed again. "What you'd learn from that young man is nothing a decent girl needs to know. Didn't Reverend Griscom warn you to stay away from the Galvan Ranch crowd?"

Beth did not hear her. Kneeling before the window, she was lost in rapturous contemplation of the slowly unfolding day, as the sun crept over the canyon rim and replaced the lavender shadows with the dazzling colors of day. She did not stir until the breakfast bell roused her from her dream; then she hurried downstairs, pinning up her hair as she went, completely unaware of the line of dust clinging to her gray serge skirt where she'd knelt.

Beth's bubbling mood of excitement gradually lost its sparkle as the long, hot morning wore on and Jerry did not appear. Even her plan to apologize to Mr. Griscom and clear the air between them was thwarted when he left abruptly immediately after breakfast, saying he had business with the Indian agent.

There were no lessons on Saturdays, but she was expected to help Mrs. Griscom oversee the girls while they made soap and worked in the laundry. It was hot, boring work and she was not surprised that the girls were usually tired when they got to her class in the afternoon during the week. After four hours Beth's black hair stuck to her forehead and her white blouse clung to her damp shoulders.

She lived for the bell that would announce dinner and the beginning of her free half day. Perhaps it was as well that Jerry hadn't come, she thought, trying to cheer herself up. She no longer had energy for anything but a bath and a nap, but the upstairs room would be stifling at noon. . . . Well, she would sit in one of the empty classrooms, then, and prepare lessons for Monday.

"Beth!" Addie Clare had been with the other girls, teaching them to put minute stitches down the breadths of muslin that were joined together to make sheets for the dormitory beds. "That man is here. He asked for you . . . and he had the insolence to take my hand! However can you stand him?" Excitement had brought a flush to her cheeks so that they matched the rosy hue of her nose.

Beth dropped the sheet she had been feeding through the mangle and wiped the hair out of her eyes with the back of one hand. "No," she said reflexively. She didn't want Jerry to see her like this—hot, damp from exertion, and her hastily pinned-up hair coming down all over the back of her neck.

"No, you're not coming with me," inquired a deep voice from the doorway, "or no, I'm not here?"

Beth looked across the busy room and saw Jerry standing at the door. He was hatless, clean, with a gleaming white shirt setting off his tanned skin and the flaming red of his hair. He was smiling, but there was a questioning look in his gray eyes. Beth felt her own lips curving in response. Suddenly she forgot her own disheveled appearance and the disappointment she'd felt at not seeing him that morning. She took a step toward him and he came into the room, hands outstretched.

"No," Beth said, feeling her mouth stretch into a most unladylike grin, "I'm not coming with you. You didn't really think I'd quit that soon, did you?" But he had come back for her. Why that should make her so happy, when she had no intention of going anywhere with him, was quite beyond her.

The Indian girls backed away, tittering with their hands over their mouths, as he stepped between piles of folded sheets and baskets of dirty ones. He took Beth's hands and she felt suddenly weak, as though a current of strength were running from her body to his.

"Well, now," he said, looking straight at her with that

quizzical smile, "so you decided to stick it out, missionary lady?"

Beth's chin came up. "I told you I would."

"So you did, missionary lady," he said, smiling, "so you did."

Beth was not quite sure how it happened, but somehow she found herself walking out of the steamy laundry with Jerry while Addie took over her tasks. They walked across the sandy yard, still holding hands, and paused under the shade of the lone cottonwood tree that grew by the fence that bounded the mission.

"Been a long week," Jerry said.

"Yes." It sounded like an admission that she'd missed him. "There's been so much to learn," Beth hurried on, "and I'm afraid I made some terrible mistakes, but I think I'm finding my feet at last." She paused, frowning. Was that really true?

"Long for me, I meant," Jerry said. He smiled at her and she felt a treacherous glow warming her midriff. "You ready to go? It's a long ride."

Beth stared. "Didn't you understand? I told you. I'm not going with you."

"Sure you are." Jerry's gray eyes met hers with a cool confidence that made Beth wonder if one of them was going crazy.

"Jerry." She took a deep breath, wondering if she could find any words definite enough to convince him. "Try and get this simple fact straight, will you? This is my job. I like it. I am not going to quit."

"Of course not, you already said so," Jerry agreed with a swiftness that left Beth feeling as though she'd stepped down an invisible stair in the darkness. "But that don't mean you can't take an afternoon off, does it? I already told Mrs. Griscom that you'd been invited to dinner at the Galvan Ranch, and that I'd been sent to bring you. And she said it was all right for you to go.''

Beth's pent-up breath exploded in an involuntary giggle. ''You—you rat,'' she said, leaning weakly against the sheltering cottonwood. ''Why couldn't you have said that to start with?''

''When I walked into the laundry room, you looked like you were spoiling for a fight with someone,'' Jerry explained, his lips twitching upward at the corners. ''I figured I'd let you take it out on me. Then maybe we could be nice and friendly the rest of the evening. Okay?''

His fingers rested on her arm just above the elbow, brushing the soft skin where she'd rolled up her sleeves to keep them out of the soapy water. ''Come on,'' he said softly, ''my wagon's hitched right over here.''

Beth shook her head, smiling. ''You're impossible.'' What a way to deliver a dinner invitation! But she followed him to the wagon without another protest. It was worth putting up with Jerry's teasing for the prospect of an evening away from the mission.

The horses were straining up the rutted track that led out of the canyon when Beth looked down at her dress with an exclamation of dismay. The splashes of water from the laundry had left a pattern of round soapy stains on her skirt from the knee down. ''Wait a minute,'' she said to Jerry. ''I can't go like this! I'll have to go back and change clothes.''

''Can't stop the horses on a hill,'' Jerry told her. ''Wait till we get up to the top.''

Beth felt guilty at the thought of making the poor horses go up and down the hill twice in a row. What had she been thinking of, to just walk away from the mission like that? It was all Jerry's fault, the way he'd rushed her and kept her off-balance. Somehow she always was off-balance when he was around, she thought, glancing at his lean figure with the blaze of red hair creeping out from under his hat.

When they reached the top, Jerry kept driving along the main road. "What are you doing?" Beth grabbed his arm. "You said you'd stop and go back when we got to the top of the canyon."

Jerry shook his head. "Uh-uh. I said you'd have to wait till we got to the top. I didn't say what you'd have to wait for."

"More word games." Beth felt hot and sweaty and annoyed. "Listen, I'm not going to dinner—"

"Of course not." Once again, Jerry capitulated when she was braced for a fight. He glanced at her and grinned. "Don't worry, we're not going to dinner at Galvan's. And you're dressed just fine for where we're going."

Beth's mouth fell open. "You lied to me? Why? What are you—"

"Nope. I lied to Ma Griscom. You I told the exact truth." Jerry flicked his whip, and the horses picked up their pace over the smooth portion of the road. "I said I'd told her you were invited to dinner at Galvan's, and that's exactly what I did tell her. It was the only way I could think of to get you sprung from there."

Beth glanced over her shoulder. They were not too far from the mission yet; she could easily walk back. But her curiosity wouldn't let her depart without finding out a little more.

"All right, master mind, I give up," she said. "Where are you taking me?"

Jerry turned his head and looked at her with cool, measuring eyes. "To the last day of the Night Chant," he said at last.

"The what?"

"It's an Indian ceremony. What goes on inside the medicine hogan is secret, but folks come from all over to watch the dancing outside. I thought you might like to see it.''

Beth had a vivid picture of Mr. Griscom's face, purple-splotched and quivering, as he worked himself up into a rage warning her about the Indians' disgusting heathen ceremonies. Would he fire her if he found out about this? No, they needed teachers too badly. There would be one almighty fuss, though.

''You might look on it as an educational experience,'' Jerry suggested.

He brought his team to a halt at a wide place in the road, waiting while she made up her mind. Clearly he would take her back to the mission if she insisted on it.

''Oh, go ahead,'' Beth said. ''I figure it's two educational experiences for the price of one. I've never been kidnapped before, either.''

❧ Chapter Five

The sing was being held at the foot of a line of flat-topped wooded hills. A small creek trickled down between two hills and meandered across the plain, marked by a line of slender trees. The medicine hogan, a squat, six-sided building of rough cedar logs, stood beside the stream, and to one side there was a line of cooking fires where women were turning meat on spits.

As far as Beth could tell, she and Jerry were the only whites among the crowd gathered to watch the dancing. She looked around curiously at the other wagons drawn up around the flat dance ground before the medicine hogan. Most of them, unlike Jerry's, were covered with white canvas tops that arched against the clear blue sky like sails. On the way out he'd told her that the sing lasted for nine days. The observers must have come prepared to camp in their wagons.

In the nearest wagon, a square-faced woman with smooth black braids pulled her velveteen blouse off one shoulder to suckle a baby. The strings of turquoise-and-silver beads that hung about her neck gleamed against her dark skin, and the

baby put up a tiny hand to grab at the beads while it nursed.
Two older children played quietly in front of the wagon.

The Navaho woman's dark eyes met Beth's and she realized that she had been staring. Embarrassed, she looked
away, trying to seem very interested in something at the
edge of the cleared space. After a moment, she had no need
to feign interest. The details of the scene blended for her into
one harmonious whole: the women tending the cooking fire
on the far side of the hogan, the old men with bright striped
blankets folded around their shoulders, the line of young
men who swayed back and forth, arms linked, keeping time
to a slow monotonous chant on two notes.

The chanting of the young men and the rhythmic thudding
of axes from farther up the canyon blended into a single
heavy vibration that seemed to fill the air with expectancy.
The contrast between the sun-gilded top of the cliff and the
cool shadows creeping across the clearing created another
kind of music, Beth thought, as did the zigzag slashes of
color that decorated the men's blankets and even the sharp
greasy smell of broiled mutton at the cooking fires. She
laughed at this last thought, and Jerry raised his eyebrows.

"Care to let me in on the joke?" he asked.

"I was thinking that everything here is like music," Beth
said. "Even the smells!" She waved one hand toward the
long rectangular fire, where mutton fat dripped into the
coals and sent up spirals of pungent, greasy smoke.

Jerry shook his head slowly from side to side. "Lady,"
he said solemnly, "if the stuff on that cook fire is singing to
you, you must be hungrier than I thought! Don't they feed
you at the mission school?"

"We skipped dinner," Beth reminded him. On the long
ride out to the place where the sing was being held, she had
not been conscious of hunger, but now as the sun went down

the cool air and the smell of broiled meat were tempting her appetite.

"I figured on starving you," Jerry told her, straight-faced, "until you were so hungry you wouldn't complain about eating Indian cooking. Didn't think it'd work this quick, though. Come on. We'll get fixed up, then you can watch the dancing in comfort."

He led her across the cleared space to a wagon drawn up close by the cooking fires. A tall Navaho woman, graceful in her heavy skirt of twenty yards of flounced calico, was just pulling a Dutch oven out of the coals with a forked stick.

"*Ahalani,*" Jerry greeted her.

The woman looked down and murmured a barely audible reply. Jerry said something in Navaho and jerked his head at Beth. The woman looked up, smiling and holding one hand before her mouth, and bobbed her head at Beth. "Owdoyoudo," she whispered, running the sounds together to make one word out of them.

"This is Mary Neez's mother," Jerry told Beth. "I told her you were the new teacher lady at the mission."

Beth held out her hand. "How do you do, Mrs. Neez. I'm very glad to meet you. Your daughter is a charming little girl, and she's doing very well in the primary class."

"Owdoyoudo, owdoyoudo," Mrs. Neez repeated, nodding and smiling behind her hand and making no move to shake hands with Beth.

"Mary's mother doesn't speak much English," Jerry explained.

"But she sent her daughter to school anyway. So she's not against education!" Beth felt she had scored a point over Jerry, with his constant denigration of everything connected with the mission school.

"Not exactly," Jerry said. "Mary's father's dead. She

remarried, and now she's got three kids younger than Mary, and the stepfather isn't too crazy about taking care of another man's kids. And Mary's too little to herd sheep. So he gave her to the government agents last time they came through.''

Beth bit her lip. "I . . . see," she said slowly. "Is that why you brought me over here? To make a point?"

"Hell, no," Jerry said cheerfully. "I brought you over here to get something to eat." He handed Beth a dripping mutton rib, still hot from the fire, encased in a thick flap of bread from the Dutch oven. "And," he went on, glancing at her, "to let Mary's mother get a look at you."

"Why? To make another point?"

"You might say so." Jerry took a bite of the steaming meat and chewed with maddening deliberation. "She didn't feel so good about letting Mary go to the boarding school. Doesn't know much about white people. I wanted to take Mary to the sing, let them visit, but old Griscom said it was against school rules and he'd charge me with kidnapping if I took the kid outside the fence. But I thought she could meet you, anyway; maybe she'd feel better if she knew what sort of lady was teaching at the school."

"Well!" Beth felt a little dashed at Jerry's blunt explanation. She'd thought the sing was an excuse for him to take her out and for them to get to know each other better. Instead it turned out she was only a substitute for a Navaho child. "You're a very kind man," she said at last, "to make this long drive just to cheer up Mrs. Neez."

Jerry finished off his piece of mutton and wiped his hands on the last of the bread. "Now, schoolteacher lady. I didn't say that was my only reason. I was going to take you anyway."

"You were?" Strange how much better that made her feel.

"Sure. Just another part of my altruistic nature. Providing educational experiences for the schoolteachers. And getting in ahead of all the lonesome men in the territory who might want to take you to the dance."

"Dance?" Beth looked at the line of young men shuffling back and forth with their arms about each other's shoulders. It was a far cry from the dances she'd been to in Iowa.

"Oh, not this," Jerry said. "But you never know, there might be a real dance got up sometime. In which case, remember I asked you first."

Beth wasn't sure how to answer this. He had to be teasing; nobody would make an engagement for some hypothetical dance that wasn't even planned yet. But there was no laughter in the level stare of his gray eyes, and he was watching her as though her answer meant something to him.

"Of course," she said lightly after a moment, "and I'll save you the first waltz on my dance card, too!"

"You do that," said Jerry. He nodded once, firmly, as if something had been resolved; then he murmured a few words to Mary Neez's mother and took Beth's arm. The firm, warm clasp of his fingers gave her an unexpected shiver of delight.

"The ceremony's about to start," he told her. "Let's go back and sit in the wagon. I brought blankets to wrap up in."

That didn't sound so good to Beth, but she found that he meant for each of them to roll up in separate blankets—like cigars in a box, she thought. At first, under the balmy evening sky, the idea seemed ridiculous. But after they'd sat for an hour listening to some monotonous chanting that Beth couldn't distinguish from the practice sessions, the chill of the desert night began to get to her, and she was happy enough to wrap up in the blanket Jerry had provided.

"Bored?" Jerry murmured in her ear.

"A little," Beth admitted. Not having any idea what was going on, she couldn't get much out of the shuffling steps of the dancers and their rhythmic chant.

"Oughta pick up pretty soon," Jerry promised. He pointed to the far side of the circle of wagons, where two Navaho men were gesturing for the people who stood among the wagons to move back. A third man came from behind the hogan with an armload of dry wood, and the central fire flared up in a sudden blaze of light.

Suddenly a high-pitched cry sliced through the monotonous notes of the chant, and five masked figures came running out of the hogan. The firelight was sufficient to show Beth the first figure in some detail. His head was covered with a soft leather bag, ornamented across the top with a stiff red crest of hair and dyed feathers, and a cloak of whitish leather draped his body. As he moved quickly around the fire, hooting softly, the light danced off heavy silver bracelets on his wrists and chunks of raw turquoise tied around his neck and ankles.

"Yebetchai," Jerry whispered, "the grandfather of the gods."

"Who are the others supposed to be, do you know?" Beth asked, pointing to the four men who followed Yebetchai, their faces likewise masked in leather bags, but their bodies bare to the waist and gleaming with sweat and white paint.

Jerry shook his head. The medicine man was leading Yebetchai and the others toward the lodge now, strewing a path of cornmeal before them. As they neared the structure of rough-cut cedar logs, the flap over the door lifted and an old man wrapped in a blanket came out, leaning against the outer wall for support.

"That's the patient," Jerry told Beth. The medicine man raised his voice, intoning a long prayer, and the masked gods formed a semicircle around the patient and kept up a slow dancing step throughout the chant. In a low voice, halting when he didn't know a word, Jerry translated scraps of the prayer for her.

"House made of dawn light, house made of evening light, house made of rain cloud, where the . . . lightning . . . stands, where the god lives. . . .

"They say that bit over and over," he interpolated. "I kind of got to understand it from hearing it so many times. Now the next bit . . . I don't get it. . . . Oh, here we are."

He took up the translation again.

"Come to us with the lightning over your head, come to us with the rainbow over your head. Come to us soaring with the lightning on your wings, come to us soaring with the rainbow on the ends of your wings."

Beth began to feel the power of the chant, this slow layering of phrase on phrase, calling to sky and earth and the mysteries that the Navaho saw behind the face of the land. Was it so different from a psalm? "Take the wings of morning," the psalmist had sung. This was no less noble, in its own way.

As the medicine man's prayer drew to an end, his voice sank and the dancing gods drew back, looking up to the sky as if they expected the god whom they invoked to come soaring on his wings of lightning. Beth looked up, too, and saw that night had fallen while she was watching the chant. The fire in the center of the dancing space was a little circle of reddish light, holding the hogan and the dancers and the people in the wagons together. Outside, beyond that circle, was nothing but the velvety blackness of the night, a darkness that swallowed up every line and feature of the desert and made the stars hanging overhead seem closer than the mesas that had disappeared into the night.

"I walk with beauty before me, I walk with beauty behind me; I walk with beauty below me, I walk with beauty above

me; I walk with beauty all around me. In beauty it is finished. In beauty it is finished. In beauty it is finished.''

The medicine man's voice stopped abruptly, leaving the
last words hanging in the night air. Beth could almost imagine that she understood them without Jerry's murmured
translation: what else could that particular pattern of syllables have meant? She drew a long, shaky breath and looked
up at Jerry. ''I'm glad you brought me,'' she said.

The solemn mood of the prayer was broken by a swift
rush forward; all the masked dancers formed a line and bent
low to shake their rattles and stamp the ground. A sharp
chant with a pounding, demanding rhythm gave the time to
their stamping dance. People began to move among the
wagons and talk in low voices; Beth sensed that the sacred
moment had passed.

''Like it?'' Jerry's face was a shadow lit by the sparks of
firelight reflecting from his eyes. The strangeness of the
scene swept over Beth all at once. What was she doing here,
out on the desert surrounded by Indians, with a man as
strange to her as one of the masked gods in the dance?

''Yes,'' she said, ''very much.''

Jerry's teeth flashed white in the firelight. ''Thought you
would, if I could get you out here. I was afraid old Griscom
would have given you his speech about disgusting pagan orgies first, though.''

''He did,'' Beth admitted.

''And you came anyway! Well, well, missionary lady.
Making up your own mind about what you see, huh? You
may have possibilities.''

The patronizing tone of his approval stung Beth. ''Sometimes I wonder who's the missionary out here. You want me
to believe the Indians are just wonderful and ought to be left
alone in their dirt and ignorance. Reverend Griscom wants
me to believe they're savages who have to forget everything

they ever loved before they can be civilized. Why don't you both just give me a chance to make up my own mind, like you said?''

"I am, missionary lady, I am," Jerry said. "Just seeing to it that you've got a little more evidence to go on. Besides, I always liked to educate a pretty girl in a wagon under the stars.''

His hand brushed hers as if by accident. Once again Beth felt a thrill of pleasure mixed with fear. She snatched her hand away and pulled the blanket tighter about her, thinking that Jerry was altogether too attractive and too sure of himself. And, she admitted ruefully, too good at keeping her off-balance. Just when she thought he'd only brought her to the sing to prove some point in their ongoing argument, he came out with some flirtatious statement that she didn't know how to respond to.

"Has anybody ever written down translations of these chants?'' she asked. That was a nice safe subject. They could talk about Indian lore for a while and perhaps he wouldn't make any more of those puzzling, ambiguous compliments. "I'd like to learn more about their beliefs.''

Jerry shook his head. "Might make a good spare-time project, missionary lady. Of course, you'd have to learn Navaho first. That'd take a few years.''

"I wasn't planning on quitting anytime soon," Beth said, suspecting he was about to tell her again that she'd never last at the mission school. "And maybe some of the children at the school could help. . . . No, I guess not,'' she thought aloud, remembering Mr. Griscom's reaction to a similar project.

"You sound unhappy about something. What's the matter?'' Jerry shifted slightly, and one arm came snaking out of his blankets to curve around her shoulders. Beth let that pass, telling herself that putting an arm around a girl co-

cooned in three layers of blankets couldn't possibly lead to anything. It couldn't possibly be making her feel a little dizzy and short of breath, either. Must be the altitude.

"Oh, nothing," Beth said. "I had a little trouble at school about something like this. . . . . That's how I got the lecture about pagan orgies, actually."

As different teams of fantastically costumed dancers succeeded one another, each repeating the original pattern of the gods' dance with variations of their own, Beth told Jerry about her idea of having the senior English class practice their writing by translating some of the Navaho legends. He listened with a grave interest that made her feel better.

"Good idea," he commented when she'd finished. "Too bad you won't be able to do it."

"Oh, I don't know," Beth said. Just having somebody take her ideas seriously gave her renewed confidence. "Maybe I'll be able to persuade Mr. Griscom. Don't you think, if he came to a sing, he'd understand better?"

Jerry snorted. "You *are* a missionary," he said. "Only I'm just not sure who you aim to convert. You really think you could get Griscom out among the savages at all, let alone make him listen to the words of the chants?"

"Maybe I'll kidnap him." Beth laughed. She felt strangely intoxicated by this unusual night under the stars, the cold air scented with piñon smoke, and the thumping beat of the ritual dances. When she looked up at the stars wheeling overhead, she felt as if she could do anything at all. "And maybe I'll just go on with the project on my own time, and not tell him about it."

"That wouldn't be a good idea," Jerry said slowly, reluctantly, as they walked toward the wagon.

"Why not? Even if he finds out, he can't do anything but tell me to stop."

"He could fire you."

Beth shook her head. "They're too short of teachers. I'd have to do something blatantly immoral to get dismissed."

"And you don't think teaching the kids to respect their own religion is blatantly immoral." Jerry shook his head and let out a long, low whistle eloquent with disbelief. "You surely are something else, missionary lady. I kind of hate to let you go back there. Reminds me of Daniel walking into the lions' den."

At Beth's surprised glance, he rubbed one hand over his spiky red hair in a sheepish gesture. "Well, missionaries aren't the only folks who can read the Bible," he mumbled. He clucked to the horses and tugged at the left-hand reins to get them moving the wagon around in a tight circle.

"If you've read that story," Beth said, "you know that Daniel came out of it better than the lions did. Do we have to go now?"

"Not if you think you can stay out all night without getting fired," he responded. "They're going to keep up the dancing until dawn, and I have a feeling that you sneaking back into the mission at sunrise would fall into the 'blatantly immoral' category in Mrs. Griscom's eyes."

Beth nodded in resignation. It did seem a pity to leave, but Jerry was right. If the Griscoms found out where she'd really been that evening, there would be trouble enough. No sense in compounding it by staying out until all hours.

"Moon's rising," Jerry explained as they left. "Gives enough light to see the track by. Good time to set out."

As they rode away from the Navaho meeting place, the distant echo of singing and drumming blended with the small creaks and jingles of the harness and the soft thuds of the horses' hooves in the sandy trail. The rising moon flooded the path before them with soft light, and the sweet and pungent scents of sage and juniper perfumed the crisp night air.

"House made of evening light . . ." she murmured, remembering the words of the chant.

Jerry nodded. "Kinda like poetry, isn't it? Makes you think. . . . I guess they know something about living in this country. Something we whites haven't caught on to yet."

"Yes," Beth said, remembering her feelings that everything fit together, the drumming and the bright splashes of color and the line of red hills against the sky. "Yes, they belong here. Do you think we ever will?"

Jerry rubbed the back of his neck with one hand. "I don't know. But I aim to keep trying. Ever since I drifted onto the edge of Indian territory, I've wanted to stay here. First time in my life I ever wanted to stay put . . . I've always been a wanderer." His voice trailed off at the end, sounding lonely and far away.

"Tell me," Beth said.

The long ride back seemed to take no time at all as Jerry told her about his parents and their little farm in Missouri; his first job at the age of thirteen, when an uncle had taken him to Texas to help with a cattle drive; the years of wandering and drifting since then.

"Kind of got moving on in my blood," he said apologetically. "Always hankering to see something new. . . ."

"Yes," Beth said. "Yes, I know!" She remembered the limitless freedom of her childhood, the sense of walls closing in when her father had informed her it was time to grow up and start acting like a young lady, to trade in her gun and her pony for long skirts and dance cards. "When I was a kid I thought I'd go around the world when I grew up. But it's not so easy for a girl to travel."

Jerry glanced at her, eyes shadowed under the rising moon. "Well, you're doing it now, aren't you? I reckon a girl who'd come this far out west on her own could do pretty near anything she wants."

If only he knew how far from the truth that was! Beth almost felt like confessing the failure that had sent her here from Iowa. But it was so seductively pleasant to have somebody think well of her. Between the scene in Iowa and the Griscoms' disapproval, she'd begun to feel as if she couldn't do anything right.

"Oh, I don't know about that," she said at last, trying to turn the compliment into a joke. "If I can get to where I can say two words in Navaho without the whole school laughing at me, maybe then I'll feel all powerful. Right now I'm just a poor, struggling schoolmarm. Did I tell you what happened in class the other day?"

She made an amusing story of her struggles with the Navaho language, not mentioning the lecture she'd received from Mrs. Griscom for trying to learn Navaho at all. Her story reminded Jerry of a time when a friend of his who knew no Spanish had mixed up the words *huaraches* and *borracho,* leaving him with a powerful hangover instead of the pair of huarache sandals he'd been trying to buy.

They swapped stories all the rest of the way back, and the turnoff to the mission took Beth by surprise. She'd enjoyed laughing and talking with Jerry so much that she hadn't realized they were almost back. At the beginning of the steep path leading down to the mission, Jerry stopped the wagon for a moment, just as he'd done the previous week when he'd driven her out. Her heart thudded wildly as he turned to her. The moon was setting behind his head, and all she could see of his face was a black profile against the cool pale light on the rocks beyond them.

"You're . . . something special, missionary lady," he murmured. One hand brushed her cheek, hard and warm and curiously unsure. "More than I figured on, that's for sure. What am I going to do with you?"

Beth felt her breath becoming ragged and uneven. All this

way, laughing and talking, she'd not felt the slightest nervousness with Jerry. Now she was intensely aware of how alone they were, the deep silence of the desert night enfolding them, the lights of the mission down in the canyon seeming as far away as the stars that hung over the mountains. She felt as though something were about to happen that she wasn't ready for—something that could overwhelm her. She sought words that would keep her safe without offending Jerry.

"I hope," she said at last, "you'll be my friend."

Jerry nodded and took up the reins again. "Okay. I guess that'll do—for a start."

❦ Chapter Six

The next week of school passed slowly, but without any more open disagreements. Beth felt quite proud of her new tact. At last she had learned that the way to get things done was not to get into open fights with authority, but just to quietly work at doing what you knew was right. So she and Lucy Tso worked together after class each day on translating the legend of Changing Woman. Lucy's English improved marvelously and Beth began to acquire a deeper understanding of the Navahos' beliefs. She felt confident that when they had finished this one project, she would be able to talk the Griscoms into letting her continue it. All she would have to do would be to show them the translated legend, let them see there was nothing evil or obscene in it. Then she'd explain that this project was the reason Lucy's English had gotten so much better.

All the same, she felt it would be best not to say anything until the time was right. She told Addie and the Griscoms that Lucy was having trouble with her grammar and needed extra tutoring. It seemed a small untruth for a good cause.

The only trouble was that keeping up the lie made her feel

just a little bit uncomfortable all the time, like having something pressing on the top of her head; like a cloudy day just before a thunderstorm. She counted the hours until her Saturday afternoon off, then reminded herself that Jerry hadn't said anything about coming back, then counted the hours again.

And even then, he managed to take her by surprise, coming up behind her just as she was shepherding the line of children into the dark, steamy dining hall. First she felt a cool breeze on the back of her neck, then she turned and saw him grinning and fanning her with his hat.

"You look as if you need a rest, missionary lady," he greeted her. "Why don't you come out and sit under the trees with me instead of going in there?

"I'm not aiming to do you out of your dinner again," he added as she hesitated. "Got a picnic lunch in the wagon. How about it?"

The little spring at the head of the canyon was no more than a trickle of water running between tumbled red rocks and over a sandy bottom. Beth perched on one of the rocks and trailed her fingers in the cool water while Jerry spread out a heavy wool blanket in the shade of the two trees that grew at the head of the spring. She'd formed the habit of coming out here with a piece of bread and cheese whenever she wasn't required to monitor the children at dinner. But it would be even more pleasant to picnic with Jerry and tell him all the things she dared not mention at the school—Lucy Tso's translation work, the new words of Navaho she'd picked up, and . . . oh, lots of things!

But just now, she couldn't think of anything to say. She studied the fluid grace of Jerry's movements as he spread out the blanket, the easy motion of a man accustomed to working with his whole body. Long, competent hands, taut hips, and muscled thighs bore witness to the strength he must exert daily in her work around the ranch.

And yet, she thought as she watched him, there was more than strength there. She'd not seen him riding, but she felt intuitively that his touch on the reins would be gentle and sure, his knees applying just the pressure necessary to guide his mount.

He looked up and his gray eyes locked onto her black ones with a searching look. "Seen enough?"

Beth felt heat flooding into her face. So he had known she was watching him. And she knew, now, that her thoughts had not been exclusively of horse taming. But he couldn't know that . . . could he? To cover her confusion, she knelt and pretended to examine the blanket he had just laid over the uneven ground for them to sit on. After a moment, no pretense was necessary: the bright, compelling patterns were almost hypnotic in their dazzling intensity.

"What beautiful colors," she said, fingering the closely woven wool blanket. The intricate design of red-and-blue diamonds bordered by black lines seemed to leap out like lightning from the cool gray background.

Jerry nodded and began setting out food from a tin box in the back of the wagon. "Mary Neez's mother made that," he volunteered. "Sold it to some friends of mine that run a trading post up in the mountains."

"It's absolutely beautiful!" Beth exclaimed. "I must tell Mary how much I like it. Maybe her mother would make one for us to display in the classroom."

Jerry gave her a sardonic glance. "Savage tribal patterns polluting the Griscom outfit? You gotta be kidding."

Beth dropped the blanket and sat down on it. "I wish you wouldn't talk that way, Jerry."

"You've been there long enough to know it's true."

"Yes." Beth sighed. "But . . . they mean well. They want to help. And the children do need schooling, Jerry! That much of what the mission does is worthwhile, even if you don't like the way they do it.'' She was arguing, she realized, as much to convince herself as him.

"Anyway, I'm not going to run out on this job just because I had a few little differences of opinion with the Griscoms. I'm going to stick it out and make this work.'' All it took was a little tact, learning when to keep her mouth shut. She didn't intend to have another fight with either of the missionaries; surely she could keep that resolve.

Jerry squatted on the blanket before her, searching her face with concerned eyes. "If I were a kind of a man," he said, "I'd tie you up and throw you on my wagon and get you out of here, just in case—" He stopped in midsentence and pressed his lips together.

"In case what?" Beth asked.

"Oh . . . in case you get ready to leave next week, when I'm not here.''

"I won't be ready to leave," Beth insisted. And that wasn't what Jerry had been about to say . . . but she was too tired to press the point. She watched while Jerry set out food from the covered basket he'd brought from the wagon. There was cold beef wrapped in soft, greasy flaps of bread, a bottle of green tomato pickles, and a pie. "Dried peaches,'' he volunteered, jerking an elbow at the pie.

"I didn't know you were a cook," Beth said appreciatively. Just looking at the flaky crust of the pie set her mouth watering after a week of institutional stews and puddings.

He grinned. "Lily—that's Nathan's wife, my friend up at the trading post—she put up the pie and the pickles for me, couple of days back. Seemed to think I might need something a little better than trail food.''

Beth nodded over a mouthful of cold beef. She had suddenly discovered that she was not too tired to eat after all; in fact, she was ravenously hungry.

"Lily washed a couple of shirts for me, too," Jerry remarked, studying the pattern of the blanket intently.

Beth felt a flash of jealousy. This Lily seemed mighty helpful for a married lady. She watched Jerry's bent head and wondered what he was thinking about.

Even staring at the bright zigzags of the blanket, Jerry found that Beth's face seemed to come between him and the pattern. Just as it had come between him and everything else he'd looked at this week. He'd been counting on this visit to get her out of his system, remind himself that she was just another girl—and a straitlaced missionary teacher at that. It didn't seem to be working. The more he was around her, the more he ached to hold her in his arms and tell her all sorts of things that a homeless cowpoke had no business telling any woman.

"Lily said I'd need a clean shirt if I meant to come courting." Damn! Why had he let that remark slip out? Lily had been teasing him, and that was all right, but there was no point in giving this girl ideas. He could take her for a picnic, maybe to a dance, but he wasn't in a position to get serious with anybody. A man who owned nothing but his bedroll and a couple of half-wild mustang ponies wouldn't stand much chance against the bankers and ranchers and miners of Gallup, once they got wind of a new girl in this corner of the territory.

But then, maybe she wasn't the kind of girl who cared about those things. Jerry raised his head and looked directly at Beth for a moment, then dropped his eyes back to the pattern on the blanket. He couldn't look at her without wanting to do more. A lot more. That, he thought with a touch of wry humor, was going to make their social relations rather complicated.

The flash of gray eyes unnerved Beth. She swallowed suddenly and nearly choked as the tough beef went down. It seemed very quiet here in the shadows; the trickle of the stream falling over a rock was the only sound. Her hands were shaking.

"And . . . are you?" she asked as casually as she could. "Courting, I mean?" What a thing to say to a man. Where had her practice in flirtation gone when she needed it? He'd be shocked.

"That depends," Jerry mumbled, still staring at the blanket.

"Depends on what?"

"Oh . . . a lot of things."

"I feel," Beth said with spirit, "like a piece of merchandise on the counter, being spread out and turned this way and that while you decide whether or not to take me!"

It was an irresistible opening. Jerry's self-control crumbled like a sand dam before a flash flood.

"Oh, no," he said gently, reaching out one hand to cup her chin. The pulse in her throat fluttered like a wild bird trapped, but she didn't turn away from him; just raised her head and stared at him with those magnificent dark eyes. "Lady, there's nothing I'd like better than to spread you out and turn you this way and that." He relayed her own words to her and saw her cheeks burn at the double entendre now that she heard it. "But I don't have to spend any time deciding whether to take you."

Beth felt weak and dizzy as his thumb moved caressingly over cheek and chin. He was coming closer now. She ought to move. He wasn't holding her with any force at all.

"I didn't mean . . ." she protested. "I don't want you to . . ."

"No?"

Jerry's voice held only gentle amusement, and his face was so close that she could feel his warm breath on her cheek. She could no more have moved away from his touch than she could have stopped breathing. Eyes closed, she waited for the inevitable—for, she admitted in one flash of honesty, what she had been dreaming of ever since he'd left her a week ago.

His kiss was as gentle as the hand under her chin, probing, exploring every corner of her mouth, slowly, thoroughly. Beth's head whirled and she put up one hand to steady herself, holding on to his shoulder, feeling the lean hardness beneath the clean fabric of his shirt. His tongue flicked out to taste her mouth; her lips parted and she felt the warm firmness of his mouth covering and possessing her. The blood raced in her veins and she longed for him to hold her, pull her against his body, and take her with all the strength she felt behind his restraint.

Instead, his hand fell away and he raised his head slowly away from her. His mouth was set in harsh lines and his chest rose and fell in an uneven rhythm that mesmerized her.

"I'm sorry," he said. "I didn't mean for that to happen."

"Neither . . . did I," Beth whispered. She was having some trouble getting her voice back under control.

Jerry put his hands behind his back as if fighting off the temptation to hold her again. "Look. I think I did this all wrong, and I wouldn't blame you if you turned me down now. But . . . there's a dance on tonight. If I promise to behave myself, would you go with me?"

"Where?" Beth asked, thinking that it wasn't so much Jerry's wandering hands that worried her; it was his tendency to head off into the trackless desert at a moment's notice. She didn't want to agree and then find out the dance was in Albuquerque!

Jerry's tense face relaxed slightly. "Galvan's. Eleuterio's having a horse race and dance to celebrate his oldest boy getting his law degree. I was going to ask you to come with me." He picked up a flap of bread wrapped around some beef and bit into it. It was easier to keep his face full of bread than to keep it expressionless while he waited for her answer.

Beth folded her hands and watched him eat. After a few moments of silence she inquired, "Well?"

"Well what?" Jerry inquired indistinctly.

"Are you asking me," Beth said patiently, "or aren't you? Forgive me, but I'm not quite clear on where we stand."

Jerry put down the improvised sandwich and gave her his full attention. "Would you go if I asked you? Or would you act like an insulted lady?" Maybe she hadn't figured out where her best interests lay. "The Griscoms don't approve of me," he pointed out. "It won't enhance your standing with the good folk of the mission."

"The Griscoms don't run my social life," Beth riposted, "and I haven't screamed and run back to the safety of the school yet." Her dark eyes danced and she tugged at a curl that lay loose over her shoulder. "If you promise to take me back to the school, and don't get any funny ideas about making me quit, I'll go."

Riding across the mesa, at night, with Jerry. The image stirred her blood with dark, sensual longings that thrilled and frightened her. What was it she'd thought about this picnic site? Chaperonage! That was the answer.

"If," she qualified her acceptance, "Addie Clare comes, too. The two of us together ought to be safe from your wiles, don't you think?" Oh, she shouldn't have said that. He would think she was thinking about . . . well, what she was thinking about.

Jerry reached across the blanket and shook her hand gravely. "It's a deal, missionary lady. You pry Addie Clare loose from her piano, and I'll take the both of you to Galvan's dance."

Beth cut a generous slice of Lily's dried-peach pie. "What if I can't pry her loose from the piano?"

Jerry grinned. "Then I'll just have to take the piano, too. Are you keeping your mouth full so I won't kiss you again?"

Beth nodded. "Safety in numbers," she mumbled. "You, me, and Lily's peach pie."

"Oh, you're safe . . . for the moment." Beth felt a flash of disappointment. Jerry stretched, yawned, and lay back on the blanket with his arms behind his head. The rough fabric of his clean blue work shirt stretched taut over his chest, making Beth aware of the firm, hard lines of his body. "I'm too tired to assault you, anyway."

In repose, his face showed white lines of exhaustion under the tan. "What's the matter?" Beth asked.

Jerry shook his head. "Nothing for you to worry about. . . . A little trouble up on Galvan North, that's all. Eleuterio had asked me to look into it last week. I packed the supplies up so anybody watching would figure it was just a normal trip. Didn't want them to know we were concerned."

"Who?"

"Not sure. I told you, nothing to worry about." But the line between his red eyebrows belied that statement.

"No?" Beth finished off the last bit of peach pie. She decided to risk a guess, putting together some of Jerry's earlier statements. "If it makes you so eager to get me out of here, don't you think I ought to know what it is?"

Jerry ran one hand through his red hair until the crisp curls seemed to be shooting off sparks of fire. "Hell! Was I that danged obvious?"

Beth nodded.

"And you ain't going to give up, are you?"

Beth shook her head.

"Well, then." Jerry took her hand. "Want to lie down against the tree? It's a long story." The thick red brows wagged up and down. "You might want to catch some rest."

"Thank you," Beth said, primly and untruthfully, "I'm

quite comfortable as I am.'' Her hand was sending strange, darting messages of delight up into her arm. If only Jerry's thumb weren't stroking her palm in that caressing way, perhaps she could manage to think straight and get the story out of him.

With a pained sigh, Jerry leaned back against the tree and closed his eyes. ''Like I told you, the Galvan Ranch got split into two sections when they extended the reservation. The main house is down on Galvan South, not too far from Gallup. Galvan North is higher ground, good for grazing, no good for farming. Nobody but a rancher'd want it. And even Eleuterio can't do much with the northeast corner. Land's so full of salts they call it Alkali Meadows. Rest of it's pretty sweet land, though.

''Well, anyway. Only good road—well, usable road, can't call it good—goes through the reservation. By Blue Mesa trading post. So we like to keep on good terms with the Indians.

''There've been reports of trouble up on Galvan North. I went up to check it out. Sheep killed on the Navaho side. Property destroyed—well, an old shack, no big deal, but the boys were keeping their harness and spare gear in it—burned on our side. Couple of cattle killed. Not for the meat or anything. Just mutilated. And one of the boys found this by the corpses.''

He twisted around and dug a silver object out of his hip pocket, a disk with serrated edges and a turquoise set in the center. ''Navaho silver work. Looks like a little back and forth revenge raiding. They run sheep over on our grazing land, the boys get excited and chase 'em off and kill a few, they come back and burn and kill whatever they can find.

''Only thing is, the wranglers up there say they haven't killed any sheep. So I went up to Lily and Nathan's trading post to ask if they'd heard anything about raids. The word there is that old Hosteen Chee—the local chief whose people found the dead sheep—put the word out that they weren't to do any raiding back. He said he'd talk to Galvan himself, try to straighten it out. He was heading down Gallup way, last they heard of him. Probably stopped off to visit a few relatives along the way.

"Before he got there, we got word about the burnings. Eleuterio wanted me to go up and check it out. Didn't get too far, though. Found that surveyor fellow—Carruthers—you remember?"

Beth nodded. "I never did understand why you were set on running him out of town, though." Maybe at last he was willing to explain to her.

"Because he said Lawrence Hudson hired him." Jerry bit off the words as though that would explain everything.

"So?"

"So, Hudson's been after Eleuterio to sell Galvan North. First he offered a low price. Then he offered a high price. Then he tried to get the courts to disallow the original Spanish land grant—claimed the boundaries described in the grant only cover the south half of Galvan's ranch. Judge McCullough threw the case out, said Hudson didn't have enough evidence to cover a rat's ass—uh, I mean, he didn't have enough evidence. So I figured he hired this surveyor fellow to sneak around up there and make up another case."

Beth thought the story over. There seemed to be a few things missing from it. "Mr. Hudson must be a very determined man. But why does he want Señor Galvan's ranch so badly?"

Jerry shook his head. "Beats the hell out of me. It's inconvenient to get to and it was badly overgrazed a couple of generations ago. Take time and money to get it back in good condition, and even then that one corner is so heavy with salt deposits that you can't grow or graze anything on it. Eleuterio's got a sentimental attachment to it because the original Galvan Ranch house was up there. Don't see what anybody else would want with it, though.''

A line creased his forehead as he stared up at the canyon rim with narrowed eyes, head tilted back against the tree. Beth watched his red hair curling against the crumpled gray bark of the tree and almost didn't hear what he was saying.

''I wouldn't be surprised if Hudson's behind this latest trouble, too. He might figure if he can make enough trouble up there, Eleuterio'll get tired and sell out to him. But I can't prove anything. I been scouting around all week and didn't find anything except word of a couple of strange men moving through the pass. That's not much evidence.''

''No,'' Beth said quietly, ''it isn't.'' She found it hard to believe that Lawrence Hudson could be involved in anything like that. He was so successful and sure of himself— why would he bother with a petty land squabble? Perhaps Jerry lived such a violent life that he thought everybody went around with a gun on one hip.

''On the other hand,'' Jerry said, ''could be that we're fixing to have a little Indian trouble. In which case I don't like you staying here. Too isolated. And if I were a Navaho, and felt like shooting somebody—''

''Let me guess,'' Beth interrupted. ''Reverend Griscom.''
Jerry chuckled. ''You've got it.''

''I've felt that way myself once or twice,'' she admitted. She rose to her knees and began packing their leftovers back into the basket. ''But I think you're wrong.''

''About the mission? Or about Hudson?''

''The mission. The Griscoms are trying to help. In their own way. And if the Navahos trust them enough to send their children here, I'm sure they wouldn't attack us.''

''Let me take that.'' Jerry took the basket from her hands and swung it up into the back of the wagon. ''Don't be too sure of your conclusions. Some of these kids were taken away from their families with the Indian agent and a troop of soldiers watching. And if they run away, they get punished. You'll find out—since you're so damn set on staying. And if there's an uprising, some of those families might just come down here to get their kids back—and they won't say please and thank you and 'scuse me, missionary lady!''

Beth shook her head. ''You don't really believe there's Indian trouble, do you? You think Hudson's faking it for his own ends.''

''Hudson's doing something,'' Jerry corrected. ''Even if I can't pin it on him yet. Whatever he's doing just might rile the Navahos enough to stir up some trouble none of us can stop.'' He gave her a hard, unsmiling look. ''If it gets bad, I want you out of here. Understand?''

''I'll make up my own mind about that,'' Beth said, ''when and if the time comes.''

For a moment they glared at one another, unmoving. Then Jerry's face relaxed and he reached for her. Beth stepped back just in time to evade his grasp.

''You're cute when you're mad,'' he told her.

Beth made a face. ''I'm cute all the time. Wait till you see me in my party duds!''

''Okay.'' Jerry stretched out on the blanket again. ''You go get Addie, and you two girls pack up your party clothes, and come back out here when you're ready. I'll just take a little nap until then.''

His eyes closed and his limbs relaxed as he finished the sentence. He seemed to be asleep immediately.

''Don't take too long,'' he called as Beth turned away. ''The horse race starts at six.''

Beth had anticipated some difficulty in persuading Addie Clare to go with her, given her disparaging comments about ''the Galvan Ranch crowd.'' To her surprise, the other girl not only agreed to come immediately, but she volunteered to tell Mrs. Griscom of their invitation in a way that was certain to raise no objections. Beth overheard only a few words of Addie's speech; she seemed to be saying something about the opportunity to spread a good word for the mission among the ungodly.

Addie's cooperation became clearer when the two girls packed their things.

"Don't wear your party dress over," Addie told her. "It'll just get all dusty. We'll wear our plain serge skirts over there, and there'll be a room set aside for the girls to change clothes and get fancied up in. They always do that at these affairs, because people come from so far away."

She delved into the narrow closet at the side of her bed and came out holding a frilly dress in a rose-and-blue-plaid silk. "It's new," she confided. "Mama sent it out for my birthday, and I didn't have the heart to tell her we don't wear such frivolous things at the mission. But now I guess it'll come in handy." She held the dress up before her and spun in a half circle to make the skirts fly out, humming softly to herself.

Beth smiled. So that was why Addie had been willing to come to the party! What woman could resist the lure of a new dress?

She herself had nothing more suitable than a yellow cotton frock that had already done duty through three summers of Iowa picnics and socials. Beth spared a fleeting thought for her father's luxurious home, the rows of dance dresses he'd ordered to celebrate her eighteenth birthday party. For five years those silk dresses had been hanging there, gracefully going out of fashion. After their blazing quarrel on the night of the party Beth had proudly announced that she would never take another penny of his money beyond what was necessary to see her through the two years of teachers' college.

Another impulsive decision, and one she'd not regretted—until now. She consoled herself with the thought that the soft yellow fabric draped becomingly and that the color set off her blue-black hair and deep blue eyes to perfection. Beth hummed a waltz tune to herself as she packed a basket with the dress and other necessities, following Addie's advice as to what to take.

Chapter Seven

As Addie had predicted, one of the upstairs rooms in the Galvan Ranch house was set aside for the use of the visiting ladies. And after the hot, dusty ride to the ranch, Beth was grateful for the chance to slip upstairs and sponge off with the tepid water in the washstand bowl. They had the room to themselves, as most of the other guests had arrived earlier in the day to enjoy the barbecue and games before the dance. Beth and Addie helped one another into their dance dresses and smoothed their hair before the cracked mirror that was set into a high wardrobe in one corner of the room.

Beth caught her breath with pleasure when she saw her reflection. A week in the desert sun had given her skin a deep glow that the yellow cotton dress accented. Above the low ruffled neckline, her hair gleamed with blue shadows in its blackness, and her eyes seemed even larger and darker than usual.

She glanced at Addie and shook her head. The soft rose-and-blue dress set off Addie's delicate coloring and the gentle flush of her cheeks, but that depressed-looking brown bun, sliding down the back of her neck as usual, fairly shouted "schoolmarm!"

"Let me try your hair another way," she suggested. "Looser, maybe, with a few locks around the face. . . ."

Addie sniffed. "It won't stay up any other way. I've tried. Besides, I don't want to look like a fancy woman."

Beth laughed, her fingers already busy with the tight knot. "Nonsense, no one will criticize you for looking a little more relaxed. This is a party, not an examination for higher standard certification! Oh—"

She gasped in admiration as Addie's brown tresses fell down from their knot. Her fine hair was like a silken cloak, framing her face and softening the sharp, pinched features.

"You see?" Addie pushed the waves of light brown hair away from her face with a fretful gesture. "I can't do a thing with it."

"You don't need to!" Beth said. "Why don't you just leave it down like that?"

There was a loud popping sound outside, from just under their window. "What's that?"

A series of louder bangs followed, with high-pitched voices yipping in chorus. Beth dropped the clinging masses of Addie's hair and rushed to the window. She leaned out and saw a circle of grinning faces below. Addie peered over her shoulder, pushing her even farther out of the window.

"Raid!" one of the men hollered up. "We hear Eleuterio's keeping the two prettiest girls for himself, and we're going to come up and get y'all if'n you don't get downstairs to watch the race!"

He drew his pistol and fired it into the air a few times to punctuate the threat. Addie squeaked in alarm and both girls jumped back from the window.

"Oh, my goodness," Addie cried, "what shall we do?

They're so wild, I knew I shouldn't have come. What if they come upstairs and see me practically naked?''

Beth looked at her in surprise. Addie's dance gown was cut a whole inch lower around the neck than her schoolteaching outfits, but somehow that didn't seem to merit such concern.

"I don't have my stockings on!" Addie explained.

"Well, put them on, for goodness' sake," Beth said, trying to conceal her smile, "and let's go downstairs before they come up to drag us out of here." The shots had startled her, but Jerry had warned them both that newcomers could expect a little rough teasing. Besides, it was flattering to know that the cowboys were so eager to meet them!

She hustled Addie through the finishing touches of her toilette so fast that they were halfway down the stairs before Addie realized that her hair was still floating loose about her shoulders.

"I can't go down like this," she wailed. "It's not decent."

"Sure it is." Beth gave her a little push to start her moving again. "Why, you're better covered than you are at school. You know, Addie," she tried to imitate Mrs. Griscom's prim tones, "it's hardly decent for a young girl to show her ears the way you do when you put your hair up."

Addie looked back over her shoulder with a glance of utter horror. "Oh, my goodness, I never thought of that! Do you suppose the dear Reverend—oh, no, he wouldn't—but still . . ."

She stumbled over a loose stair rod and Beth had to grab her arm to keep her from falling. "Don't worry, Addie. It was a joke. You always look perfectly respectable."

As they neared the bottom of the stairs, Beth heard trampling feet and suppressed snickers from the wide porch that ran around three sides of the house. She raised both hands over her head. "Don't shoot, boys," she called, "we'll come quietly."

Another fusillade of shots greeted their entrance onto the porch. Addie squeaked again and buried her face in the nearest safe object. It happened to be Eleuterio Galvan's velvet waistcoat.

"There, there, señorita." Eleuterio Galvan managed somehow to pat Addie on the shoulder, kiss Beth's hand, and bow to both ladies at the same time. "There's nothing to be frightened about. Why, Señorita Clare!" His tone changed to one of surprise as Addie lifted her head. "I did not recognize you at first. You look . . ."

His snapping black eyes swept over Addie's slender figure outlined in the soft thin fabric and rested on the soft masses of brown hair that tumbled about her face. "Different," he concluded. "Very . . . different."

He bowed again and offered Addie his arm. "This is my son, Jaime." The slender, dark young man standing beside Eleuterio bowed to Addie, but his eyes rested on Beth. "Would you care to come with me and meet the rest of my guests, Señorita Clare?"

Jerry was standing just behind Eleuterio. He grinned at Beth over his employer's shoulder but had to wait until Señor Galvan and Addie moved away before he could take Beth's hands. His smile faded and his gray eyes widened as he got his first good look at her in the yellow cotton dance dress. His lips parted as if he wanted to say something, but he only looked at her as if he were trying to imprint every line of her face on his memory.

She was lovely, a dark-haired beauty in a dress the color of the sun, but that wasn't all that brought the singing joy to his heart. He'd been to enough dances to know the girls brought out their prettiest clothes for such occasions, pleated silk and rustling taffeta underskirts and big velvet bows. But all she had on was a simple yellow dress, without even a necklace to emphasize the glorious line of neck and shoulders and breast that the low neckline exposed.

She must come from a poor home, with nothing to support her but her teacher's salary. He'd somehow been thinking her people were well off; only rich girls moved with that kind of unconscious assurance. Now he knew renewed hope that almost stopped his heart. She wasn't much better off than he was, besides being educated. Maybe she wasn't beyond the reach of a poor cowboy with nothing but his monthly salary to offer.

There was a turquoise necklace he'd seen on the pawn rack at Blue Mesa. Next time he'd buy it for her and put it around her neck, and it would echo the blue lights in her hair. He was certain she wouldn't scorn the gift, as a girl who had gold chains and ruby pendants in her jewel box might.

But he wouldn't wait until then to get down to serious courting. He'd take her out back tonight, and . . . There was the hint of that section manager's job Eleuterio had mentioned, but he'd never been interested, not wanting to be tied down. That was a long way off, of course, but if she had the grit to stick it out and wait for him, then she'd have what it took to stand the hard life. . . . But he wanted to see her smile when he gave her the necklace—

His half-formed thoughts and plans collided like half a dozen glittering soap bubbles bursting into thin air, and he laughed at his own tongue-tied confusion.

"What's the matter?" Beth asked, remembering how he'd teased her once for staring like that. "I got smut on my face or something?" She pirouetted, and the three layers of ruffled yellow skirt belled out around her.

Jerry caught her hands to stop the pirouette. Momentarily off-balance, she tripped and leaned against his arm for support. His arm tightened around her and for one dizzying moment their lips were inches apart. Then she recovered her balance, he let her go, and the moment was past. But she could not forget the feel of his arm encircling her, the roughness of his shirt sleeve, the corded muscle beneath it, and the warmth of his body.

"Oh, I reckon you'd pass in a crowd, missionary lady."

As a compliment, it lacked something, but the pressure of his hand on hers, the light in his eyes, the way he kept glancing at her as she took his arm and stepped down from the porch, all said what he hadn't put into words. Beth felt regal and beautiful and filled with a strange, bubbling excitement, as though something wonderful were going to happen this evening. She stole a glance at the man beside her.

He'd used the short interval since their arrival to splash the dust off his face and slick down his unruly red hair, but he was still wearing the well-worn white shirt and blue denim pants in which he'd ridden from the mission. The close-fitting clothes, molded to his body from long use and many washings, emphasized the strong lines of his broad shoulders, narrow waist, and long, slightly bowed legs.

He wasn't dressed richly like Eleuterio Galvan and his son Jaime, both sporting black velvet suits ornamented with hammered silver buttons. And he didn't exude wealth and power like the Anglo ranchers who were gathered under the trees by the barbecue pit, their tailored suits setting them apart from the wranglers who worked for them. But every inch of his body proclaimed the raw masculine power that made him the equal of any man there.

Jerry glanced at her again and she felt his arm trembling slightly beneath her fingers. He desired her. She knew that, and the knowledge flooded her body with waves of fear-filled longing. It was, she told herself sternly, a good thing that Addie Clare would be riding back to the mission with them. A very good thing. Beth wrenched her thoughts away from what might happen otherwise and studied the scene before her.

The wide expanse of hard-packed dirt before the ranch house was dotted with brightly dressed men and women, laughing, talking, and eating. As Señor Galvan led them toward the great pit where joints of meat were being roasted over coals, Beth noted that there seemed to be three separate groups of guests.

To her right, beyond the barbecue pit, several wagons with rude canvas covers were drawn up in a semicircle. Indian families were gathered in the shade of the wagons. The women, dressed in bulky calico skirts with velveteen jackets, stared shyly at the white guests and giggled occasionally; the men came up to the barbecue pit from time to time and took chunks of meat back to share with their families.

To the left, under a spreading cottonwood tree, several Anglo ranchers were seated with their families at one of the trestle tables that had been set up for the occasion. Beth noticed Lawrence Hudson in this group and blinked in surprise.

"Somehow I hadn't expected to see Mr. Hudson here," she murmured to Jerry, indicating the banker's distinguished figure in his light gray silk suit. "Does Señor Galvan know you think he's responsible for the problems you've been having on Galvan North?"

Jerry nodded. "No evidence," he murmured back, barely moving his lips. "Hudson's a prominent citizen. Eleuterio don't want to offend him without cause. Anyway, I hear he invited himself to this shindig. Some deal about a thoroughbred mare he imported from back east. Wants to run her in the horse race and show us locals what a real horse can do."

Beth studied Hudson's confident figure as he stood under the trees, talking with two other men who were strangers to her. His lightly tanned face and splash of yellow hair stood out in pale profile against the dark cluster of tree trunks. She could not read his expression, but even from this distance, his relaxed stance and emphatic gestures spelled confidence.

As she watched, he turned and waved as though some sixth sense had told him of her observation. Beth smiled and waved back vigorously, then felt the muscles of Jerry's arm tighten slightly under her hand.

She glanced up at Jerry. "And will he show you up?"

"Maybe—maybe not." Jerry's lips clamped down over the last word. "You trying to set us up in competition?"

Beth shook her head. "I think you two butt heads enough without any help from me," she said quietly. "Can't we just enjoy the race and the dancing?" Looking at Hudson's self-assured figure, she found it hard to credit Jerry's suspicions of him. But she didn't want to argue. "Tell me more about the race," she suggested.

"Well," Jerry drawled, "you'll be glad to hear it won't be just me against Hudson. There's a dozen fellows racing, but I don't figure any of us stand much of a chance against that knock-kneed, swaybacked horse of Red Singer's, but we like to get up a little race now and then, just to keep him in practice. I won two concho belts and a saddle blanket from some Indians at a sing in Chelly last year by betting on Red Singer."

He took her arm and steered her toward the barbecue pit, where the third, and by far the largest, group of guests stood. "Come on and get your plate loaded, and meet the boys. They look like they're going to shoot to kill if I don't give them a chance to meet the new teacher."

Clustered around the barbecue pit and the surrounding tables were the wranglers who worked on the Galvan Ranch. Some were Mexican, some Anglo, and Beth noticed at least one young man whose aquiline features, dark slanting eyes, and bright red head cloth reminded her of the Navahos squatting in the shade of their wagons.

"Red Singer," Jerry introduced that young man, and Beth nodded. "Shorty, Three Holes Jim, Felipe, Red, Big

Dan, Jose. Get out of the way, boys, and let the lady get something to eat if you haven't finished it all up.''

"Okay, Jerry," drawled the rotund, merry-faced boy introduced as Shorty. "You can watch the lady eat if'n you want to. I'll take my turn when the dancing begins."

Jerry loaded Beth's plate high with piles of beef, red beans dotted with chili, bread, and roasted ears of corn.

"I can't possibly eat that much!" she protested.

Jerry shrugged. "Suit yourself. Eleuterio don't like to see anybody go hungry."

"What about you?" Jerry had taken almost nothing.

"Oh, I'm racing." Jerry's eyes flicked up and down Beth's figure in the soft yellow dress with a warm look that left her blushing. "I'll just have to have my fun some other way."

As they made their way to one of the long trestle tables set up in the shade, a group of musicians under the trees struck up a dance tune. Beth found her feet tapping in time to the lively music.

"Miss Johanssen." Lawrence Hudson, immaculate as ever, bowed and sat down on her other side. "You are truly looking lovely today. I am reminded of a yellow rose I once saw opening into full bloom, blushing in the radiance of its own beauty."

Beth's eyes sparkled at the elegantly turned compliment. So Hudson could talk about something else besides the glorious future of the territory! He might have more possibilities than she'd thought. She glanced at Jerry, a little piqued that he hadn't said anything half as nice to her, and caught a brooding scowl that sent her eyes to the laden plate before her.

"Thank you, Mr. Hudson," she said demurely.

"Call me Lawrence." Hudson placed his hand over hers. "I must apologize for abandoning you so rudely at the train station that day. I did not realize that you were in need of transportation to the mission school, or I should have been happy to offer you my services. It is a blot on the growing reputation of our fair city that the loveliest flower in the desert should have been forced to ride to the school in a rough wagon. You would have found my buggy much more comfortable—and a more suitable setting for your beauty, Beth.''

His eyes raked her figure with a lingering glance that made Beth feel distinctly aware of how closely the old, soft cotton dress followed the lines of her body. Strange—she didn't mind when Jerry looked at her that way.

''Miss Johanssen to you, and the lady doesn't need your help,'' Jerry drawled. ''I'll take her anywhere she wants to go.''

''The lady might,'' Hudson said, ''have her own preferences in the matter.''

The two men glared at each other behind Beth's back; she could almost feel the short hairs on the back of her neck sizzling where their glances crossed.

''I'm sure it's a very nice buggy,'' Beth said, removing her hand and busying herself with the steaming mountain of food before her. ''But Addie and I came with Mr. Dixon, and he's kindly offered to take us back after the dance.''

''Then perhaps you will honor me by coming for a ride some other day.'' Hudson tried to recapture her hand, but Beth moved so that his fingers closed over the fork instead. ''You don't need to be shy, Miss Johanssen,'' he chided. ''A lovely girl like you must be used to the attentions of men.''

''I'm not shy,'' Beth said. ''Just hungry.'' She removed her fork from his grasp and wiped the tines on a napkin. She turned her head toward Jerry, giving Hudson a fine view of her back. ''Do tell me more about the horse you are racing, Jerry.''

''Yes, Jerry,'' Hudson broke in, ''don't you have to go off and pay some last-minute attention to whatever sorry specimen you've dragged off the desert for tonight's event?

Don't let us keep you. I'll be happy to entertain Miss Johanssen while you go about your rustic pursuits.''

Jerry scowled at Hudson. "Miss Johanssen don't need your brand of entertainment. And watch where you put your hands. We got ways of dealing with rustlers like you.''

Hudson's toothy smile spread across his face. "Really? But you haven't been doing so well with rustlers recently. Did you ever catch up with the Indians who've been mutilating your cattle?''

Beth caught her breath in shock and then sat very still, hoping she hadn't been too obvious. How could Hudson know about the mutilations? Jerry had just come back from Galvan North that day. For the first time she began to believe his suspicions of Hudson. She looked at Jerry but could find no sign in his impassive face that he'd understood the import of Hudson's remark.

Jerry shook his head. "Don't even know for sure if it's Indians.'' His cold gray gaze hardened. "Just understand this, Hudson. Anybody goes after my property, I know how to take care of them.''

"I'm sure Miss Johanssen must be delighted to be considered property," Hudson said. "I do hope you manage to take better care of her than you do of Galvan North.''

He slicked back his smooth yellow hair with one immaculately manicured hand. "Perhaps Eleuterio should just forget about trying to ranch that northern section. It's just too much trouble, isn't it . . . what with having to go through the reservation to get there, and having the Indians raid all the time.''

Beth had stiffened when Hudson mentioned the mutilated cattle. Now she jumped when he dropped his arm over her shoulders. "Relax, Miss Johanssen," he told her. "I'm sorry you had to be frightened with this talk. It's too bad that some irresponsible people are stirring up trouble with the Indians.''

As he spoke, his hand wandered idly to the front of her dress, where his thumb rubbed back and forth against the satiny skin exposed by the low-cut bodice. Beth tried to shrug his arm off her shoulders, but he only tightened his grip.

"Don't be shy," he murmured into her ear. "I can take much better care of you than this illiterate cowpoke. Really, a fellow like that, with nothing to offer a girl, should know better than to raise her hopes with a courtship that can go nowhere." The last words were spoken loudly enough to attract Jerry's attention.

Jerry responded at last to Hudson's baiting. He stood up, his lean height shadowing the table. "Take your hands off the lady," he ordered.

Hudson laughed. "Really, Dixon. That's for the lady to say . . . isn't it?"

Beth peeled Hudson's arm off her shoulder and dropped it in his plate. "If you two are going to fight," she requested politely, "would you please do it somewhere else? You're interrupting my dinner." She speared a chunk of beef and chewed it defiantly, refusing to look up at the two men glowering over her.

"Hey, Dixon!" A tall, bearded man with his ten-gallon hat pushed back at a rakish angle swaggered over and clapped Jerry on the back. "You want to race or fight? If you ain't going to run that little mustang of yours, I'll ride her while you beat up the banker."

"You!" Jerry scoffed, dusting off his hands. "You'd ride her into the ground, Barb." He nodded to Beth. "This sorry specimen is Barbed Wire Bob, so called on account of a memorable encounter between his hind end and a snarl of wire, and he's too clumsy to fall off a rolling barrel without help."

Beth swallowed the beef in an indigestible lump and acknowledged the introduction. Her heart was pounding with relief. Did this Bob know just how opportune his intervention had been? Whether or not, she was grateful to him and greeted him with enough warmth to show it.

Jerry clapped Bob on the shoulder. His other hand brushed across the top of Beth's head in a feather-light caress. "Sorry to leave you alone for the race. I got this little mustang I brought down from Galvan North last winter. Been gentling her for a cow pony, but she's got a nice turn of speed on her. Thought I'd run her in this race of Eleuterio's."

"Mustangs and Indian scrubs," Hudson sneered. Some of his color had returned. "You'll both be looking at my new thoroughbred's heels."

Jerry laughed. "You riding her yourself, Hudson? Thought not." He gave the banker a scornful glance and strode off to the corral, where the racing horses were tethered.

Hudson lingered, looking down at Beth with an unusually warm expression. "Miss Johanssen, I know the mission doesn't approve of betting, but if you want to pick up some easy money, Bill Garvey over there is holding the bets on my thoroughbred, Mother Lode. I know the mission doesn't pay you girls very much, and this is an easy way to get yourself some pin money."

He smiled and one hand moved out as though he wanted to touch her again but didn't dare complete the gesture. "Perhaps, if you win a wager on Mother Lode, you'll feel more kindly toward me."

Beth had not yet been paid for her work at the mission, but she still had three ten-dollar gold pieces in her purse, the remnants of her Vinton salary after she'd bought her fare out to the New Mexico Territory. She'd meant to hoard the money in case she needed to pay her way home again. But watching Hudson's confident face, she made a snap decision.

After all, Beth reasoned to justify the betting impulse,

even if she lost, she meant to stay at the mission for some time. She was determined to make a success of this job. So there was really no need to hang on to a going-home stake. And if she could double her money on the horse race, she'd have enough extra to buy books and pictures for the children to brighten the drab schoolroom.

"Thank you," she said politely. "Which gentleman is Bill Garvey?"

Hudson pointed out a white-haired, prosperous-looking man with a gold watch chain stretched across the rounded expanse of his generous stomach. Beth nodded her thanks again and strolled over to the group of ranchers when Hudson departed to check on his horse.

From the knoll where the ranchers were gathered, Beth could get a clear view of the racecourse. After she placed her bet, defiantly laying down all three of the precious gold pieces, she moved to the front of the crowd, smiling and nodding as the ranchers and their wives introduced themselves. They were a friendly, jovial crowd, and none of them seemed to have much doubt that Hudson's Mother Lode would win. Behind her back, Beth heard one man say, "Time somebody showed the greasers what real horseflesh can do."

She felt uncomfortable with this group. Why did they accept Eleuterio's hospitality if they despised him? She glanced almost furtively around her, hoping that Eleuterio Galvan wouldn't notice and misinterpret her standing with these people who had obviously come only to celebrate Hudson's victory in the horse race.

Looking across the flat stretch that had been marked out for a racecourse, she caught sight of Eleuterio Galvan being very attentive to Addie. The Galvan wranglers surrounded them, and beyond there were the bright skirts of the Indian women who'd come down to the edge of the course to watch

Red Singer race the whites. Beth wished suddenly, passion-
ately, that she were watching the race from the middle of
that laughing, rowdy bunch, instead of standing here with
Hudson's friends. But it was too late to change now. They
were about to start.

The horses and riders were bunched at the starting line, not
far from their viewing post. Beth picked out Jerry's red head
but couldn't see the horse he was riding. She could see that
most of the horses were scrubby little half-wild cow ponies,
not much like the sturdy Morgans and quarter horses she was
used to seeing in her father's stables. She was disappointed to
see what a poor showing they made beside Lawrence Hudson's tall thoroughbred. Much as she hated to admit it, Hudson
was right. What could a bunch of desert mustangs do against a
true racehorse imported from the East?

Lawrence Hudson gave some last instructions to his rider
and came striding back up to the little mound where the
spectators were gathered. He stood just behind Beth.

''That's my horse—easy to pick out, eh?'' He pointed out
the tall bay mare. ''Isn't she a beauty?''

''She is,'' Beth admitted. She'd never seen better stock,
even in her father's stables. ''Have you raced her before?''

Hudson chuckled. ''Not against these wranglers and
sodbusters. But she did well as a two-year-old in New York.
I saw her there when I was back east on business and arranged to have her shipped out. After she's won a few races
for me I'll use her for breeding stock; she's much too valuable to waste on these penny-ante events.''

He put one hand on Beth's back, just above her waist, and
she tried to move away from him but was trapped by the
pressure of the crowd. His hand didn't move as she'd
feared; just remained there, making a hot, damp spot on the
back of her dress, asserting his right to touch her. Beth
gritted her teeth and concentrated on the start of the race.

A red bandanna dropped from Barbed Wire Bob's outstretched hand was the signal for the start. Straining at the bit, the horses thundered away from the starting line in such a cloud of dust that Beth was momentarily blinded. As they passed the knoll, she saw that Hudson's Mother Lode was indeed in the lead, while the two horses closest behind were ridden by Jerry Dixon and Red Singer.

"They have to go a quarter of a mile out, to that post." Hudson pointed out the stump of a dead tree toward which the riders were racing and used the gesture as an excuse to leave his arm around her shoulders. "They'll turn around it, come back, and finish at the starting line."

His breath was warm on the bare back of her neck, and his hand kneaded her shoulder as the horses raced for the inside turning position. Beth wriggled forward, away from his touch, on the pretense of trying to see better.

As the horses drew near the turning post, it seemed to Beth that the bay mare, though still ahead of the other two, was too far out to get the inside track around the post. Behind her, Jerry Dixon and Red Singer competed for that position. The cowboys and ranchers were shouting encouragement to their favorites so loudly that Beth felt enclosed by a continuous blur of sound and motion.

"Come on, Jerry!" she cried, jumping up and down in her excitement. In her desire to see him win, she didn't even care if she lost her carefully hoarded gold pieces. "Come on!"

In the dust of the turning, it was impossible to see who was nearer the post, Jerry or Red Singer. But Mother Lode was clearly unwilling to make the quick turn required. She loped around the turning post in a dignified half circle that left her far behind the quick little cow ponies.

As they came down the straightaway, Jerry and Red Singer were neck and neck. Just behind them, Mother

Lode's rider lashed the thoroughbred with his quirt in a vain attempt to catch up the ground he had lost at the post.

The mustangs plunged past the starting line and Barbed Wire Bob raised both hands. "Red Singer, by a nose!"

Beth was shaking with excitement and disappointment. So Jerry had not won . . . not quite . . . but anyway, he hadn't been beaten by Hudson's imported thoroughbred! She turned her head to give the banker a sympathetic smile and was startled by his black scowl.

"Dirty tricks!" he muttered. "Not decent, having redskins compete with white men." He saw Beth looking at him and forced a smile. "Sorry about your wager, Miss Johanssen. I hope you didn't lose more than you could afford. I'll make it up to you."

"There's no need," Beth replied truthfully. She nodded to Hudson and went over to Bill Garvey to settle accounts with him.

As the crowd dispersed, more than one of the Anglo ranchers shook his head as if agreeing with Hudson. Jerry, ambling over to the mound to reclaim Beth, heard Hudson complaining that Red Singer had cheated somehow in that dusty turn when none of them could see what was going on.

"Don't be a sore loser, Larry," he urged, clapping the banker on the back. "We train the cow ponies to turn on a dime. Your Mother Lode not being what you'd call a practical working horse, she wouldn't know that little trick."

Hudson brushed off his coat with fastidious care, flicking his fingers over the immaculate surface as though to remove the contamination of Jerry's touch. Still scowling, he gave Beth a curt nod, turned on his heel, and left without a word. Most of the ranchers followed him, drifting off toward the ranch house in twos and threes.

Jerry shook his head with mock sorrow as the banker departed. "Sore loser," he murmured.

"You're certainly not that," Beth said. Jerry's gray eyes were dancing with little lights and he was tapping his foot with barely restrained energy.

"Oh, I never had a chance against Red Singer," Jerry said. He grinned at her, visibly shrugging off the tension of the race. "I just hope Hudson didn't con you into putting too much down on his mare."

"No," Beth said. "How could you think I'd bet on his side?"

Jerry's dusty grin faded. "You mean you put your money on me? And I lost it for you. Damn. I can't make it up to you the way Hudson could."

"You don't need to," Beth said, smiling slightly. "I won. I bet on Red Singer."

She patted the newly filled purse at her elbow. The Anglo ranchers who came to witness Hudson's victory must not have heard about the Indian races where Red Singer always won. The odds on Hudson's horse were so high that she'd made a positively indecent profit. Bill Garvey had said that if he paid off in gold, her reticule strings would break from the weight, so instead he'd peeled off a dizzying number of crisp new greenbacks and stuffed them into her purse.

Jerry laughed and put one arm around Beth, squeezing her tight. They stood together on the grassy mound and watched people trickling back toward the ranch house for the dancing. "What sort of loyalty is that? You're supposed to think I'm the best at everything."

"Love you, love your horse?"

"Well," Jerry allowed, "I wouldn't go that far. Na'acoci—that means 'Gambler' in Navaho," he explained, "well, he's kind of a hard case. Reared on the mesa, been running loose all his life, not exactly a lady's horse."

Beth glanced up at Jerry's lean, lantern-jawed face

through her lashes. "Sounds as though you could be describing yourself as much as the horse."

"Could be," Jerry conceded. "Told you, Beth—I'm not a good catch."

"That's not what I meant." She could feel her face turning red. "Do you think I came out west looking for a rich man to marry?"

Jerry crooked one red eyebrow at her. "You wouldn't be the first."

Beth threw up her hands in disgust. "Oh, you twist everything around!" she exclaimed. "I came out here to teach school. I came to this party to dance. Can't we leave it at that?"

She spun around and started toward the house, but Jerry put his hands around her waist and held her on the grassy mound, standing before him. "Is it really that simple?" he asked. "I don't think so, lady. I think you came out here looking for something, maybe you don't know what, but whatever it is, you won't find it at the mission school."

Beth turned in the loose circle of his open hands and looked at his level gray eyes searching her face with no hint of a smile. What was she doing there? A girl with any sense would turn around and run the other way when a man like Jerry approached her, so free with his hands and his kisses, so tight with his words. Instead, she was just standing there, smiling up at him and feeling her knees turn to water when he drew her closer.

"And what about you?" she murmured. "Are you . . . looking for something, too?"

Jerry shook his head. "Not any more," he said, and his arms tightened, bringing her so close that she could feel the heat of his body.

The grassy knoll was deserted now, and the blue light of evening was around them. A warm breeze floated in from the desert and surrounded them with pungent air. Despite the warmth and the heat of Jerry's hands on her waist just above the wide sash of her dress, Beth shivered. There was a new, demanding certainty to the way his hands moved on her body; something she wasn't quite sure how to handle. "We should go in."

"Do you always do what you should?"

Beth glanced toward the ranch house, where women hurried along the porch, applying matches to some curious earthenware pots with pierced openings in their sides. As the candles in the pots were lighted, they filled the porch with dancing patterns of light and shadow, looking like gold filigree set against the blue of early evening. More candles, inside, illuminated the grand *sala* that Beth had only peeked into on her way upstairs earlier, and the enticing sound of fiddles tuning up carried across the dusty yard to where they stood under the tree.

"I want to dance," she said, firmly, to cover the confusion of her senses and the part of herself that wanted to stay out here with Jerry.

She was both relieved and disappointed when he released her. "Okay, missionary lady. Let's dance."

Chapter Eight

They reached the grand *sala* just as it was cleared for dancing, with the heavy leather sofas and Indian rugs pushed back against the walls to expose a floor of broad oak planks. The few girls in their bright, full dresses were each surrounded by a crowd of wranglers and ranchers. At one end of the long, low room, the musicians were grouped behind a piano as if they felt the need of a shield from the boisterous crowd.

Beth recognized Jim Maxwell, the station master, standing near the musicians. As the lead fiddler nodded, Mr. Maxwell ascended a chair and clapped his hands for quiet.

"All right, boys," he shouted. "The music's ready and the floor's cleared. In a minute I'm going to let you lead your pretty little sage hens out to dance. But first, Señor Galvan wants me to issue a gentle reminder. This here room has the best dancing floor in Gallup and he would appreciate it if the gents would take their spurs off before strutting their stuff. Second, leave your shooting irons outside. We may be gathered here to celebrate his son Jaime's elevation to the bar, but Jaime wants you to know that he ain't so desperate

111

for customers that he needs to represent any of you on a murder charge.''

A roar of laughter greeted this statement, and Jaime's slender, black-suited form reeled under the hearty back slaps given by the men standing next to him. "Tell Barbed Wire Bob to take his breath outside," one of them yelled. "After all the onions he et this afternoon, that's the killingest weapon in this here room."

"So what?" Jim Maxwell shouted back. "You ain't planning to dance with him, are you?"

Before any more hecklers could start, he raised both arms. "I hereby declare this great social event open!"

The fiddlers launched into the lively polka they had been practicing earlier, and Beth felt Jerry's arm slid around her waist. She leaned back against that hard support and gave herself up to the music.

The room spun around her in a dizzying whirl as they circled the floor. "First the heel and then the toe," Beth hummed, "that's the way the steps do go! First-the-heel-and-then-the-toe . . .''

As soon as the dance floor was filled with couples, the musicians increased the speed of their tune. Faster and faster the dancers whirled, trying to keep up with the lively steps, until first one couple and then another collapsed, laughing and gasping for breath. Beth was ready to give in after three times around the floor, but Jerry's arm tightened around her waist and he laughed at her for being an eastern softie. "Out here in the West," he told her, "we can ride all day and dance all night! What's wrong with you?!"

"First-the-heel-and-then-the-toe . . .'' the caller sang out.

"Oh, we've got to stop," Beth begged. "I've got a stitch in my side!"

Jerry ignored her pleas; then placed both hands around

her waist and lifted her off the dance floor, spinning her around and around until he was too dizzy to stand up. As they collapsed against the nearest wall, the musicians brought the song to a rousing finale and immediately started a spirited square dance tune.

"Oh, mercy," Beth pleaded when a square brown hand grasped her wrist and tugged her away from Jerry. It was the boy called Shorty. He'd failed to secure a partner in the first dance and was full of energy now.

"No rest for the ladies," Shorty told her, and whirled her away before Jerry could protest.

"But I don't know how to square dance!" she wailed as they took their places in the set.

Shorty waggled his thick dark eyebrows. "You don't need to know, silly. Caller tells you what to do!"

Beth's momentary relief evaporated when she heard the caller's actual words. "Allemande left! Sashay right! Do-si-do!" If these were instructions, they might as well have been in Navaho. No, worse than that. She knew at least three Navaho words.

Shorty yanked her in more or less the right direction. Their opposite numbers laughed when they got all tangled up because Beth didn't know how to chain across, and when the square ended in hopeless confusion, she could see that nobody else was doing much better.

The next dance was a waltz, and Jerry claimed her again, with a few uncomplimentary words to Shorty about people who would jump a man's claim just because he took a moment to catch his breath.

"All's fair," said the unrepentant Shorty. "You think Addie Clare would waltz, or don't the missionaries allow it?"

"Eleuterio's got her," Jerry pointed out. Galvan had talked to Addie through the first two dances while wranglers hovered around them, not daring to interrupt the boss's conversation. Now he and Addie were circling the floor with smooth turns that sent Addie's cloud of brown hair floating around behind her.

"It's a cut-in dance," Shorty said, and as he departed to try his luck with Addie, he tossed back, "And I reckon you're about to find that out!"

A moment later Beth understood what he meant, as Lawrence Hudson's smooth blond head appeared behind Jerry. He tapped Jerry's shoulder and took his place with Beth so smoothly that neither of them had a chance to protest.

"I was beginning to think I would never get a chance to dance with you," Hudson murmured.

He held her closer than Jerry had; she could feel the pressure of his stocky body against hers. His hand was too firm on her back for her to move away, and he guided and twirled her about the floor with casual expertise, never missing a step.

"We dance well together." Hudson gave her a toothy grin. "It's a good omen for other forms of cooperation."

"Is it?" Beth deliberately let her steps drag, trying to disturb the swaying rhythm of the waltz, but Hudson's firm hand forced her around and backward in a series of dizzying turns so that she had to cooperate in order to keep her balance.

"Aren't you bored yet with your rustic swain?" Hudson asked as they dipped forward and back in time to the music. "I'm a much better dancer than he is."

"I'm bored," replied Beth, "with being manipulated like a doll. Please don't hold me so close." She gasped as Hudson reversed the direction of their steps and swept her into another backward turn.

The music came to a stop and Hudson released her, though his open palm lingered for a moment, reluctantly, on the wide sash that outlined her waist. "In Gallup," he said,

"I call the tunes and lead the dance. You might think about that when deciding whom you prefer for a partner."

The smile now reminded Beth less of a rabbit than of some ocean predator showing its teeth, a big fish serenely confident that all the little fish would swim into its jaws. "A wrangler on a Mexican sheep farm," he said, "is hardly a suitable partner for a beautiful young lady from the East. An unemployed wrangler would be even less suitable, don't you think?"

"Actually," Beth said, "I understood that Señor Galvan had more cattle than sheep."

Hudson seemed just slightly taken aback by her literal reply. He bowed and was gone just before Jerry came up to her. Beth stood with one hand pressed over her wide sash where Hudson had touched her, feeling the tight bodice absurdly constricting.

"What was he saying to you?"

Beth forced a smile. "Nothing. . . . Social pleasantries. You know the sort of thing." She didn't think it was the right time to risk telling Jerry about Hudson's threat to get him fired. Besides, it was an empty threat . . . wasn't it? Eleuterio Galvan wouldn't fire Jerry just on Hudson's recommendation . . . or pressure.

"No," Jerry said somberly, "I don't know much about social pleasantries. And I don't reckon I want to, either, if they make you look as sick and washed-out as all that."

Beth laughed. "Trying to seduce me with compliments, you silver-tongued devil? It's too hot in here, that's all. Let's go out on the porch for a moment and get some fresh air."

There was a crowd of people talking at the door to the *sala* and a knot of men smoking on the front part of the porch. Jerry took Beth's hand and cleared a way through them. Her head spun briefly with the fumes of cigar smoke,

then they were through and standing around the corner
where the porch wrapped around the side of the ranch house.

"Now," Jerry said, leaning stiff-armed against the wall
as if he thought Beth would try to push past him and get back
to the crowd just around the corner.

Beth felt an uncontrollable flutter of excitement in her midriff as she looked at his dark form outlined against the velvety
blue sky. He was so close that she could feel his warm breath
on her cheek, but all she could see was his black outline block-
ing the stars. Around the corner she heard a few laughing
words in a liquid, incomprehensible language.

She put up one hand to push his arm aside. It was as
firmly planted as the root of one of the twisted piñon trees
that clung to the edge of the canyon. "I think I'd better go
back to the dance."

It was hard to breathe, harder to talk, and when his arm
relaxed against her pressure she felt a sharp stab of disappointment that he was going to take her at her word. But instead of moving back to let her pass, he was closer, pressing
her back against the wall of the house, his hands burning
through the thin soft fabric of her dress.

"First," he murmured, "we've got some business to finish." Then his lips covered hers and she was shaking her
head in protest. But it was exactly what she wanted and her
body knew it and relaxed, went treacherously limp against
the demands of his mouth and hands, which played on her
senses until she could think of nothing else.

It was like a new dance to which she was just learning the
steps, and they fitted together as no two partners ever had
before. His kisses trailed glowing fires across the curve of
her neck and shoulder, and her head fell back against the
wall so that the only thing holding her up was the pressure of
his lean body against hers.

His hands moved upward to mold the curves outlined by

her tight cotton bodice, and everything they had done or said before now seemed like children's play. Beth felt her skin flaming under his touch, felt an aching deep inside her that could not be assuaged by kisses. She clung to him and wantonly kissed him back, dimly registering the erratic thud of his heartbeat as if it were her own.

A woman's giggle, shrill and high-pitched, warned them someone was approaching, and sure enough it was followed by the thud of booted feet coming around the corner. Jerry released her and slipped against the wall with catlike speed, lounging with his back against the wall as if they'd only been watching the full moon that rose over the jagged black cutout of the mountains in the distance.

A man and a woman came around the corner of the porch and paused beside the railing. Addie's face was white in the moonlight, and her unbound brown hair billowed around her like a cloud. Eleuterio Galvan was a shadow beside her. Neither of them noticed Beth and Jerry standing silently in the deep shadows by the wall.

"It's so beautiful here!" Addie exclaimed with forced vivacity, leaning out over the rail as if all she cared for was to admire the mountains.

"If you were to stay over until tomorrow," Eleuterio suggested, "I could show you around the ranch. Do you ride, Señorita Clare?"

Addie giggled and pressed one hand to her throat. "Well . . . a little; but I really shouldn't . . . ."

"There is a very docile, sweet-tempered mare in my stables," Eleuterio said. "A lady's mount—we call her La Doña. You would be doing me a favor to ride her; I am afraid my rough wranglers will make her quite unfit for civilized treatment."

Beth clamped her lips together hard over the laughter bubbling up inside her. La Doña would need to be very docile indeed if Eleuterio meant to get Addie to ride her! Addie was even intimidated by the poor, raw-boned horses kept at the mission.

Galvan spoke in a low, confidential tone, assuring Addie that there would be no impropriety in her staying overnight, as several of the ranch families would be doing the same thing and all the girls would share the room upstairs where she and Beth had changed clothes. He would be happy to provide her with transport back to the mission on Sunday afternoon. "Or, if Miss Johanssen also chooses to stay, you girls can ride back together."

"Oh, no," Addie said, "Beth will have to go back tonight. The Griscoms would be terribly worried if neither of us returned. But she can explain to them that I decided to stay over."

Eleuterio Galvan raised her hand to his lips. "Then you have decided to stay. My house is honored."

"Well . . . yes. That is, I don't know. . . ." Addie fluttered. She gave an ineffectual tug, trying to free her hand. "Maybe we should go back to the dance, Señor Galvan."

"Call me Eleuterio," Galvan suggested, tucking her hand under his arm and leading her back toward the front of the house.

As they passed out of sight, Beth found that Jerry, too, was shaking with silent laughter. She shook her head, bemused by the implications of the scene. One implication in particular set her blood to pounding through her veins in a most disturbing way.

"Well, missionary lady," Jerry whispered beside her, "looks like you just lost a chaperone for the ride back."

That was too dangerous to think about. Beth quickly changed the subject. "Did you hear him saying to call her Eleuterio? She'll never manage it." Addie had trouble enough with the Americanized names of the Navaho children, names like Tso and Begay and Teez. What she would do with a tongue twister like Eleuterio Galvan was beyond Beth's imagination.

"She'll think of something," Jerry asserted. "Your Addie is coming out of her shell right fast, ain't she? If Eleuterio can pry her loose from the mission crowd, she might turn into a real woman."

"You seem to forget that I'm part of the 'mission crowd'!" Beth snapped, suddenly irritated by Jerry's patronizing tone. Was that how he saw her and Addie—as innocent little girls who needed a man's help to become "real women"?

Jerry's eyes shone in the moonlight. "No. I haven't forgotten. But I kind of hoped you were beginning to see another side of the story."

Beth had meant to talk to him about her problems at the mission, her confusion and her concern for the children. But at that moment it became impossible. "I think," she said, tilting her chin so that her eyes met his, "Addie had the right idea. It's time we rejoined the dancers."

For the rest of the evening, Beth saw to it that she had no chance to talk either to Hudson or to Jerry. It was easy enough to keep busy. There was perhaps one girl at the dance for every ten men. Beth found that she was in constant demand. Spinning in a wild stamping dance called the varsoviana, waltzing with Shorty, or taking Jerry's hand for a romp down the line of couples with their arms arched overhead for a line dance, she laughed, gasped for breath, and avoided any more intimate moments.

But always, whether she was in his arms for a dance or glancing across the room, Jerry's gray eyes were on her, promising and demanding at once and making it impossible for her to forget that the end of the evening awaited them. Dancing, flirting, or drinking the sweet-sour lemonade that

Señor Galvan had provided for the ladies, she was constantly aware of his presence. By the last, slow, swaying
waltz that indicated the end of the evening's amusement she
could think of nothing but Jerry.

When the dance was over, the ladies left for the long ride
back to Gallup or went upstairs to spend the night. The men
who stayed behind settled in the card salon for some serious
drinking and playing that would occupy them till dawn. Exhausted, sleepy, but oddly exhilarated, Beth bade farewell
to Señor Galvan and jumped into the high wagon that Jerry
had brought from the stables.

The moon that had been just rising above the mountains a
few hours earlier now hung in the sky like a last white lantern left over from the dance. The desert air was crisp and
clear with night. Beth shivered and was grateful for the
richly embroidered silk shawl that Eleuterio Galvan had
pressed upon her for the ride home.

Beside her, Jerry seemed to be devoting all his attention to
the horses, but Beth could feel his occasional glances at her
like so many electrifying caresses. The pale light stripped
Jerry's red hair of its fire and threw his features into sharp
relief. Behind them, the few remaining lights of the ranch
house slowly dwindled into pinpricks of light, like strayed
stars resting at the foot of the mountains.

In the silence of the desert night, the small sounds of their
movement rang out clearly: the wagon wheels creaking, the
soft clip-clop of the horses' hooves sinking into the sandy
road, the chink of the harness. Jerry looked over at Beth and
drew in his breath as though he were about to say something. She waited, tense, but he exhaled again and stared before him at the ruts marked out like lines of ink across the
silvery whiteness of the road.

"It was a nice dance," Beth said. Her voice sounded
clear and tinny in the silence, and her breath made a white

puff of vapor before her face, She pulled the shawl closer around her. "Thank you for taking me."

The ranch house was far behind them now; they were alone in the shallow bowl of the desert, with its jagged rim of mesas before them, mountains behind. When Beth closed her eyes, she remembered all the intoxication of those stolen moments on the porch of the ranch house. When she opened them, she looked at the perfect stillness of Jerry's tall form and wondered when he would touch her again. Out here, under the stars that seemed to swing as low as the lanterns at the dance, she felt as if the usual laws were suspended. Anything could happen here. And she knew she wanted something to happen. Beth shivered even though she was not cold, and Jerry put his arm around her shoulders.

"Cold?"

"Yes," she lied. Now he would stop the team, turn to her, and kiss her again . . . and then?

But they kept moving, and he kept one hand on the reins. Beth felt a queer disappointment. She straightened her shoulders and moved slightly away from him.

Jerry felt the slight withdrawal and immediately released her. "You mad at me or what?" he asked. "Way you've been keeping clear of me for the last half of the evening—maybe you'd rather have gone home in Hudson's shiny new buggy."

Beth stared at him, her eyes dark and unreadable, her lips parted in a tempting way that made him ache to kiss her. "I didn't want to go home with Lawrence Hudson."

So much for the "what." Maybe she was scared of him— afraid he might demand more than she was willing to give. Jerry felt the ache of desire for her in his loins and wryly admitted that she might have something to be scared of. Except not Beth, never Beth; he'd never do anything to hurt her. Didn't she know that?

"Some folks," Jerry said, staring at the black lines of the

reins looped over his hand, ''would take advantage of a situation like this—escorting a girl home from a dance alone, and all.''

Beth remembered their first ride to the mission, the miles wasted in bickering argument and that searing, dusty, gritty, blazing kiss just before they'd reached the mission school.

''But I suppose you wouldn't,'' she said.

Jerry nodded. ''Right.''

''You were free enough with your hands a couple of hours ago.''

''There were folks within call then,'' he pointed out. ''Look, all I'm saying is, I respect you. You got nothing to be afraid of. And you know that, or you'd have made some excuse to stay overnight so you wouldn't have to ride out alone with me.''

Beth supposed he was right. The quiver of fear with which she'd looked forward to their ride back was gone now. So was the excitement.

''So,'' Jerry finished with only the minutest quiver at the corner of his lips, ''seeing as you're perfectly safe with me, you might as well move closer and get warm.'' He raised his arm invitingly, and after a moment Beth moved over to cuddle next to him on the hard wagon bench.

''I wasn't afraid anyway,'' she lied.

''Of course not.'' Jerry flicked the reins expertly to guide the horses a little to the left, around a deep wagon rut that yawned black in the moonlight.

''And we have to talk.''

''Go ahead.'' Was it only her imagination, or did he sound disappointed?

Clasping her hands lightly together under the cover of the silk shawl, willing herself to forget the disturbing sensations of his body next to hers, Beth plunged into a rather tangled and confused exposition of what Lawrence Hudson had said to her about the trouble on Galvan North.

Jerry nodded a few times, but she felt he wasn't really listening. "Don't you understand what this means?"

"Uh-huh." His arm tightened about her. "Means you like me better than Hudson, or you wouldn't be telling me this."

Beth shook her head. "And they say women make everything personal! Listen, Jerry. This is important."

"*We* are important," Jerry corrected her. "I figure you've found what you're looking for. What you're really telling me is, you've made your choice." He tried to plant a kiss on her forehead, but she ducked away and scooted along the bench out of his reach.

"And *you* accused *me* of trying to set you two in competition!" Beth waved her hands in frustration. "Don't you even want to hear the evidence I got on Hudson?"

"Yeah, all right, I heard it," Jerry told her. "And it wasn't anything I hadn't already figured out, and it ain't anything I can act on without some proof."

"Well, now you've got proof. Why don't you tell the sheriff and make him stop it?"

"What Hudson said to you?" Jerry shrugged. "That ain't what I'd call proof. Except what I already knew. We'll have to wait."

"You already knew what he was up to," Beth marveled, "and you won't do a thing to stop it."

"Schoolteachers!" Jerry made the innocent word sound like an expletive. "What makes you think you can team me around like one of the kids in your classes? Can't you trust me to work this out in my own way?"

Beth folded her arms. "You're right. I don't understand this territory. Where I come from, if something's wrong, we try to fix it."

"Like you're fixing the Indians?" he drawled. "Yeah, that mission school of yours is fixing them real good, isn't it? Why don't you calm down till you figure out how things work around here, missionary lady? I never said I wasn't going to do anything about Hudson. Just said it didn't make no sense to have the law on him for two words he said to some girl at a dance. Nobody'd believe you, anyway."

"Well, thank you very much!" Beth felt a flame of pure fury within her. "It's certainly enlightening to know just how much you trust my word."

And to think she had been trying to help this infuriating man settle his mystery! But no, he didn't want help from a mere woman. Didn't even believe her! Suddenly it seemed impossible to endure the rest of the creaking ride back to the mission. She put one hand on the side of the slow-moving wagon and jumped out before Jerry could stop her.

Standing ankle deep in the soft sand that sifted into the wheel ruts, she glared up at him. "Please don't trouble yourself to take me back to the school. I'd rather walk than take a favor from a man who thinks I'm a liar. Besides, you need to save your horses. They're likely to be all you've got left after Lawrence Hudson burns down Galvan North and gets you fired!"

Turning her back on Jerry, she plodded up the side of the sandy trail. The moonlight cast all the little uneven places and pebbles and ruts into sharp relief, exaggerating their outlines so that she had to watch carefully where she put her feet.

After ten steps she knew that her soft dancing shoes would be ruined by the sand that sifted over their tops at every step. Never mind. Nothing, she told herself, would induce her to turn back and ask for help from that impossible man. Grimly determined, she moved on, thinking impolite words to herself and trying to ignore the creaking of the wagon behind her.

Chapter Nine

"Beth!" Jerry called out behind her in a low voice as he leaned forward to urge his horses up the hill. "Dammit, you can't—I didn't mean— Goddamn it to hell, woman, get back in this wagon and sit down!"

They had reached the crest of the hill, and the horses trotted easily to catch up with her. Beth glared over her shoulder at the wagon and was startled to see Jerry sitting far over on the right side of the bench while the reins fell slackly to the floor. He leaned down, his right arm scooping out in a curve that brushed her shoulders. One hand clamped hard under her ribs and she was dragged back toward the wagon, losing her balance, her feet knocked from under her. Just before she fell, his other hand caught her under the full skirt of the yellow dance dress and he lifted her bodily into the wagon and across his lap.

"*Now.*" He glared at her, spitting out the next words like chips of flint. "You going to be reasonable, or do I have to deliver you at the mission all tied up in a neat parcel? And don't think I wouldn't do it," he warned, fingering the knife

in his hip pocket and casting a warning glance at the coil of
rope that lay with other odds and ends in the wagon bed.

"I see," Beth said between clenched teeth. "You can
take action fast enough when you only have one helpless girl
to deal with. It's just rich bankers and like that that intimidate you." She was breathing hard, and that had nothing to
do with the force that had yanked her back into the wagon.
His thighs were hard under her, and the nearness of his body
was unlike the closeness of the dance, and her heart was
thumping so hard that he must feel it against his chest.

"Helpless. Girl." Jerry said several words that a thoroughly nice-minded girl wouldn't even have recognized;
Beth hoped the moonlight did not show her fierce blush.
"Lady, you are about as helpless as a poor little prickly pear
showing its flowers to attract victims."

His arm tightened around her and his free hand slid under
her chin, tilting her face up to the moonlight. He studied her
features as though he had never seen them before, as though
some secret vital to his life were concealed there. "But more
tempting," he whispered.

Too tempting. He surrendered to the desires that had been
tormenting him all evening. It shouldn't be like this,
dammit, in a wagon under the stars—she was all silk and
honey, this sweet, maddening girl, and he had no place to
take her, no place of his own but the bunkhouse he shared
with a dozen other cowboys. And he shouldn't be making
love to her when this was all they could have, when he was
years away from being in a position to marry. But he was beyond reasoned restraint, had been ever since he'd scooped
her up from the sand and felt her supple body in his arms.

Beth could feel his anger shift to something else with the
release of tension in his hands. She drew in her breath
sharply, afraid of her own unthinking response to his touch.
But the pounding of her blood grew stronger with every

breath and was now far louder than the distant voice of her
anger. His mouth came down on hers, hard and demanding,
and her own desire was what held her still to meet his kiss,
not the hands on her body that tightened with the first touch
of their lips.

Beth felt velvet and tasted honey. The stars were wheeling around them in dizzying pinwheels. When he released
her mouth so that he could move on down to her neck and
shoulders, her breathing sounded thick and ragged in her
own ears. He was taking her apart inch by inch, sliding the
soft yellow cotton dress down her shoulders and following
its path with kisses that left her exposed to more than the air.
Her veins were filled with something lighter and more vola-
tile than blood, something as light as the dancing wisp of a
fiddle tune, and the expert movements of Jerry's mouth
against her bared skin were what gave the music its
compelling undertone.

"*Beth.*" Only that, and then his fingers were pulling at
the ribbons on her embroidered chemise, letting the lacy
white work fly loose as a wisp of cloud in the wind. His
thumb moved lightly back and forth across one nipple and
she shut her eyes at the wonder and the glory of it, the sweetness that made her breast ache for more, a demanding pleasure that was almost painful. She ached for Jerry's touch
everywhere.

It's not my fault, she thought defensively as she went
down open-mouthed under another of his probing, burning
kisses. I tried . . . Addie was supposed to come with
us. . . .

"Jerry, darling," she murmured, putting one hand up to
cup the short red curls at the back of his head. His body was
pressing against her now, lean and hard and eager, and his
hands were hard on the softness of her breasts, but she didn't

mind, she was his now, and always. "My love," she said aloud without thinking, "my dear, dear love."

The movements of Jerry's questing mouth stilled, stopped. Beth hung quivering in some space between the stars and the desert. Time stopped; she knew she had done something wrong, something was broken, but as long as she didn't move and didn't feel then it could be put right—it could be as if it never happened.

"No," Jerry said. Slowly, painfully, he sat up. "No. Don't love me."

Eyes averted, he tossed the shawl at her.

Beth sat up, too, her heart aching with loss even while other parts of her body still ached for the sweetness that had been broken off so quickly. The night air flowed as cool as spring water across the skin exposed by Jerry's caresses. Her breasts were aching with desire and the nipples, taut and erect from Jerry's touch, puckered and contracted slightly in the chill of the desert night. She pulled the silk shawl over her bare shoulders and huddled into it. The underside of the embroidered work, the knots of silk and the threads of silver, was rough against her soft skin like the calluses on Jerry's work-hardened hands.

"I'm sorry," Jerry muttered, hunched over the reins and staring fiercely in front of him. "Didn't mean for that to happen."

Beth felt a chill that had nothing to do with the night air. Under the cover of the shawl, she fumbled to pull her dress back up over her shoulders. He didn't want her. She was a wicked, forward girl, and she was throwing herself at a man who didn't care about her at all; all his passion was reserved for abstract issues like Indian rights and the Galvan land grant.

"Here," he added, eyes fixed on the horses.

The first stirrings of hope were revived in Beth's mind.

Whatever was going on, it was more complex than Jerry's getting scared she would carry a flirtation too far. He'd been like this at their picnic, too, she remembered—carried away, then drawing back, possessed by some inner fears.

It was not entirely bad to know that she had the power to disrupt his personal schedule and break down that iron will, even momentarily. As he glanced at her, his mouth taut with desire denied, she felt a light, bubbly happiness spreading through her veins. She laughed aloud. "And just where were you planning for it to happen, pray tell?"

Jerry looked straight at her for the first time since he had roughly broken off the embrace. The moonlight turned his face into an unreadable collection of sharp white planes and black shadows, but she thought she saw a quiver of amusement at the corner of his lips. "Well, not in a wagon halfway between Galvan Ranch and the mission school, that's for sure." He paused, frowning as if it hurt him to go on.

"You—you're worth better'n that. Better than me, if it comes to that. You could do better for yourself than a footloose wrangler." He paused again and looked away from her. The wagon heaved and creaked as they moved from the soft sand trail of the valley to the irregular rock bed that ran along the top of the mesa. Beth held her breath, but it seemed he meant to say no more.

"Is that why you don't want me to love you?" But he had spoken no word of love. Beth felt fear chill her veins in the uncountable seconds while she waited for an answer. The last man she'd refused, laughing, in Iowa, had called her a proud beauty and prophesied that she'd get her comeuppance some day. At the time his melodramatic words had only made her laugh again. Now she wondered if this was what he'd meant. Did everyone have to tumble into love, once in their lives, with someone who could no more respond to their feeling than he could fly to the moon?

"That and . . . other things," Jerry said finally.

Beth decided that if she could feel like hitting him over the head with something heavy, she must not have a broken heart. Not yet, anyway. Why couldn't he ever say anything straight out? Was he trying to let her down gently, or what?

"Lawrence Hudson would agree with you," she said at last, hoping to goad Jerry into some expression of feeling. "He says I can do better for myself. Maybe he thinks I should set my cap for a banker."

Jerry glanced at her, his dark-shadowed eyes unreadable. "Yes? Well, he's right. You want to stick with Hudson and the good people of the mission. That's where a nice girl from back east belongs."

There it was again. The good people of the mission. The lines were drawn in this part of the world, and the mission school and Lawrence Hudson and the rich Anglo ranchers were on one side, and on the other was a ragged coalition of men like Jerry and Red Singer and Eleuterio Galvan.

And she was on the wrong side. Or was she? "I don't know, Jerry," she said quietly. "I'm not so sure I belong at the mission. We—we don't see eye to eye on everything." It was as close as she could come to confessing all the problems she'd been having. And even that, it turned out, was too close.

"Good," Jerry said promptly. "When you going to quit?"

And go home? Beth frowned at her clasped hands as though they could provide some sort of answer. Was that what he wanted? A quick flirtation, a few stolen kisses, and then let the crazy lady go back east where she belonged?

"I . . . don't want to leave this territory," she said. The quiver in her voice betrayed her real thought. The desert was where she belonged—but it was Jerry she didn't want to leave.

Jerry looked up at the ragged black line ahead where the mesa broke off and the road dipped down into the canyon where the mission school sat. "Well," he said slowly. "Wrangler's one thing. But Galvan's been talking about making me a section manager, if I stick with him another six months or so. There'd be a house goes with that."

Beth felt a pounding ache at her temples. A house. Jerry. Leave the school. It was too soon! How could she ever feel at peace with herself if, after the disaster in Iowa, she ran away from this job after only two weeks?

"I never stayed one place that long before," Jerry added. "But with you . . . And we might be able to get the house earlier, if I told him we needed it. Not much of a place," he warned her. "Two rooms, adobe. Not the sort of thing you'd be used to."

She thought of a little adobe house somewhere far out on the Galvan Ranch. Two rooms, one dark-shadowed, smelling of fresh clean linen on the bed and piñon logs on the fire; a room lit only by the sparks from the hearth, and Jerry there, alone with her. Something dark and frightening—and wonderful—stirred in her blood.

Against that, she envisioned the school, the dreary attic room she shared with Addie, the weary round of bells and prayers and meals and trying to find some way of reaching the dark-eyed Indian children without annoying the missionaries. How much easier it would be to run away from that to the shelter of Jerry's little adobe house! Just as she'd run from Iowa to the territory.

That was a sobering memory. Was she always to be running away from failure? Beth's spine straightened. No, she wouldn't give up so easily. She would finish her teaching term at the school. No one would be able to say she'd run away from this job in disgrace.

She opened her mouth to break the silence that had gone on too long, but Jerry spoke before she had a chance.

"It's a pretty isolated life for a girl like you, used to living in town. If you think the mission school is lonely—this'd be worse. I can't blame you for not wanting it." His hands were tight about the reins, the only sign of the tension he must be feeling. After a brief pause he said, "Or is it the waiting? Not knowing when we could get the house? Because I could maybe get a job in town. . . ."

Beth put her hand over his, willing the tension from his clenched fingers. "You'd hate that, Jerry. And I would, too. It's not that. But . . . I don't want to give up my job at the school yet." She couldn't just walk out on two jobs in a row, then go and live with Jerry and never do anything of her own. She had to have some success of her own first. But if she tried to explain that, wouldn't he think she was complaining about the isolation of the life he offered her?

Beth longed with every fiber of her being for that magnificent, lonely world of the red-rock desert and the shining mesas. And Jerry. But she wanted to go to it of her own will, after succeeding at the task she'd taken up. Not to run to him as a refuge from failure.

"I—the school isn't all that bad," she said lamely. Thank goodness she hadn't told Jerry all the details of her clashes with the Griscoms! If he knew half of what went on, he'd think she was crazy to stay there. Maybe she was. "It's doing some good, even if it's not all it could be," she insisted, as much to herself as to him. "Don't you think it's worthwhile to educate the Indians?"

Jerry gave her a wry smile. Her heart twisted at the pain she could sense behind it. "Educate—or cripple?" He sighed and flicked the reins over the horses' backs to hurry them across the plain. "Never mind. You got ideals. You want to live like civilized folks, and I don't blame you. It's what a girl like you oughta have.''

"It's not like that at all!" Beth almost shrieked in her frustration. "Don't you see?" But how could he see? She'd never told him about why she came out here. Maybe she should tell him now. No, they were starting the rough descent into the canyon. A single lamp twinkled in the mission house; Mrs. Griscom must be waiting up for her. This was no time to start with lengthy explanations. She clasped her hands together, longing to reach out to him again, knowing she must not distract him as he maneuvered the wagon down the steep trail to the canyon floor.

"Jerry, please trust me," she said quietly. "There is something I have to do here, and I think it is worth doing. I want to finish out my term at the school. Then . . . there is nothing I would like better than to be with you."

Jerry flicked a dark glance at her over his shoulder. "Straight?"

"Straight," Beth affirmed.

He heaved a sigh, but his shoulders straightened, and his hands held the reins loosely again. "Shoulda known better than to get mixed up with an uppity eastern woman." He sighed again. "What are you, a career girl or something? Next thing I know you'll be tellin' me how to vote!"

Beth felt a rush of relief. He did understand. He would wait for her.

"Next thing you know," she said, speaking lightly to cover the deep relief she felt, "we'll have the vote. And then you men will have to watch out, or you'll be saying 'Yes, ma'am,' and 'No, ma'am,' to a lady judge in Gallup!"

"Judge Beth Johanssen?"

"Could be!"

They had reached the fence that marked the mission

boundaries. Beth slipped out of the wagon to open the gate, paused with one hand on the top rail. "Don't bother to bring your wagon in any farther," she said in a low voice. The light in the mission house was moving from one room to the next, as though Mrs. Griscom were coming downstairs to meet her. She wouldn't be pleased to hear that Addie had stayed behind, and seeing Jerry would do nothing to sweeten her temper. She stood on tiptoe to give Jerry a quick, unsatisfactory kiss on the cheek.

"I'll be back." Jerry accepted his dismissal with a grin, which surprised Beth. She hadn't expected him to settle for that token embrace and was obscurely disappointed. "To . . . talk politics."

"Right!" Beth raised her hand to wave good-bye and found it caught in a warm, hard clasp that kept her prisoner.

"But first," Jerry murmured, jumping from the wagon bench while he held her hand fast, "I'm going to say a proper good-bye to my girl. Just so you remember, if Larry Hudson comes sniffing around next week, I've already staked my claim."

His mouth covered hers in a bruising kiss that sent quivers of desire racing deeply through her body, pressed to his and aching from the strain and the moment of separation that was coming. Would he understand why she had to stay on at the school? Would he doubt her, once he had ridden back to the ranch? Would she even see him again? All Beth's doubts and questions were swept away in the urgency of the flames that ignited between them. She clung to him, exulting in the bruising pressure of his arm about her waist and the hard lines of his body pressing against hers.

"Well!"

A pallid circle of lamplight danced around them. Shocked, Beth pushed herself away from Jerry to see Mrs. Griscom, a massive black pillar in her crackling bombazine, holding up a lantern in one hand and glaring at them both. The only indications she had not been sitting up, fully dressed, all evening were two buttons fastened awry on the front of her dress and some wisps of hair sticking out of a hastily twisted bun.

"Well!" Mrs. Griscom repeated, as though she were too shocked to say more. "Fine goings-on in the very courtyard of God's house, Miss Johanssen. I knew I should never have agreed to your going off with those publicans and sinners—chaperone or no chaperone. Addie Clare has not the strength of character to control your kind." She peered suspiciously into the empty bed of the wagon. "And where is Addie? What have you done with her?"

Her tone suggested that she thought Beth and Jerry might have stopped on their way home to dispose of Addie in some nameless pagan orgy. Beth felt untimely giggles shaking her. No, she implored herself, not now! Don't laugh in her face, it's the one affront she'd never forgive!

"Addie stayed behind at the ranch, Mrs. Griscom," she said, twisting her hands in the thin cotton skirt as if that action could control the threatening quivers in her voice. Beside her, she felt Jerry's hand slide around her upper arm in a warm, comforting hold. Steadied by the touch, she went on smoothly, "She was fatigued by the journey and the noise, and felt one of her sick headaches coming on—or, we thought, it might have been the measles," she improvised. "Didn't you say she had a rash, Jerry?"

"Definitely flushed," Jerry agreed. "Feverish, you might say." His voice was shaking slightly. Beth shifted her weight and leaned back hard on his toe, giving him a warning glance. This was no time to play with words.

"She feared to bring an epidemic back to the school, so Señor Galvan kindly offered to let her stay overnight and to bring her back tomorrow if it should prove to be nothing serious.''

''Well!'' Mrs. Griscom exclaimed for the third time. ''How inconsiderate of Addie, to get sick just when I need her help with the new children that are coming in.''

Beth exhaled a very small sigh of relief. At least Mrs. Griscom had accepted her story. Now she had only to catch Addie on her return tomorrow and warn her to back up the story of a sudden indisposition.

''You'll just have to watch both classes tomorrow,'' Mrs. Griscom warned. ''Day of rest it may be, but they always get difficult when there's new children brought in. I don't want these wild up-reservation Navahos that Griscom's bringing in to upset the others. First thing we know we'll have a flock of runaways on our hands.''

Jerry's hand tightened on Beth's arm until she let out a squeak of pain. Ignoring her, he leaned forward and addressed Mrs. Griscom. ''Up reservation, ma'am? Your husband's gone out to kidnap some more children, has he?''

''No concern of yours,'' snapped Mrs. Griscom, ''and you can hardly call it kidnapping to rescue them from their heathenish ways. But since you're so interested, yes, he's gone up Blue Mesa way to clean out that nest of no-account Navahos that hang around the trading post. Should get ten, maybe twenty kids. Indian agent's with him, so they won't get any ideas about resisting. And we should get double the appropriation next year. New buildings!'' Her eyes flicked over the shabby adobe buildings. ''Maybe even a deeper well. I can expand the garden.''

Jerry swung around and gripped Beth by both arms. ''Blue Mesa! That's old Hosteen Chee's people. Next to Galvan North. If there wasn't Indian trouble on that section before, there sure will be now. I bet Hudson put them up to this.'' He was staring right through her, talking to himself.

Beth felt chilled by the faraway look in his eyes, as though he were staring at horizons too distant for her to see.

He dropped his eyes to her face and studied her for a moment. "You'll have to come with me now," he stated.

His restrained anger was like the flames of a brush fire crackling around her. She stood in the center of the fire, feeling the burning touch of his hands on her, but somehow she remained cold. Her mouth felt dry. She didn't understand. She moistened her lips, tried to tell Jerry that she must have time to think, but the words wouldn't come. She could only shake her head.

"You see what sort these folks are? Filling up the school and building up their appropriation by stealing kids. You want to be a part of that?" He shook her lightly as though he thought she were already part of it.

"Unhand Miss Johanssen!" Mrs. Griscom clawed at Jerry's back, trying ineffectually to pull him away from Beth. "You can't talk to my schoolteachers like that."

"Go away," Jerry flung over his shoulder. "This is between me and Beth." He turned back to Beth, his hands now resting lightly on her shoulders, his face a white mask in the moonlight, which turned his curly red hair to an inky shadow that spilled over his forehead. "Well? Get your things. I'll wait here. Just yell if the old harpy tries to stop you."

"She's not going anywhere with you!" Mrs. Griscom tugged at Jerry's arm, trying to drag him away. "Just get back in your wagon and get out of here, young man, and stop trying to tempt a God-fearing young woman out of her duty."

Duty. That word rang in Beth's ears, as heavy and harsh as a blacksmith striking an iron bar. And solid. Something she could hold on to. Slowly she raised her eyes to Jerry's implacable face. "I'm sorry, Jerry. I can't just run off with you like this.'' He couldn't really have expected her to. They had just agreed that she would finish her term at the school. But his face was hard and still, a collection of white and shadowed planes with no more life in them than a statue in a museum.

"Make up your mind,'' he said, slowly stepping back. His hands fell away from her shoulders, and she felt the cold bite of the desert air on her skin where he had held her. "Or . . . I guess you already made it up, didn't you? Play it safe. Stay with the good people. Wait to see who wins this round—Hudson or Eleuterio.''

Beth shook her head, trying to force words through her dry lips. Why was he talking about waiting and winning? A moment ago he'd been asking her to marry him—if she understood him—and now they were fighting over something she'd thought already settled.

She couldn't just up and quit her job because of some incomprehensible quarrel between his Indian friends and the missionaries. But he was vaulting up to the high wagon seat now without a backward glance for her.

He couldn't just leave like that, without a word of explanation.

He was leaving. The creak of the wagon wheels was the loudest sound in the desert night.

"You are not fair!'' she cried after him, released at last from her paralysis. "You expect me to make a decision when I don't know what's going on. You expect me to walk out on my job just because you say so. You—''

The wagon rolled on, away from the mission, until it was only a moving shadow among the shadows below the cliff. Beth felt something warm and moist on her bare arm. It took a minute for her to realize that Mrs. Griscom was patting her arm.

"That's all right, dearie,'' she said. "I knew you'd

choose the right path in the end, even if you have been flirting with temptation. Best you come inside now. You'll need your rest before Griscom comes back tomorrow.''

Numbly, Beth followed Mrs. Griscom into the little house. She felt drained and empty inside, as though Jerry had taken the best part of her away with him, leaving nothing but an aching hollow. How could he just leave her like that? How could it hurt so much?

''The first couple of weeks are always hard.'' Mrs. Griscom was offering her a mug of something hot and bitter. Beth took the mug in both hands and gratefully gulped down the steaming beverage. The first couple of weeks. Had it only been two weeks? How could a man she'd only seen three times have the power to hurt her so?

''I must have been mad,'' she said aloud, oblivious to Mrs. Griscom's presence. ''I can't marry him. I don't even know him. And he's completely unreasonable.''

'' 'Course he is,'' Mrs. Griscom agreed comfortably, taking the empty mug from her hands and nudging her toward the stairs. ''And you don't have to marry anybody. You just stay here with us and help with the school. You've been reckless and disobedient, but you show Griscom a proper spirit of penitence, and we'll just make a fresh start.''

A fresh start. Helping with the school. Through the waves of sleepiness that suddenly assailed her, Beth wondered as she climbed the stairs why these words suddenly seemed so empty. It was all she had wanted two weeks ago, but now she couldn't stop thinking about Jerry.

''He didn't mean it,'' she told herself as her head hit the pillow. ''He lost his temper. You both did. People can make up after they lose their tempers. Happens . . . all the . . . time. . . .''

Chapter Ten

The optimism with which Beth had drifted into sleep had deserted her by the morning. She was tired from the dance and the long ride back, and it seemed like an intolerable effort to get dressed and drag herself downstairs to help Mrs. Griscom oversee the children at breakfast. She no longer felt sure that Jerry would come back; his blazing anger the night before was the clearest thing in her memory.

Remembering how he'd shouted at her to come away with him, Beth's lips compressed and angry spots burned in her cheeks. As if she could throw up her job on a moment's notice whenever he whistled! Oh, he'd pretended to understand that her work mattered to her, even agreed that she should finish out her term, but when it came to the point he was just like any other man. "Do exactly what I want, *now*, or I withdraw the lordly light of my countenance from you!" Beth muttered in bitter parody as she ladled out glutinous oatmeal into the children's bowls. "Well, I'm not having any of that."

"Me, neither," said one of the senior boys with a cheeky

grin, and Beth realized with a start that she'd been muttering aloud. ''Don' like oatmeal.''

Beth let him get away with an extra piece of bread to replace the disdained oatmeal. She could hardly blame him. The thick, gooey mixture of oats and chaff was about as appetizing as the white paste they used to glue book covers back on, and probably less nourishing. She would have to ask Mrs. Griscom about this appropriation they received for each child. Surely better meals could be contrived.

On this grim morning, teaching at the mission school seemed like a poor thing for which to have given up Jerry's love. Beth's chin tilted upward and she surveyed the shabby dining hall with a challenging glare that quite frightened several of the younger children who'd been thinking about wriggling about on the hard benches. Very well, she resolved; if teaching was to be her life, then she'd make it into something she could feel good about. No more truckling to the Griscoms!

She scraped the big pot clean for the last child and thankfully escaped to her own seat with a piece of bread and a cup of black coffee. She nibbled on the bread, dipping it in the coffee to soften it, and let Mrs. Griscom's continuous soft monologue about the troubles of dealing with the Indians wash over her unheeding ears while she scanned the rows of children and sorted out her own thoughts.

''Where's Lucy Tso?'' she asked abruptly, interrupting Mrs. Griscom's complaint that some of the senior boys were sneaking out at night to go to the forbidden ''sings'' in the mountains.

Mrs. Griscom flushed and smoothed the ruffles ornamenting the front of her Sunday gown. ''Lucy was impudent,'' she said. ''She is being punished. It's no concern of yours.''

''What did she do?'' Beth had a horrible, sinking feeling

that she already knew. Somehow, Mrs. Griscom had found out about the translations she and Lucy were working on.

Mrs. Griscom shook her head. "It doesn't matter. I don't blame you, Miss Johanssen. You are new here and do not understand how we do things."

That seemed to be a constant refrain from everybody she met in the territory, from Jerry to the Griscoms. But this was a school, and Beth was a schoolteacher—probably for the rest of her life, it now seemed—and she was tired of being warned off. "Lucy is one of my students," she said evenly. "It is my responsibility to maintain discipline. *What did she do?*"

"You know perfectly well what she did!" Mrs. Griscom retorted. Her flabby neck turned red with indignation and the loose skin shook as she attempted to stare Beth down. "And it's no use your attempting to shield her. She gave you the idea of translating their heathen legends in the classroom, knowing perfectly well it was against all our policies, but she thought she could take advantage of a new teacher. And she's been going on with it all this week! Writing down disgusting heathen tales!"

Mrs. Griscom held up one hand as Beth attempted to speak. "Don't attempt to shield her. I heard all about it from Ethel Yazzie. She came directly to me when she found out what Lucy was doing."

"I just bet she did," breathed Beth. "The little sneak!" She'd never cared for Ethel, a sly-faced girl who leaned over the others' shoulders to sneak looks at their work. Beth had tried to fight down her dislike, telling herself that a teacher shouldn't have favorites.

Mrs. Griscom folded her hands before her on the table. Beth stared at the pudgy white fingers, the thin gold wedding band half-buried in the flesh. "Ethel is a good girl and knows her duty. And Lucy showed no sense of shame when

when I confronted her with her transgressions. She said she was proud of her people and their stories. Proud! After all our work to eradicate these superstitions!''

"Ethel got the story wrong," Beth snapped. "Lucy may have mentioned the Changing Woman legend to me, but it was entirely my idea, Mrs. Griscom, to have the class translate those stories. And Lucy was continuing with the translations at my request, because I decided it was a good way for her to practice her English."

The anger roared within her, deafening her to Mrs. Griscom's attempts to interrupt. "But you couldn't talk it over with me, could you? It could have waited until today, but you couldn't wait to punish the girl for something I had instigated."

There was a sour taste in her mouth, and her hands were shaking, but she could not stop. She pushed back her chair and leaned over Mrs. Griscom, her eyes flashing. "What did you do to Lucy?"

Mrs. Griscom seemed to shrink into her chair, like a puffball mushroom that had been squashed under someone's foot. "I locked her in the storage basement to reconsider. She can come out when she is ready to apologize."

Beth felt sick at the picture of Lucy shut into that tiny, windowless space, a half room dug out of the earth under the mission house. She'd glanced down there once when Addie showed her around the school. There were spiders—Beth had a particular aversion to spiders and all clinging, crawling things that left strands and webs where they might brush against your face. She wondered if Lucy had the same aversion.

Mrs. Griscom shrank back in her chair, and Beth realized that the woman was afraid of her.

"All right, she's been punished," she said quietly. "Now you're going to let her out. Aren't you, Mrs. Griscom? Oh, never mind. You don't have to do it yourself. Just give me the key. Now!''

The single word was snapped out like a military order. Mrs. Griscom handed over her heavy ring of keys without a word and Beth marched out of the hall, her head high.

Her mood of righteous anger had softened into dismay by the time she'd unlocked the trap door that led down into the storage basement and scrambled down the steps to lead Lucy out. The girl was quiet and trembling, her flesh was cold to the touch, and a sour smell told Beth that she had vomited in the corner. As she helped Lucy up the stairs, the girl's hand brushed a spiderweb and she flinched violently.

"I don't like spiders, either," Beth said in a firmly cheerful voice. The hot glare of the sun was a relief after being in that earthen-walled closet for just a few minutes. And Lucy had been there all night. She looked closely at Lucy, worried about her passivity and the strange leaden tint of her complexion.

"I don' mind spiders," Lucy whispered. "But they say that place's—a man died in there. *Chindi.*"

Jerry had told Beth something of the Navaho horror of the spirits of the dead, a fear that led them sometimes to abandon perfectly good hogans because a relative had died in one. It would have been torture for Lucy to spend the night in such a place. Beth put her arm around the girl's frail shoulders and hugged her reassuringly. "You don't believe that, do you, Lucy?"

"Of course not." Lucy straightened and shrugged off Beth's arm. Beth felt the girl's will rejecting her touch. "That's ignorant superstition. I'm an educated Indian. I don' believe old stories."

"Good!" said Beth with false heartiness.

"Maybe good, maybe not," Lucy muttered, staring at the ground.

"What do you mean?" Beth put one hand on Lucy's arm. It would do the girl good, she thought, to talk about her fears and the night underground. "Tell me, Lucy. It will help to talk about it."

Lucy spun around and shook off Beth's hand. "Too late to talk!" she said in a low, passionate voice. "You talk in class—see what happens? Nothing happens to you, but it costs us."

"It . . . cost me something, too," said Beth, a queer little ache in her heart as she thought of Jerry.

Lucy ignored her and went on speaking in a low monotone, the words rushing out as if they'd been held back for too long and now she could not control what she said. "All right, I don' believe in *chindi*, that's good, I wear a pretty dress and you teach me to cook in a shiny kitchen with a big iron stove. What good does that do me? I can't go home. I can't go back to cooking over a smoky fire and wearing the same old calico skirt and everything smelling like sheep's wool. I can't go to the sings anymore, I don' believe in them. You going to get me a nice house wit' running water and a shiny kitchen, Miss Johanssen? Huh? You think that Mrs. Griscom, she gon' treat me nice like a white lady and curtsy when she see me on the street? No, here in school it's 'forget your pagan ways,' but when I go to town it's 'dirty Indian, get back to the reservation.' "

Beth stood silent and helpless in the face of Lucy's outrage.

"I graduate next term," Lucy said at last. She turned and started across the yard to the long dormitory where she slept.

Beth reached after her. "Wait, Lucy! I didn't know you were worried about what to do after you got out of school. Maybe I can help."

Lucy looked back over her shoulder. The passionate anger of a moment ago was gone, replaced by the mask Beth was used to seeing on the faces of all her Indian pupils. "No, Miss Johanssen," she said. "I don' need any more white people help."

She paused for a second and fired one parting shot. "No, I don' believe in *chindi* spirits anymore. But maybe I wish I did. Then I could go home. Then I'd belong somewhere."

Beth stood helpless in the glare of the morning sun as Lucy marched away from her and entered the shabby dormitory building without looking back. Lucy's outburst had mirrored everything Jerry had said to her about the harm that the mission schools were doing. Perhaps they were right. Perhaps she was no better than the Griscoms. They openly hated and feared the Indian culture, but she, too, was working to change it.

Up to this day, she would have called Lucy Tso one of the successes of the system—bright, neatly dressed, almost fluent in English. Now she wondered what did happen to girls like Lucy when they left the school. The Griscoms mentioned proudly one girl who worked as a maid for a rancher's family, pursed their lips and sighed about the two who worked in the hotel in Gallup, and shook their heads over the majority who went "back to the blanket."

But where else could they go? Beth remembered Hudson's anger at losing the horse race to an Indian, his outburst that they shouldn't be allowed to compete with white men. All too many of the ranchers at Galvan's party had nodded their heads in agreement.

She shook her own head. The weight of her own thick black hair, piled high and held by long pins, suddenly seemed too much to bear. Her head ached unbearably and the glare of the sun blinded her eyes. The one thing everybody seemed to agree on was that she didn't belong here.

"You don't understand the problems."

"You won't be able to take living in the desert."

"You don't understand our ways."

All the critical voices she had heard blended into one accusing chorus in her head. The barren schoolyard was blurred by the tears in her eyes. Beth rubbed the back of one hand across her aching forehead and plodded back to the meal hall. She had to give Mrs. Griscom back her keys. She would have to play the piano for divine service, since Addie was not back yet. One step at a time. Just do what you have to do, she thought. Stop trying to make the universe right for everybody; it doesn't work.

Her chastened mood persisted through the short service of hymns and prayers through which Mrs. Griscom led the uncomprehending children, most of them with no object but to sing louder and faster than their neighbors. Beth's amateurish piano playing was drowned out in the cacophony of tuneless voices; no loss, she thought, bringing the pedals down for a final crashing chord to the last hymn. She massaged her aching forehead with tired fingers and wearily braced herself for the next task in the endless day.

Mrs. Griscom was already outside, urging the children back to their dormitory, where they were expected to spend the rest of the hot, airless Sunday reading their Bibles—except for the boys, who tended the vegetable garden. The trickle of muddy water that ran through the garden's rows must not be ignored, even on Sunday.

There was the jingle of harness outside and the whinny of a horse. Jerry had come back! Beth's fatigue dropped from her like a dusty traveling cloak. Picking up her serge skirts, she hurried to the door of the chapel and paused for a moment, almost blinded by the sunlight reflecting off the bright metal and gleaming leather of the buggy that stood in the courtyard.

Lawrence Hudson was standing beside the buggy, his golden hair gleaming as brightly as the polished hinges of the doors. He held a shiny black beaver hat in one hand and was gesturing with it as he put some argument to Mrs. Griscom. Beyond them, Addie hurried toward the mission house, her head bowed and her shoulders hunched as if she expected a scolding.

Beth felt a sinking sensation in the pit of her stomach. She gripped the edge of the door to steady herself. She had unconsciously been counting on Jerry to bring Addie back, thinking that would give her a chance to make up with him.

"Oh, Miss Johanssen," Mrs. Griscom called as Beth paused in the doorway. "Do come and join us."

Incredibly, she was smiling as though she and Beth were the dearest of friends.

"Mr. Hudson has kindly invited you to go for a ride with him," she said when Beth had crossed the yard to join them, "and since it is a day of rest, and Addie is back to help me oversee the children, I have given my consent. You will be back, of course, in time for the evening meal."

"Oh!" Beth looked at the shiny buggy and at Lawrence Hudson's confident grin. She didn't like Hudson. But the thought of being away from the school for a couple of hours was a powerful temptation. And how could she refuse, when he'd come all this way?

"You had business in this area, Mr. Hudson?"

"Call me Lawrence," Hudson suggested with a smile that flashed in the sunlight. "And my only business, Miss Johanssen, is to see more of you—and, of course, to admire the progress made by these excellent people in their fine work here." He bowed slightly toward Mrs. Griscom, who accepted the compliment with a simpering smile that sat oddly on her square face.

"Go on, Miss Johanssen," she urged. "You should enjoy your free time. We'll all be busy tonight when Griscom gets back."

Still numb from her disappointment, Beth let Hudson slide his hand under her elbow and help her into the buggy. He treated her with respect, not swinging her up bodily the way Jerry had, but the lingering touch of his moist palm was more unpleasant than Jerry's brisk clasp about her waist. "I don't know—" She started to think of an excuse, but it was too late. The horses were moving and Hudson had tipped his hat in farewell to Mrs. Griscom.

"I hope you understand, Beth, that my only object in coming here was to see you. I told you last night that we ought to get better acquainted." He gave her a fleeting smug smile before one of the frisky horses claimed his attention for a moment.

"I stopped overnight at Galvan's ranch," he went on once the horses were under control again, "and in the morning, since I was coming here anyway, I told Señor Galvan that I would be happy to convey Miss Clare back. Stop that, dammit!" he shouted as the near horse pulled sideways to sniff at a fence post.

"Oh!" Beth repeated. She was still stunned by her disappointment. "You—you told Señor Galvan that you were coming out to see me?"

"Actually," Hudson corrected, "it was that wrangler of his I spoke with. Young Dixon."

Beth felt sick. After the way she'd flirted with Hudson at the party, Jerry might think they'd arranged this meeting today.

"I had anticipated some hostility on his part," Hudson added, "but he seemed to think well of my chances with you. Perhaps the night gave him time to realize that a homeless wrangler has no place courting a girl when he has nothing to offer her."

"Jerry's going to have a house," Beth said swiftly. "Señor Galvan promised him a job as section manager."

Hudson raised his eyebrows. "My dear girl, I think it very unlikely that Galvan will have a job to offer Jerry in six months' time, let alone a house. The day of the Mexican sheepman is over. This territory belongs to true Americans, who will develop it as it deserves to grow."

The steep rise of the trail leading out of the canyon forced Hudson to lean over his horses and coax them up the rough road. Beth sat on the edge of her seat as the buggy swayed from side to side, prepared to leap out if it overturned, as seemed likely. The high-sprung buggy and frisky horses were showy, she thought, but not so well adapted to the territory as Jerry's wagon and mustangs.

"There!" They reached the mesa top and Hudson mopped beads of sweat from his brow with a white linen handkerchief. The red dust was settling on his gray silk suit. He must have stopped just before reaching the mission to dust himself off and wipe the buggy's woodwork. The picture made Beth smile.

"It's an unseasonably warm day, is it not? You'd not object if I removed my coat?" Before Beth could give her assent, Hudson had tossed the coat into the back of the buggy. His immaculate white shirt and grey silk vest were marred by dark circles of perspiration under the armpits.

"A barbarous country, fit for none but Indians," he muttered, looking around at the expanse of red and ochre rocks glowing against the intense blue of the sky. "It will be my pleasure to take you away from all this."

"I don't think we can get very far this afternoon," Beth replied, deliberately misunderstanding him. "Remember, I have to be back in time to help with supper."

Hudson's response was a self-satisfied grin that exposed the gleaming, perfectly even row of his prominent front teeth. He definitely looked better with his mouth shut. Beth stifled an impulse to hand him a carrot to chomp on. "My dear girl, you don't understand. A man in my position needs a wife—a hostess, a companion, a consort, if you will. I have decided that you will be eminently suitable."

Beth bit back a gasp at this arrogant pronouncement. Her first impulse was to say something scathing about *his* utter lack of suitability as a husband for *her*. She clamped down hard on her unruly tongue. Tact, tact, Beth, she reminded herself. Think before you speak, and all that. What did a ladylike girl say in response to an unwelcome proposal? Goodness, she'd turned down enough limp young men in Vinton, Iowa, without offending them or hurting their feelings. Surely she could deal with Hudson the same way. No need to get annoyed; the man didn't realize how obnoxious he sounded.

And, Beth realized, to some extent she'd encouraged this proposal. Last night it had seemed like fun to pit her two suitors against one another. Now she knew, too late, that there was only one man she cared about. She couldn't even remember why she had thought Lawrence Hudson attractive.

"Mr. Hudson," she said at last, folding her hands in her lap and twisting the fingers together hard, "I am deeply honored, but I do not feel that we should suit one another as man and wife."

Hudson merely smiled and nodded, and Beth felt a momentary relief that he'd taken her refusal so well. She was too soon relieved, as his next words revealed.

"Don't be so modest, Beth. I understand that you're overwhelmed at the thought of such an important social position, but I will be happy to teach you your duties. You have beauty; that is all that is required."

Beth gritted her teeth. "Mr. Hudson, you don't understand. I don't want to marry you."

Hudson patted her hand. "There, there. Don't be afraid.

A young girl is not expected to have the same judgment in these things as a mature man—indeed, it would be most unsuitable that she should. A girl is a delicate blossom, unfit for the harsh currents of life which men must navigate. In your innocence you cannot judge what is best for you. Your parents are far away; let me be your guide.''

''I don't,'' Beth said with her hands tightly clenched together, ''need a guide.''

Hudson gave her a blandly inquiring look. ''No? You must be aware that your position at the mission school is not entirely secure. Mrs. Griscom tells me she has the gravest doubts as to your suitability for the teaching life. But she would not, of course, question the character of my affianced bride.''

The touch of his hand on hers, damp and soft, was not to be endured. Beth moved away from him until she was pressed against the side of the buggy. They were on smooth, level ground now, the horses moved tirelessly forward and the buggy rolled too fast for her to jump out. Besides, where would she go? She had not been paying attention while they drove and had no idea how to get back to the mission school from here.

Hudson went on talking in a soothing monotone. His words barely penetrated her consciousness. Her blaze of fury at the way he ignored her plain statements had died down to a dull, tired ache of hopelessness. Everything was slipping away from her—Jerry, the teaching work she cared about so much—she was a failure at everything she tried.

Perhaps she should give up and let some man like Lawrence Hudson take care of her and shelter her. Perhaps he was right, women were too weak to make their own way in this world. Another clash with the Griscoms like the one this morning, and she'd be thrown out of the school, left with a choice between marrying Hudson or swallowing her pride and going back to her family to admit her mistake. At least, if she accepted Hudson's offer, she could stay out here and write glowingly happy letters home and never admit what a failure she was.

But would the man never quit his maundering! Beth's head was aching intolerably. If only she could sit quietly in the buggy for a little while, feeling the breeze on her face and contemplating the ever-changing line of the red-and-purple mesas, perhaps she could find her own way out. But no, Hudson had to tell her about all the advantages she would enjoy as his wife. A two-story house on the edge of town, silk dresses, afternoon teas with the other ladies of Gallup, yearly shopping trips to Kansas City or even Chicago . . . The list went on and on, and the longer he talked, the more Beth felt choked and stifled by the picture of the luxurious life he promised.

"But I like the desert," she said when he began promising to take water from the irrigation ditch to make her an enclosed green garden.

Hudson flicked an irritated glance at her. "To look at, perhaps. But to live in? No, Beth, the only thing that makes living out here bearable is the hope that it can be transformed into a garden suitable for a lovely flower like you to grace." He paused for a moment. "And that, Beth, takes wealth. Great wealth."

"I . . . didn't realize your bank was so profitable," Beth said.

Hudson smiled and she realized her mistake. He thought she would be more interested in him if he could convince her of his wealth. "It isn't. Not yet. But I have other plans. Great plans, Beth, and you can share in them. I've spoken to you of the mineral wealth lying beneath the surface of this desolate land. Did you ever hear of the Dry Lake gold?"

Without waiting for an answer, he went on, "I've been

studying the records, and listening to the old tales. There was a party of two prospectors came through Gallup from the north, fifteen years ago. They paid for their drinks with a nugget of pure gold, saying they'd found it in a dry gully wash. Left the next morning, heading back north. Their bones were found not far from this very spot. Indians—or rivals. Where did that gold come from? Eh?'' He slowed the horses so that he could lean over to Beth and repeat the question. *"Where did that gold come from?"*

"I've no idea," Beth said with perfect truth.

It seemed to be the right answer. Hudson laughed and patted her on the knee. For once Beth was grateful for the muffling, stifling layers of serge skirts and cotton petticoats and knitted stockings. She could barely feel his touch. "Ah, but I have! The original owners of the Galvan land grant were fabulously wealthy. How else could they have gotten rich from this barren desert? There had to be mineral wealth—wealth that they kept a secret from the Spanish king. When the original branch of the family died out, the secret died with them. But I've been over the records, and I had a man of my own out surveying the territory—until they threw him off. It's somewhere on Galvan North. I'm certain of it. A lost gold mine, right under that fool Galvan's nose, and he wastes his time raising sheep and cattle!''

Beth felt a wild new life running through her veins. She looked away from Hudson, afraid he would see the flash of excitement in her eyes. "Galvan North? There's gold there? Are you sure?"

"Didn't I just tell you so?" Hudson snapped with a flash of irritation.

Beth's hands were trembling. So this was why Hudson wanted to get Galvan North at any price! The missing piece of the puzzle was in her hands. Wait until she told Jerry. . . .

The excitement ebbed, leaving her stranded on a dry shingle of disappointment. She would be telling Jerry nothing. He cared so little for her that he could wish Hudson good luck in his courtship. This information wouldn't change that. How could she even tell him? He probably would never come out to the school again.

But there was still Eleuterio Galvan, who deserved better than to have his family home attacked by this greedy little speculator without even knowing why. And when she found out enough to accuse Hudson and make the accusation stick in court, wouldn't Jerry be sorry! Beth took a deep breath and looked up at Hudson with wide dark eyes. She had to slouch a little against the seat in order to maintain the pose, but that wasn't too much of a sacrifice for a good cause—though being nice to Hudson might turn her stomach if she thought about it.

"I don't understand," she said in an innocently adoring tone. "If the gold is on Señor Galvan's land, how will that make you rich?"

Hudson's tolerant laugh set her teeth on edge. "It won't be Galvan's land when the gold is discovered, Beth. I think I can safely promise you that much!"

"But I thought," Beth said, trying to keep all expression out of her voice, "that he had refused to sell his ranch to you?"

Hudson favored the horizon with a small, tight, private smile. "I have reason to believe he'll change his mind soon."

"Oh? Why?"

He gave her a sharp glance. Beth hoped nothing but vapid curiosity showed on her face. "Why do you care?"

She twisted her hands together and forced out a nervous giggle. "Well, if we're going to be rich . . ." She let the sentence trail off, slouched down a little farther so that she could look up at Hudson through her lashes, and giggled again.

Hudson chucked her under the chin. Beth thought about biting his finger and regretfully decided that would spoil the impression of girlish innocence and greed she was trying to project. "Don't worry yourself about business matters, dear girl. You are too young and lovely to be sullied with men's business dealings. Trust me. I'm going to be the richest man in this territory . . . and you're going to be my wife."

In the interests of information gathering, Beth did not contradict this statement. But evidently she had already asked one too many questions, for Hudson abruptly changed the subject as he turned the buggy to take her back to the mission. All the way back across the mesa he held the horses to a discreet jog trot while he favored Beth with a detailed account of his rise from banker's son to independent banker, the wisdom of his decision to relocate out west, and the glowing prospects that were shortly to descend on the territory of New Mexico with the development of her mineral wealth.

"Statehood is just around the corner," he vowed. "And then . . . well, the new state will need prudent men, men who can think ahead."

Men who can make whopping big contributions to somebody's campaign coffers, Beth added silently.

Just before the road turned downward to lead into the canyon, Hudson pulled the buggy to a halt. Beth, dreaming of how she would expose Hudson's schemes and win Galvan's—and Jerry's—undying gratitude, was slow to recognize his intention. When his arm went around her waist and his warm, moist lips brushed her cheek, she was revolted. The scene was like a bad parody of Jerry's first kiss, here on this same bluff. She tried to push Hudson away, but his stocky body concealed a surprising strength.

"Don't fight it, Beth," he muttered as he pushed her down against the seat. "You're meant for me. Can't you feel it—can't you tell? Just like the Dry Lake gold. Two treasures waiting for me." His hand closed over her breast, squeezing painfully tight. Beth knew a moment of chilling fear. Hudson's eyes were glazed over and he didn't seem aware of the strength he was exerting.

As she twisted to avoid his lips, one of the long pins that held her hair up jabbed into her scalp. She worked her free hand up, pulled the pin out and struck down at Hudson's arm.

He gave a yelp of surprise and let go for a moment. The horses stirred at his cry. Beth leaned forward, grabbed the reins that he had left loose, and yelled at the top of her lungs. The horses jerked forward and launched the buggy on a breakneck descent down into the canyon.

Beth's arms ached with pulling on the reins to guide them. Her hair tumbled about her face and was blown back. She glanced to her side, saw a white-faced Hudson clinging to the buggy seat, and laughed with mad exhilaration. All the pent-up frustration of the day was released in this crazy ride that required every bit of her driving skill to get them to the bottom in one piece.

Even the soft sand at the canyon bottom didn't stop the horses in their headlong rush. Beth let them wear out their excitement in the sandy track, only twitching the reins slightly to guide them through the mission school gate without brushing so much as the rim of a wheel against the fence posts. And a mercy the gate was open, she thought as they came to rest before the mission house.

Before the buggy had quite stopped rolling, Beth gathered up her heavy serge skirts and jumped out. "In case you didn't understand, Mr. Hudson," she called up, "I'm refusing your kind offer. I hope that's perfectly clear now!"

It was unwise to tease the man, but Beth had felt her precarious self-control eroding through the long, hot, disappointing day. Now, braced for Hudson's anger, she was disappointed again. He was staring past her. Beth followed the direction of his gaze and for the first time realized why the gate was open. Mr. Griscom's tall wagon with its slatted sides had just rolled in, back from his excursion to Blue Mesa.

But the wagon was almost empty. There were only two small children, a boy of perhaps eight or nine and a girl two or three years younger. The tall, spare missionary had to stoop to hold one hand of each child as they wriggled and tried to pull away.

"Well, I'll be damned," Hudson breathed. "Old Griscom stole Hosteen Chee's grandkids! I wonder how he pulled that off."

"Hosteen Chee." That was the man Jerry had said was the leader of the Navahos around Blue Mesa—the man he wanted to confer with, to see if they could keep Indians and whites on both sides of the reservation line from breaking out into more violence.

She sagged limply against the side of the buggy while Mr. Griscom accepted Hudson's congratulations.

"Yes," he was saying, "a great catch. Chee's the most obdurate savage in the mountains. If I can tame these two, the rest will follow."

"I'm sure they will," Beth said weakly. "I just hope they don't follow with tomahawks, that's all. Or whatever your local Indians use."

❧ Chapter Eleven

$\mathcal{T}$he little girl tugged hard at Mr. Griscom's hand, freed herself, and sat down with a plop in the sand. She opened her mouth as if to cry. The boy glanced down at her and barked out a single harsh phrase. She clamped her mouth shut with both hands.

Beth wanted to cry herself, sensing the children's fear and bewilderment at this strange place. Mr. Griscom began proudly explaining how the other Indian children had been hidden by their parents, but he'd picked these two up while they were herding sheep. It must, Beth thought, have been a terrifying experience for the children—far out on the desert, out of call of their families, to be carried away by this tall, harsh man whose language would be strange to them.

Later she could worry about the rights and wrongs of Mr. Griscom's action, think about its possible consequences. Right now, there were two frightened children before her who needed comfort. It was too bad she didn't speak Navaho, but at least gestures were a universal language. Beth knelt and held out her hands to the children. Two pairs of dark, shining black eyes stared back at her, opaque and hard as pebbles.

"Come with me," she said softly. "You must be tired and hungry. There's food inside." A few of the words from her impromptu language lesson came back to her. "*Atoo*—stew," she tried.

The little girl looked up at the familiar word, but the boy's expression did not change. "We don' eat your food," he announced in slow, careful English. "We don' stay here. My grandfather will come for us. He is a great warrior. I will be a warrior, too. I will not stay with the Black Coat." He folded his arms and glared defiantly at Mr. Griscom.

Beth drew a deep breath and let it out slowly. How could she deal with this child's unrelenting hostility? Perhaps she could appeal to his pride. "I'm sure you will be a great warrior," she said. "I already know you are clever, because you speak English so well. But even a great war leader may be taken captive, and a clever warrior will eat when he is a prisoner so that he does not grow weak."

The boy frowned, then gave an abrupt jerk of his head. "You are right," he announced. "Where is this food?"

Beth stood up and nodded to Mr. Griscom. "I think it's better if I take them now, don't you?" she murmured.

The missionary was happily telling Lawrence Hudson the tale of his dangerous journey to Blue Mesa. He spared Beth only a preoccupied nod.

She led the way to the dining hall. The windows of the dormitory that faced the dining hall were alive with dark heads and muffled giggles, but so far none of the boarding-school children had come out to see the new arrivals. Beth was grateful for that. It would be easier if she could get the children fed and calmed down first.

She didn't venture to take the boy's hand, but the sound of soft footsteps behind her reassured her that he was following. As they neared the dark, open doorway, a small hand was thrust into hers, and the little girl looked up with wide dark eyes. The boy uttered a harsh phrase and the girl blinked but did not withdraw her hand.

"My sister is scared," he announced. "She's only a stupid girl. She didn't see a big hogan like this before. I know all about white people hogans. I go to the trading post at Blue Mesa many times. I live with the white trader for a year." He stuck out his chest and swaggered through the door ahead of Beth.

Mrs. Griscom flatly refused to have the children in the dining hall until they had been bathed and dressed in clean clothes. Beth anticipated a struggle over this, but the boy was unexpectedly helpful. Not only did he cooperate himself, but he explained to his sister that these were white customs and not harmful. At least, that was what he said he was telling her. Watching the little girl's eyes roll up when she saw the tin tub full of lukewarm water, Beth suspected that he had added a few embellishments of his own. But at least both children were quiet while she bathed them and searched out the smallest clothes in the mission store for them.

Supper was not ready yet, but she slashed off large hunks of the bread left over from dinner and stole a jar of jam from the pantry. While the children were stuffing their mouths with the unfamiliar, sweet, wonderful food, she managed to learn a little more about them.

The boy was called Riding Boy—because of his skill with untamed ponies, he boasted—and his little sister, who spoke no English, was called Wind Flower because of the great wind that blew when she was being born. Their parents were dead and they lived with their grandfather, Hosteen Chee. Just now he was away in the south and they had been staying with a step-aunt. Hosteen Chee was supposed to come back soon and Riding Boy was confident that he would come with a war party to destroy the mission as soon as he found out what had happened to them.

"But I will not let him kill you," he finished. "In the old days, when the warriors made raids, they took women of the other tribes for slaves. I will make him keep you."

Beth gave an uneasy laugh. Jerry had told her that the Navahos had not made war on the whites since Kit Carson had defeated their chiefs, thirty years before. But she was not entirely sure that the Blue Mesa Navahos knew this.

While the children were finishing their bread and jam, Beth heard Hudson's buggy driving away. She breathed a quiet but heartfelt sigh of relief. She just didn't have the energy for another confrontation this day.

Or so she thought.

Mr. and Mrs. Griscom came in and sat down on either side of Beth. Mr. Griscom looked tired but very well pleased with himself. His thinning gray hair was plastered to his scalp with sweat and there were new lines in his face, but he smiled and nodded at the children with satisfaction. "A good trip—a most satisfactory trip," he said, rubbing his hands together. "And to think I feared, at first, that it would be a total failure!"

As he recounted the tale of his adventures once again for Mrs. Griscom's benefit, Beth gathered that the Indians who normally lived around Blue Mesa had mysteriously vanished just before he arrived. "Almost as if they knew what to expect," he added, glaring at Beth as though he found her personally responsible.

It had been sheer chance that he'd found Chee's grandchildren. The main road back to the mission was in such poor condition that after Mr. Griscom had parted from the Indian agent, he'd taken a back way home that detoured around the far side of Blue Mesa. There he'd seen the children herding sheep. They'd been afraid of him, but when he'd feigned wagon trouble the little girl had drawn close out of curiosity. Once he'd captured her, the boy had come along rather than let his terrified sister be taken away alone.

"And their people don't know they are gone yet?" Beth exclaimed. Somehow she had not really taken in Mr. Griscom's earlier accounts—she had envisioned him going up to an Indian encampment with the agent, much as a truant officer would visit homes in Iowa. The account of this brutal kidnapping shocked her, and she was too tired and worried to conceal her feelings. "That's cruel. You must send a message at once. They will think the children are dead or injured."

Mr. Griscom gave a heavy, patient, tolerant sigh and shook his head. "Miss Johanssen, you are new here, and—"

"I know," Beth interrupted. She spoke the next words in time with him. "I don't understand how you do things. Right? But it's not a local custom anywhere to steal children away from their homes, Mr. Griscom!"

"It is here," the missionary corrected. "How else do you think we would get them? They would all be ignorant, naked savages forever. A little kindly force, Miss Johanssen, to lead them into the right ways. You'll see. After a while, they will calm down and be quite happy here. Why, most of our older children don't even want to go home!"

Beth thought about Lucy Tso, complaining that the missionary school had made her unfit to live in a hogan without giving her a place in the white man's world. But she didn't have time to sort out the question in her own mind. Riding Boy had been listening while the missionary expounded his views. Now he burst into furious speech.

"We are not ignorant. My uncle is Sings All Chants. He knows all the Night Chants and the names of the gods. You are the one who is ignorant. You don' even know how to cover your trail. When my grandfather comes back he will

follow your tracks and come here to get us. He has said that
no one of his clan shall ever go on the white man's road.
Slayer of Enemy Gods will protect us.''

"Silence!" Mr. Griscom thundered. He rose from the
bench and glared down at Riding Boy, who planted both
fists on his hips and continued shouting in a bewildering
mixture of Navaho and English while Mr. Griscom tried to
shout him down. The missionary's tall, black-clad figure
towered above the boy and wisps of gray hair blew around
his shoulders. Beth thought that he looked like an Old Testa-
ment prophet rebuking the heathen.

"You were brought here to be educated, and the first lesson you will learn is obedience and respect to your elders!"
Mr. Griscom shouted.

"My grandfather will go on the war path to rescue us!"

Mr. Griscom's large, bony hand shot out and gripped
Riding Boy by the nape of the neck. Wind Flower screeched
and threw herself on the missionary and bit his hand. Mrs.
Griscom slapped the little girl to the floor and Beth pushed
her way between them.

"Please," she said breathlessly, "please don't shout at
the children. You're upsetting them. Let me explain. . . .''

But Riding Boy had become a snarling, spitting bundle of
defiance to whom nobody could explain anything. Mr.
Griscom transferred his grip to the little boy's arm and
hauled him across the floor of the dining hall.

"Into the storage cellar with both the little heathens," he
panted. "Give them time to cool down and remember their
manners." He scooped up Wind Flower under his free arm
with unexpected strength.

"No!" Beth cried. "No, you can't do that!"

She started after Mr. Griscom, but Mrs. Griscom's stocky
form blocked the door. Her husband's return seemed to have
given the fat woman a new infusion of strength. "Can't do

that, missy?'' she mocked. "Wait and see! I guess we've had about enough of your Indian lover ways around here! Now you'll see how we deal with rebellious spirits."

Beth tried to physically push Mrs. Griscom out of the way, but it was like pushing a small mountain. All her furious energy was swallowed up in pushing at the woman's soft, squashy, heavy body. Before she had gotten out the door, Mr. Griscom was back, jingling the key ring around one finger and smiling with satisfaction. "That'll soon calm them," he said.

"Are they scared? Are they crying?" Beth demanded.

Mr. Griscom's smile faded slightly. "Not they! The little heathens scratched and cursed all the way across the yard. A night in the cellar, and no breakfast. They'll be ready to apologize at morning prayers tomorrow."

"And if they aren't ready?"

"Then," Mr. Griscom said with sweet patience, "they'll stay in there until they are properly submissive."

Beth's hand shot out for the key ring, but Mr. Griscom was too quick for her. He caught her wrist and forced her arm downward with a vicious twist. Beth bit her lip to keep from crying out with the pain.

"Obedience to properly constituted authority," he said in the same calm, sweet tone, "is one of the cornerstones of our civilization. Don't you agree, Miss Johanssen? Don't you?" He smiled as he spoke, and Beth gritted her teeth. She had not realized before that Mr. Griscom enjoyed inflicting pain in the exercise of his authority. It explained much of what was wrong with the school.

With each question he forced her arm farther back. Waves of pain shot up to Beth's shoulder, filling her with a sick dizziness that kept her from saying anything more.

"She's overwrought, Griscom," Mrs. Griscom intervened. "Put her up in the attic room overnight. Addie can sleep downstairs. After a night of prayer and meditation she'll see the error of her ways.''

Mr. Griscom's iron-hard grip warned Beth that overt resistance was useless. When he pushed her toward the door, she straightened her back and walked quietly across the yard to the mission house. With Mr. Griscom on one side of her and his wife on the other, there was no chance of getting away, and she preferred not to be dragged struggling across the yard in view of all the schoolchildren who were watching from their dormitory.

Pride and anger kept her head high and prevented the tears of frustration from brimming over until she was actually in the hot little attic room that was to be her prison. But when she heard the key twisting in the door, she felt desolate and entirely alone—and very much a failure. She sat on the bed and nursed her aching wrist, rocking back and forth like a child.

What a distance she'd fallen from the high hopes with which she'd come out to this teaching position! Beth remembered the bright-eyed idealistic girl who'd stepped off the train in Gallup station and gave a dry laugh. She'd been all set to convey the blessings of education to some vaguely pictured people called ''Indians'' or ''noble savages'' or ''dirty redskins,'' depending on whom you talked to.

Instead, all she'd brought was more trouble. Dry-eyed, Beth faced that fact and her own humiliation. If she hadn't jumped in to interfere between Mr. Griscom and the children, both sides might not have gotten so angry. Now the Griscoms were likely to punish the children even more harshly, just to show Beth where the power lay. And Lucy Tso—she, too, had been punished because of something Beth had started.

Everything she did seemed to annoy the Griscoms. And

they took it out on the children, who were utterly in their power.

This school is a bad place, she thought. But does it have to be that way? Can't the children learn without being browbeaten and scared?

The Griscoms obviously didn't think so. And they'd been here longer than she. As they—and everybody else—seemed fond of pointing out, Beth didn't know how things worked in the territory.

But one thing she did know, she thought. It was wrong to force children away from their families and beat and terrify them. She imagined Riding Boy as he would be in ten years, his blazing pride reduced to a sullen glow of anger such as she'd seen in Lucy Tso's face. She couldn't stay and watch that happen. She would have to forget all her proud resolves, leave this school, go home, and confess to her family that one more attempt had ended in failure.

Running away again, a mocking voice sneered in her mind. Ignoring the voice, Beth pulled her straw case from under the bed and began cramming a few necessities into it. The trunk could wait until she sent for it—or it could wait forever; she didn't particularly want to see those thick serge skirts and sensible, schoolteacherly shirtwaists again. All she wanted to do was to give her notice and get out of here.

She stopped with her brush and comb in one hand and sank back on the narrow bed. The bedframe gave a dispirited creak in harmony with her thoughts. Where did she think she was going? The Griscoms had locked her in. She would have to wait till morning, when Mrs. Griscom came to let her out.

That reminded her forcibly of two frightened, lonely children, waiting until morning in that dark cellar with its dangling spiderwebs and horrible scurrying things on the floor. Beth clenched her fists in impotent fury. "No," she said aloud, hardly realizing she had spoken. "No, I won't wait here like a bad little girl until it pleases the Griscoms to let me out. And I won't leave those kids in the cellar, either."

Brave words. But how was she to carry them out? And even if she and the children got away from the school, where would they go?

The answer to the second question, at least, was easy. It would be humiliating, but she knew where to get help. And the answer to the first came only seconds later, in the form of a gentle scratching on the door.

"Beth?"

It was only the strained, fraying thread of a voice, but the sound brought Beth to her knees at the other side of the keyhole. "Addie?" Who else could it be?

"I heard what happened." Addie's voice was curiously muffled, as if she had a cold. "I brought you some supper."

"Thanks," Beth whispered. "But I'm locked in." Dare she ask Addie to steal the key? Would she have the courage?

Then, incredibly, she heard a grating sound in the lock. There was a rusty squeal of protesting metal. On both sides of the door, the girls stiffened and held their breath for a minute. Then Addie twisted the key again and the door swung slowly inward. She edged sideways into the room, carrying a bowl of stew before her in both hands, and pushed the door shut again with her foot. Her eyes were red and swollen as if she'd been crying.

"I heard everything," she whispered, "but I didn't dare interfere. The Reverend is terrible when he's in one of his moods—I was afraid. Oh, Beth, what will you do? He's dreadfully angry."

"Do?" Beth felt her half-formed resolves crystallizing at Addie's miraculous appearance. The way was opened this

far; she felt no doubt that she would overcome the other ob-
stacles before her. "Do? I'm going to leave. With—"

She stopped short. No telling how far Addie's loyalty
could be trusted. Better not to tell her any more than she had
to.

"You can't do that," Addie protested.

Beth almost laughed. "Addie. They're going to fire me in
the morning anyway. Why should I wait?"

Addie was shaking her head. Her thin lips were pinched
together and she lowered her head, giving her a look of mul-
ish stubbornness. "He won't fire you. He said he'd like to,
but it might not be wise since you're going to marry Mr.
Hudson."

"I'm not going to marry Mr. Hudson." Beth felt invisible
nets of convention closing about her. How long could she
keep fighting what everybody around her took for granted,
from the treatment of the Indian children to Lawrence Hudson's high-handed disposal of her future? No, she had to get
away now. And she needed Addie's help. "Addie? Where
did you get the key to our room?"

"Oh, I've always had one," Addie said with a touch of
pride. "He never thought to take it away from me. But I
couldn't leave you alone up here all night without your dinner."

"Oh . . . yes. Thank you." Belatedly, Beth acknowledged the bowl of congealing stew with its grayish blobs of
fat. "Listen, Addie. This is important. Do you know where
Mr. Griscom keeps his keys?"

"Why, he hangs them on the nail next to the pantry
door," Addie replied, and then her red-rimmed eyes widened and she backed up against the closed door. "Oh, no,"
she whispered. "I'm not going to take dinner to the children, too. What if he caught me?"

"Fine. I'll do it." As she spoke, Beth shrugged into her

heavy traveling cape. If Addie thought all she meant to do was smuggle food to the children and then come meekly up to the room again, so much the better.

Addie blocked her passage, the obstinate look back on her face. "No, Beth. I can't let you go, either. He's angry enough with you as it is."

"Do you think I care about that?" Beth felt curiously light-headed and gay as she cast aside the last hopes of preserving a respectable position. "Move, Addie." Addie's thin shoulder bones under her hand felt as light and fragile as a bird's skeleton. A gentle push was all it took to get her out of the way. Addie had never stood up to anybody in her entire life and it was far too late for her to start now.

"What about me?" Addie wailed. "If he catches you, he'll find me out, and then he'll be angry at me for letting you out. Beth, if you go out that door, I'll go right downstairs after you and tell the Reverend on you. I'll have to!" She was almost pleading as she made her threat. "Don't you see? You're leaving me no choice!"

"No, Addie," Beth said gently. "There's always a choice. Only it takes some of us too darned long to find it out!" It was herself she was thinking of, not Addie, but she blamed her careless words when Addie's eyes filled with tears. She put a consoling hand on the other girl's shoulder, feeling again the frightening fragility of her slender frame. It wasn't Addie's fault. She needed to be protected and cherished. She wasn't a big healthy girl like Beth, the sort that everybody expected to stand alone.

Beth swallowed hard over an unexpected lump in her throat and forced herself to grin at Addie. "Don't worry, Addie. You don't have to make any choices. I'm going to do you a big favor and relieve you of the responsibility." With a lightning dart, she got the door key out of Addie's limp fingers and edged through the half-open door. "I'm going to lock you in."

Over Addie's outraged gasps, Beth closed the door very gently and put the key in the lock. Before she turned it, one more thought occurred to her. She opened the door a crack and whispered, "I wouldn't bother screaming for help. Mr. Griscom will just think it's me, and ignore you."

She closed and locked the door, then tiptoed down the narrow flight of stairs that led from the garret down to the living quarters of the house. The sharp edges of the key cut into her palm where she clenched her hand about it, all her muscles tense now, alert to any sound as she passed the missionaries' bedroom. Moving as slowly and cautiously as a hunted animal, she felt her way to the massive house door and lifted the latch, a quarter inch at a time.

When she finally slipped outside and felt the cool night air on her face, she felt like turning her face to the rising moon and uttering a prayer of gratitude. Not yet. There was too much to be done. Slipping from shadow to shadow, and at last darting across the naked courtyard in the full moonlight, Beth made her way to the dining hall and found the ring of keys hanging beside the pantry just as Addie had said.

She made her preparations before returning to the mission house to free the children. Fortunately the cellar entrance was outside the house. She raised the trapdoor slowly, prepared to call out to silence the children if they made any noise. But there was no sound from within.

"Riding Boy?" Beth whispered.

No response. For a moment she felt an uprush of relief. One of the missionaries must have relented and let the children out of their confinement. She wouldn't have the responsibility for taking care of them—no one could expect her to sneak into a dormitory and steal them out of it in the middle of the night.

Then she realized that she couldn't leave without search-ing the cellar and making sure the children were not there. And she didn't have a lantern. All she could do was go down and feel around the spidery interior with her bare hands.

Setting her teeth, Beth propped the trapdoor open and de-scended into the cellar, one shrinking step at a time. What were a few spiders? she asked herself. High time she got over this silly aversion, anyway; she was supposed to be a competent adult, not a nervous little schoolgirl. Besides, she was more than halfway down the steps and hadn't encoun-tered a—

Something webby brushed against her face. Beth gave a strangled, involuntary shriek and clawed at her face with both hands. There was a snuffling noise from the bottom of the stairs. Her face was clear of the spiderweb now, but the rustling, sighing sounds went on. Beth felt a cold sweat dampening her forehead and palms.

"Chindi," murmured a frightened voice out of the dark-ness.

Beth tardily recognized the rustling sounds as the move-ments of children awakening from sleep. "No," she said in a low, clear voice, praying that the missionaries wouldn't hear her through their bedroom window. "No, I'm not a spirit, Riding Boy. I am Beth Johanssen—remember? I've come to get you out of here."

She was feeling her way forward and down as she spoke. Her foot touched solid earth with a jolt when she'd been ex-pecting to go down one more step. Small hands scrabbled at her skirt, and she heard a sniffle. Stooping and reaching by instinct, she scooped up the tiny form of Wind Flower. The little girl wrapped both legs around her waist and clung to her neck, almost choking her. Beth adjusted her burden slightly and reached out a hand to Riding Boy, who took it without speaking. Slowly they mounted the stairs out of the cellar.

At the top, Beth put a finger to her lips to warn the children that they must not speak. She led the way to the rickety stable behind the vegetable garden, where one of Reverend Griscom's wagon horses stood already saddled. She'd hoped to get both horses, but the other one was fastened in its stall with a catch that her fumbling fingers could not manage in the darkness, and at last she'd decided that time was more important.

"That old horse for the two of us?" Riding Boy whispered. Even in a foreign language and talking under his breath, he managed to convey his sense of outrage.

"One horse for the three of us," Beth corrected. "I'm going with you. And we won't have to ride one horse very far—I hope."

Riding Boy gave her a disdainful look. "You don' need to. I can find my way home."

"Of course you can," Beth said. It wasn't just tact; she devoutly hoped he could find his way back to Blue Mesa, for she certainly couldn't! "But I'm going with you anyway."

"Why?" Riding Boy stood before her, legs straddled and arms akimbo, a miniature image of defiance.

Beth didn't care how independent Navaho children were supposed to be, she wasn't about to let any eight-year-old kid go off across the desert on his own. But if she told Riding Boy that, it would only start an argument that they couldn't afford to have until they got clear of the mission school. "Well . . ." she said slowly, then spoke more quickly as inspiration came to her. "I can't stay here, can I? After letting you out? The Black Coat will be angry with me. He might lock *me* in the cellar." Her shudder was not entirely feigned. The skin on her face still crawled with memory of that clinging spiderweb.

Riding Boy thought it over for a few minutes, frowning, then gave her a curt nod. "Good," he said. "You are my responsibility now. I will take care of you."

Beth couldn't resist the temptation to give him a quick hug while she was helping him up before her on the horse. "We'll take care of each other—okay?"

Riding Boy grinned and made a circle with his thumb and forefinger. "Okay!"

Chapter Twelve

The moon was almost down by the time they reached the sleeping Galvan Ranch. All the lights were out in both the main ranch house and the bunkhouses that stretched out to one side. Beth slid off the bony horse with gratitude. The gelding's only gait was a sloppy, bone-crunching amble that had jarred her spine with each step. She certainly hoped Jerry would be able to provide them with better horses.

If he wanted to help at all, that was. And if she could find him! Beth bit her lip. On the way to the ranch she had been so worried about the embarrassment of meeting Jerry again, admitting she was wrong and asking for his help, that she'd omitted to think about just how she was to get hold of him.

Only now, looking at the dark bulk of the buildings before them, did she realize the gap in her planning. She didn't even know where he slept! And she could hardly go around throwing gravel at selected windows. Before she ever reached Jerry she'd be explaining herself to a housekeeper, two maids, three cowboys, Señor Galvan . . . "And a partridge in a pear tree," she whispered to herself, hovering on the edge of a hysterical giggle. Behind her, she could feel the anxiety of the two children on the horse. They were whispering to each other in Navaho.

"Wait here," she whispered to Riding Boy, leading the horse back behind an outlying storage shed, where it—and the children—wouldn't be seen from the house if anybody should wake up and glance out a window. Beth slithered to the corner of the shed and peered around it, hoping desperately for some clue to let her know where Jerry might be.

The ranch house and the bunkhouses were as dark and unwelcoming as ever. Beth twirled a loose strand of springy dark hair between two fingers and tried to think what to do now. Perhaps she should just march in and demand Señor Galvan's help. No, that was too risky, with the children waiting just outside. What if he sent them back? He might disapprove of the mission schools as much as Jerry did—or he might not. She didn't know him well enough to say. And as a local rancher, he couldn't afford to get mixed up in her problems with the school.

Beth had been staring at the house, absentmindedly tapping her foot, while she tried to think what to do next. A flicker of movement in the moonlight caught her attention. She froze against the corner of the shed, praying that her dark dress and hair would blend in with the adobe walls. Her heart thudded in her chest as a lean figure moved slowly out of the shadows and toward the storage shed. Behind her, the tired horse breathed out a great snorting sigh that must surely have been audible yards away. Beth closed her eyes and prayed to become invisible.

When she opened them, the wandering cowboy was closer to the shed. The last glimmers of moonlight hovered about his lanky form and the crisply curling hair that spilled over his forehead.

"*Jerry,*" Beth whispered on a long exhalation of relief.

Her palms were sweaty and her knees wobbled as she moved away from the shed to greet him.

"Beth?" Jerry's eyes widened momentarily. In two strides he was beside her, holding her in his arms and kissing her hungrily. His hands were spread against her back, holding her close to him, so close that the pounding of his heart amplified her own. His lips, warm and demanding, covered her eyelids and mouth and throat with desperate kisses. The storm of passion in his blood spread to her as if by contagion. Her own arms tightened about him and she exulted in the possession of this lean, hard body, all taut muscles and long bones and neat, practiced movements.

Too practiced. In a moment she would forget what she'd come for. Beth wound her fingers in the curls at the back of Jerry's neck and pulled his head away from her breast.

"Ow!" Jerry put up a hand to see if all his hair was still there. "I guess I'm not dreaming." He gave her a rueful, indignant look. "Well, what did you come here for, if you didn't want to kiss and make up?"

Beth felt silly, gay laughter bubbling up like a refreshing spring inside her. It was going to be that easy, then. "I do want to make up," she said. "I was wrong."

"So was I," Jerry allowed. "Shouldn't have expected you to run off from your job like that. I wouldn't quit Eleuterio on a moment's notice—I should have known you wouldn't quit the school that way."

Beth smiled and shook her head. "I did."

"Did what?"

"Quit the school. Tonight."

As Jerry's mouth fell open, Beth hastened to get the rest of her story in before he started kissing her again and the rest of her sense went flying out the window. "Mr. Griscom came back with two Indian children that he'd kidnapped from Blue Mesa. They say they're Hosteen Chee's grandchildren. I'm taking them back to their grandfather. But we need horses and supplies. I thought maybe you could help us.'' She took Jerry's hand and led him back around the corner of the storage shed. The two children stared at him solemnly from the back of Reverend Griscom's bony gelding.

Jerry stared back for a moment, then guffawed and slapped his knee.

"Hush!" Beth whispered. "Do you want to wake the whole ranch?" She looked at him uncertainly. The moon was behind the mountains now, and he was only a dark column against the slightly lighter sky. "What were you doing out here, anyway?"

"Couldn't sleep," Jerry said. "Thinking about things."

"Oh!" Beth didn't examine why this laconic statement made her feel so cheerful. "Well, as long as you're up, would you mind helping me, uh, borrow a couple of Señor Galvan's horses?"

Jerry slid his arm around her waist. "We'll see. So you didn't come to make up with me, huh? Just came to turn me into a horse thief?" His tone was teasing and warmly affectionate. "What changed your mind so fast, missionary lady? Last night you were all set to become a pillar of society. Now you're a horse thief and a kidnapper."

Beth shook her head. "I'm only borrowing the horses. And I'm not kidnapping the children. Mr. Griscom did that. I'm just returning them to their family. There's a big difference!"

"Big difference might not look so clear to the law," Jerry drawled. He slipped his other arm around Beth's waist, holding her fast in front of him. "Beth. You've done enough. You go back to the school now. I'll see that Hosteen Chee gets the kids back."

Beth shook her head. "You have your work to do. I have this." She looked up at his shadowed face, searching for the words that would make him understand. "Please, Jerry. I have to do this. I have to . . . make up for—'' A lump in her throat choked her.

Even to Jerry, she couldn't explain all the feelings that Mr. Griscom's abuse of the children had awakened in her. If she hadn't come to help at the school, would he have grown ambitious enough to kidnap more children? She should have listened to Jerry's warnings about the Griscoms from the very first day. Now she had to do everything she could to atone for that mistake.

Jerry's arms abruptly fell away, releasing her to the chill of the night air. ''All right. We'll need a couple of good horses— one for each of us, the kids can ride in front of us. Wait here.'' He turned and began walking back to the stables.

Beth ran after him and clutched his arm. ''Wait a minute,'' she whispered. ''What do you mean, *we* need horses?''

Jerry halted in midstride. ''You're not going alone,'' he said, and began walking again.

Beth followed him all the way to the stables, arguing in whispers. It was about as effective as arguing with one of the rocks on the mesa. Jerry didn't even deign to answer her until he had two horses ready to go, with bedrolls and supplies slung behind the saddles. He scrawled a brief note on a scrap of paper sacking and attached it to the saddle of Mr. Griscom's horse when they led the bony gelding into the stables.

''Now,'' he said when they were out behind the storehouse again. ''That note was to tell Eleuterio that I'm quitting. Said I was bored, going down south to look for work. Both these ponies are mine, so there'll be no problem about them being stolen.''

It was Beth's turn to stare open-mouthed.

''That way,'' Jerry explains, ''anybody wants to bring in the law on this, they can't sue Eleuterio. I'm just a private citizen—nothing to do with the Galvan Ranch.''

Beth shook her head. "No, Jerry. I can't let you do this for me."

Jerry took her by the shoulders and pulled her close to him. "Get this straight. I don't like you going up to Blue Mesa area. Not after the trouble we've been having up there, not after what Griscom just pulled. If I were any kind of a man at all, I'd tie you up and leave you in the stable and take the kids back myself. Only reason I don't is because I'm afraid you'd never forgive me. But no way am I going to let you do this alone."

Beth nodded. "You got one thing right, anyway. I'd never forgive you. But listen, Jerry, there isn't any Indian trouble up there. You were right—it's all Hudson. I didn't have time to tell you what—"

A cock crowed and Jerry held up his hand for silence. "We got to get moving," he whispered. He helped Beth mount and handed up Wind Flower to sit before her, taking Riding Boy on his own horse. As the horses moved silently away from the sleeping ranch, Beth felt the cool early morning breeze spring up, and she saw that the sky behind the mountains was just perceptibly lighter than the black horizon.

It was midafternoon when they stopped, still more than a day's ride from Blue Mesa. Jerry had suggested that they ride south at first and then swing around in a half circle that would take them right off the reservation territory, past the old ranch house on Galvan North, then back to the reservation near Blue Mesa.

"That way," he explained, "if Griscom thinks the kids ran away on their own, he'll head straight towards Blue Mesa to catch 'em up, and we'll miss him. And if he follows you to Galvan's, it'll look like you and me headed south like I said I was going to."

Riding Boy spoke up at this point.

"He will track you," he said.

Jerry laughed. "You think a Black Coat can track an Indian?"

Riding Boy stuck out his narrow chest proudly. "Not an Indian," he said, "but anybody could track you! You leave a trail like a wounded Mexican." He scowled for a moment, squinting backward along the path they had traveled since leaving the ranch. "Better let me take care of you."

Jerry laughed, but Beth noted that he acceded to Riding Boy's instructions, taking the horses across stony paths in one place, in another confusing the trail with a brush of juniper twigs drawn through the dust. Once he caught her eyes on him as he knelt to replace a stone on the path and shrugged with a deprecating smile. "Can't hurt—might help," he muttered. "The kid could be right. I never tracked anything but a strayed cow."

"I am right," Riding Boy insisted. "No white eyes know how to cover a trail. You break twigs, and Skinny Trader at the post is even worse. His woman is not so stupid, though," he added, a slight reminiscent smile curving his lips. "She speaks the language of the People, and she walks lightly. And she has hair like the sun."

"That's my buddy Nathan and his wife, Lily, he's talking about," Jerry explained to Beth. "Last year when Riding Boy was sick, he stayed with Lily and Nathan for a while."

"Oh, is that why you speak such good English?" Beth asked the boy. "I wondered."

Riding Boy thrust his skinny shoulders back and raised his chin proudly. "The white eyes language is ugly, but I can learn any language. It is much harder for you to learn the tongue of the People. Nathan's woman, Sun Hair, is the only one who speaks our tongue well, but many Navaho have learned English. That proves that we are more smart than you."

"Perhaps it does," Beth allowed.

As they rode along, she beguiled the time by getting Riding Boy to teach her a few more words of Navaho. But as the sun rose higher and higher, her head ached, her eyes smarted with dust and light, and she could no longer concentrate on the words as he pronounced them.

Wind Flower leaned back against her, the small hot body making a sweaty patch on the front of her dress, and Beth kept one arm around the little girl for fear she would fall asleep and tumble off the horse. Riding Boy's head remained high, but the pinched look about his mouth and nostrils made Beth wonder if the strain of the long night and day were not getting to be too much for him.

Only Jerry seemed unaffected by heat and fatigue. Mile after mile his lean figure sat comfortably in the saddle, moving slightly with the horse, looking as if he had been born on horseback and had never known thirst or exhaustion. Beth kept glancing at him, wanting to beg for a rest stop, but the words stuck in her throat. The country through which they were riding was strange to her. She would have to rely on Jerry's judgment to know when it was safe to stop.

Finally, when the sun was well past noon, they came to a narrow canyon whose slides sloped together to form a deep white V of rocks at one end. There were trees growing out of the cleft, and when they drew closer Beth heard the unmistakable dripping of water.

"We'll rest here," Jerry said, "and go on tonight—after moonrise." He handed Riding Boy down from his horse, helped Beth and Wind Flower dismount, and began unsaddling. Beth stood unsteadily on the rocky ground, feeling a whole new series of aches and pains begin in her legs from this change in position. She longed for a hot bath and a clean bed with white sheets.

What you'll have, she told herself, is some nice cold

spring water and a blanket that probably doesn't harbor too many fleas. And not even that till the horses are taken care of.

Her father had drilled into her from an early age that no rider ever rests until his horse is cared for. Now the habits of her early years came back. Beth went through the motions of unsaddling the horses and leading them to the spring almost mechanically, her head spinning with waves of tiredness. She missed Jerry's grunt of surprise as she went about her tasks with automatic competence.

By the time the horses had been given a drink and a handful of oats each, Jerry had the bedrolls spread in the shade. Beth collapsed onto her blanket without even thinking about washing her face or combing her hair, then sank thankfully into the oblivion of sleep. Through her exhaustion, she was dimly aware of Jerry squatting beside her, chewing a leaf from the tree and looking up the canyon. His watchful presence was a guarantee of security that she carried with her through her dreams.

When she woke, the sun was almost down, and Jerry was tending a small fire some distance from the bedrolls. Riding Boy and Wind Flower were sleeping in a tangled heap, arms and legs sprawled out, like a pair of exhausted puppies. Beth straightened her clothing and tiptoed away quietly so as not to disturb them.

She went up the canyon a little way, to the source of the spring, and splashed the clear water over her face and hands. The high pile of her black hair was a disaster; after some thought she pulled out the pins, combed her hair out with her fingers and made a single thick braid over one shoulder, tying it with the red ribbon she had been wearing at her throat.

Jerry raised his eyebrows in greeting when she came back from the spring. "What's this! Indian braids? Want me to get you a squaw dress?"

"It's practical," said Beth shortly. She was still tired, and Jerry's gentle teasing rubbed her the wrong way. She didn't particularly need to be reminded of how much she'd thrown away in this mad escapade. The children, she told herself—they're reason enough for everything. Just think of that.

But she couldn't help worrying over the matter in her own mind, wondering if there wasn't some way she could have helped Riding Boy and Wind Flower without seeming to defy the Griscoms. Perhaps if she'd stayed calm, tried to reason with the missionary later when he was not so angry, they could have worked something out—mitigated the school's harsh policies, arranged for all the boarding-school children to spend holidays at home with their families, so that they didn't lose touch completely.

Beth shifted her cramped limbs with a sigh, trying to find some comfortable way of sitting on the hard ground when her legs ached from hip to ankle. She stared into the glowing coals and shook her head. She didn't have the tact and patience necessary to work with Mr. Griscom and slowly change his idea of what the school should be. Any more than she'd been able to take things slowly in Iowa. What was so terribly wrong with her, that she kept getting into quarrels with the people who were supposed to be on her side? Tears filled her eyes and slowly plopped down on her cheeks, one by one, unnoticed.

While Beth stared into the fire, lost in thought, Jerry had been quietly watching her face in the uneven glow of the small flames. He felt a strange contentment as he studied the tanned oval of Beth's face, the generous mouth now drooping slightly, the wonderful dark eyes under strong brows. The firelight and the twilight competed to shade her face in purplish shadows and golden highlights.

With the single, thick black braid lying over her shoulder, giving her strong features a slightly Indian cast, she looked

like the spirit of the desert. Everything that had drawn him
to this harsh, dramatic country—the shifting colors and
changing moods, the force of the summer flash floods and
the endurance of the patient land—all were gathered together and brought to life in the face of this one girl who had
walked off a train and into his heart.

From that first meeting, when she'd jumped in front of
him to protect a perfect stranger who could mean nothing to
her, he'd known that she was the girl he'd always been waiting for. There was a reason why he'd been a loner all these
years, drifting from ranch to ranch across the red-rock desert
country of the western territories without ever settling
down. The reason was waiting for him at the Gallup train
station—a girl just his height, with curling black hair and
melting dark blue eyes and a saucy, generous mouth that
begged to be kissed. And she'd been waiting for him, too,
only she didn't know it at first. Now, he reckoned, she had
to know it. Why else would she've come to him for help?

He noticed the way she shifted about, trying to get comfortable. Poor girl, her legs must be aching after that long
ride. He rose and stepped lightly over to the blankets where
the sleeping children lay. Folding one blanket over two or
three times, he brought it back to the campfire and spread it
on a flat piece of ground. "Sit here," he invited Beth in a
low voice, "you'll be more comfortable." His intentions
weren't entirely altruistic. It was time to get her away from
the far side of the fire and next to him where she belonged—
and there was just enough room for two people to sit rather
close together, the way he'd folded the blanket.

Beth took the place he'd prepared but kept her face turned
away from him. Peering at her averted profile in the golden
light, he saw glistening traces of tears on her cheeks. "Hey,
missionary lady." Without thinking, he gathered her to his
chest in an enveloping hug. "What's the matter?"

Beth stiffened at first, then relaxed against the comforting warmth and solidity of Jerry's body. Her throat and chest ached with the effort of holding back tears. "I'm a failure," she choked out eventually.

"Not in my book." Jerry stroked her back with one hand. He couldn't help enjoying the smooth curve of her back, couldn't help stroking on down along the flowing line of her hips. Her body seemed made to fit in his arms, under the curve of his palm. Under those rather awful, schoolmarmish skirts, she'd have to be the softest thing he'd ever touched.

Jerry felt his natural urges responding in an all too predictable way. He shifted his weight, hoping Beth wouldn't notice anything. Crude cowpoke, he berated himself. Couldn't he think of any but the one thing to do with a girl? This one needed comforting, not lovemaking. "I think you've just done a pretty brave thing," he said. "Nothing to feel bad about. You should be proud."

Beth lifted her head from his shoulder and pushed the damp strands of loose hair away from her face. "You don't understand," she cried. "I should have been able to explain to Mr. Griscom—to work things out—but I always get in a fight! I always run away," she wailed. "What's wrong with me? I can't get along with people, I wanted so much to be a teacher, and everything I try turns out all wrong. It's just like Iowa all over again. Oh-h-h. . . . I'm sorry—" She bit her lip, trying to regain some composure.

Jerry pressed her head back down against his shoulder as the tears broke out afresh.

"Crying all over you like this. . . ." she whispered between sobs. Her whole body was shaking in his arms. Jerry held her tightly, trying to stop that shaking, trying to make her know with his body what she couldn't, right now, take in with his words—that he was here for her, that he'd always be here with her.

"Don't worry," he said after a while, as she seemed to be calming down. "Hey, this is a desert, remember? We could all use a little more water. In fact, if you're through watering me, that juniper bush over there says it would like a little attention."

Beth gave a damp giggle and sat up. Jerry's hands around her waist anchored her, strong and secure. He rubbed his cheek against the top of her head in a wordless caress. Under all the emotional storms, Beth was conscious of a faint surprise. Jerry had seemed so strong and hard. She'd never imagined he could be tender like this.

"So," he said after a few minutes. "What went wrong in Iowa, that had you in such a tizzy about doing this job right?"

"Pretty much the same thing." Beth sighed. Her shoulders sagged as she recalled the weight of the town's disapproval, the visit of the school board to her rooming house, and the formal notice that she was relieved of her teaching duties. "Only the situation was the reverse of this area. I insisted on enrolling a child that the school board didn't want to have in school."

"Why not?"

"The child's mother," Beth said, "was a . . . er . . . lady called Whiskey Kate. She lived in a shack on the edge of town, and I don't have to tell you what her business was."

Jerry gave a long, low whistle and shook his head. "I guess you're just a natural-born troublemaker, lady." The warm affection in his words robbed them of their sting. "What ever made you think you could get along with the missionaries?"

"I didn't think about it much," Beth admitted, staring into the flames with troubled eyes. "I thought I could get along with Indians."

"Noble savages?" Jerry chuckled.

"I guess." Beth could laugh now at her own naiveté. "I wasn't really thinking. When I got my teaching certificate my family stood around me in a large circle and solemnly predicted disaster. They said I was too hotheaded and impatient to teach. So I didn't want to come home with my tail between my legs, admitting I'd been fired. It seemed like a much better idea to come out here." She sighed. "I guess I'll have to go home now, though."

"I can think of other alternatives," Jerry murmured into her left ear. He pulled her back against him, his arms encircling her waist. Drained by her emotional storms, Beth was content to lean back against him, secure in the circle of his arms.

"For the record," he said into her tousled hair, "anybody who can't get along with old Griscom is all right with me. I knew all along you were too good for his outfit. Didn't figure on you seeing it so fast, though. You're smarter'n I thought. Maybe too smart for a wrangler."

Beth chuckled. Jerry's calm acceptance was easing her troubled spirits already. She'd been imagining what her family would say about this latest venture. It was a relief to find that Jerry, at least, didn't seem to think she was disgraced for life. She twisted in his embrace and pretended to scowl at him. "All right. You were right about the mission school. I already admitted that much. How long am I going to have to listen to you saying 'I told you so'?"

Jerry held her slightly away from him and looked into her face with grave eyes shadowed by the darkness around them. "What I had in mind," he said, "was something like the rest of our lives."

Beth felt dizzy and shaken with happiness. How could something so wonderful as Jerry come out of all the trouble she'd caused? "I think I could stand that," she whispered.

The words ended on an involuntary squeak as his arms tightened about her, forcing the breath from her lungs.

"Not so tight!" she protested, but Jerry only grinned and informed her that she'd have to give him a kiss for every quarter inch of breathing space he allowed.

"I'll suffocate!" Beth dropped a kiss on his chin and his arms relaxed a fraction. "Am I turning blue yet?" She made a darting foray toward his eyebrow. "The rest of our lives together won't be very long," she threatened, "unless you let me breathe." She wriggled around and kissed the top of his shoulder. The worn fabric of the shirt, soft with many washings, did little to conceal the strong male body beneath. Beth's lips lingered, pressed against him again, and Jerry groaned.

"You got enough breath to talk," he whispered, "and enough sassiness to drive me crazy!" With a deft move, he flipped them over so that she lay on her back on the folded blanket, pinned down by his body. "Now it's my turn to do a little missionary work," he challenged her.

His lips brushed the tip of her ear, sending strange, feathery shivers of excitement through her. Moving lower, he gently nipped her earlobe with his teeth, then buried his face in the soft curve of her neck. His tongue flicked in and out, rousing her to throbbing sensitivity in parts of her body she'd never even thought about before, and his hands followed the curves of her body under the sensible thick skirt that she'd been wearing for too long.

The tantalizing touches were everywhere, possessing the back of her knee, the hollow at the base of her throat. Fingers and then lips lightly brushed one throbbing nipple that ached for a fuller caress. Beth's senses swam in a new world that seemed to be full of soft, intoxicating movements and dreamy caresses.

The night air was cold on her shoulder blades and the heat of the fire bounced off her leg. Dimly she realized that her clothing must be somewhat disarranged. But it didn't matter. Nothing mattered except Jerry, moving over her with expert hands and lips, bringing her nearer and nearer to total surrender with nothing more than a tingling touch here, the pressure of his leg there—

A sleepy murmur from the blankets on the far side of the campfire froze them both.

"The children are awake," Beth whispered to Jerry.

He sighed and shifted his weight so that she could sit up. "Just wait," he whispered back while she hurriedly straightened her clothing. "Day after tomorrow we'll give 'em back to Hosteen Chee and you'll have to think of some other excuse. Chow time, kids," he called in a normal voice. "Then we'll hit the road again, okay?"

Jerry kept up a steady stream of inconsequential chatter while he built up the campfire and passed around their supplies of hard biscuits and canned peaches as if they were a sumptuous feast. Only his eyes, constantly meeting Beth's over the flames, held a quiet glow of their own that said he was only waiting until he could truly be alone with her.

The climax of the feast, for Beth, came when he produced a battered tin coffeepot from his inexhaustible saddlebag. He shoved it into the glowing coals at one side of the fire while they ate, then poured steaming black coffee into a tin mug, which he and Beth shared. The bitter, sugarless brew, so hot it scalded her lips and so strong that she was surprised it didn't eat a hole right through the mug, was the best thing she'd ever tasted. It put new heart and strength into her and made the prospect of the moonlight ride before them seem less impossible.

Jerry touched her arm when she rose to her knees, wincing at the strain on her tired muscles. She began packing things back into the saddlebag.

"I don't want to wear you out," he said. "Me being used

to being in the saddle all day, and the kids been riding since they could walk, we might forget how rough a pace this is on somebody from back east. You want to rest a little longer, just say the word.''

Beth laughed. At least here was one place where she could meet him on equal ground, eastern tenderfoot or no. ''There was one thing I forgot to mention about my family,'' she told Jerry. ''My father taught me to ride and shoot like a boy. We got along fine until he decided I was grown up and ought to turn into a lady at the snap of his fingers.'' She bit her lip, the pain of that old fight still with her. ''I've missed riding since I started teaching school. Been longing for some exercise.''

That was true—as far as it went. It was also true that she hadn't envisioned anything as grueling as this midnight trek across the desert. Exercising her father's thoroughbreds in a nice green field was a different story. But there was no point in burdening Jerry with trivial details. Beth got to her feet, suppressing any wince this time, and heaved the saddlebag up across the horse's back herself, just to show Jerry she could do it.

''Okay, missionary lady.'' Jerry shook his head, smiling. ''Guess there's a few things I don't know about you yet.'' He tipped her head back and kissed her fiercely on the lips while they were hidden from the children by the two horses. ''But I aim to find out,'' he whispered with sudden passion. ''I'm going to know everything there is to know about you. I'm going to know things you don't know about yourself.''

Beth gave a rueful smile and took the rolled-up blankets from Riding Boy to pack them on the horse. ''That shouldn't be hard,'' she said. ''I don't think I know myself very well. I was going to come out here and be a nice, quiet, well-behaved little schoolmarm.''

"Instead of which," Jerry finished, "you wound up going on the war path with a crazy cowboy."

Beth bit her lip. "And losing your job as well as my own. Jerry, I'm so sorry to have involved you in my troubles—"

"Forget it," Jerry told her. "If you hadn't come to me, then you'd have something to apologize for." He lifted Wind Flower up to the neck of the horse while Riding Boy scrambled up onto the other horse without aid.

Jerry stood with one hand on the saddle and chuckled quietly. "Besides, I always did wonder what it'd be like. All the good Indian wars were before my time. When I was a kid, I used to pretend I was fighting in Kit Carson's forces. Never did figure I'd end up on the red man's side, though."

Beth giggled. "I used to read dime novels, too," she whispered. "How do you think I'd look in war paint and feathers?" She brought her hand up and patted her mouth in an imitation of the Indian war whoop of a circus show.

Jerry turned his routine trampling of the campfire coals into a war dance, bending at the knees and straightening and giving off his own war cry. Beth joined him and they pranced twice around the dying fire, whooping and giggling, while Riding Boy and Wind Flower watched with solemn faces from the backs of the horses.

"What are the white eyes doing?" Wind Flower whispered to her brother. "Are they crazy?" It was a possibility that had occurred to her off and on ever since the tall lady with the black hair had taken them out of the cellar.

Riding Boy shook his head. It galled him to admit that there was anything he didn't know about the whites' customs. "Must be some white people magic," he whispered back while Beth and Jerry stomped out the last glowing embers of the campfire.

❦ Chapter
Thirteen

$\mathcal{T}$he next stage of their journey carried them around in the wide half circle Jerry had planned, off the reservation and then back through Galvan North. He insisted on the utmost caution as they moved through the ranch lands, fearing that they'd be noticed by some of the hands who worked this territory. At least that was his excuse. Remembering his stories of mutilated animals and burned buildings, Beth wondered if he didn't have more to worry about than some of his friends, who surely would keep silent about their presence.

Whatever his reasons, he was adamant on the need for caution. They detoured through winding canyons for cover, waited while Jerry crept ahead to peek over a range of hills, went miles out of their way to avoid one solitary cowboy chasing a strayed calf.

As a result, the ride took longer than he had expected. At moonset they were still far from the ranch, but the faint glow of dawn gave enough light to continue.

Even in her exhaustion, Beth was struck by the beauty of the land revealed on this ride. The Galvan North grant was a green oasis in the middle of the desert, nourished by springs that allowed a thin covering of grama grass to spring up wherever the rocks had crumbled to soil. Against the patches of green, nourishment for thirsty eyes, the red-rock cliffs of the reservation formed a permanent dramatic backdrop.

In years to come Beth would retain only jumbled, chaotic memories of this flight across the ranch: the sweet smell of the grass near a spring and the bubbling of water, the curve of a green hill against the sky, the blessing of shade where another spring nourished two gnarled trees. It was enough. In spite of her exhaustion she was exhilarated by a strange sense of homecoming. Jerry at her side, the long stretches of grama grass quivering in the wind, the cliffs beyond—she knew, without analyzing it, that for once in her life she had just exactly what she needed.

Except for sleep. By the time the sun was high she was swaying drunkenly in the saddle once again, while Wind Flower sagged against her and nodded off to sleep.

"We'll rest at the old ranch house for the rest of the day," Jerry decreed. "Unless some of the boys are using it. . . . They ought to all be at the other end of the ranch, though. Eleuterio wants us all to stay away from the reservation line until this trouble's settled."

"Oh. Is the ranch house near the reservation?"

"Close enough to pi—er, spit over the line," Jerry said. His tanned face flushed several shades darker. "You wait here. I'll go up and see if the house is clear."

Beth slouched on the back of her horse, afraid to dismount while Jerry investigated for fear she would not be able to force herself up again. When he came back and reported that the house was empty, she was too tired even to feel relief that they had shelter; she felt only a stupid, stumbling resentment that he wouldn't let them go straight to the house. He insisted that they should tether the horses behind a line of junipers that marked the old corral, out of sight of the house, so that anybody riding by would not notice anything unusual.

Tired though she was, Beth cried out with delight when they left the old corral and she finally saw the ranch house. A rambling structure of native stone and massive wooden beams, it seemed to crouch low to the ground, following the contours of the gentle hill on which it rested. A row of tall, dark green junipers along the west side of the house promised shade from the worst heat of the day, and a spreading oak seemed to sprout straight up from the red-tiled roof.

"Patio," Jerry explained, jerking his thumb at the oak. "House is a big square built around an indoor terrace. Eleuterio told me once they used to build 'em that way in old Spain. The first Galvan to hold these lands married a *señorita* from the old country, who was lonely for her home. He built this house to make her less homesick."

"It looks as if it's welcoming us," Beth said softly. "Maybe the house has been lonely, too."

Jerry gave her a sardonic glance. "Oh, I wouldn't say that. It's been inhabited off and on—I found the nests when I checked it out just now."

Beth shivered. "Spiders?"

"No, just rats."

"Great. Any other details we should know about?"

Jerry nodded. "Some tramps must have broken in recently. There're traces of a campfire in the middle of the front room, and a couple of empty bottles. We'll stay in the back rooms . . . and I'll sleep with one eye open."

"All things considered," Beth said, "I'm more afraid of the rats than of the tramps." If they were tramps. But she didn't want to raise that question in front of the children.

They followed the same pattern as on their previous stop, unrolling bedrolls and flopping down exhausted almost at once. The only difference was that now they had a house to sleep in.

"Some of the rooms even have roofs," Beth commented. "Aren't you afraid I'll get soft, sleeping in all this luxury?"

She spread out blankets for the children in one of the small rooms along the back of the house, shaded by the junipers, and put her own bedroll in a corner room a little distance away. At least, she thought as she stretched her aching body out on the blanket, she and Jerry would have privacy in case . . . in case . . .

Sleep claimed her before she finished the thought.

When she woke, the mellow golden light in the patio told her that it was late afternoon. Except for the blanket she slept on, the room was empty.

Where was Jerry? Beth raised herself on one elbow, listening. The house was quiet but for the whisper of the wind in the junipers that stood sentinel over her roofless room, the rustle of some small desert animal in the rafters. . . .

Rats! Beth remembered Jerry's warning and jumped to her feet, trying to hold her skirts tight to her ankles and simultaneously peer up into the broken rafters over her blanket.

She could see nothing up there. But the thought had thoroughly awakened her, setting her heart pumping and her hands shaking. No hope of getting back to sleep now. Beth tiptoed out of her room, reassured by a gentle snoring from the other end of the corridor that the children were still sound asleep.

The arrangement of the house was as Jerry had said: a square around an inner patio. Each side of the square consisted of a series of small, squarish rooms, with narrow windows facing out and doors facing inward to the patio. Between the patio and the rooms ran a deep, shady passage,

the roof supported on stone pillars and heavy dark beams
that must have been hauled in from the mountains.

Beth tiptoed along the passageway, glancing into the
doorless rooms as she passed. In the room beside hers Jerry's bedroll, rifle, and cooking gear were neatly stacked.
She sighed. Last night his eyes had promised that he was
only waiting until they could be together in privacy. Was he
backing off now? Perhaps the house made him nervous. Perhaps he had started thinking that getting involved with a
woman meant the loss of his precious independence, a settled job, regular hours, town living, all the things he hated.

And perhaps, she told herself, he was being considerate.
Letting her sleep. Showing that he wouldn't take advantage.
He did seem to come up with scruples at the most inconve-
nient times.

Beth tried to convince herself that she was grateful for his
chivalry, but all her attempts to assume the proper maidenly
attitude failed completely. Last night she'd felt brave and
able to face anything—as long as Jerry was beside her. Now
Jerry had disappeared, and she felt lost and lonely and afraid
of the future. What was happening to her? She was losing all
the self-confidence that had carried her through life, first
getting a teaching certificate against her family's opposi-
tion, then facing down the furious school board in Iowa, and
finally making the dangerous trek out west by herself.

For all her difficulties with various authorities, Beth had
never lost confidence in her own ability to face and sur-
mount any problems that she encountered. Her father had
raised her almost like a boy, teaching her to ride and shoot
and tell the truth, implying that those qualities were all she
needed. He had been shocked to discover that the independent young lady he had reared was not about to turn into a
simpering finishing-school miss on the day he decided she

was grown up and ready to be married off to one of his friends.

Beth wandered onto the patio, lost in her memories, scarcely hearing the rustling of the dry oak leaves about her feet. The curved stone benches that bordered the patio were filthy with dead leaves and bird droppings, but the gnarled trunk and wide, low branches of the oak tree beckoned to her. Beth hitched her skirt up most immodestly and scrambled up to the lowest branch, where she sat swinging her legs and rejoicing that at least she had not lost all her girlhood skills.

She'd been so brave then, so sure of herself. When her father informed her that it was time to act like a lady and start attracting suitors, she'd faced him down in a three-day shouting match that had her gentle mother and faded aunts cowering in the sewing room.

"No penny of my money will go to waste on higher education for a daughter!" her father had bawled. "It's time you gave me a grandson to carry on the business after me!"

"If you won't pay for my schooling," Beth had yelled back, "I'll run away to New York and earn my own living!"

"What do you think you could do to earn a penny, you spoiled brat? Go on the streets?"

"Yes!" Beth had retorted, having only the vaguest notion what that meant but satisfied with the way her father turned red at the threat.

Finally they'd reached a compromise. She would dress like a lady, letting her skirts down and putting her hair up, and her father would pay for the two years of college she needed for a teaching certificate.

"Why not?" he'd said with a shrug when he'd finally given in. "It's only putting off the inevitable by a couple of years. If you don't get thrown out of the teachers' school, you'll never hold a job. You can't shout down a principal or a school board the way you bully me, young lady.''

"Who's the bully?" Beth gave her father a hug, quite friendly now that she'd won the argument and quite convinced that the world was only waiting for one Beth Johanssen to demonstrate her superior capabilities.

Beth sighed and laughed at once. How had she ever been so sure of herself? Time after time she'd been on the carpet at the teachers' college for one scrape after another, but always reprieved because she was the smartest, brightest student they'd had. Had she expected the rest of the world to be similarly impressed with her capabilities? Even the scene in Vinton, where she'd taken her first teaching job so as to be a reasonable distance from her disapproving family, had not shaken her confidence. She'd merely decided that the East was too conventional to appreciate her. But she could do anything—she would travel out west by herself and civilize the savage Indians.

Beth shook her head with a rueful smile. It seemed to her the whites in New Mexico Territory were in worse need of civilizing than the Indians. Except, she mentally corrected herself, for Jerry.

Dear Jerry. . . . Her eyes misted over. How could she have doubted him? Of course he wasn't avoiding her. He'd just thought it would be kind to let her sleep. And maybe he thought she would be shy of him, afraid that he'd take advantage of her here in this deserted house.

Beth knew that was what she ought to feel, what any nicely brought up girl would feel. But her veneer of ladylike behavior had been wearing thinner and thinner ever since she'd hit the heat-shimmering fringes of the desert. After disgracing herself at the mission school, running away with a strange man, and riding astride with kilted-up skirts for two days, she didn't have much sense of propricty left. Cer-

tainly not enough to keep her away from Jerry until some
black-coated man like Reverend Griscom said the right
words over them.

"The fact is," she concluded, staring up at the mosaic of
green oak leaves and blue sky, "I want him to take advantage of me."

She blushed once the words were out but didn't retract
them. She was not, Beth reflected ruefully, a truly nice-
minded young lady. She'd always had suspicions of that
fact, but it had taken Jerry Dixon and the red desert of New
Mexico to show her how much of a rebel she really was at
heart.

Staring up through the leaves of the oak tree, lost in her
thoughts, she failed to hear the soft rustling sounds below as
booted feet walked through the carpet of dead leaves and
broken twigs. The watcher in the patio moved slowly and
quietly, so as not to disturb her reverie. When he had
reached a point directly below the branch on which she sat,
he looked up for a few seconds, taking a most ungentle-
manly pleasure in the revealing view of long slim legs clad
in white stockings and surrounded by ruffled cotton petticoats. Then one sinewy hand reached upward to close about
an ankle and claim his prize.

Beth gave an involuntary shriek when she felt the hand on
her foot, rudely interrupting her reverie. She kicked out with
her free foot and lost her balance when that leg, too, was
caught in an unbreakable grasp. Her arms flailing for support among the branches of the oak, she slipped downward,
heard an ominous tearing sound behind her, and landed
breathless in the grasp of two strong arms that caught and
held her with ease.

On the way down she'd seen sunlight flash on a coppery
red head, and her fear had vanished. Jerry's tanned, laughing face bent over her as he examined his prize, holding her

securely against his shoulder. Beth felt like an awkward parcel, with her long legs dangling over his arm in a froth of petticoats, and her ripped skirt trailing almost to the ground.

"You had better put me down," she said. "I wouldn't want you to strain your back or anything."

Jerry grinned. "You weren't frightened, huh? Even for one teeny moment?"

"Naturally not," Beth said, lying with as much grace and dignity as she could under the circumstances. "I knew it was you all along. You startled me, that was all."

"Uh-huh." Jerry shifted his grasp slightly, so that he took most of her weight on one shoulder, and started across the patio toward the rooms at the back of the ranch house. "Might say I *took advantage* of your being so deep in thought."

A burning flush spread over Beth's face. Of course his choice of words was just a coincidence. "How long were you there?" she inquired, staring over his shoulder.

"Long enough," Jerry said.

And what did that mean? She had not long to ponder the question. A few easy strides took them to the room where Jerry had dropped his bedroll and other things. He ducked under the low stone lintel, stooping so that she wouldn't hit her head, and gently put her down in the center of the room.

He wasn't holding her tightly enough to keep her against her will, but Beth stood like a captive in the circle of his arms, trapped by the pounding pulse in her throat and the sweet tremors that ran through her at his slightest touch. She raised her lips to his and waited for the inevitable kiss.

Jerry cleared his throat. "I got . . . a few things to take care of," he said. He left her there, standing in the middle of the room, while he spread out the bedroll, patting and smoothing the blanket as though his care could turn the stone floor into a feather mattress and the somewhat smelly blanket into satin sheets.

Beth licked lips gone suddenly dry. "I thought . . . when you picked another room . . ."

"I had my reasons," said Jerry, kneeling on the blanket and brushing away nonexistent creases. "You needed your rest. And besides . . ."

There was a long pause in which Beth could not breathe or move. "And besides?" she murmured at last.

Jerry looked up, his tanned face lit by a flashing grin. "This room," he said, rising from his knees, "is much better."

"Oh?" It looked much the same to Beth—narrow window, roof half fallen in, anonymous piles of rubble in the corners.

When he moved she felt her knees going weak with anticipation. But he turned away from her, and her heart plummeted.

"This room," said Jerry gently, "has a door."

He shut the heavy warped door of oak planks and came back to her across the longest three feet of distance any man had ever crossed. This time his hands were hard and possessive and there was no question at all of her walking away from him. The urgency of desire leaped between their bodies like an electric charge, startling them both.

The heavy, hampering garments were an intolerable barrier between them. Jerry tugged at the fastenings and helped her to shrug them off. His lips and hands sought out each white, silky place on her skin as it was exposed, burning her with demanding kisses that sent pulses of liquid fire leaping through her veins. They were hasty and clumsy in their undressing, discarding clothes in a random heap on the floor, torn skirt and silver spurs, delicate lace-trimmed petticoats and scuffed leather boots in one pile. She felt the roughness of the woolen blanket against her skin, then Jerry's lean hard body moved over her, his hands roving at will and laying claim to all they touched.

Beth knew a sudden, shaming moment of fear as his rising hardness pressed against her thighs. Her arms tightened convulsively around him, drawing him close to her, wanting to get the unknown act over with quickly before she could lose her courage. But he resisted the pull, lying half over her propped on one elbow and stroking her white flesh with long, sensuous caresses that made her tremble with pleasure and fear together.

"Don't be frightened," he murmured in her ear, lifting the great weight of black curls that clung to his fingers and crackled in the dry air. "Don't worry about anything." The nape of her neck shivered in anticipation as he trailed one finger along it. He lowered his head and she pursed her lips, waiting for a kiss, but instead he moved lower yet, until his lips just grazed the tip of one breast and sent new shocks of desire racing through her body.

"I'm not frightened," she lied. Then his lips closed over her nipple, tugging at the rosy pcak until it became the center of an aching desire that shivered through her, and it was not a lie any longer. When his free hand cupped her other breast, then passed lower to brush across the dark triangle where her thighs met, she arched her body for his touch and moaned when he withdrew ever so slightly.

The delicately brushing fingertips drove her into a frenzy of desire. Eyes closed, she tossed her head from side to side, rising to meet him as his hands glided over her with sure, knowing touches, bringing her nearer and nearer to total surrender. She opened to the gentle pressure of his hand without remembering fear, only wanting those exploring touches to go on and on raising her to new heights of pleasure.

When he poised himself over her for a moment, when the

touch of his hand was replaced by something else, she was beyond knowing anything but the ache of desire deep within her. There was a moment of tearing pain; she cried out in shock and tried to get away from the pressure that hurt her, but he was holding her down now with legs and hands and lips, pressing her down and caressing her and murmuring soothing nonsense words into her ear all at once. In the aftermath of the pain, she felt him moving inside her, calling forth new responses from her depths, and she forgot that she had tried to push him away.

All her consciousness was now centered on that dark tidal rhythm where their bodies, locked together, moved without volition or planning. Mindlessly obeying the needs thrumming in her blood, she arched herself against him once more, wound her long arms and legs around his body, and thrust upward to meet his fierce thrusts in the final explosion. Her body was shaken as if by a giant hand, pulsing and contracting until she could bear it no more, narrowing to a single point of sensation that flowered into a tide of light that filled her completely.

Lost in that floodtide of delight, knowing nothing but the pounding of her blood and the slowing pulsations of her body, Beth glided slowly down from the heights where Jerry had taken her. She opened languid eyes and saw him still above her, his arms encircling her, the promise of endless love in his eyes. She reached up one wondering hand to touch his cheek, reassuring herself from the warm bristly feeling of his unshaven skin that this was really Jerry, the wrangler from Galvan's ranch, and not some stranger with supernatural powers to move her.

"Well, missionary lady," Jerry drawled, his lips curving into a satisfied smile, "you're pretty good at this, for somebody who's never done it before."

"You're not bad yourself," Beth retorted, "but I'm afraid I can't return the rest of the compliment!"

Jerry's eyebrows shot up. "You mean you're questioning my purity? Why, you shameless hussy! Don't you know nice girls aren't supposed to know about a feller's little adventures?"

Nice girls, no. But shameless girls who wanted a man to take advantage of them and said so where he could hear them . . . Beth burned with embarrassment.

"Well, look at that, now," Jerry said in tones of detached scientific interest. "I never knew you blushed all the way down to there." His finger lightly traced the path of the rosy flush on her body, which had a disastrous effect on her breasts. The nipples seemed to have taken on independent life, springing up and impudently demanding more of Jerry's caresses, never mind Beth's embarrassment.

"Want to go for a full house?" His hand moved lower, and Beth caught her breath as his fingers fastened in her and reawakened the pulsing of desire.

"I can't . . . we shouldn't . . . Oh, please!" she moaned, unable to help herself as he probed her intimately and revived the aching need for him.

"Please stop," Jerry asked, his face alight with lively curiosity, "or please go on?"

But Beth was beyond words, so he made his own decision in the matter.

This time, the first urgency assuaged, their bodies moved together slowly and gently, like an underwater ballet. Beth forgot her shame and ceased to wonder what he thought of her, lost in amazement at the way they fitted together so perfectly. She ran one hand along his shoulders, the hard wiry body and the unexpected swell of the hips, then let her hand fall away when he moaned at her touch. Without ceasing his slow, gentle strokes, Jerry captured her hand and placed it back where it had been.

"Touch me, Beth. . . . I need you to hold me, too," he whispered into the sweet-scented hollow between neck and throat, kissing the blue pulse that beat there.

She complied joyfully, reveling in her freedom to trace the lines of this taut male form, so different from her own and the source of so much pleasure. Jerry shivered under her touch and quickened his movements; she held him tightly against her and welcomed the demands he made of her with fierce upward thrusts of her own. The sweet tide of light flowed upward through her body again, loosening and relaxing her limbs, and she floated peacefully while he cried out and collapsed atop her.

"I'm a selfish son of a bitch," Jerry growled when he recovered enough strength to lift his head, "but I'm glad you haven't done this before."

Beth caught at the hand that prowled among her curls and held it to her breast. "So am I, dear love. So am I." A wicked twinkle filled her eyes. "I might need a lot of practice, though. . . ." As if by accident, she brushed one hand along his side and just grazed the curling nest of red hair between his thighs.

"Mercy!" Jerry fell back on the floor, arms and legs sprawling. "Didn't anybody ever tell you that a man can't perform forever?"

"Nobody ever told me anything," Beth said. "How should I know?"

"Well, I'm telling you now, ain't I?" Jerry groaned as she leaned over him, brushing feather-light kisses across his chest and stomach. "Do I look like the picture of energy?"

"You do seem rather . . . limp," Beth teased, placing her hand over the parts in question. "That is . . . Oh, I didn't think . . . ." She felt him rising again under her palm.

"A miracle! You've raised the dead!" Jerry rolled over and threw his arms about her waist, pulling her into his arms all helter-skelter for a kiss here and there wherever he could reach. He clamped strong thighs around her legs and cupped his hands around her breasts, holding her back against him where she could feel the evidence of his reviving desire.

"Stop!" Beth hissed, wriggling to get free.

"What's the matter?" Jerry teased. "You said you needed practice."

"Stop, I—"

A loud thump from the front of the house, followed by an equally loud curse, interrupted them.

"—think I heard something," finished Beth.

Jerry was already grabbing for his pants. "You stay here," he instructed her.

❧ *Chapter*
Fourteen

 *A*s soon as Jerry slipped out of the room, Beth threw on her blouse and skirt. She tiptoed barefoot along the passageway behind him, taking care to avoid the crackling oak leaves that littered the pavement. Halfway to the front of the house he realized she was following him.

"Get back," he whispered.

"Why?"

"I don't recognize that feller's voice. He's not one of our men."

Beth remembered Jerry's report that someone had broken into the house since his last visit and his insistence that they conceal all traces of their own presence. And her own theory that Hudson had hired men to kill cattle and burn buildings. Swallowing hard, she tried to ignore the fluttering sensations in her stomach. She shook her head. "I'm coming with you," she whispered. "What if it's something you can't handle alone?"

Jerry threw up his hands in disgust. "All right. But at least get the rifle out of my pack." He gave her a speculative glance. "I don't suppose you know how to load it?"

Beth nodded and Jerry's eyebrows shot up. "Well, well," he whispered, "a very talented missionary lady indeed!"

Feeling warmed and strengthened by his praise, Beth went back for the rifle while Jerry resumed his stealthy progress toward the front room.

The late afternoon sun was almost gone behind the mountains now, leaving only a golden trace along the top of one wall in a jagged line that followed the broken silhouette of the fallen roof. The afterglow of sunset made the blue-shadowed interior of the room seem even dimmer. She would have to load by feel.

The long barrel and utilitarian wooden stock of the rifle were cold to her hands. Beth's fingers trembled as she slid back the bolt and fumbled with the unfamiliar magazine. Cartridges now—three, four, five, and she could snap the trapdoor shut and push the bolt back. The whole operation had taken no more than half a minute, but the sweat was trickling down her forehead before she finished. Having the loaded rifle in her hand, like a live thing preparing to spring, made her feel much happier.

When she rejoined Jerry, he was crouched in the passageway between the patio and the front room, about two feet from the gap in the wall where wide double doors had once stood. He held up one hand for silence and Beth tiptoed the last few steps with exaggerated caution. She noticed that his other hand held the old Colt revolver that usually rested in a holster just above his hip. He must have picked it up when he went out to investigate the noises, when she'd been too scared even to think of getting a gun.

The voices in the front room were blurred and indistinct. Beth could tell that there were at least two men there and guessed that they'd been drinking. The desultory conversation rose and fell, long mumbled rambling sentences followed by a few words almost shouted for emphasis. They seemed to be congratulating themselves on the success of some project. She caught the words "damned interfering redskin" once, and then, "not enough kerosene," and "should of made sure they were all dead."

Beth gave an involuntary shiver. These definitely weren't Galvan men. And frankly she was terrified.

Jerry turned and squeezed her hand. His face was set in hard lines that she had not seen before. "Get back to the kids' room," he hissed. "Get them dressed and get out by a window. Go around back to the old corral and saddle up."

"But you—" Beth started to say.

"Don't argue." Even in a whisper, his voice made the order final. Beth laid the rifle down by his free hand, but he shook his head and motioned that she was to keep it. She backed away from him with cautious steps, holding her skirts bunched in one fist so that they didn't brush against any of the dry leaves and other rubble that littered the open passageway. The rifle rested cold and heavy in her other hand, ready to be whipped up to her shoulder if she needed it.

Her mouth had gone dry and there was a dark roaring noise in her ears. This was not like hunting with her father, or even like riding away from the Galvan Ranch and concealing their tracks so that the missionary wouldn't be able to come after them. The few words she'd heard left her in no doubt that the men in the front room were killers.

Her palms were damp with perspiration. She hoped her hands would not slip on the rifle if she had to use it. She changed hands on the rifle and rubbed her palm on the folds of her skirt.

She was moving along the back passageway now to the room at the corner where Riding Boy and Wind Flower were still sleeping. Indian children were quiet, disciplined—they wouldn't make a sound when she woke them. She'd seen the boarding-school children waking soundlessly and warily in their dormitory.

The children were sitting up on their blanket, eyes wide, when she tiptoed into the room. Riding Boy had a protective arm around his little sister's shoulders.

"Where is Jerry?" he whispered.

"He's coming," Beth whispered back. Thank goodness, the children had picked up the sense of danger. They would give her no argument. "Get dressed. We have to meet Jerry by the old corral. Can you get out the window?" The roof over this room was still solid; one reason she'd picked it for the children. The narrow window would be a tight squeeze for her, but she'd worry about that after she lifted the children out.

While she hoisted the children to the window, she prayed that her words had been correct. Jerry'd said nothing about meeting him. But then, he'd said nothing about what they were to do when they got to the corral, if not to wait for him. Surely a quick retreat was their only choice? He wouldn't take on two armed men by himself.

Beth saw Wind Flower drop from the window into Riding Boy's arms and breathed a sigh of relief. At least the children were safe. "Run to the corral," she whispered to Riding Boy. "Stay out of sight of the front. I'll be there in a minute." She paused, trying to think. From this window she could see the sun just sinking behind the western mountains, the sky pink and gold with reflected glory. "If I don't come, wait until it is quite dark, then take Wind Flower on your horse and ride for the reservation."

Riding Boy shook his head. "A warrior must stay to defend the women."

Beth could have shouted in vexation. She was in agony to get back to see that Jerry was all right. What if those men caught him? He had only the revolver. He might need her to back up his fire. "Riding Boy." She forced herself to speak slowly and distinctly. "You are unarmed. If for some reason we cannot join you before dark, the best thing you can do is to ride to your people, to get help."

Whatever happened here would be long over before anyone could come—and Beth doubted very much that the Navahos would care about the fights between some white people. But the excuse might serve to get Riding Boy away from the danger. "And you must see that Wind Flower is safe. That is your first duty."

Her knees sagged with relief as Riding Boy gave a solemn nod and squared his shoulders, visibly accepting the responsibility she placed upon him. He raised his hand once, in farewell, then took Wind Flower's hand and melted into the shadows of the junipers without a word.

Beth waited, straining her eyes, until she could no longer see even a flicker of movement. Then she took up the rifle, which had been leaning against the wall, and made her way back to the door opening. All this time her nerves had been stretched taut, waiting for the exchange of gunfire that would signal that Jerry had been seen. Silence was good news—but this continued silence was hell on her nerves. She peered out into the passageway, now entirely dark, and jumped at a scraping sound from the wall to her left.

"Beth?" It was Jerry's voice, low and strained in the darkness. "Thought I told you to get the hell out of here."

"I'm afraid of the dark," Beth whispered back. "I want you to hold my hand."

He chuckled under his breath. A warm hand reached sideways out of the darkness and fastened over her breast for a moment. Beth heard her own sharp intake of breath at the sudden touch and the unexpected dart of pleasure in the midst of fear.

"Sorry," came Jerry's unrepentant gesture. "It's so dark, I just had to hold whatever I could find." This time it was her hand he took in the darkness. "Come on. We'll go out through my room. I want to pick up my tack on the way out."

He stepped forward, feeling his way along the wall, and Beth followed. On the third step her hand brushed a soft, clinging web that wrapped around her fingers. Something crawled down her arm. Beth gasped and waved her arm wildly to dislodge the spider, unable to think about anything but the need to get that creeping horror off her skin at once. Her hand crashed into a broken rafter that had been leaning slowly downward with its burden of tiles for untold years. The slight shock was enough to shake loose half a dozen tiles, which fell clattering to the floor.

There was a shout from the front room, and a moment later Beth saw sparks of flame in the darkness that accompanied a thundering explosion of gunfire.

Jerry reacted immediately, while Beth was still stunned. He pushed her through an open doorway while he leaped forward, the revolver in his hand. "Fire to back me up," he whispered. Then he was gone and she had only his voice to guide her.

"Give up, Fritz," Jerry shouted, "we got you surrounded!" Beth couldn't see him in the darkness. She put the rifle to her shoulder and fired high, afraid of hitting him. A moment later his revolver spoke from the doorway down the hall, and she was able to aim lower in the darkness—just at the height of a man. Her second shot was rewarded with a cry of pain.

Jerry was shouting some nonsense. "Get 'em, boys!" he called. "Bill, you and Terry fan out and cut off the front door!"

Catching on tardily, Beth made her voice as gruff as possible and shouted, "Got it, boss!" while she fired her remaining shots into the darkness and reloaded. Jerry dodged from room to room, firing random shots to make it seem as if there were several men back here, and Beth added an occasional rifle shot to keep up the excitement.

Their ruse was rewarded by a shout of dismay and a rapid retreat. As soon as the outlaws' gunfire stopped, Jerry lowered his Colt and put one hand on Beth's arm. They heard scrambling noises from the front of the house, and a moment later the welcome sound of a couple of horses being ridden away at top speed.

Beth sagged against the wall, shaking all over. Her shoulder ached from the recoil of the rifle and her trembling hands would no longer obey her commands.

Jerry took her shoulders and pulled her to him. Their lips met in one long, consuming kiss that fed new strength into her. She leaned against him, ashamed of her shaking body but unable to command it.

"Beth? We don't have time to be scared now. Got to get out of here. Can you make it?"

Beth straightened and nodded. "Yes," she said, hoping her voice wasn't trembling as badly as her hands.

"Good girl."

The accolade was as good as a shot of brandy, flooding through her veins and warming her like his kiss. Beth found with mild surprise that she was actually able to scramble up through the broken roof in Jerry's room, take the rifle when he handed it to her, jump down, and thread her way through the junipers to the corral.

Riding Boy and Wind Flower were there, already mounted and holding the mustangs as steady as rocks. Beth felt weak with relief. She had been wondering what she and Jerry would do if the children had already ridden away.

She scrambled up behind Wind Flower and took the reins

from the little girl's cold fingers. Her own fear was wiped away by the feeling of the small, shivering body. What must it be like for Wind Flower, not understanding anything they said, yanked from her home first to the boarding school, then on the run with strange white people?

She hugged the little girl. "I'm scared, too," she told her, not caring that Wind Flower couldn't understand her words. The feeling would get across, and that was more important. "It's all right now."

"*I*," boasted Riding Boy, "was not afraid. Not even a little bit." But Beth noticed that he was clinging as close to Jerry as Wind Flower was to her.

Jerry set a punishingly hard pace out of the valley—hard for the riders, worse for the exhausted horses. In the darkness before moonrise they had to pick their way carefully, and as they entered the jagged canyon territory of the reservation Beth was continually afraid that one misstep on the steep paths would send her and Wind Flower and their horse all together down a rocky slope or over the sheer drop at the edge of a mesa.

"What's the hurry?" she asked Jerry when they finally had to halt at the top of a steep rise to give the horses a rest. "We scared them off, didn't we?"

Jerry nodded and drew her a little way apart from the children. "We did that," he allowed. "But I may have made a small mistake."

"What's that? I thought you were wonderful." Beth leaned against his shoulder and he put his arm around her. She felt warm and comforted and safe, as if she were standing in a magic circle. She drew in a deep breath, expecting to savor the combined subtle scents of leather and cotton shirt and Jerry, and instead got a strong whiff of tired horse. Oh, well. She probably smelled like a horse, too. They all did.

"When I called one of 'em by name?"

Beth nodded.

"Thought I recognized his voice. Used the name to startle him, give us a couple of seconds' breathing space. Seemed like a good idea at the time, but now . . ." He shrugged.

"You called him Fritz," Beth prompted.

"Yep. Fritz Bauer. Rode range with him once in Socorro—long time ago. Mean son of a bitch. Couple of months ago I heard he was wanted in Texas."

"What for?" Beth moved closer, snuggling gratefully into the protective circle of Jerry's arm.

"Armed robbery." Jerry paused, dragging the words out reluctantly. "Murder. Arson." Another pause. "He held up a saloon, shot the barkeep dead, and wounded a couple of other men. Kicked over a lamp on his way out and the place went up in flames. Townspeople were busy trying to put the fire out, and he got away."

He recounted the violent details in a quiet, almost detached tone, as if he were trying to make it something as remote as a newspaper account. But with Fritz Bauer and his friend out somewhere under the same stars that hovered over their mesa, the story was all too real. It could have been them—and the children—

"The wounded men?" Beth asked.

"Didn't get out in time."

Beth felt sick.

"Sorry," Jerry said. "Didn't want to tell you. Thought you'd best understand what we're up against. See, Fritz and his buddy must have been hiding out up here. Probably thought they were safe, even if somebody saw them—we're a long way from El Paso. But now Fritz knows I recognized him. When he gets over his fright and stops running, he'll figure he can't let us get away."

The peaceful mesa seemed full of frightening shadows,

every rustle in the sagebrush a potential menace. Beth wrapped her own arms tightly around her and shivered. There was something about this story of Jerry's that she had to think about. Try to think. . . . There'd been too much violence around Galvan North recently. What was the connection?

Jerry was talking again, explaining that they were not really in any danger—not at first. Fritz would be expecting them to head south for Gallup to tell the sheriff. He'd go that way in the hope of cutting them off. Meanwhile, he said, they would be riding north and west, into the mountains of the Indian reservation. They would stop at Blue Mesa trading post just long enough to leave the kids with his friends Nathan and Lily, then make their way back to the Galvan Ranch. Eleuterio Galvan could spread the warning that Fritz Bauer had been seen in the area.

"Though by that time, with any luck, he'll be over the border to Mexico, and good riddance," Jerry finished up.

Beth shook her head. "I don't think so." The pieces were falling into place now. Why hadn't she told Jerry all her news earlier? Well, she excused herself, there had been a few other things that seemed urgent at the time. . . . She blushed, remembering the exact nature of some of that urgency, and was grateful that the darkness cloaked her blushes.

"Listen, Jerry," she said, "I don't think Fritz Bauer is just hiding out here. I think he had a reason to be here—a reason to be around the ranch house. You know when they were talking about not having enough kerosene? I bet you Lawrence Hudson hired them to make trouble on Galvan North. I bet they're supposed to destroy what's left of the ranch house—burn the beams, make the whole roof fall in, make a wreck of it."

Jerry shook his head slowly. "We been over all that before. I'd like to pin it on Hudson, but there's no proof. Besides, why would he want Galvan North so bad?''

"I know.'' Beth moved to a large rock and sat down, gathering her torn and dirty skirt about her ankles. "Lawrence Hudson came courting me.'' She felt quite smug with her knowledge. "And he talks too much when he's courting. He thinks there's gold on Galvan North. Something about the old Dry Lake finds.''

Jerry laughed. "Dry Lake! That old story about the old fellows with their nugget? There's been a dozen prospectors went broke trying to follow their trail. Could be anywhere along the edge of the reservation. Why's Hudson picked on Galvan North?''

"He thinks,'' Beth said, "the existence of a secret vein of gold is the only thing that could explain the ranch's prosperity in the old days.''

Jerry smacked his fist down into the palm of his other hand. "Goddamned eastern idiot! Not you, sorry. Hudson. Didn't he ever hear about overgrazing? This whole range used to be so thick with grama grass you couldn't hardly walk through the stuff. Eleuterio's ancestors ran too many cattle and a hell of a lot too many sheep, spent the profits and went into debt on top of that. Eleuterio's trying to build the range up again, but it'll take years to get it back in condition. Meanwhile, Galvan South is supporting the whole shebang.''

Beth shrugged. "Fine. Tell that to Lawrence Hudson. He struck me as a fairly determined man, once he gets an idea into his head. And I bet you he hired Fritz Bauer and that other man to make trouble between Galvan's hands and the Indians on the reservation.''

"You already said that.''

"Yes, but you didn't believe me the first time.''

Jerry laughed and caught her hands to pull her up to him.

"So you're gonna keep telling me until I get it right? Once a schoolteacher, always a schoolteacher."

"Not any more. . . ." Beth's voice trailed away. Stupid, in the midst of all that was happening, to grieve over the way she'd blown her teaching career sky high! But that failure still hurt. She would have been a *good* teacher—she knew she would. The children liked her. If only she could get along with her superiors.

"Cheer up, missionary lady." Jerry gave her a light swat on the bottom to start her moving back to the horses. "I reckon to keep you too busy with our own kids to be worried about any others. Once I get a place, that is. . . ."

His own voice trailed off as the thoughts he'd been pushing aside overtook him. As a roving wrangler, he could have quit Galvan's outfit and drifted off to another one without giving it a second thought. But a married man with a family needed a secure place—the sort of place Eleuterio would have given him, if he'd stayed on and taken that section manager's job. Well, maybe Galvan would take him back, if Beth was right and Fritz Bauer had been hired to cause trouble up here, if he could catch Fritz and run him off the ranch for good. . . .

And maybe he wouldn't. There was no proof that Hudson and Bauer were in it together, and this escapade of Beth's would alienate a good many of the good people of Gallup. Could Eleuterio afford to keep a man who'd just royally pissed off the mission school? Jerry shrugged and mounted. One thing at a time, and their next job was to see the kids safely to Blue Mesa trading post. He and Beth could worry about the future once it was established that they had one.

While they were talking the moon had risen, and it was a little easier to see their path when they started out. But there was danger as well in the pale clear light. Every irregularity in the terrain stood out as a bold black shadow. Anybody looking for them would be able to spot their movements from miles away. And Jerry didn't know this territory as well as he used to.

"Riding Boy," he said in an undertone, "do you know the canyons that run through here? Can we get up to the mountains without showing ourselves too much?"

Riding Boy nodded. "Take longer, though."

"That's okay." His worry was that they'd be spotted. As long as Fritz didn't know they were heading this way, he'd have no reason to go north. If they stuck to the shelter of the canyons, they could take their time. Jerry cursed himself silently for having loitered with Beth on top of the mesa while the moon came up. They were silhouetted against the sky like black cutouts in a carnival shooting gallery, perfect targets for a man with a repeating rifle and plenty of time to choose his mark. Jerry felt the sweat trickling down the back of his collar as they picked their way across the mesa to the downward path that Riding Boy indicated.

It was hard going, tracing the narrow paths of summer streams and picking their way over loose pebbles and boulders washed down by the infrequent flash floods that had scored the canyons over millions of years. The hours of the night passed with agonizing slowness, and every time they broke cover Jerry was tense with listening. When they reached the mountains where trees grew thickly on the lower slopes he felt somewhat better. There were miles between them and the ranch now, and with any luck more miles between them and the outlaws, who should—if they had any sense—be waiting to ambush them on the trail to the south. Now they had only the grueling climb over the pass before them.

At dawn they came over the pass, to a semicircular dip like half a broken teacup set against a sheer cliff. The unpretentious log frame of the mountain trading post, set back against the cliff, looked like sheer heaven to Beth. Perhaps they could stop here long enough for her to bathe—perhaps Jerry's friend Lily would be able to lend her some clean clothes. At the moment she couldn't at all understand the appeal of the gold for which Hudson was willing to kill and burn. A clean blouse that didn't smell like a horse would be infinitely more valuable to her than a sack of gold nuggets.

The corral before the post was empty. Were Lily and Nathan gone?

"Guest corral," Jerry explained. "They keep their own horses back of the post, out of sight—and temptation." He grinned. "Some of their visitors have a fondness for good horseflesh and an inadequate sense of private property."

Riding Boy frowned. "Jerry, why—"

Jerry was already unsaddling. "Just a minute," he said over his shoulder. He helped Beth to dismount. Her legs were so stiff that she almost fell when her feet touched the ground. Jerry held her for a moment until she got her balance. "You go on in," he told her, "and sit down. I'll see to the horses."

For once Beth was tired enough to let Jerry do her work for her. She hobbled toward the post, wishing that she didn't have to meet the beautiful and accomplished Lily when she was such a mess. She twitched at her skirt and tried to smooth the one tangled braid of her hair, but it was no use. Nobody could look presentable after two solid days of riding.

As she approached, she felt a tremor of apprehension at the sight of the closed door and dark windows. What a time to come calling! She looked over her shoulder and saw that Jerry was coming toward her. The children dawdled at the corral. They were shy. She could sympathize. She wouldn't press them to come in yet.

But why should Riding Boy be shy of Lily and Nathan? Hadn't he boasted of spending almost a year with them?

The question flitted briefly across her tired brain, to be shelved with all the other unsolved puzzles of the journey. Thank goodness, the door of the trading post was opening. Someone must have been awake to see their arrival.

Beth stepped up to the door with renewed confidence. As it swung open a bare twelve inches, she was surprised to see a narrow, unshaven face with a long nose and pinched features like a weasel's. Well, she told herself, Jerry had never said his friend Nathan was handsome or clean.

"Good morning—" she started to say.

The owner of the unshaven face reached out one grimy paw, grabbed her arm, and hauled her bodily inside the trading post, immediately slamming the door again. Something hard pressed against her ribs and she recognized a voice she had heard only once before in her life.

"Glad to see you could join our little party," said Fritz Bauer.

❦ Chapter Fifteen

$\mathcal{H}$e was standing in the corner by two oddly shaped long bundles. As he spoke, he turned and leveled the gun in his hand on Beth's midriff. The barrel shook slightly, going around in tiny circles that had a hypnotic effect on her. She felt dizzy, and the dim interior of the trading post seemed to be going dark and light in rhythmic pulsations.

"Don't just stand there, Danny," Fritz barked to the man who held her, "tie her hands."

Beth felt a stab of pain in one shoulder as her captor roughly yanked her arms back and tied her wrists with something cold and hard that bit into the skin when he twisted it tight. The pain helped to clear her head. Her vision steadied and, now that her eyes were adjusted to the dim light, she could see that the two long bundles behind the counter were people, tied hand and foot and gagged. One of them had yellow hair that gleamed against the dark wood of the counter.

"All right." The man called Danny gave Beth a shove that sent her stumbling forward toward his partner. Fritz caught her and used the excuse to run one hand over the front of her blouse as he steadied her.

"Okay, pretty girl," he told her, "you just behave and nobody gets hurt. You going to be good?"

Beth nodded vigorously. Fritz seemed to be amused by her terrified compliance. "Good. Just don't say nothing when your boyfriend comes in, okay? We got a little surprise party planned for him, see."

Danny was peering through a tear in the yellow calico curtains that covered the trading post's one window. "He ain't coming in," he complained. "Nosing around the corral. Mebbe he noticed something wrong."

Where were the children? Beth's stomach twisted at the thought that she and Jerry might have brought them into something much worse than what they were running away from. She tried to edge nearer to the window, to look for herself, but Fritz stopped her with a jerk on the wire that bound her hands.

"Aah, let the little lady look," Danny said. "Mebbe she'd like to invite her boyfriend to join the party."

Fritz thought it over, rubbing the blue-black stubble on his chin with one hand. "He coming yet?"

When Danny shook his head, Fritz turned Beth around so that she faced the door, giving her another lingering caress as he did so, and shoved her back across the narrow space to Danny's waiting hands. Danny grabbed her by the waist and aimed a slobbering kiss at her mouth. Fighting nausea, Beth ducked her head and butted him in the chin. He yelped with pain and grabbed her bound wrists and pushed them up until she whimpered at the stabbing ache that went shooting through her shoulder blades.

"Cut it out," Fritz ordered. "You can play later. You!" The word was barked at Beth; his gun was pointing at her again, aimed just at the silver buckle that belted her torn skirt. She shut her eyes. She didn't want that wavering black

hole to be the last thing she saw on earth. Numb with fear
and pain, she waited for the explosion to tear through her.

"We want your boyfriend in here," Fritz was saying.
"You're going to help us."

Beth shook her head. The gun lifted a fraction of an inch.
Fritz walked slowly forward until the muzzle was pressed
against her left breast. "You got one chance to change your
mind."

Beth's mouth was dry with fear. She nodded and Fritz
snickered, but the gun stayed where it was, heavy and
menacing. "Okay. When Danny opens the door, you call
your man and tell him you need him inside. Got it?"

Beth opened her dry mouth. "Y-yes," she croaked in a
half whisper.

"Say it nice and clear."

"T-take the gun away," she whispered. "I'm too
scared. . . . Please! I'll do whatever you say."

Fritz studied her white face for a moment. Then, with a
nod of satisfaction, he stepped back two paces. The gun remained in his hand, but it was pointing at the floor. Beth let
out a deep sigh of relief. "I'll call him," she promised in a
voice that quavered only a little. "Open the door!"

When Danny pushed the door open a crack, she hung
back. Her knees were trembling visibly. Danny cursed and
pushed her forward by her bound wrists. He stood directly
behind her in the door, between her and Fritz. "Call!" he
growled in her ear.

Beth threw her weight at the crack of daylight showing
through the door and shouted, "Don't come in, Jerry—it's a
trap! They're—"

She fell to her knees in the open door and rolled sideways,
hoping desperately to avoid Fritz's shot. Jerry was running
toward her. A gunshot exploded inside the trading post,
deafening her, and a sharp pain shot through her shoulder.

She was lifted from behind and hurled down on the floor of
the trading post. The door slammed shut.

Beth lay with one bruised cheek on the floor, breathing
shallowly and somewhat surprised to find she was not dead.
Fritz stood above her with the revolver in his hand.

"Get him?" Danny asked.

"Naah. Son of a bitch moved too fast."

Slowly Beth realized that the ache in her shoulder must
have come from being knocked against the doorpost when
they'd dragged her back into the store. Fritz had fired at
Jerry, not at her, and her attempt to warn him had only
drawn him into more danger. But he'd escaped—or had he?
Sick with fear and worry, she struggled to her knees.

"Okay. You won't help us one way, you will another.
Seems like the cowboy must like you some, way he come
running when you yelled."

Beth felt cold with terror at the look in Fritz Bauer's eyes.
Still holding the smoking revolver in one hand, he reached
down and twisted his free hand in the thick hair at the nape
of her neck. He hauled her to her feet with casual strength
and pushed her toward the window.

He stuck the barrel of the gun in between the yellow calico curtains and the rod they hung on, and yanked downward. The bright flowered stuff parted from the rod with a
tearing sound, baring half of the window.

Fritz pushed Beth up to the window and held her there
against the cold glass with one hand. He pointed the gun at
her neck, moving it closer and closer while he watched her
terrified eyes with a smile of satisfaction. The hot tip of the
barrel rested on the hollow at the base of her throat,
scorching her. Beth flinched away, but Fritz's hand in her
hair held her firmly.

"Open the door again," he told Danny.

"The cowboy's got a gun," Danny whined.

"Well, hell, I didn't say to hang your ugly face out there like a duck in a shooting gallery! Just open it a crack and tell him we want to parley. Get him to come close enough where he can see the little lady, here."

Danny slithered over to the door and opened it a bare crack, keeping his body firmly pressed behind the solid door. "Cowboy?" he shouted. "We got your girlfriend. You want to talk?"

Beth sobbed aloud with relief as Jerry's voice shouted back. She couldn't see him, but he sounded very much alive. "Let the girl go, Fritz. Then we'll talk."

Fritz shook his head at Danny, who yelled, "No!"

A long silence followed. "Make him come in," Fritz prodded.

Danny shrugged. "You didn't tell me what else to say."

"Aaah, nincompoop," Fritz snarled. "I have to do everything myself? Tell him—aah, never mind. You hold the girl. Think you can do that much, or you scared she'll beat you up?"

Danny glowered from underneath his jutting brows, but he sidled over to the window and took over Beth and the gun. She was relieved by the change. Danny held her rather gingerly by one arm, as if he was afraid she might explode, and he treated the revolver in much the same way, letting it dangle limply from his free hand.

"Not that way, stupid. Goddammit, she will beat you up. Hell, she's more of a man than you are; she ain't whimpered yet. I oughta get rid of you and take her for a partner."

Fritz grabbed Danny's hand with the gun in it and pushed both up against Beth's breast. He gave Beth a tight, mean smile while moving Danny's hand so that the tip of the revolver barrel caressed her breast in a long, lazy spiral. "How about it, sweetheart? Want to join up with a real man?"

He didn't wait for an answer.

"Okay, cowboy," he called through the half-open door, "you just do what we say, nobody's going to get hurt. Now listen good. First you throw your gun belt out where we can see it. Then you come out nice and slow, hands up, and walk into the post. Got it?"

The seconds crawled by while he waited for a response.

"You got ten seconds to make up your mind," Fritz called. "Then I'm going to start on your girl. I was just going to shoot her in the head, but now I'm figuring to start lower down and work my way up." He went on to describe in obscene detail exactly what he planned to do to Beth if Jerry didn't surrender.

The thump of a gun belt in the cleared space before the post interrupted Fritz's foul tirade. All three of the people at the front of the trading post stopped and waited with bated breath. A lean figure stepped out from the shelter of the rocks at the side of the post. Beth squeezed her eyes shut over silly, meaningless tears of relief. Then she forced herself to open them again, to take in what would be her last sight of Jerry alive.

Nothing happened.

Jerry walked slowly and deliberately toward the trading post, his hands over his head. When he reached the door, Fritz pulled it open and beckoned him in with a smirk.

Jerry's eyes went to the window where Beth stood like a statue in Danny's grip, the gun pressed into her side.

"No funny business, cowboy," Fritz warned. "Put your hands behind your back. Goddammit, Danny, don't we have any more rope?"

"You made me use it all on them two," Danny whined, jerking his head behind the counter.

"Well, cut me some of that up there." Fritz pointed at the

coils of rope hanging from the beams at the back of the store.

Danny shrugged, put down his gun on the windowsill, let go of Beth, and fumbled for the knife at his belt. The minute Beth was out of danger, Jerry threw himself at Danny, hitting him between the knees and thighs and knocking him back into a bag of flour in the corner. Danny reeled out of the flour sack in a cloud of white dust and launched himself back at Jerry.

Beth had been knocked to the ground when Danny was bowled over. She struggled up to her knees and saw the revolver on the windowsill, just at eye level. If only her hands were free! Fritz was reaching for the gun now, edging past Jerry and Danny as they wrestled in the center of the store. Beth tried to block his motion with her head. He laughed and slapped her face aside, filthy fingers spread over her mouth and nose. The stink of his hand made her feel sick. She bit down hard on a finger. He howled, snatched his hand away, and swung at her with the hand that held the gun. The shiny, blue-black barrel swung toward her and exploded against her head in a shower of sparks.

A ringing noise filled Beth's head and the post went black for a moment. When she came to again, the brief fight was over. Fritz was holding the gun on Jerry while Danny, whining and apologizing, tied his hands. A freshly cut coil of rope lay on the floor.

"Put 'em over there with the others," Fritz instructed Danny. Two hard hands grabbed Beth by the armpits and dragged her backward across the floor.

"I'd rather walk," she protested, twisting her head in a vain attempt to catch Danny's eye.

Fritz swore again. "Walk! Goddammit, Danny, why didn't you tie her feet? Hell, if I didn't think of everything, it wouldn't get done. And pick up that damn flour sack. It's

dry enough here without choking on a damn dust storm of
flour.'' He aimed a casual blow at Danny, who had bent
over to drag Jerry behind the counter. Danny straightened
and glowered at Fritz. Beth held her breath, hoping that
they'd quarrel. But Fritz stared his partner down, and Danny
returned to his task, grumbling under his breath.

''Danny do this, Danny do that,'' he muttered as he
dumped Jerry's inert form beside Beth. ''Pick up here, run
over there. I don't know if I'm a partner or a goddamn
slave.'' He ambled over and made a fuss about straightening
the flour sack, dumping the spilled flour back in with his
hands and making rather more of a mess than had been there
to start with. When he'd finished, he twisted the top of the
sack closed and sat down on it, arms folded, glowering at
Fritz.

Beth lay perfectly still, hardly daring to move for fear
Danny would remember that he hadn't tied her ankles. She
cherished every scrap of freedom she could retain. She
turned her head sideways by slow degrees until she could
look at Jerry. His face was bruised and purpling over one
eye, and his lip was split, but he closed the other eye and
gave her a slow wink. ''You oughta see the other fellow,''
he whispered.

''Oh, Jerry . . .'' Beth felt perilously near to tears. ''The
children?''

''Run off.''

''How?'' But Jerry's eyes were looking past her, at the
two other victims whom she'd nearly forgotten in the last
few minutes.

''Lily? Nathan?'' he whispered. ''You all right?''

From where he lay, Beth realized, he couldn't see the
movements of their breathing, or the gags that filled their
mouths. Dared she whisper a reassurance to him?

There was a tiny, metallic clink from the other side of the

post, where Fritz sat. The high counter shielded him from their sight. Beth held her breath as Danny got up from the flour sack, stretched, and ambled across the post. "Gimme some o' that," he whined.

"What'd you ever do to deserve it?" But the gurgling sounds suggested that a bottle was being passed from hand to hand.

If the high counter kept them from seeing Fritz and Danny, it must also shield them from their captors. Moving with infinite caution, Beth wriggled her shoulders up the rough wall of pine boards behind the counter, using her feet to brace herself and push. Once a splinter caught in the back of her blouse and tore the fabric and she froze, afraid the small sound would attract attention. But Fritz and Danny were too happy to notice by now, laughing over past exploits and renewing their partnership in the haze of whiskey.

When she was sitting up, she twisted her shoulders toward Jerry until her bound hands behind her were at a level with the blond woman's mouth. She felt behind her with fingers that were already going numb, caught hold of the filthy bandanna that had been used as a gag, and tugged it downward.

"Aah." A thankful gasp told her that her effort had succeeded. Beth leaned back against the wall. "I'm Lily Reiberg," the blonde whispered, "and this is my husband, Nathan."

Nathan was a short, wiry man with green eyes and black hair so curly that it was almost fuzzy. He nodded over his gag in Beth's direction. "And you must be Jerry's friend, Beth?" Lily went on. "He's told us about you."

Fritz and Danny were shouting out some kind of obscene drinking song now, rocking back and forth on the barrels and thumping their feet on the floor. Beth hoped the song had many verses; it was excellent cover for their talking.

"Pleased to meet you," Beth whispered back. "I wish it could have been under better circumstances."

Lily grinned through lips that were bruised at the corners from the tight gag. "I must apologize for our rude visitors. We weren't expecting company. Ah . . . friends of yours?"

Beth decided that she could get to like this spunky little blonde very much, even if she was delicate and petite and fluent in Navaho and a fantastic cook. "Not exactly." She scooted down the wall until her shoulders were propped between the wall and the floor and prepared to tell Lily exactly how they had gotten into this fix and how sorry she was to have involved her and Nathan.

"I hate to interrupt this hen party," Jerry murmured in Beth's ear, "but you reckon we could make some plans first, and dig up past history later?"

Beth wanted to shrug, but her shoulders hurt too much. "Plans? Like what?"

"Like getting at the knife in my back pocket."

"Oh!"

Jerry turned over so that his back was to her, and Beth wriggled around until she could just feel the handle of the knife with her fingertips. It took countless minutes of anguished maneuvering to grasp the knife and draw it out, but finally it clattered to the floor. All four of them held their breath for a minute and let out a silent prayer of thanks when the raucous singing resumed. But by then Beth had discovered a new problem.

Every time she tried to pick up the knife, it slipped out of her fingers. She could barely feel now, and her stupid fingers wouldn't grasp anything. "My hands are too numb to hold the knife." She swallowed hard to hold back tears of rage and disappointment.

Lily nudged Beth, and she painfully turned her body until she could see the other girl. Beyond her, Nathan was wriggling around, trying to sit up. "Nathan can wriggle around," Lily whispered, "if Jerry can cut him loose."

Beth relayed the message without asking how Nathan had communicated to Lily through his gag.

Under cover of the singing, Jerry picked up the knife and held it behind him while he inched his way around until he was lying at Beth's feet, with his face against the back of the counter. Nathan wriggled the same way until their bound hands met behind their backs. The look of agonized concentration on Jerry's face was Beth's only clue as to how the cutting was going.

Something hard and dark came flying over the countertop. It hit the floor beside Beth and exploded in a shower of glass splinters and whiskey fumes. She had closed her eyes and ducked instinctively when the missile came over the countertop. When she opened her eyes, Lily's cheek was cut and bleeding from a glass splinter, and there was broken glass all over the floor.

"Goddammit, Fritz," Danny complained, "what'd you have to go and do that for? You just made me clean up the flour, and now you got glass all over."

Fritz laughed. "Who cares? It'll all be the same in a few hours."

"Then why'd you make me clean up the flour?"

"Because I don't like a messy house!" Fritz roared. There was a smack of flesh on flesh and a series of crashing thumps. Then scrabbling sounds, like a man unsteadily hauling himself upright by holding on to whatever he could reach.

"Aw, Fritz, why'd ya knock me off the barrel?"

"Aah, shut up."

One of the men—Fritz?—began a tuneless whistling, while the other one paced up and down. Beth could just see his cracked leather boots each time he reached the door and turned around. She prayed he wouldn't take it into his head to glance around the high counter.

There was a quiet snapping sound and Jerry gave a sigh of relief. Beth had been so wrapped up in listening to the outlaws' wrangling, she'd forgotten to watch Nathan and Jerry. Now she saw that Nathan was free. He had jerked the gag loose from his mouth and now was moving his arms cautiously, slowly, stretching the cramp from them. There were ugly red marks scored deep into his wrists. Looking at them made Beth think about the pain in her own arms, so she looked away while Nathan took the knife from Jerry, sat up, and began working on the rope around Jerry's wrists.

The cracked leather boots paced up and down the small room with wearying monotony. Three steps away from them, pause, turn, three steps back, and he was standing inches from them. Then he would turn and pace back three steps and return.

"Cut it out," Fritz growled. "You're driving me crazy."

Beth silently seconded the motion.

"Well, I'm nervous," Danny whined. "Whyn't we get it over with now?"

"I told you. We got to wait till some Indians come down to trade."

Beth wondered why. Evidently Danny knew why, for he didn't question this dictum of Fritz's. He just whined and complained that he was tired of waiting and it could be three days before anybody showed up to trade at the post.

"It won't be," Fritz said. "Trust me. Wasn't I right when I said we had to wait outside the ranch and track these dudes? They had you scared so bad you was going to run clear back to Gallup and throw yourself in the sheriff's arms for protection.''

"You was scared, too," Danny whined. "If you hadn't of fallen off your horse, you'd've been in Gallup before me."

There was a crack as if Fritz had hit Danny with the back of his hand. "Shut up! And wasn't I right when we spotted them, and you wanted to trail them through the canyon, and I said they had to be heading here and we could get here first and wait for them? And wasn't I right when I said we could take out the dumb Jew trader here without no trouble?''

There was a strangled hissing sound from Nathan. Jerry, his hands free now, clapped one hand over Nathan's mouth while his face turned bright red with indignation. When Nathan had calmed down, the two men started working on freeing their legs.

"So I'm right about this, too," Fritz finished triumphantly. "We wait until the Indians show, then we can take care of these folks and do another little job for Hudson at the same time."

Hudson! Beth suppressed a gasp at this confirmation of her theory. She looked at Jerry, who nodded somberly while he sawed at the rope around his legs. He gave one overly energetic push and the knife slipped out of his hands and clattered against the floor.

"What's that!" Chair legs thudded down, booted feet approached. Jerry and Nathan had no time to get back in their original positions. They dropped down on the floor and lay like logs. Jerry had his back to the counter, so that they wouldn't notice his hands were unbound.

"They been wriggling around back here," Danny announced. He aimed a casual kick at Nathan. Beth winced in sympathy as the boot hit Nathan's shoulder.

"Aah, what the hell," Fritz growled. "Can't do much with their legs tied together."

"I never tied this one's legs." Danny stooped over Beth with a speculative smile. "Could have a little fun."

Beth felt sick as his whiskey-laden breath hit her. Her eyes slid sideways and met Nathan's. There was a mute plea on his face. His gag was off, and so was Lily's, and the handle of the knife could quite clearly be seen protruding from under his prostrate body. If Danny looked away from her, he was bound to notice that something was wrong. She forced herself to smile.

"Getting bored, big boy?"

"Hey-y." Danny's filthy hands fondled her breasts through the limp cotton blouse. "Feeling friendly, huh? I guess you don't get enough from the cowboy here."

Beth kept her lips stretched in a grimace that surely couldn't deceive anyone. "I can be real friendly," she murmured in what she hoped was a seductively husky whisper, "if you're nice to me." She pouted. "My hands hurt real bad."

Danny's smile was a horror of rotting, yellowed teeth. "We-ell, now. Reckon we could work something out."

"Yeah, bring her over," Fritz called. "We got to change that wire on her hands anyway."

"Why?" Danny pulled Beth to her feet and guided her out from behind the counter.

"Wire," Fritz said, "don't burn."

Beth couldn't quite follow that, but she wasn't going to argue with anything that got Danny's attention away from the men at this crucial moment.

She glanced surreptitiously around the interior of the trading post. Was there anything she could use for a weapon? A cleaver, an axe, anything hard and sharp?

Her survey was disappointing. She was standing in the

middle of the small open space where Danny had been pacing up and down. The rough plank floor was bordered on three sides by the tall wooden counters that left no place to run and hide, even if her hands had been free. She would just have to delay and distract these two until Jerry and Nathan got their bonds off.

Seated in front of her, Fritz tilted a wooden chair back against the counter and looked her up and down while Danny twisted the wire loose from her wrists. When Fritz reached out and began fondling her breasts, Beth bit her lip and concentrated fiercely on her surroundings, trying to ignore his sly glances at her face.

The countertop was bare except for a tin can half-full of loose tobacco and a box of papers. Behind the counter on two sides were shelves piled high with trade goods: canned tomatoes, sacks of flour and coffee, stacks of bright velveteen and calico. Nothing useful there, even if she could have reached over the high, wide countertops. Nothing that would cut Fritz Bauer's hands off at the wrists, for instance. He reached inside her blouse and her skin crawled with revulsion at the touch of his grimy hands. She stared upward, trying to think of something—anything—else.

The hooks suspended from the roof beams were more promising. Coils of rope, black iron cooking pots, tin kettles, tanned hides, cooking and gardening tools hung from hooks and nails all around the room. Beth's eye was caught by a gleaming heavy cleaver with a nice solid wooden handle. It was balanced across two nails in one of the wooden posts that supported the end of the counter, above Fritz's head and just tantalizingly out of reach.

"Hey! Look at me when I'm talking to you!" Fritz tweaked her nipple through the soft cloth of the blouse, bringing tears of pain to Beth's eyes.

"Talking? Is that what you call it?" she said in glacial tones.

"Watch your mouth." Fritz slapped her across the mouth and she tasted blood.

Danny gave a final twist and at last the wire dropped away from her wrists. She brought her hands before her with a feeling of inexpressible relief at loosening the strain on her arms and shoulders. Her fingers were totally numb at first, but as the circulation returned they began to tingle painfully.

When Fritz reached for her again she stepped back reflexively and bumped into Danny. He chortled and fastened grimy hands about her waist. "Looks like she likes me better," he gloated. "I'll go first this time."

"The hell you will!" Fritz rose and reached over Beth's shoulder to fasten a hand on Danny's throat. Danny let go of Beth and flattened himself against the counter on the opposite side of the post.

"Hey, now, Fritzie, I didn't mean nothing," he pleaded.

Fritz took the gun from his belt and waved it threateningly in Danny's face. "Out," he ordered. "You can come in and get yours when I'm finished with her."

Danny ducked, one arm over his head, and scuttled to the door. Before it had closed behind him Fritz put his gun down on the counter and reached for Beth again. As his hand closed over her shoulder she twisted away. His fingers caught on the cloth of her blouse and he pulled her around in a half circle until she was backed up against the counter. There was a ripping sound as the overstrained cloth parted. Fritz pushed her backward over the countertop and his free hand fumbled inside the torn garment, closing over her bare flesh.

An unreasoning horror seized Beth. She struggled uselessly as Fritz's face came down on hers. He thrust his tongue between her lips but was unable to force the barrier of her teeth clamped shut. "Open your mouth," he ordered. One hand was fumbling between her legs now.

Beth's fear vanished in a wave of clear, cold anger that left her feeling oddly detached, as if she were watching all this happening to someone else. One hand was pinned between her back and the countertop. Fritz was pressing against her now, and she could feel his hardness. He was forgetting to be careful as lust overwhelmed him.

Beth shifted her weight very slightly, so that her left foot was planted solidly on the floor. Fritz was pulling her skirts up, awkwardly, with one hand. When he had them raised almost to her waist, she jerked her right leg up sharply. He howled with pain and let go of her to clutch at his bruised genitals.

Beth reached up without looking and felt the handle of the cleaver solid and satisfying in her hand. She brought it down in a long, full-armed sweep that should have intersected Fritz's head, but he jumped away at the last minute. He clawed at her hand and she brought the cleaver down again. This time it hit the countertop with a solid thump, and something pale and wriggling jumped across the counter where the shiny blade fell. Fritz screeched and then screamed again as Jerry rose from behind the opposite counter, coming straight at him like an avenging fury. He bolted for the door and barely made it out ahead of Jerry.

Beth reached the door and slammed it before Jerry could pursue Fritz outside. She dropped the heavy bar into its slot and leaned against the closed door, gasping. Jerry grabbed her by the shoulders and crushed her against his chest. "Are you all right?" he demanded. "Are you—"

"I'm f-fine," Beth said shakily. "Ow! Don't hold so tight!"

Jerry released her and Beth tried to pull the torn edges of her blouse together. She peeped around the corner of the tall counter and saw that Nathan was working to free Lily. As soon as the ropes around her arms and legs were cut, Lily sat up and said perkily, "My, haven't we had an *interesting* morning!"

"May get more interesting yet," Nathan warned.

But their situation seemed pretty good. Fritz and Danny were securely locked out of the trading post and Fritz's gun was on this side of the barred door.

"What about Danny?" Jerry asked. "Doesn't he have a gun?"

Nathan's lips twitched. "They were arguing about that before you rode up. Seems he's afraid of them."

They all exploded in slightly hysterical laughter. Beth wiped the tears from her eyes and listened to Nathan apologizing for having let those two catch him off guard.

"Usually have the gun behind the counter, where I can stop anybody wants to make trouble," he explained. "But . . ."

"But his fool wife had borrowed it for target practice and didn't put it back in the right place," Lily interrupted. She hugged her husband. "It's all my fault, Nathan, we might as well say so right off. And I would *never* have forgiven myself if those—those—"

She was evidently unable to find a word suitable to express her contempt for the outlaws.

"Snakes," Beth suggested.

"Sonsabitches," was Jerry's contribution.

Lily gave a decisive nod. "Thank you. If those sonsabitches had killed you because of my carelessness. It would have haunted me for the rest of my life!"

She turned to Beth. "You cannot imagine how terrible it was," she said earnestly, "lying there behind the counter and listening to them plan how they were going to trap you and Jerry when you rode up here. Jerry's one of our oldest and dearest friends, and he's told us so much about you that

I felt as if I knew you already. I tell you, I was praying that they were wrong and that you weren't coming here at all, or that you'd notice something funny when you were outside.''

"Almost did," Jerry said. "Leastways, Riding Boy was trying to tell me something, but I was too tired to pay attention. Then he dragged his sister up on my horse and took off. I was about to light out after them when the party started.''

"Riding Boy!" Lily exclaimed. "You've found him? He's been lost for days, and Hosteen Chee has been just about going out of his mind. He's down here just about every day to inquire if we've heard any news of him.''

Jerry put one arm around Beth. "Well, Beth can tell you about that better than I can. If the kid gets home okay, Hosteen Chee will owe her a big debt.''

Lily looked Beth up and down again and nodded her head sharply. "I'll hear about that later," she promised. "But right now, I'm famished.''

"Me too," Beth said with surprise. It seemed ages since she had thought about food. It also seemed ages since she had had any. She thought with longing of a steaming hot cup of coffee, sweetened with condensed milk.

Lily crossed to the far counter and was reaching over the shelves for a can of tomatoes when she noticed something on the counter and gave a cry of surprise. "My goodness, Beth, whatever is that?''

She backed away from the red-and-white thing on the counter, pointing at it with a disgusted expression.

Jerry looked and started to laugh. "Well, I'll be damned! Hope you never get mad enough to settle our differences with a cleaver, missionary lady.''

It was one of Fritz Bauer's fingers.

"I don't think," Beth said faintly, "that I'm so hungry after all.''

Chapter Sixteen

$\mathcal{B}$eth felt as if she just might faint. "Go ahead," Lily advised. "It's all over, why deny yourself the pleasure?" But Beth settled for sitting down on the one wooden chair, feeling weak and dizzy, while Lily bustled around preparing an impromptu meal of canned tomatoes, canned peaches, and soda crackers. Setting the food out on the top of a barrel, she disappeared into the back room and came out triumphantly bearing a scrap of butter on a blue willow-pattern plate.

"Nathan built me a cold storage cellar," she confided to Beth. "Just a hole scraped into the dirt back of the post, really, where the building backs up into the hill. But it's real convenient having it right inside where I can get at things."

"Especially today," Beth agreed. She, for one, felt absolutely no desire to go outside until they were sure that Fritz and Danny had given up and left.

Jerry and Nathan hoisted themselves up to sit on the high countertop, while Lily perched on another barrel and tried to persuade Beth to nibble a cracker.

Their situation seemed so good, compared with the stark terror of a few minutes ago, that they were all silly and light-headed with relief. Lily and Nathan told competing versions of their courtship. Lily's version was that she had inherited a trading post and didn't know till she got out to Blue Mesa that she'd also inherited her father's stubborn assistant, who refused to move out. "So, after a season with this fellow ruining my reputation, what could I do but marry him?" she asked.

Nathan wrinkled his nose. "You missed a few points, *schatzie*. Truth is, I felt honor bound to stick around and help this empty-headed bit of fluff out of all the scrapes she was bound to get into." He illustrated his point with some stories that had Lily red in the face and the others giggling.

One of Nathan's stories reminded Beth of something that had happened on her father's thoroughbred farm, and before long she was enmeshed in a complicated anecdote involving a black racehorse, a diamond necklace, and her own debu-tante ball—a last concession to her father before she went to teachers' college, though she left that part out of the story.

Jerry sat a little to one side, watching her animated face as she waved long, shapely fingers to emphasize one point or another. Diamonds, he thought. Racehorses. What was this girl doing in Indian territory, slaving away for a mission teacher's pittance? Wearing one of her old wash dresses to parties? Was it some kind of complicated masquerade?

He had never felt more alien from the world of wealth and privilege that Beth described. She got so caught up in her story that she was completely unaware of how much she was revealing about her background. A girl like that, Jerry thought, she might come out west for a season to play at being poor, but it wouldn't last. Yes, and while she was playing she might prefer the poor cowboy to the banker. Why not? It cost her nothing—it was only a game. But she wouldn't stick it out.

His heart twisted as he watched her telling her story. The

girl he'd always dreamed of and waited for, and when she finally appeared, she was not for him. The carefree laughter of the other three grated painfully on his nerves.

"Ain't you celebrating a little too soon?" he broke in on the conversation. "We're not free yet." He jerked his head toward the window. "Nothing to say those two ain't still hiding outside."

"Yes, but I don't think they can give us any serious trouble," Nathan said. "We've got food and some water. These walls are too thick to shoot through. I saw to that myself when we had to build the new post. Besides, we've got Fritz's revolver."

"And he's got my gun belt," Jerry pointed out.

Nathan moved quickly away from the window.

"My good curtains," Lily mourned the ripped calico. "Nathan, if I stitch them up real quick, maybe we could hang them again. I don't like bare windows, especially if there are sonsabitches outside waiting to get us."

"I wish you wouldn't teach her new words, Jerry," Nathan said with resignation. "You know she doesn't have any sense about what she says." He ruffled his wife's yellow hair fondly. "And no, *schatzie*, this is not a good time to be playing around with window decorations. What if they decide to take a shot in at the window?"

"Ha!" Lily disputed him immediately. "Didn't you hear what Jerry and Beth said? Jerry knows that Fritz Bauer. He's wanted in Texas. He won't dare hang around when he knows all of us could turn him in. They'll be hightailing it for Mexico."

"Maybe they should be," Nathan said, "but they aren't. I can see them from the window. They're laying up behind the rocks at the corner, but every once in a while one of them sticks his head up." He hefted the trading post revolver. Lily had absentmindedly laid it among a stack of dress goods when she'd finished her target practice, giving Nathan a nasty shock when the two outlaws had swaggered into his post and he'd reached into the drawer under the counter only to find it empty. Nathan felt much happier now that the revolver rested in his hand. Now he raised it toward the window. "Those heads popping up and down would make fine target practice," he said wistfully.

"Nathan Reiberg, you get away from that window!" Lily screeched. "What do you think Fritz and Danny will be doing while you stick your fat head up to get a shot at them? I didn't marry you for the pleasure of watching bullets bounce off your thick skull!"

She shooed Nathan back from the window while Jerry gave a meditative nod. "Lily's got a point," he said. "We got this far without anybody getting hurt. Maybe they've had about enough."

He opened the window a crack. "Hey, you guys," he shouted, "you better leave before somebody comes to trade. You go peaceful now, we'll forget we ever saw you."

A burst of raucous laughter greeted this proposition. "Hey, dummy, all we're waiting for is a couple of customers," Fritz called back.

Jerry shook his head. "Loco," he muttered.

"Yeah," Danny chimed in, "all we need is one dead Indian to set the scene. Too bad you couldn't fight them all off when they burned down the post last night!"

Jerry swung the casement shut on the laughter that followed this statement.

"So," he said to no one in particular. His face had changed subtly, looking harder and older, with the laughter lines around his eyes and mouth erased. Beth felt more afraid when she looked at him than when Fritz and Danny were in the post. "So that's their game. Do a good turn for

Lawrence Hudson and get rid of the evidence at the same time.''

Beth shook her head. "I don't understand."

"You know what Fritz and Danny are wanted for in Texas," Jerry said slowly.

"Armed robbery."

"And murder. And"—he dropped the last word slowly, reluctantly, like a stone breaking the ice on a frozen pool—"arson."

Beth's mind shattered with the word. She shook her head violently, and her long black braid whipped back and forth. "No." She did not want to understand. But she could not forget Jerry's story of the shoot-out in El Paso that had sent Fritz and Danny on the run: the wounded men, the saloon sent up in flames merely as a diversion. Pictures of crackling flames filled her mind. She could almost smell the smoke, feel her skin blistering.

Nathan nodded. "They're going to burn down the post. But they're going to wait till somebody comes to trade. Figure a few dead Navahos outside will add to the picture of Indian trouble in this area. They get rid of us, Hudson pays them for another job, everybody's happy. Neat solution." The savage sarcasm in his voice startled Beth, and she welcomed it, anything to distract her from those too vivid pictures.

Nathan went over to the barrel where Lily perched and put his arm around her. "It's all my fault," he said. "I should have sent you back east when you came out here, all bright and perky in your lace dress, to run your trading post all by yourself. You could be sitting in some nice big house with lace curtains and velvet sofas right now, drinking tea and counting your dividends."

Lily put her arms around Nathan's neck and pulled him

down to her for a fierce, lingering kiss. "Don't you know that the only place I want to be is with you?"

Beth looked across the room and met Jerry's eyes. "That goes for me, too," he said quietly. "I shouldn't have let you come along on this crazy excursion. You don't belong here, anyway."

Beth deliberately ignored the twinge of pain his last statement caused her. He hadn't meant it that way—he was only worried for her. And there was only one possible answer to that—the one Lily gave Nathan. But something about Jerry's stillness prevented her from getting up and going to him. "It was my excursion," she reminded him, "and I shouldn't have let you come along."

Lily wiped her eyes and released Nathan with a shaky laugh. "Anyhow, it's all my fault, if we're sharing out blame. . . . When we built the new post, Nathan was going to make it of adobe like Dad's old place, but no, I had to have log walls and a plank floor." Her lips trembled slightly. "All those weeks you spent cutting down trees and hauling logs and sawing planks, Nathan, and soon it's all . . . going . . . to go up in smoke." Her voice quavered and she broke off, reaching blindly for Nathan's hand.

Somehow, nobody felt much like talking after that. Jerry and Nathan, discussing the matter in low voices, concluded that they had best keep watch on the rocks in the hope that Fritz or Danny would break cover long enough for one of them to get a clear shot. They opened the window slowly, an inch at a time, and took up positions on either side of it.

The morning dragged on interminably. It was hot and stuffy inside the cramped, closed-in trading post, but nobody complained about the heat. Lily foraged around among the trade goods, found a needle and thread, and offered them to Beth to patch her blouse together. It seemed a pointless activity when they were probably not going to survive the day, but as Lily said, they might as well keep busy.

Beth retreated behind a counter with a length of velveteen wrapped around her and squatted on the plank floor, stabbing the needle through the blouse fabric and scowling at the resulting tangle of stitches. After watching her for a few minutes Lily took the blouse away and snipped away the rat's nest of thread and knots that Beth had created. She drew the torn edges together with neat, precise stitches.

"I never learned to sew," Beth confessed. She felt grubby and clumsy next to Lily's delicate femininity.

"But you can ride and shoot. That's more useful out here," Lily said.

"It would be a lot more useful," Beth said gloomily, "if I had Jerry's rifle in here." She'd left the rifle slung to the saddle of Jerry's horse; presumably it was now halfway into the depths of the reservation with Riding Boy and Wind Flower. At least they were safe! She tried to recapture the sensation of relief she'd felt on hearing that news, but it was hard to think about anything besides the men waiting outside to kill them. "Thank you, Lily."

She took the neatly mended blouse and wriggled into it. "I wish we could spare water to wash it," Lily said regretfully, "but I guess we'd better save whatever water we have in case . . ."

"Yes." Beth knew they should be making intelligent plans for what to do when Fritz and Danny fired the trading post, but fear and exhaustion combined to paralyze her. Besides, their choices didn't seem very good. They could stay in the post and be burned to death, or run out—assuming Fritz and Danny hadn't blocked the doors—and be shot.

Or worse. She remembered Fritz's hands groping inside her clothes, and her skin crawled with revulsion. She stood up abruptly and went to the corner where Jerry stood on one side of the window. She leaned her forehead against his back, feeling the warmth of breath and bone and muscle. What a waste, what a stupid waste! "Jerry?" she murmured. "If you don't get them before they start the fire?"

"Yes?"

"I . . . don't want to be burned." It was as close as she could come to making the request that he shoot her rather than let the fire—or Fritz—get her.

Jerry's hand gripped hers so tight she thought her bones would break. "You won't. You won't die. I'll work something out."

"Don't worry," Nathan quipped from the other side of the window. "My mother always said I was born to be hanged. I wouldn't have the nerve to die in a fire and disappoint her."

Beth forced herself to smile. "Samuel Johnson says the prospect of being hanged concentrates a man's mind wonderfully."

Jerry squeezed her hand again. "Right. And we're all going to get out of this, find the sheriff, and give Fritz and Danny boy a little something to concentrate on. Just as soon as I figure out how. . . ."

Lily had returned to her barrel-top perch, where she was now busily mending the torn curtains. Her yellow head shone all the brighter for being bent over a sea of yellow-flowered calico. "Cellar," she said.

"Cellar?" Nathan repeated.

"Where we store the milk and butter—when there is any."

Nathan shook his head. "*Schatzie,* that's not even big enough to hide you in. Besides, the smoke'd likely still get you."

"I know that," Lily said impatiently. "My goodness, Nathan Reiberg, do you think I'd hide in the cellar, anyway, knowing all my friends are being burnt up just outside? But remember when you expanded it last year? And you said you couldn't dig it any bigger because when you went down you hit solid rock and if you went up you'd weaken the soil and the whole thing would cave in on us?''

Nathan nodded.

"Well," Lily said, "if it caved in, we could get out back while they're busy shooting and lighting fires and all up front.''

Light dawned on Nathan's face. "Damned if you ain't right!" Leaving his post, he plucked Lily off the barrel by the waist, spun her around, and kissed her two or three times. "You take the gun," he said. "You and Beth can keep watch by the window. Jerry and me got some digging to do." He thrust the store revolver into her hand and clambered on top of the barrel himself to reach for a shovel that hung from wire loops along one of the heavy roof beams. He thrust a short hoe into Jerry's hands and beckoned him into the back room.

"Oh, Lily?" Nathan's curly head popped up around the door frame. "If you see anything, don't aim. Okay? Just stick the barrel out the window and pull the trigger. As long as you got the right end pointing out the window, I don't *think* you can hit any of us." He chuckled and disappeared again.

"Wise guy," Lily said without rancor. "Just because I wasn't a very good shot when I came out west.''

Nathan's head appeared again. "Hah! Ask her sometime how I got this nick in my ear when she was supposed to be at target practice." He pushed his frizzy hair aside to reveal a white crease that gave his left ear a distinct point, like a leprechaun's. "The Indians used to call her Woman Who Sprays Bullets Like a Goose Sprays Sh—''

Lily started to wave the revolver around and Nathan

ducked back behind the door, laughing too hard to finish the sentence.

"I'm a better shot now," Lily said, resting the revolver barrel on the windowsill and eyeing Beth as if she expected her to challenge this statement. "Some better, anyway. . . ."

"It sounds as if you two had a stormy courtship," Beth said.

Lily giggled. "Sometime I'll tell you all *my* stories. . . . Not when Nathan's listening, though." She squinted out the window. "Do you think they're still there?"

"Yes." Beth hefted Fritz's gun and wished she could take a few sighting shots, just to get the feel of it.

The sun rose higher and Beth's eyes began to water from squinting interminably at the bright rocks. Sometimes her vision wavered with the strain and the whole scene seemed to quiver as if under water. Water! she thought with longing. The knowledge that they had to ration what little they had to throw on the fire gave her a raging thirst which canned tomatoes and peaches could not assuage.

Muffled thumps and curses from the back room did little to calm her nerves. It sounded as if Jerry and Nathan were finding it hard to dig through and enlarge the cellar. She longed to go back and see how they were doing but dared not leave her post.

"I guess you don't get much business here," she said to Lily. It must be well past noon by now, and there had been no sign of anybody coming down the steep mountain path that she watched alternately with the rocks.

Lily frowned in puzzlement. "More than this, usually. . . . This is a good location. Most of Hosteen Chee's people graze their sheep here all summer. Why, some days I can't get my housework done for all the women coming in and wanting to pick out dress lengths for new skirts and blouses! I don't understand why nobody's come yet."

Nathan came around the counter. Sweat was dripping from his forehead and dampening the curly black hair on his head and forearms, and his shirt was damp and grubby. He leaned against the counter, taking deep breaths.

"Jerry's spelling me," he said. "Gets kinda short of air down there."

"How's it going?" Lily asked.

He shook his head. "A few problems. . . . Don't you worry, though. We'll get there."

"What kind of problems?"

"Rock," Nathan said reluctantly. "Can't expand up where I wanted to, we hit a big slab of rock. Don't worry, though. We'll work around it."

"If we have time," Beth murmured. "Why don't they go ahead and fire the post? They must know we'll think of something if they leave us in here long enough!"

"I guess they really want to set the scene with a few dead Navahos," Nathan said. "Indians are kind of superstitious folks, you know; they don't like trading at a post that's going up in flames. Might be bad for business if they set the fire too early."

He kissed Lily on the forehead. "I'd better get back to work. Try not to shoot yourself in the foot, *schatzie,* and keep praying for business to be as bad this afternoon as it was this morning. This is one day I could stand to do without customers!" He winked and crawled back behind the counter.

"Maybe," Lily said hopefully, "even if somebody does come to trade soon, it'll be someone they couldn't possibly accuse of killing us. Like Red Singer's wife and her two babies."

"In which case," Beth said, sighting on the crack be-

tween two rocks where she kept hoping to see a head appear,
"they'll probably kill them quietly and wait for someone
else."

That put an end to that line of conversation, and Beth was
sorry she'd said it. The waiting time was even longer now
that they'd run out of things to talk about. The minutes
seemed to crawl by while Jerry and Nathan thumped and
sweated and cursed in the narrow store.

When Jerry came out to take a breather, he reported that
they had managed to tunnel around the rock outcropping.
The question now was whether they would hit more rock
when they dug upward again to break through the soil behind the trading post. They didn't want to make the attempt
ahead of time for fear Fritz and Danny would notice something. But when they did try to break out, there would be no
second chances.

"Going to take careful timing," Jerry summed up. "If
you girls see anybody coming down the mountain path,
you fire a shot to warn them. If they come up the other
way . . ." He shrugged. Their first warning then would be
when Fritz and Danny attacked the unsuspecting Indians on
their way to the trading post.

In either case, once Jerry and Nathan heard the shooting,
they would dig furiously. If they didn't hit rock, and if the
earth didn't cave in so fast that it buried them, then they
should all be able to get out while Fritz and Danny were
busy at the front of the post. Then, if Nathan's horses were
still in the back corral, they might be able to get away entirely.

A lot of ifs, Beth thought. "Best if we wait till dark," she
said aloud. "They'd be less likely to notice us then."

Jerry nodded. "If we can. Kind of funny nobody's
showed up yet."

He took over from Lily at the window, standing on the

opposite side from Beth. Their free hands met below the casement. His warm, firm grasp was like a lifeline that she could hold on to. Beth leaned her head against the window frame and shut her eyes for just a minute. She was so weary of this interminable watch!

As the first long shadows of the mountains began to creep across the clearing, she began to hope. Miraculously, they had passed an entire day without anyone coming to the trading post. Perhaps they would be able to escape in darkness after all.

"I better get back to the digging," Jerry said, confirming her unspoken thought.

It was a physical pain, sharp and nearly intolerable, to let go of his hand. She allowed herself the luxury of one glance at his tall back and lean hips as he walked across the floor to resume his digging task.

From the corner of her eye she saw a flicker of movement at the near side of the rock closest to the trading post. She swung back to the window and fired without taking time to aim, fired again, and knew she was too late.

A moment later and it was too late indeed. She could hear surreptitious scraping sounds along the wall of the trading post. Which of the outlaws had risked himself to dash across the few feet of clear space? Beth could have cried with disappointment and frustration. So many hours of watching, and she had failed them all when the time came.

"Lily," she said, her voice low to keep the man outside from hearing, "I missed. He's at the wall around the corner. Is there any chink in the wall there?"

Lily shook her head. Nathan had built the trading post well and solidly.

"Guess they're not going to wait for their dead Indians," she said as Nathan emerged from the cellar. "Should we start digging?"

Nathan shook his head. "Sounds like he's working his way around the post. Don't want to start a cave-in while he can see it."

A moment later a pungent aroma filled Beth's nostrils. She sneezed and waved her hands in front of her face to clear away the fumes that were making her eyes sting. It seemed to be coming from the half inch of open space between the casement window and the frame.

"Kerosene," Jerry said, sniffing the air. "Must have brought it with them. What every well-equipped arsonist needs!" He laughed without humor.

Nathan nodded. "If they're pouring it all around the post . . . I don't know how far away from the building we'll be when we break through, you know? Could be a tad difficult."

That, Beth thought, had to be the understatement of the year. She pictured the sheet of flames rising around the post, engulfing them all.

"The water," Lily said suddenly. She moved toward the bucket that contained their precious supply. "We should all soak our clothes and tie rags over our mouths." She took a bolt of bright blue velveteen from the shelf and began cutting it into wide strips.

At least it was something positive to do. It seemed to Beth that she had been telling herself that all day. She dipped her strip of velveteen in the bucket and stood passively while Jerry wielded the tin dipper to pour streams of tepid water over her head and shoulders.

The small supply of water was used up all too soon, and they helped each other adjust the dampened masks of blue velveteen. Lily looked them over and giggled. "We look like a desperate gang. I'm glad I don't have to meet us on a dark night!"

Then there was nothing to do but huddle by the entrance

to the cold store while Nathan wriggled down and forward with the shovel, ready to strike upward into the earthen ceiling with the blows that would either open the way to freedom or bury him under the fallen rocks and dirt. Beth waited by the window until the last minute, hoping that one of the outlaws would grow careless and expose himself to her fire. Even in the dusk, she promised herself, this time she would not miss.

The smell of kerosene was stronger now. The fumes made Beth giddy and confused her. There seemed to be a kind of distant humming in her ears. She shook her head, but the humming sound only grew louder and stronger. "Listen!" Lily held up one hand.

"Do you hear it, too?" Beth asked.

Lily nodded.

Nathan inched his way backward out of the cold store. "I felt the ground shaking."

Jerry put his arm around Beth's waist and held her close to him. Their water-soaked clothing clung to them, and little droplets formed where their bodies met, rolling down and falling from the soggy hem of Beth's skirt with a rhythmic splash, splash, *splat!* The tiny rhythm of the dropping water blended with the distant thrumming. The sound reminded her of a sunlit morning at home when she'd watched her father and the stable lads exercising a dozen mounts at once.

"Horses!" she said.

"Hoofbeats," Nathan said at the same time. They looked at each other and laughed nervously.

Now Beth could hear a shrill yipping sound mixed with the drumming hoofbeats. "What's that other noise?" she asked Nathan.

He turned to his wife. "How about it, Sun Hair? Ever hear a Navaho song like that before?"

Lily shook her head, frowning. A lock of fair hair fell over her forehead and she tugged at it as she concentrated. "Sounds a little like the Night Chant," she said. "Not quite right, though."

"Ahu-u-u! Ahu! Ah-ah-ah-hu!" came the wailing sound, quite close now.

Lily shivered. "No," she said with finality, "I've never heard anything like that before. And I don't want to! It's downright eerie!"

There was a spatter of rifle fire outside the post and Beth jumped. "We should have been shooting our guns," she accused herself. "We didn't warn them."

"Those shots came from up on the mountain path," Jerry contradicted her. He ran across the cabin and pressed his face to the windowpane.

"Jerry! Get back!" Beth shrieked. She ran after him and tugged on his arm, terrified that Fritz or Danny would shoot through the window.

He acceded reluctantly to her tug, grinning. "I think," he told Beth, "the U.S. Cavalry just came to the rescue.

"So to speak," he amended a moment later as a tide of horses bearing half-naked, fearsomely painted warriors swept into the clearing.

❦ Chapter Seventeen

*H*eedless of danger, Beth pressed her face to the window. In the gathering dusk she could just make out the figures of the Indians who came galloping down the mountain path, yipping shrilly and letting off their rifles as they came.

In the forefront of the war party was a very old, wrinkled man whose long gray braids fluttered crazily in the wind as he charged down on the rocks where Fritz and Danny hid, shouting a war cry and brandishing a long black lance decorated with tattered eagle feathers. A black-painted leather shield decorated with zigzag white lightning designs hung around his neck, bouncing from side to side as he rode.

There was a spatter of gunfire from behind the rock, marked by brief explosions of sparks from Fritz's gun. The old chief fell backward in his saddle and was lost to Beth's view as other warriors swept past him. These younger men were armed less traditionally with rifles.

Beth's hands twitched with longing for the shiny new Krag carbine carried by a young man who seemed to have taken over the lead from the fallen chief. He fired from horseback at the cleft between the two rocks. There was a cry of pain from behind the rocks and Fritz rose into view, clutching at his chest, then spun around and fell backward across the rock.

"Oh, good! Get him! Get him!" Beth was dancing up and down with excitement when Jerry's big hand brushed her away from the window.

"Get your face out of there before you get hurt," he ordered her, usurping her place and pressing his own face to the glass. Behind him, Nathan and Lily crowded to look.

The firing from behind the rock continued sporadically for a few minutes.

"Danny must have gotten over his fear of guns," Lily murmured.

Jerry's hand caressed her golden curls in an absentminded gesture. "Don't worry," he said. "Who's that?"

He pointed back behind the rock, where a single warrior, his face fearsomely smeared with red and yellow paint in zigzag streaks, crept from boulder to boulder on the hillside with Hosteen Chee's eagle-feathered lance in his hand.

"Long Spear," Lily identified the figure, and Jerry laughed.

"Reckon the name suits him, then. . . ."

"It doesn't refer to his weapons of war," Lily said with an impish grin. "At least, that's not what the Navaho girls say. They say—"

"All right, Lily," Nathan interrupted. "I guess we can all figure it out." He rolled his eyes at Beth with a mock sigh. "Never will civilize her," he muttered.

They fell silent with tension as Long Spear crept up on his unseen foe. He was standing only a few feet above the large rock when his face changed.

"Goddamn murderin' savage!" They heard the yell, saw the sparks as Danny's gun went off. Long Spear staggered

back, recovered himself, and fell forward still holding the
lance. Beth held her breath when he disappeared from view
behind the rock.

A moment later the young men on their horses were all
around the rock. Something waved high in their midst—
the eagle feathers bound to the tip of Hosteen Chee's
lance. The tips of the feathers were dark now, as if they'd
been dabbled in blood. And there was Long Spear, holding his shoulder, obviously in pain and just as obviously
determined not to show it as he limped out to greet his
admiring comrades.

"Whoo-ee!" Jerry emitted a high-pitched yell that startled Beth. Wheeling away from the window, he grabbed
Lily around the waist and kissed her. "We made it!"

"Sounds to me like our friends the Navahos made it,"
Nathan remarked. He shook hands with Beth, his face
grave, but there was a twinkle in his eye. "Can't say that we
were much help to them. Lily, you want to let down the bar
and welcome our good friends into the post?"

Lily had her arms around Jerry's neck, squealing with excitement as he swung her around with her feet off the floor.
Nathan sighed. "Guess I'll have to do everything myself
. . . as usual!"

Beth doubted that either Jerry or Lily heard his teasing
comment. They were too excited. She stood by the window,
feeling awkward and not sure what to do with herself, while
Nathan wrestled with the heavy bar that kept the door
closed.

The tall, bronzed men came crowding into the store as
soon as Nathan swung open the door. Jerry put Lily down
and she ran to greet them, fussing over Long Spear and
insisting on washing and bandaging his wound at once.
The other men came in slowly, smiling but serious. They
touched Jerry's and Nathan's hands with brief greetings.

"Ahalani."

"Ahalani," Nathan responded. *"Ukehe."*

The low-voiced murmur of Navaho words, with Lily's bright voice twining in and out like the chirping of a happy bird, only added to Beth's sense of unreality. She felt as if she were watching a magic lantern show—as if she weren't quite there. Of course, she didn't belong there the way the other three did. She couldn't even understand what they were saying.

The memory of Jerry and Lily's exuberant kiss was a dull ache inside her. Of course it was just the excitement of the moment—but she wished he had turned to her instead of Lily.

She wished he would come to her side now, to tell her what they were talking about. She hadn't even realized he spoke Navaho. But he was deep in conversation with the gray-haired warrior. That must be Hosteen Chee. How had he escaped unhurt? Straining to get some meaning from the unfamiliar faces and words, Beth only felt more and more out of place.

Lily had lit a lamp and the golden light shone on bronze skins gleaming with grease and paint, long black braids tied with ribbons, black-and-gray-and-red-striped blankets casually draped over the wearers' shoulders. While Lily fussed over Long Spear's shoulder, an older man was gravely smearing his face with charcoal. What was that about? For that matter, what was any of this about?

Plucking up courage, she made her way through a gap in the crowd and boldly took Jerry's arm. He looked at her with surprise, as if he had momentarily forgotten her existence.

"What happened?" she demanded. "Where are Fritz and Danny?"

"Dead."

Beth's knees felt weak with relief. Until that moment she had not felt truly safe.

"Then . . . everything's going to be all right?"

"I guess. I don't know."

Beth felt as if he were withdrawing from her into some secret world where she could not follow him. It must be only her imagination. She was tired, she told herself, and her nerves were overstrained. They were all tired. She slipped one arm about Jerry's waist and leaned against his shoulder. "As long as we're together," she murmured, "it's all right."

"Yeah." Very gently, Jerry disengaged himself. "As long as . . . Beth. We got to talk."

"What's wrong?"

Her voice was getting shrill, the Indians turned to stare at them. Jerry raised his hand. "Hush! Lily's speaking."

Nathan hoisted his diminutive wife onto the tall countertop. She stood above the Navahos, looking like a bedraggled fashion doll in her damp lace blouse and soggy skirt, and said a few words in Navaho.

"She's thanking them for coming to our rescue," Jerry interpreted, "and inviting everybody to dinner."

"Yes, but what *happened*?"

Before Jerry could answer, Lily had jumped down from the counter and pushed her way over to them. Her fair hair was hanging loose in damp ringlets and her piquant little face was alight with excitement. "Beth, can you help me? We've got to set out food for all these folks. Start by opening the canned tomatoes, I guess, and Jerry, if you'd start a fire for coffee . . . Excuse me, Long Spear, I need to get at that cracker barrel."

Lily bustled around her little domain, capably setting out food for twenty men on the counter, and Beth followed her around while following her orders.

"Could you reach me that case of strawberry jam?" Lily asked. "I know we don't have bread to spread it on, but that's all right, they love sweet things. Just hand out spoons all around."

After Beth had found the spoons in a drawer full of bent nails, string, and other necessities, she played truant from Lily. It was too painful to watch Jerry avoiding her in the cramped space of the store. She went outside and saw Nathan squatting by a small fire. Perhaps he would tell her how the Indians had come so opportunely to their rescue—that would give her something to think about, anyway.

Nathan was busy patting out flat loaves of bread and frying them on a three-legged iron skillet that sat in the coals. "Squaw work," he explained with a grin. "Want to take over?"

"Only if you'll tell me what's going on." Beth gestured at the dark faces around them, the horses penned in the corral. "Where did all these people come from? How did they know we were in trouble?"

The smile faded from Nathan's face. "Well, I don't rightly know yet. Those two thugs of Hudson's are dead, I know that, and I asked Hosteen Chee how he knew to come help us and he said to wait until the bread was ready. He wants to make a speech and tell us all about the victory in old-time Indian fashion, praising everybody, and I reckon he's entitled to do it that way if he wants to."

"Will you," Beth asked carefully, "be able to translate the speech? While he's talking?"

Nathan shook his head. "I'll get the gist of it, though, and then I can tell you later. Now, about this bread . . ."

"No translation, no bread making," said Beth decisively. She walked on, ignoring Nathan's cry of dismay.

She was just a few steps past the fire when a small hand slid into her own. Startled, Beth looked down and saw tiny

Wind Flower looking up at her with wide, delighted black eyes.

"Wind Flower!" She knelt and hugged the little girl. "I'm so glad you're safe. . . . And oh dear, I wish you could tell me all about it." She couldn't bring herself to let go, so she picked Wind Flower up and settled her on one hip. The little girl's delicate bones were no weight at all.

"*I* can translate," piped up a confident little voice from her other side.

Beth looked down and Riding Boy thrust his chest out, thumped himself on the breast bone, and did a little swaggering dance. The tattered shirt and pants supplied by the missionaries had disappeared now; he wore nothing but some cut-down leggings and a few swipes of ochre paint.

"I know everything that happened," Riding Boy boasted. "I would tell you now, but it is better to let my grandfather speak first. Besides, a great warrior does not praise his own deeds. So I will let him tell you how I saved the post. I can tell you everything exactly as he says it."

"Riding Boy," Beth said, "you're my friend for life. How would you like some canned peaches while we're waiting for the speeches to start?" She didn't intend to let the kid out of her sight until he came through with the promised translation.

Riding Boy ducked his head and grinned. "That is good. I am not tall enough to reach up to the counter with the men. They are getting all the good food."

"We'll fix that," Beth promised. Still carrying Wind Flower and holding Riding Boy's hand, she made a quick raid into the trading post and came away with a random assortment of goodies for the three of them to munch on while they waited.

They settled themselves on a flat rock just to one side of

the trading post door and Beth spread out the feast. Riding Boy and Wind Flower helped themselves to beans, stewed tomatoes, and strawberry jam with relish, but Riding Boy spat out the tinned sardines after one bite and politely said that he would leave the dead fish for Beth, since white people evidently liked these things. ''White people spoil good food with salt,'' he confided, stirring a spoonful of strawberry jam into the beans.

They had almost finished their feast when Nathan rose, clapped his hands for silence, and brought out a tin trunk for Hosteen Chee to stand upon. He had gotten his lance back to use as a staff. Leaning the butt of his long black lance on the ground, he began a long, quavering oration.

''Now he is telling about our ancestors of the Salt clan,'' Riding Boy informed her.

It seemed to Beth, as Riding Boy labored through a word-for-word translation, that Hosteen Chee had far too many ancestors and that they had all performed far too many great deeds of war.

After a lengthy peroration, Hosteen Chee paused for breath, threw back his shoulders, and began speaking in a quieter tone of voice.

''Now he is telling about you,'' Riding Boy said.

''Me?'' Beth was startled.

Riding Boy picked up the translation again as Chee recounted how his grandchildren had been stolen by the white eyes while he was far away in the south. They would have been taken from their clan and family to follow the white man's road; they would have forgotten how to live as the People lived, and they would not have known of their great ancestors whose deeds he had just recounted. But a woman of the white tribe who was as brave as a warrior had brought his children back. She was pursued on the trail by evil men of her own tribe and barely managed to reach the Blue Mesa trading post in safety.

As Hosteen Chee went on, he pointed at Beth and the dark faces gathered around the fire turned to inspect her. She wiped a smear of strawberry jam off the corner of her mouth and sat up very straight between the two children, feeling remarkably foolish. "Jerry was there, too," she muttered to Riding Boy. "Why doesn't your grandfather point at him for a change?"

"Hush," Riding Boy commanded her sternly. "Show respect."

Once again Hosteen Chee's tone changed, and now Riding Boy's skinny little chest expanded until Beth thought he would burst open from pride. "Now he is telling about how I rode away from the trading post to get the men of my clan and bring them to the rescue."

"You did that? Oh, Riding Boy!" Beth impulsively hugged the boy until he wriggled out of her embrace. "You saved us!"

"It is not good for a warrior to boast of his own deeds," Riding Boy reproved her. "Listen to my grandfather, he is telling how I was *very* brave and rode *very* fast. He says if it were not for me, all the white people in the trading post would be dead. He says . . ." He paused and frowned.

"What is he saying now?" Beth nudged him.

"Oh, just talk about this useless girl." Riding Boy reached around Beth and scuffed the top of Wind Flower's head. She giggled and ducked under Beth's arm. "He is saying how I was very clever to leave her here, so that she could warn the people who came to trade and turn them back."

"That little thing stayed here all alone?" Beth gasped.

Riding Boy pouted, seeing some of Beth's attention being diverted from its rightful object. "Yes, but she would never have thought of it by herself. I had to tell her what to do. She is only a stupid girl, after all.''

"Someday," Beth said thoughtfully, "we are going to have a long talk about the relative stupidity of boys and girls, Riding Boy. What's your grandfather saying now?''

"Oh, just a bunch of stuff about gathering the young warriors, and how he had to show them how to paint their shields because they have never been on the war path since Kit Carson made peace, and they are all stupid anyway and couldn't do anything without their bang-bang guns, and it's a good thing he was in front because he knew the prayers to sing over his shield and he was protected with the sanctified pollen and the bad men's bullets bounced off his shield and did no harm," Riding Boy summarized in one breath. He listened for a moment longer.

"Oh, and the bad men are both dead, and fortunately they died outdoors so the trading post will not be haunted by their spirits, and,'' Riding Boy finished triumphantly, "if you were not a stupid girl, you would understand what he is saying for yourself and I would not have to tell you everything!''

Beth laughed. "All right, Riding Boy. You're a walking advertisement for the value of a good education.''

"And you use too many big words.''

Beth was thinking up a cheeky reply when Jerry's approach struck her dumb. Hosteen Chee had finished his speech and was now standing just inside the trading post, gravely accepting the thanks of Nathan and Lily. The Indians who had accompanied him were melting away into the darkness, untying their horses and preparing to ride away with a lack of fanfare in strange contrast to their whooping, yelling appearance a scant hour earlier.

Beth got to her feet as Jerry walked toward her. Her mouth was dry at the sight of his unsmiling face. What was the matter? She didn't understand. Why couldn't they celebrate as Nathan and Lily were?

"You hadn't ought to stand out here in those wet things," Jerry said. "I brought you a blanket." He unrolled the soft woolen blanket he had been carrying under one arm and dropped it over her shoulders, wrapping the ends around so that she was encased in a cocoon of warmth. "Lily said to tell you they'd cobble up some white-woman clothes for you in the morning."

"Oh . . . how kind," Beth said inadequately. Suddenly she was near tears. "When I nearly got them killed and the post burned down! How can Lily be so *nice*, and she's pretty and dainty, too, and she speaks Navaho, and . . ." She trailed off in trembling consciousness of her own inadequacies. Next to Lily she felt so big and clumsy, good for nothing except to handle a gun and get into quarrels with her supervisors. And she knew how Jerry admired Lily. The contrast between them must have been painfully evident to him when they were all together at the post.

"Yes," Jerry agreed, "Lily's quite a lady. Nathan's a lucky man." There was an undisguised note of longing in his voice as he looked at the golden rectangle of light where the trading post door stood open. Beth followed the direction of his glance and thought she understood. He was trying to tell her that whatever was between them meant nothing compared to his longing for his friend's wife. She felt more inadequate than ever and longed to get out of the situation. But she could hardly jump onto one of Jerry's horses and ride off into the night like the Navahos.

"Well," she said, "I guess I'll just go and find some place to sleep. I'm pretty tired."

Jerry gripped her arm as she started back into the trading post. "Not in there."

She stared at him. "Why not?"

Jerry shrugged. "I figured Lily and Nathan might want to be alone."

He didn't sound the least bit sad about it. "Don't you . . . mind?" Beth asked tentatively.

"Hell, no. Why should I?"

"Well, you . . . and Lily . . ." Beth stopped, completely unable to explain that revealing moment when she'd seen their kiss in the post. "I saw you kissing her," she said at last.

"And you're going to throw a jealous twit about it, is that it?" Jerry's fingers were hard, bruising her arm. He shook her lightly. "What's gotten into you, anyway? Damn it, Beth, you know Nathan's my best friend."

"I know," Beth said miserably. "I didn't mean you'd do anything to hurt him. But I could see . . . anybody could see . . . and you said there wasn't any future for us. . . ." Her voice was quavering abominably. She wished she could turn away from him, to hide the tears that must be glistening on her lashes, but he held her arm too tightly.

"Look," Jerry said at last, "I don't know what kind of sick ideas you got in that missionary school. Sure, I kissed Lily. I was kind of excited about the idea we weren't all going to be dead in half an hour."

"So why couldn't you kiss me?" Beth cried. "Why are you acting as if you don't even like me anymore?"

Jerry's face twisted and he looked away from her. "Like you? I don't even know who you are."

"What do you mean?"

"Why didn't you tell me you were rich?"

"I'm not." Beth shook her head in confusion. "Oh, do you mean the money I won betting on Red Singer's horse? But you knew about that already." She felt as if she were trying to bat down wisps of fog with her bare hands to get to Jerry.

"No, I don't mean that," Jerry growled. "I mean the big house, the white columns, the stable of thoroughbreds, the diamond necklace, the debutante ball. A few little things you never mentioned, lady."

Beth stared at him. "Why, no. It didn't seem relevant. Would you have thought more of me if I'd paraded around in my old dress, telling everybody that my stockings might be darned in three places but my father was rich and I'd been used to better things?"

"It would have been more honest," Jerry said. "I thought you were like me, making your own way in the world. I thought we could work things out together, but I wasn't counting on some girl who'd lived soft all her life and had that kind of home to run back to if things didn't go her way. Even if I got that section manager's house, what kind of a life is that for you? You were just playing a game with me."

Beth felt totally drained, as if the exhaustion of the last three days had all caught up with her at once. She had no feeling left, no fire—only this sad, aching emptiness where Jerry's love had once warmed her. She sat back down on the rock and gathered the blanket about her. "It's no game," she said dully. "My father and I quarreled when I left home to teach school. He said I'd be running back home in three months. I haven't taken a penny of his money since I got through teachers' college. I wanted to prove myself."

She looked up at Jerry's dark profile against the night stars. "But I never can prove myself to a man, can I? No matter what I do, I'm just a silly girl and you know I don't really mean it, won't stick it out. Damn it, Jerry!" Her voice rose as anger began to warm her. "I taught for three years in Iowa and lived on my salary. I came out west by myself. I've just ridden across the most god-awful country in the world for two days and helped fight off an attack on the trading post. How *dare* you tell me I won't stick it out here, can't take the life? How much more do I have to take?''

Incredibly, he was laughing. One hand reached down and caught her wrist. As he hauled her to her feet, she struck out at him ineffectively, wanting to claw at his eyes. ''Know me?'' she spat at him. ''You're right, you don't. You don't know the first thing about me! You—''

Jerry's mouth came down on hers in a hard demanding kiss that shut off her words in midstream. She twisted and fought, but his hand at the back of her neck forced her into acceptance, and the subtle pressures of his lips and tongue lit the fire within her that she'd thought was gone forever. When he finally raised his head, she was beyond resistance.

''Beth.'' The laughter was still there, an undercurrent in the strong stream of his voice. ''You crazy missionary lady, don't you know what you're taking on? I'm just a dumb wrangler. What sort of a life can I offer you? I don't own anything but my boots and saddle and a couple of half-broke cow ponies. And as of two days ago, I don't even have a job.''

''Oh, Jerry.'' Beth felt as if her insides were dissolving under the steady pressure of his hand, the nearness of his hard body. ''You don't have to offer me anything—but you. Don't you know that?''

Jerry drew her nearer until their faces were a scant inch apart. ''Don't you know that?'' he murmured, playing her own words back to her. ''Don't you know that all I want is you, missionary lady?''

Beth smiled. ''Riding Boy was right,'' she said softly. ''I'm just a stupid girl. You might have to tell me a few more times before I get it right.''

"I got another way to convince you." Jerry's hands slid to her waist, and as their bodies met in the now empty clearing, the blanket dropped to the ground unheeded. Beth felt as if she were on fire wherever they touched. Jerry covered the tips of her breasts and her thighs and her neck with desperate, urgent kisses, until he reached her mouth and his lips clung there for uncounted minutes.

He sucked at her lips, nibbled them gently, thrust his tongue inside to taste the sweetness of her mouth. She clung to him for balance and felt all her worries and all her good sense flying away. Lost in the delight of belonging to him, she was no longer capable of questioning why he wanted her. It was doubtful, she thought with the one corner of her mind that retained some sanity, whether she was even capable of standing up without help. And if he didn't stop brushing one hand over her thighs and bottom while he kissed her, she wasn't going to be good for anything at all. Except . . .

"Bed," she murmured shamelessly when they came up for air. "A large, large bed. A feather bed—"

Jerry's lips covered hers again, ravaging the last tremor of sensual excitement from her, demanding more than she had ever known she could give. When he finally released her, her knees were trembling and her body ached for him. "There," Jerry said, holding her against his shoulder. "Do you think I kiss Lily Reiberg like that?"

"I didn't know you could kiss anybody like that," Beth said. She lifted one shaking hand to caress his bristly cheek. "What other skills have you been holding out on me?"

"Come to the guest hogan," Jerry suggested, "and I'll demonstrate." He stooped and lifted her with one arm under her knees before she knew what he meant to do. With the same motion he grasped the blanket and threw it into her lap.

The guest hogan was a traditional six-sided building of

cedar logs, set a little ways back from the clearing among deep resin-scented shadows. Jerry paused at the door, kicked it open with one booted foot, carried Beth in, and deposited her on a rustling corn-shuck mattress.

"It's not exactly a feather bed," he apologized, "but it's private." He closed the door and Beth blinked in the total blackness of the interior.

"Where are Hosteen Chee and the children staying?" Suddenly she felt afraid of this new, confident Jerry. She wanted to talk for a little while, until she got her balance back, until her pulses stopped throbbing so outrageously.

"In the trading post." There were more rustling sounds as Jerry peeled off his clothing in the darkness.

"But I thought you said Lily and Nathan wanted to be alone!"

Jerry chuckled and felt his way to the bed. "Well, you can't always get what you want. They're an old married couple. Do them good to restrain their baser urges until tomorrow." He reached for her and one hand fell upon her breast. He gave a soft, satisfied chuckle and pulled her to him. "Haven't you got out of those wet things yet?" While he spoke, his hands were busy with the tiny buttons down the front of her blouse. Beth sighed with pleasure as the inside of his wrist grazed one nipple through the damp cloth.

"What about . . . your own . . . baser urges?" It was difficult to speak. His lips at the base of her throat were doing something strange to her breathing and something even stranger to the moist spot between her legs.

"I don't think," Jerry murmured into her throat, "I can restrain my urges . . . much . . . longer. How the hell does this unfasten?" He gave an impatient yank at the blouse and the thin fabric parted right over the line that Lily had darned with such painstaking little stitches.

His hand slid under the torn rag to cup her breast, and

Beth caught her breath at the warmth of his touch on skin that was chilled from the damp clothes she had been wearing. As gently as if he were exploring some hidden treasure, he lifted the soft weight in one warm, dry hand while his thumb rubbed back and forth over the sensitive tip, sending shudders of ecstasy through her. When his lips found the taut peak, sucking and nibbling to bring her to even greater heights of desire, she sobbed aloud with pure pleasure.

She slid one hand downward along his body in the darkness and felt his hardness under her fingers, warm and full and demanding. She stroked along the length of the throbbing shaft and felt his whole body quiver against hers. "Beth," he murmured thickly, "Beth, you're driving me crazy."

"It's mutual." Beth's other hand spread among the crisp red curls on the back of his head, holding him against her breast. She felt the shudders of desire pass through his frame and prolonged the embrace, savoring the sweet torment on the edge of fulfillment, until he fumbled at the waistband of her skirt with fingers made clumsy by haste and desire.

"Beth . . ." He pushed the skirt away. The heavy fabric, cold and damp and stiff with the splashes of water, was cold and rough against her thighs. Then there was only Jerry, warm and hard against her, demanding the entrance that she willingly gave with parted thighs and lips and open hands to stroke along his bare back. The smooth perfection of their union shocked her so that she cried out in the darkness and was surprised by her own voice. She clasped him fiercely with arms and legs, holding him close against her, wanting the closeness even more than she wanted him to slake her fires of desire.

Then he moved again, swift and certain, and she felt such pleasure she could hardly hold still. She was shaking against

him and her whole body quivered with deep tremors of un-
bearable sweetness.

"*Mine.*" He rested above her on knees and elbows, and
she could still feel him hard within her. "All mine, missionary lady. Don't forget that. I've staked my claim."

"Is that how you do it?" Beth giggled. "I had no idea
mining was such a rewarding profession. Why don't you
take it up full-time?"

With a movement too swift to anticipate, Jerry grasped
her by the waist and rolled over on his back, pulling her on
top of him without separating their bodies. "I reckon it'll
take me all my time and energy to tend this one claim," he
told her, pulling her facedown until her lips met his. As the
heat of his mouth enveloped hers, Beth felt him stirring deep
within her.

"Seems like you've got some energy left," she teased.

Jerry let go of her and flopped back on the corn-shuck
mattress, arms and legs limply outspread. "Nope. All
gone."

"All?" She bent over him and let the tips of her breasts
trail over his chest, savoring the light prickling of the curly
red hair that was sprinkled over his chest, enjoying her
power to stop or start the teasing circular movements as she
wished. Her hips moved with the rest of her body, and Jerry
drew in a sharp intake of breath and caught her by the hips
and held her down against him.

"You started it," he told her, "you do something about
it."

"Mmm. Maybe I'm tired, too." But she could not stop
the tremors that raced through her body as his fingers dug
into her hips and moved her back and forth. Didn't want to
stop them. Gave herself up to the new rhythm, never notic-
ing when his hands fell away and his eyes closed while she
knelt above him and his lean hips arched to drive deeply into

her from below, taking her more thoroughly this time than ever before.

The darkness seemed to be lit by rings of colored light radiating out from some interior source within her, rings that grew and swelled and exploded and left her floating, weightless, gasping, over Jerry's long body. His arms reached through the space and the darkness and gathered her in to his chest, and she rested there, knowing nothing but the perfect peace and contentment of his love. What did the future matter? Their present was enough for her.

❦ Chapter Eighteen

In the morning Beth awoke to the scent of juniper and cedar, flecks of sunlight coming through the chinks in the walls and roof, and the roughness of a wool blanket over her. It was very quiet in the hogan; Jerry was gone, and her clothes were neatly draped from a projecting pole in one wall. She put on the limp, tattered garments and tried to pull the edges of the torn blouse together to cover herself decently. It was impossible, and this time the blouse was beyond Lily's mending. Shrugging, she wrapped the blanket about her shoulders and went out to see what was happening.

The trading post was guarded by Riding Boy and Wind Flower. They directed her into the back room, where Nathan and Lily lived. There Beth found Lily, flushed by her exertions over the fire, setting out a massive breakfast of fried mutton chops, biscuits with syrup, and coffee. Hosteen Chee sat on the floor to one side of the fireplace, watching Lily's efforts with grave approval.

"Where's Jerry?" Beth asked.

Lily pushed a damp wisp of yellow hair off her forehead

and swung the heavy three-legged frying pan off the fire with casual expertise. "Jerry and Nathan went down to Galvan North. They want to see if somebody can take a message to Eleuterio. It might," she said with uncharacteristic understatement, "be a little complicated to explain things to the sheriff in Gallup."

"It might," Beth agreed. "Especially if the sheriff is currently looking for whoever kidnapped two children from the mission school." She felt disappointed that Jerry wasn't there, but Lily told her that the men would be back by night. Apparently it didn't take so long to get to Galvan North if you weren't trying to avoid possible ambushes.

"Hosteen Chee stayed to talk to you," Lily said. "I'm supposed to translate. After breakfast," she added firmly, taking the biscuits out of the Dutch oven.

Beth ate one of Lily's fluffy biscuits and watched with awe as Hosteen Chee stirred half a cup of sugar into his coffee and drank down the steaming, syrupy concoction in one gulp, then disposed of half a dozen greasy chops while waiting for Lily to boil the next pot of coffee. Finally he wiped his fingers and pushed himself away from the table with an expression of deep contentment on his wrinkled face. Beaming at Beth, he addressed a few incomprehensible words to her.

"He wants to thank you for everything," Lily translated.

Beth began to suspect that Lily's Navaho wasn't as fluent as everyone made out. "Shouldn't that be the other way around?"

Lily shook her head, laughing, and repeated Beth's comment to Hosteen Chee. This elicited a longer speech from him.

"He says," she reported, "that he appreciates your bringing the children back safely, but he is even more grateful for the opportunity to lead his people once more in war against the enemy. The young men of today are soft because they have no fighting to do, but he was once a great war leader and it is his duty to train them so that if the need arises—as it did last night—they can perform almost as valiantly as he did.''

Beth nodded and tried to keep her lips from twitching up at the corners. She could certainly see where Riding Boy got his self-confidence from!

"Sun Hair tells me that you are a teacher," Hosteen Chee continued through Lily's interpretation. "That is good. Our people need to learn the ways of the white men.''

Beth stared. ''But he just thanked me for bringing the kids back!''

Hosteen Chee clarified his statement. He did not want his grandchildren to forget their heritage. But he wanted them to learn to read and write and to keep their own accounts. He had heard that the whites had schools where their young men learned better ways of farming. He intended to send Riding Boy to such a school when he was older.

Beth shook her head, marveling at the resilience of this old man whose life had spanned two such diverse cultures. Last night he had been a vision of primitive vengeance, face and body streaked with paint, riding down on the enemy with his black lance decorated with eagle feathers, counting on chants and sacred pollen to deflect bullets from his body. Now he was stoking himself with syrupy coffee and telling her about his plans to send Riding Boy to agricultural school.

"What about Wind Flower?" she asked.

Before Lily had finished translating the question, Hosteen Chee's dismissive wave of the hand gave Beth the answer. "Let me guess," she said. "She's only a girl. Doesn't need education. Right?''

Lily shook her head, smiling. "Wrong. Navaho women

own their own property. He says she doesn't need to read and write books, but she had better learn arithmetic, because she inherited a lot of sheep from her mother and she has to keep count of her property."

Beth leaned forward and studied the old man's wrinkled face with renewed interest. He nodded emphatically three times and one forefinger shot out and tapped her on the chest while he boomed out a long, sonorous pronouncement. Then he sat back, arms folded, and smiled while Lily translated.

"He says that you are a good teacher. Not like the Black Coat who hates and fears his people and wants to turn them into whites. He watched you last night. You are new to this country, but you showed no fear when his warriors came into the post."

"Well, of course not!" Beth exclaimed. "They were here to help us!"

"He says you will stay here and teach the children at Blue Mesa."

Beth shook her head regretfully. "Lily, you know I can't do that. After the way I ran away from the mission school, I'd never get a permit to teach on the reservation."

"He has already thought of that," Lily said after another interchange in Navaho. "He says you should find some land on the borders of the reservation, like the place that fat Mexican—oops, I mean Señor Galvan—owns. That would be close enough for the children to come and go; even if they have to stay at the school for several days at a time, it is better than going far away and forgetting to be Navahos like the children who are taught by the Black Coat."

Hosteen Chee nodded once more as Lily finished her translation. Beth felt a silly lump in her throat. Her own school! She could imagine nothing better. But she would have to go where Jerry went. And it didn't seem very likely

that Eleuterio Galvan would promote him to section manager after this escapade, so they might have to go to one of
the ranches down south after all.

"Lily, would you thank him for me? And say . . . Oh,
you know how it is with Jerry and me. I don't even know if
we'll be able to stay in this part of the country." Ridiculous
to get all teary about leaving a place she'd known for such a
short time. But she couldn't ever imagine feeling so at home
anywhere else.

After Lily's translation, Hosteen Chee nodded, stood up,
and walked into the trading post with slow, measured steps.
Beth felt a little hurt that he'd dismissed her so completely,
as though she were worthless if she didn't agree to his plan.
She followed Lily into the store. The children were already
outside, getting their horses for the journey home.

Hosteen Chee produced a handful of silver dollars from a
buckskin bag and laid them down on the counter in front of
Lily.

"He wants to redeem some of his pawned jewelry," Lily
told Beth. She went to a rack at the back of the counter and
began sorting through strings of turquoise and silver,
chatting as she did so.

"They bring this stuff in to pawn for food in the winter,
then when the sheep are sheared they bring in their wool and
get the jewelry back and we freight the wool to Gallup and
sell it. It makes keeping accounts kind of complicated, but
Nathan's good with numbers. Unusual to have anyone redeem their pawn in the off season, though. Maybe he's
going to a sing and wants all his finery."

She pulled out a magnificent string of silver flowers ornamented with turquoise and coral centers and held it up.
"This one?"

Hosteen Chee nodded and took the necklace from her
hand. Stepping toward Beth, he lifted the string of silver

flowers in both hands and dropped it over her head. The silver was cold and heavy on her shoulders.

"He wants you to have this," Lily said quietly as Beth fingered the necklace, "not as payment for his grandchildren, but as a token of friendship between you."

"Oh." Wordless, near tears, Beth fingered the heavy silver necklace. It was a magnificent piece of work, gleaming with smooth curves and mysterious symbols. "I—I don't have anything to give him."

Lily translated. "He says that you know what he wants, and you will give it when the time is right."

Hosteen Chee nodded and went out to where Riding Boy held the horses ready. "Wait," Beth said, "I haven't thanked him properly. I—I—"

But the Indians were already gone.

"Come inside," said Lily, repressing a grin at the incongruous sight of the beautifully crafted Navaho jewelry over Beth's filthy, tattered blouse. "We'll have to make you a new blouse to go with that pretty necklace."

It was a long, slow day for Beth, sitting indoors and trying to emulate Lily's neat stitches while she wondered how Jerry and Nathan were doing on their errand. Fortunately the trading post was quite busy that morning, as word of the fight had spread on some invisible grapevine and every family within a twenty-mile radius had to come in and see the scene of the great battle for themselves. Lily was kept busy popping up and down to wait on the Indians who came in to trade, and Beth enjoyed the excuse to put her needle down and watch the customers. The women in their velveteen blouses and full calico skirts, jangling with silver and coral and turquoise, were most picturesque. But Beth was even more charmed by the shy black-haired children who clung to their mothers' skirts or raced up and down in the clearing, reenacting the fight with shrill cries.

"Ahalani," she ventured to one daring little girl who came up close enough to touch her skirt.

The little girl giggled and whispered, *"Ahalani,"* before darting back and burying her head in her mother's skirt. Every few seconds she peeped out, giggled, and hid again.

Beth dreamed for a few minutes about a school full of black-eyed children who drifted in and out with the seasons as their people migrated with the sheep and the rains. How would you teach such a class, never knowing from day to day which children would be there or what they'd remember from their last visit? She mentally tossed McGuffey's *Graded Readers* out the window and set about planning just how she would handle her dream school. It would be a challenge, no question about that.

The mental exercise kept her occupied until, at noon, Lily shooed the few remaining customers out of the post and set out a cold meal in the back room. "I *refuse* to be jumping up and down to get tobacco or nails or coffee while I am having lunch," she declared. "It's very bad for the digestion. Go away!"

That last was tossed over her shoulder in the general direction of the front room, where someone was pounding on the door.

"You also refuse to jump up and let your husband in?" a voice inquired.

"Nathan!" Lily squealed and almost overturned the luncheon dishes in her haste to get to the door. Beth was close behind her. Why was Nathan back so soon? Had something happened to Jerry?

That fear, at least, was settled when the door opened and she saw Jerry's red head behind Nathan. And with them—

"Eleuterio!" Lily's squeal was just as loud and delighted as it had been for her husband. She launched herself into Señor Galvan's arms and gave him a loud, uninhibited kiss.

Beth's last lingering shreds of jealousy blew away. Obviously Lily kissed everybody that way. Well, if Nathan could put up with it, so could she.

"Where did you come from? What happened? Is everything all right at the ranch?" Lily shepherded them all into the back room and began setting out extra plates, bubbling over with so many questions that nobody could interrupt to give her an answer.

"Let the man sit down and eat," Nathan declared, rumpling his wife's hair as she passed between table and cupboard. "I don't know about the ranch, we didn't get that far, met Eleuterio halfway here. Sit down yourself, stop getting so excited, everything's fine."

"*Is* it? Eleuterio? What are you doing up here, anyway?" Lily plunked herself down at the table, leaned on her elbows, and waited.

Galvan seated himself gingerly in a straight wooden chair that creaked under his weight. He closed his eyes and moaned softly. "What about a little of your peach pie, Señorita Lily? That's a long ride for an old man like me."

Lily whisked a pie plate out of the corner cupboard, cut Galvan a massive slice, and poured boiling coffee into a thick white mug. "Then why did you make it?"

Galvan opened one reproachful eye. "You're supposed to tell me I'm not an old man."

"You're not an old man," Lily said promptly, resuming her seat. "*Please*, Eleuterio."

Señor Galvan heaved a mighty sigh and took a forkful of the peach pie. "I was tracking Jerry, of course."

"What!" Beth sat up straight. "But I thought—" She turned to Jerry, confused. "Didn't you leave a note?"

Galvan waved his fork through the air. Beth stared at the bite of peach pie impaled on the tines of the fork. "Sure, he left a note. You're not a very good liar, Jerry. I didn't believe that story of yours about quitting and going down south for a minute.'' He snapped the last bite of pie off the fork and washed it down with hot black coffee. "Well, maybe two minutes." He leaned back with a sigh of repletion. "But that was before Reverend Griscom arrived on my doorstep, demanding the return of this young lady.'' He nodded at Beth.

Jerry chuckled. "Sorry about that, Eleuterio. Maybe I should have warned you that would happen. But I figured you were better off not knowing anything about Beth being on the ranch.''

Señor Galvan sighed. "Perhaps, perhaps not. I am afraid Reverend Griscom did not believe my denials in any case. He insisted on searching the premises very thoroughly.''

"And you let him?'' Jerry's eyebrows shot up.

Eleuterio Galvan smiled and fiddled with his black mustache. "It seemed advisable. To keep the peace . . . and to keep him busy. Before he'd got halfway through his search of the bunkhouse, he had uncovered enough evidence of sin to keep him in sermons for the next six months. Six empty beer bottles,'' he summarized, "three pictures of lovely *señoritas* in various stages of undress, and one . . . er . . . lacy undergarment tucked into Barbed Wire Bob's bunk.''

Jerry chuckled. "I didn't know Bob wore lace! Have to give him some grief about that when I get back.''

Eleuterio Galvan coughed gently. "Er . . . we have to talk about that,'' he observed.

Beth felt her heart sinking. He was going to fire Jerry! "Señor Galvan, that isn't fair! Jerry's been more help to you than anybody else could possibly be, and you know it! Didn't he tell you about the men Lawrence Hudson hired to burn your ranch, and—''

Galvan waved her into silence with one placid gesture.

"Enough, Señorita Johanssen. Please allow me to tell this story in my own way."

Lily and Jerry both directed quelling glares at Beth and she subsided, inwardly fuming, while Eleuterio Galvan went on to tell the rest of his story. It was quite simple, really. While Reverend Griscom had been haranguing the boys in the bunkhouse about their sinful ways, he had taken a good horse and tracked Jerry and Beth to Galvan North. It had been obvious to him that Jerry's disappearance had something to do with Beth and the Indian children, particularly when it became apparent that both horses were carrying extra weight.

"You tracked us?" That point had been bothering Beth since the beginning of the story. Riding Boy had been most insistent about the devices he used to hide their tracks.

"Sure," Galvan replied offhandedly. "Oh, I saw where you'd made some efforts to obliterate the trail, but my blind grandmother could have picked it up again."

Jerry choked into his coffee. "Do me a favor. Don't say that in front of Riding Boy. He's right proud of his tracking skills. And I guess he's got something to be proud of, at that. Did I tell you how he rode for help while we were penned up in the post here?"

"You did," Galvan said. "Three times."

"Then you know about Fritz and Danny?" Beth asked.

Galvan nodded. "I had not imagined that Señor Hudson could stoop to hiring such scum." He spat out an incomprehensible Spanish phrase and reddened slightly. "Forgive my language, señorita." He bowed to Beth.

"That's all right," Beth said. "I don't know Spanish."

"I do," Lily piped up. "It means—"

"*Lily!*" Nathan scowled across the table and, to Beth's amazement, Lily subsided at once. "Act ladylike," Nathan warned her. "In case you didn't notice, we've got a nice young missionary schoolteacher visiting us. You want to shock her?''

"I owe you something for discovering them, Jerry,'' Galvan said. He sighed. "Paying this particular debt may be . . . complicated.'' Beth noted that although his mouth was drawn down in sad lines under the black mustache, his eyes twinkled as though he were amused by some private joke.

"Is it because of me?'' she asked quickly. "Is Reverend Griscom going to . . .'' She paused. What could he do to her, exactly? Was she going to wind up in jail on a kidnapping charge?

Galvan shook his head. "No, señorita. He has not connected your disappearance with that of the children. In any case, the time of that particular boarding school is past. The Indian agent will not want to make trouble for you; he has trouble of his own. Washington is not pleased with his highhanded kidnapping of reservation children. The new policy is to let them alone, not to drag them in by force.''

Beth felt relieved to know that the children around Blue Mesa would not have to go into hiding again. "I hope that lasts,'' she said.

Galvan shrugged and smiled. "It will last at least six months, then there will doubtless be a new ruling. . . . But let us not beat our heads against Washington's policies tonight, my friends. This particular boarding school will cease to trouble us. Reverend Griscom has decided to return east, since both the young ladies who worked as his schoolteachers have been seduced by the wicked men of the Galvan Ranch.'' His smile broadened until his face seemed to be nothing but white teeth and twinkling black eyes.

"Addie?'' Beth breathed.

He nodded. "Señorita Clare has done me the honor of consenting to be my wife. I should have been coming to Blue Mesa in any case, to invite you to attend our nuptials.''

Jerry shook Galvan's hand and gravely tendered his congratulations, while Beth enjoyed a momentary glow of achievement. If she hadn't tricked Addie into letting her hair down, she thought, Eleuterio would never have noticed her. At least one thing she did hadn't turned out badly.

"Now"—Galvan brushed aside Lily's excited questions about the wedding—"we have a few other small matters to settle." His eyes skimmed all their faces before settling on Jerry. "I am not going to make you a section manager, Jerry."

Jerry's face was set in the masklike lines that he used to conceal emotion. "No. I didn't think you would." He reached under the table and squeezed Beth's hand. "I reckon I can get a town job. That'll be better for you, won't it, Beth?"

"No," Galvan said. "No town job." He paused, palpably enjoying the way they all hung on his words. Beth began to hate him.

"I want you to take over Galvan North for me."

Jerry's jaw dropped a good inch. Lily giggled and clapped her hands. "Wonderful! Now you and Beth will be our neighbors."

"Eleuterio?" Jerry inquired in a husky, uncertain voice. "You—you don't mean it?"

Eleuterio beamed. He looked like a chubby, dark-complexioned Santa Claus, Beth thought, and she forgave him his pleasure in power for the equal pleasure he found in fixing their lives up. "Oh, but I do. You know, these actions of Hudson's have created some tension between my men and the Indians. Unfair, but true. I need to place someone here who can deal with both sides. Nathan tells me that your prospective wife happens to be in very high standing with Hosteen Chee's people at the moment."

"Translation," Jerry said, grinning. "I got the job be-

cause I'm marrying a lady with connections." He lifted
Beth's hand to his lips.

"If," Eleuterio said cheerfully, "the lady will accept the
position? The old ranch house is not in good order—I will
see that you have men and materials to work on it, but it's
not a modern residence—and the location is somewhat isolated. . . ."

Jerry looked worried. "I don't know, Eleuterio," he
said. "You know there's nothing I'd like better, but it's not
much of a place to bring a lady to, and that's a fact. Can't
get into town in winter because of the snow, can't get in half
the time in summer because of floods. . . ." His voice
trailed off and he looked at Beth with a question in his gray
eyes.

"Lily likes it okay out here," Nathan put in.

"Yeah, but . . ."

"Why don't you ask me first, before you go and turn it
down?" Beth interrupted. As if she'd turn down a chance to
live in the most beautiful place she'd ever seen, in an old
Spanish mansion alive with history! She could have laughed
with happiness, but Eleuterio Galvan deserved a more serious answer than that.

"Señor Galvan," she said, "there is no place on this
earth I would rather live than Galvan North. I loved the old
ranch house from the moment I saw it." And it already had
precious memories for her. She glanced at Jerry and saw
from the warm glow in his eyes that he, too, was remembering their first night together, under the stars in one of the
roofless rooms of the old house. But his worried look was
still there.

"One other problem," Jerry said. He paused, drumming
the fingers of his free hand on the table. "I feel like an un-
grateful hound bringing all this up, Eleuterio . . . but have
you figured how we're going to deal with Hudson?" He

looked around the table, making sure he had everybody's attention, before he went on. "He still wants the land. And I don't see where he's going to stop, just because a couple of hired guns got killed. We got no evidence connecting them with Hudson. So there's no way to stop him pulling the same trick, or worse, again."

"Oh, I think there might be." Galvan smiled. "Now that we know why he wants the property. . . ."

Jerry shook his head. "Yes. He thinks there's gold on it. What good does that do?"

"If Señor Hudson wants gold," Galvan said, "we'll just have to help him find some, won't we?"

"How?" Jerry demanded. "Why? What good is that going to do?"

Galvan gave him a benign smile. "Don't ask so many questions. I have some ideas." He explained his plan, and by the end of the brief speech everybody around the table was smiling.

"Think it'll work?" Lily gave a delighted giggle. "Oh, wonderful! I can just see his face. . . ."

"There's just one thing," Galvan cautioned her. "To take the map in, we need somebody Hudson trusts absolutely—somebody whose word he would never think of questioning."

Beth sighed. "Wonderful. You don't happen to have a judge or a minister in your back pocket, do you?"

"Better than that." Galvan rose to his feet, bowed to Beth, and kissed her hand while she looked up at him with surprise and horror as his idea dawned on her. "I have the only person to whom Hudson ever confided the secret of his search for gold. I can't think of a better person to carry the message, can any of you?"

They were all looking at her.

"Oh, no," Beth said. "No. Absolutely not!" She began

to feel helpless. No matter what she said, the message wasn't getting through—she could tell by the way they kept looking at her.

"Oh, yes," Nathan corrected her. "As Eleuterio says— who could be better?"

"No," Beth told him, more weakly this time. All those expectant eyes on her reminded her of the morning she'd walked into her first schoolroom, quaking internally. She made one last try. "You don't know what he's like. The man is not normal. And I insulted him badly last time we met. I wouldn't go to see him if I had a whole regiment of cavalry backing me up."

"You don't need a whole regiment of cavalry," Jerry said. "I'll be following you in case there's any trouble."

Beth shook her head. "He's obsessive. Last time I barely got away from him. I wouldn't be alone with him for all the tea in China. I'm sorry, Jerry, we'll have to think of some other plan."

"It's okay," Lily said. "From what you've told us, he doesn't lust after you nearly as much as he lusts after gold. You can just quietly slip away while he's fondling his nugget." She giggled. "Oh, dear, that sounds terrible! He really ought to have two of them, don't you think, like—"

"Lily." Nathan gave his wife a threatening look. "Pipe down before you shock everybody again."

Lily piped down.

Chapter Nineteen

Three days later, in front of Lawrence Hudson's elegant house on the outskirts of Gallup, Beth dropped the reins of Eleuterio Galvan's second-best buggy and nodded with a pleasant smile to the boy who ran out to take charge of her horses. The smile was pasted onto her face by sheer willpower. Force of will could do nothing about the interior shaking she experienced as she stepped up to Hudson's front door, or the dampness of her palms under the driving gloves, but fortunately those things were not visible.

"Miss Johanssen!" Hudson answered the door himself. They hadn't been counting on that. Surely there were servants in the house? Beth felt extremely reluctant to walk into the dark building where she would be alone with Lawrence Hudson. Of course, she wouldn't be exactly alone. She suppressed the desire to glance over her shoulder and make sure that Jerry was waiting around the corner as he'd promised. He would have to stay out of sight in any case, so looking for him would do nothing but betray her nervousness.

And perhaps she wouldn't be able to get in to see Hudson. Instead of opening the door wider and inviting her in, he was standing in the crack, looking her up and down with distinctly suspicious eyes.

"I certainly hadn't expected to see you in Gallup," he said.

"Oh, Mr. Hudson," Beth quavered. No need to fake the tremor in her voice; that was genuine enough. "I've been so foolish. I do hope you can help me." She twisted Lily's lace-trimmed handkerchief in her gloved hands and dabbed at dry eyes. "You're my only hope. Please . . . Lawrence?"

It was rather a difficult trick to look coyly through her lashes at a man several inches shorter than she was. The difficulty of the pose kept Beth from thinking about other, more frightening things. She glanced up and down the street. The bottle-brush tree at the corner of the house quivered slightly, reassuring her. "If anyone were to see me here . . ." she murmured, dabbing at her eyes again.

"Of course, come in." Lawrence Hudson seemed to have recovered from his initial surprise. He took her by the arm and drew her into the shadowed entrance hall. "Forgive me. I was only surprised to see you. After our last parting, I scarcely dared hope you would be so . . . friendly . . . as to come and visit me at home." The sarcastic curl of his lips warned Beth that he meant to make her pay for being rude to him at their last meeting.

"Do come into the parlor," he urged her. "You are unescorted?" His eyes flicked up and down her figure, neatly outlined in the new basque with black velvet ribbons that she and Lily had sat up through two nights to stitch together.

Lily had been quite right when she'd insisted on making the bodice an inch smaller, Beth thought with a blush. She couldn't take a deep breath in this damned garment, but it was certainly attracting Lawrence Hudson's attention. And that was what they wanted—wasn't it?

"Oh, Mr. Hudson," she murmured·as he escorted her into a parlor luxuriously furnished with maroon plush chairs and velvet curtains, "I do hope you're not shocked that I came to see you. But I am quite alone in the world, and I did not know where else to turn." She did, however, know better than to join him on the purple plush settee toward which he was steering her. Beth chose an isolated, straight-backed chair whose tilted horsehair seat kept her sitting straight up for fear of sliding off altogether. She clasped her hands together in her lap and looked up at him with big, tear-filled eyes.

"Poor little girl," Hudson murmured, bending over her solicitously. "You must have been through so much."

Beth wondered exactly what he thought she'd been through. She hadn't had a chance to tell him her story yet. Of course, there must be all kinds of fascinating gossip going around town by now. If she hadn't had a mission to perform, it would have been interesting to let Hudson tell her exactly what she'd been through.

"Let me get you a cordial—something to refresh you."

It wasn't an innocent cordial in the tinted crystal glass he handed to Beth, it was straight brandy, and if she drank half of it she'd be too dizzy to remember half the lies they'd made up. Beth pretended to take genteel sips and waited until Hudson turned away to pour his own drink. Then she recklessly dumped the contents of the glass into a potted cactus beside her chair.

"Good girl! That'll put the color back in your cheeks." Hudson smiled when he saw her empty glass. "Here, let me offer you a drop more. Don't be shy, dear, there's plenty more where that came from, and it's only a tonic to give you strength."

Tonic, hell, Beth thought, you're trying to get me drunk and into bed without even listening to my sad story, you lecher. Perhaps she should drop the map in front of him, that would get his attention fast enough. Crude, though. Better to sniffle her way through the story as planned. She raised the glass to her lips and waited for another chance to dump the contents.

"Now, dear." Hudson drew up another straight-backed chair right next to hers, sat down, and put his arm around the back of her chair. "I'm so pleased that you've turned to me in your trouble. Er . . . what exactly is your trouble?"

"I—I don't know where to begin," sniffled Beth. She sat up a little straighter, set her nearly full glass down on a polished mahogany table, and launched into a confused rambling tale about having been deceived by Jerry's promises of marriage into a midnight elopement. Instead of taking her to a town where they could be married, she complained, he'd taken her to the deserted ranch house at Galvan North.

"Terrible!" Hudson's eyes were gleaming and his small, pink tongue darted in and out to moisten his lips. He leaned over her; Beth leaned away and encountered his groping right hand on the other side of the chair. She sat very straight and tried to ignore his breath on her neck and his fingertips brushing the tight fabric of her bodice. "And so he had his way with you? Terrible, terrible. You were quite helpless—I understand that—no one will blame you, my poor girl."

"Well, no," Beth said.

Hudson looked disappointed.

"I'm sure he meant to," she said, "but we were . . . interrupted." It was easy enough to give Hudson a vivid description of the two men who had camped in the front room of the old ranch house, her terror, and the aura of violence around them. She noticed that Hudson paled and stopped

licking his lips as she described Fritz and Danny in enough
detail for him to recognize them.

"Did you—you didn't happen to overhear any of the ruf-
fians' conversation?" he asked in a hoarse voice.

"As a matter of fact, I did," Beth said. "They were
arguing about a gold vein they'd found. One of them, the
little whiny one, wanted to go back and tell you about it, but
the big mean one said it was all theirs. Then he pulled out a
gun and shot the little one."

"The cheating son of a bitch!" Rising from his chair,
Hudson smacked a clenched fist into his open palm and
stalked around the room. "Pardon my language, Beth, but
you know how important this matter is to me."

"Yes," Beth said, unable to keep the sarcastic edge from
her voice. "I know." Only too well, she thought. "I don't
know what happened then. I was so frightened that I fainted.
When I came to, Jerry Dixon was cleaning his gun and the
big man was also dead. Jerry said the big man had heard me
fall when I fainted and he would have ravished me if he
hadn't shot him. Of course, I was terribly grateful to Jerry for
saving me from a fate worse than death, but he didn't seem
to care about me anymore. He was all excited about something he'd found in the big man's pockets," she pouted,
"and he wanted to go back to Galvan's right away."

Hudson cursed. "Damn the luck! Now Eleuterio knows
everything. He'll never sell the land now."

"No," Beth contradicted him. "He doesn't know. He
hasn't talked to Jerry yet."

"Why not?"

Beth looked down and blushed. "When we were going
back to the ranch, Jerry got—he tried to get familiar with
me. I was so frightened!" She clasped her hands to her
bosom and batted her eyelashes rapidly to conceal the ab-
sence of tears.

"Yes, yes, to be sure," Hudson said impatiently. His apparent concern for her troubles seemed to have vanished completely. "Very sad, but young ladies who run away with strange men must expect these things. It's too bad you are ruined. . . ."

"But I'm not," Beth protested. "I was so scared that I hit him over the head with a big rock and ran away. But before I ran away, I went through his pockets and found the things he took from those awful men on Galvan North. I didn't know what to do. I was afraid to go back to Reverend Griscom because he would be mad at me. And Señor Galvan is probably just as bad as Jerry Dixon. I couldn't trust him! So I came to you."

She rummaged in her reticule and drew out the crumpled map that Jerry and Eleuterio had carefully forged. A splotchy, incomplete sketch such as Fritz Bauer might have drawn, the one thing clearly marked on it was the location of the Dry Lake gold vein.

Hudson snatched the map from her hands so eagerly that it tore across one corner. He scanned it with greedy eyes. "You say Galvan doesn't know about this yet?"

"I don't see how he could," Beth said. "I took the buggy and both horses, so Jerry would have to walk."

Hudson smiled. Beth wondered whether he didn't realize that a man left alone in the dry lands between Galvan North and Gallup would very likely die of thirst and heat before he could walk to civilization. Or was it that he simply didn't care? With an internal shiver, she decided the latter was more likely.

"You're a good girl," he commended her. "Don't worry about anything. I'll take care of you. Er . . . you'd better wait here while I go see Eleuterio and get this matter finished off."

Beth pouted. "Can't we both go?" She stood up and put

her hand on Hudson's sleeve, pressing herself up against him and batting her lashes again. "I do so want to see you get the gold mine. After all, you've worked so hard for it, you deserve it . . . Larry."

Hudson breathed deeply and Beth wondered if the perfume Lily had sprinkled over her was bothering him as much as it was her. He slipped an arm around her waist and she gritted her teeth in revulsion. But he had to believe she was entirely his, otherwise he might start questioning the entire plan.

"On second thought," Hudson said huskily, "there's no great hurry about seeing Eleuterio. I can go out to his ranch a little later, when it's cool. Why don't we go upstairs and, er, rest for a while?"

On the other hand, there were limits to just how far she would go in making this act convincing. Beth peeled Hudson's arm off her waist and stepped back. "Not until we're married," she said coldly.

"Married!" Hudson laughed. "You're making a mistake. A gentleman in my position doesn't marry a . . . a soiled dove."

"I told you," Beth protested. "Jerry Dixon never touched me."

Hudson eyed her and gave another unpleasant laugh. "Yes, you'd have to stick to that story, wouldn't you? Frankly, I don't care whether it's true or not. The whole town will think of you as the wrangler's leavings when this story comes out, and I've no mind to be laughed at for taking what even a cowboy couldn't be troubled to marry."

"But—but I brought you the map to the gold mine," Beth whined. She let her lower lip tremble artistically. "Don't you owe me something for that?"

Hudson folded the map and stroked it lovingly. "To be sure, and I mean to give you a nice little position for it. But

not as my wife—you're not good enough for me now, dear.
I'll set you up in your own suite of rooms at the Gallup
Hotel, though, and I won't be mean about new dresses or
trinkets—so long as you don't entertain anybody but me.''

"That's not fair. I thought you'd marry me if I brought
you the map!'' Beth snatched at the folded paper and Hudson knocked her away with a casual backhanded slap. Her
lip tingled and she tasted salt.

"Go to your cowboy lover,'' Hudson advised, tucking
the map into an inside vest pocket. "Maybe he'll take damaged goods. I can do better.'' He went to the door of the parlor, turned, and looked back at Beth. She was leaning
against the table, one hand to her swollen face. "Or you can
stay here, if you like. Your spitfire antics have put me out of
the mood for you now, but if you're prepared to be nice
when I've finished my business, I'll still take care of you.''

Beth waited, holding her hand up before her face, until
she heard the front door slam behind him. She exhaled a
deep sigh of relief and made her way shakily across the
room. On the way she passed the mahogany piecrust table
where she had left her second glass of brandy. She took it up
and drained it at a gulp. She was entitled to something to
calm her nerves, she thought, after playing a scene like that.

Suddenly the front door slammed and steps resounded on
the polished floorboards of the entry hall. Beth froze with
the empty glass in her hand. Hudson back already? Had he
suspected the trick? She searched back through her memory
of their conversation, wondering what she'd said to make
him suspicious and how she could repair the damage.

The parlor door flew open and Jerry erupted into the
room. "Beth! You all right?'' His eyes took in the swelling
bruise on her face and his red hair bristled until it seemed to
be shooting off sparks. He knocked down the piecrust table
and the brandy decanter in his haste to get to her, and his

boot heel caught in a tasseled fringe under the plush settee and ripped several yards of gold braiding free.

Beth found herself in his arms without any clear notion of how she got there, laughing and crying at once, and dizzy from the fumes of the spilled brandy that rose all about them. Everything about him, she thought, was just right, the lean hardness of his body, the way his shoulder was just the right height for her to rest her head on, the strength of his arms around her. Even the rather strong smell of leather and horse that clung to his working clothes was preferable to Hudson's genteel toilet water.

"I was worried sick when Hudson came out without you," Jerry told her unnecessarily. "I thought the idea was for you to ride out to the ranch with him and then stage a quarrel."

"It was," Beth agreed shakily, "but he's too easy to quarrel with. I couldn't wait. Don't worry, though. He swallowed it!"

Jerry's finger traced the lines of her swollen lip. "I owe him something for that," he said softly.

Beth shook her head. "Never mind. I was asking for it—he said . . ." Somewhat tardily, it occurred to her that she had better not quote Hudson's exact insulting words to Jerry. Her redhead just might lose his temper entirely, and a fight between him and Hudson at this point would do nothing to improve the overall plan.

"Said what?" Jerry's arm tightened around her protectively.

"Oh, nothing much," Beth evaded. "I can't remember. I'm too drunk. He was going to ply me with brandy and ruin me, you see. Except then we quarreled. But I figured I deserved the brandy, after he left. Good for the nerves, you know."

Jerry shook his head. "So while I've been squatting out

there behind a bottle-brush tree, worrying my fool head about you, you've been in here swilling Lawrence Hudson's liquor! No wonder it smells so rich in here." His lips brushed hers lightly. "Never know what'll happen when one of these prim schoolteacher ladies kicks over the traces, do you?"

"This particular schoolteacher lady," Beth said, "wants to get out to the Galvan Ranch and hear the last act."

"From lies to drinking to eavesdropping." Jerry shook his head again. "Lady, it's just terrible what has been happening to your moral fiber. I am truly shocked."

Beth snuggled into the curve of his arm. "Are you? Already? That's too bad. I can think of a lot more ways I'd like to shock you."

Because of the time it took them to discuss those and other matters, they did not arrive at the ranch in time to eavesdrop on Lawrence Hudson's talk with Eleuterio Galvan. In fact, Jerry barely drove up to the ranch in time to hide the buggy before Hudson came out onto the covered porch, shaking hands with Eleuterio and smiling. They watched from the concealment of the barn while Hudson drove away, fondling a crinkling paper that he clearly loved too much to stow away in his vest pocket with the map.

Eleuterio was shaking his head sadly when Beth and Jerry hurried up to the house.

"Terrible, the way these clever Anglos take advantage of a poor Mexican," he mourned. "So smooth-talking, so quick. How can we ever keep up with them? . . ."

"You sold him the land," Beth stated.

Eleuterio's smile broadened. "That map of yours was a masterpiece of indirection, Jerry. He must have been unable to decide which part of the salt flats the gold vein is supposed to be on, because he offered to buy everything north of the Little Canyon."

"So what did you sell him?" Jerry asked.

"All of it," Eleuterio said simply. "And I only asked twice what he originally offered for the whole of Galvan North."

Jerry threw his hat into the air with an exultant whoop. "You dumped the entire salt flats on Hudson? Eleuterio, you're a genius! He can spend the rest of his life looking for his Dry Lake mine up there. And the money should be a big help in getting Galvan North profitable again."

"Half of it," Eleuterio said. "I have other plans for the rest."

"What?"

"Wait for dinner. We're having a celebration feast."

That night all the candles were lit in the massive wagon-wheel chandelier that hung over the old oak dining table. Eleuterio Galvan's housekeeper had brought out the antique lace tablecloth from Spain and the silver service from Mexico, while the cook had worked all afternoon preparing a feast for what she understood was an engagement party for Señor Galvan and the Anglo *señorita* from the mission school. Addie's eyes sparkled in the candlelight as Beth and Jerry, Lily and Nathan, and Eleuterio's son Jaime all toasted her. With her brown hair flowing about her shoulders like a silken cloak, she looked almost beautiful, and Eleuterio beamed with pride every time he looked at her.

Eleuterio banned all talk of Hudson and his plot until the chilled caramel flan was served for dessert and the servants withdrew. Then he leaned back in his high carved chair, wistfully fingered a cigar that he was too polite to light in the presence of the ladies, and told them of the additional safeguard he'd devised on Hudson's future behavior.

"He didn't know you had recognized those two *hombres* as the men who did that job in El Paso, Jerry," he explained. "And he was real eager to get a look at their personal things. Maybe he thought there'd be a better map, or some other clue, in their saddlebags." He chuckled richly and rolled the unlit cigar between his fingers.

"So I asked very innocently if they'd been working for him and he said yes, they had. I told him I'd be happy to turn their effects over to him, but I needed a paper to cover me in case the next of kin showed up."

Eleuterio spread his hands with a disarming grin. "You know, I'm only a stupid Mexican, I'm afraid of getting in trouble with the law!" He pulled out a piece of paper with Hudson's handwriting on it and waved it like a banner of victory.

"I'll be damned," Jerry said wonderingly. "He signed a paper?"

"Saying they were working for him," Galvan confirmed. He shrugged. "Who knows? Maybe he truly didn't know who they were. But Fritz Bauer had some letters in his wallet. I kept those—proof of identity. If Hudson gets tired of searching the salt flats, and starts to make trouble again, those letters plus his signed statement ought to convince him to calm down."

Jerry nodded. "You didn't think of mentioning that little twist to me ahead of time."

Galvan waved his unlit cigar airily. "A sudden inspiration. Besides, I had witnesses."

Lily giggled. "I was under the piano."

"I," said Nathan, "was on the porch beside the open window."

"And I was behind the door," Addie said with a blush that spread across her cheekbones and deepened the rosy tint on the tip of her nose.

"Too bad you two missed all the fun," they said in chorus.

Jerry's foot reached out and brushed Beth's under cover

of the tablecloth. "Oh, I don't know," he said, looking at her with a secret smile.

Later, when Jerry invited Beth to walk out with him and admire the stars before she retired to the room she shared with Addie, he thought of one last question that hadn't been settled.

"How can you think of money at a time like this?" Beth exclaimed. She removed his hand from her breast.

"Just wondering," Jerry said. "I can wonder about lots of things at the same time. Like how many buttons you got on this darned basque, or whatever you call it."

"We're getting married tomorrow," Beth said.

"That makes it practically legal. Anyway, I can think about that and still wonder what Eleuterio's going to do with the rest of the money he conned Hudson out of. I'm not just a dumb wrangler, you know. I'm a ranch manager. I can hold one skittish little heifer down and make business plans at the same time."

His lips caressed the white V of skin revealed by her unbuttoned bodice and Beth shivered with pleasure. "Are you sure you're thinking about business? How many things can you do at the same time?" She caressed the back of his neck where the close-cropped red hair was right with curls. A little more, and she would lose control of her senses entirely, right here on the front porch.

"I'm a very talented man," he murmured, his breath warm on her neck, "and very curious. I want to know if you're wearing anything under this."

"I'm not," Beth said, vainly trying to refasten the buttons his curious fingers had freed. "I left all my underwear at the mission. You're going to have to buy me a trousseau."

Jerry grinned and slipped one hand under the basque to cup her breast. "Maybe I'll just keep you in a blanket. Unwraps easier. . . . Beth? You sure you don't mind living up at the old ranch house?"

Beth pulled his hand away and refastened her buttons.
"That deserves a more serious answer than I can give when
you're doing that," she told him. "Jerry, you know I love it
up there."

"Yeah, but . . . well, I know how much the school
teaching meant to you. . . . If I got a town job, you could
keep teaching."

"I intend to," Beth told him. "Eleuterio and I had a little
talk after dinner. He's going to donate some of the money he
got from Hudson to build a school up on Galvan North, next
to the reservation border." She fingered the silver and turquoise necklace Hosteen Chee had given her. "I've already
got two pupils."

Jerry laughed and hugged her. "Damn, you're persistent,
missionary lady! How'd you work it out? Oh, tell me tomorrow. I don't want to be serious tonight." He kept one arm
firmly around her, imprisoning both her arms, and set to
work on the buttons down the front of her bodice again.

"Don't *do* that!" Beth moaned as his mouth fastened on
the rosy tip exposed by her half-opened bodice. She gave an
involuntary sigh of pleasure. "You'll drive me crazy. You
know I'm sharing a room with Addie tonight."

Jerry substituted his thumb and forefinger for the action of
his lips, gently tugging at the sensitive tip until Beth shud-
dered as ecstasy flared through her.

"I'm persistent, too," he told her, "and I'm not sharing a
room with anybody. I just want to help with your school
plans, that's all."

"School plans!" Beth's half-closed eyes snapped open as
surprise warred with the delicious languor that flooded her
body. "How do you figure this is helping?"

"I want to help you get more pupils," Jerry explained
gravely. "Takes a little longer this way, of course. We'd
better get to work on it right away."

About the author

Kate Ashton is also known as Catherine Lyndell and Kathleen Fraser. She holds a Ph.D. in linguistics from the University of Texas and speaks not only French, German, Greek, and Arabic, but also Swahili, which she learned while living in Africa as a Fulbright fellow.

The idea for SUNSET AND DAWN came to her when she took a vacation in New Mexico and immediately fell in love with the dramatic landscape of red rocks, green valleys, Indian reservations, Spanish missions, and Texan entrepreneurs.

At one time Kate taught mathematical linguistics and Swahili at UCLA, but she now lives with her husband in Austin, Texas, where she writes full time.

Voyage to Rom

Win A Romantic Caribbean Cruise!

On November 9, 1985, the luxury liner *Carla Costa* will embark on a special romance theme cruise to the deep Caribbean's most exotic ports of call, and you can be on board! Four lucky Pinnacle romance readers and their guests will set sail with us as winners of the *Voyage to Romance* Sweepstakes. Sponsored by Pinnacle Books and Costa Cruises, the *Voyage to Romance* theme cruise will visit San Juan, Curaçao, Caracas, Grenada, Martinique, and St. Thomas. Top romance authors, like Heather Graham, will be on board to conduct writing workshops and give island tours. And to get our guests ready for romance, there will be fitness and nutrition experts, cosmetic and fashion demonstrations on board. So, enter today and get ready for romance on Pinnacle Books' *Voyage to Romance!*

1. NO PURCHASE NECESSARY. On an official entry blank or plain 3″ x 5″ piece of paper, print your name, address and zip code. Mail your entry to: VOYAGE TO ROMANCE SWEEPSTAKES, Post Office Box 5, New York, NY 10046. Enter as often as you like but each entry must be mailed in a separate envelope.

2. One (1) winner of a cruise for two will be selected on a monthly basis, May through August, for a total of four cruises. These winners will be selected in random drawings from entries received under the supervision of Marden-Kane, Inc., an independent

ance *Sweepstakes*

judging organization whose decisions are final and binding. All entries received by the last day of the month will be eligible for that month's drawing, with the final receipt date being August 31, 1985.

3. *PRIZES:* (4) GRAND PRIZES of a 7 day cruise for two to the Caribbean aboard the ms Carla Costa. Cruise includes round trip air transportation from winners' home to point of embarkation. Cruises must be taken on dates to be specified by sponsor. No substitution or transfer of prizes. Winner consents to use his/her name and/or photograph for publicity purposes. One prize per family. Winners will be required to execute an Affidavit of Eligibility and Release. Odds of winning depend upon the total number of entries received.

4. Sweepstakes are open to residents of the United States, 18 years of age or older, except employees and their families of Pinnacle Books, their affiliates and subsidiaries, advertising agencies and Marden-Kane, Inc. Void where prohibited or restricted by law. All Federal, State and local laws apply.

5. Winners will be notified by mail. For a list of Grand Prize Winners, send a stamped self-addressed envelope to: VOYAGE TO ROMANCE WINNERS, c/o Marden-Kane, Inc., Post Office Box 106, New York, NY 10046.

Name_____

Address_____(No. P.O. Box)

City_____State_____Zip_____

Name of Bookstore_____

City_____State_____